The Sugar Man

Born in Britain to a Spanish father and a French mother, Nicolás Obregón grew up between London and Madrid. Nicolás lived in Los Angeles for six years where he was a creative mentor in the youth incarceration system. He wrote and narrated the USG-Universal podcast *Faceless*, which was nominated for best title at the New York Radio awards and his work features in the award-nominated anthology *Both Sides*, focusing on the humanitarian crisis on the US/Mexico border. Nicolás is a graduate of the acclaimed Birkbeck Creative Writing Masters course and a former bookseller for Waterstones. He lives in Madrid.

The Sugar Man

NICOLÁS OBREGÓN

MICHAEL JOSEPH

PENGUIN MICHAEL JOSEPH

UK | USA | Canada | Ireland | Australia
India | New Zealand | South Africa

Penguin Michael Joseph is part of the Penguin Random House group of companies
whose addresses can be found at global.penguinrandomhouse.com

Penguin Random House UK,
One Embassy Gardens, 8 Viaduct Gardens, London SW11 7BW

penguin.co.uk

Penguin
Random House
UK

First published 2025
001

Set in 13.4/16pt Garamond MT Pro
Typeset by Six Red Marbles UK, Thetford, Norfolk
Printed and bound in Great Britain by Clays Ltd, Elcograf S.p.A.

The authorized representative in the EEA is Penguin Random House Ireland,
Morrison Chambers, 32 Nassau Street, Dublin D02 YH68

A CIP catalogue record for this book is available from the British Library

HARDBACK ISBN: 978-0-241-34542-9
TRADE PAPERBACK ISBN: 978-0-241-34543-6

Penguin Random House is committed to a sustainable future
for our business, our readers and our planet. This book is made from
Forest Stewardship Council® certified paper.

MIX
Paper | Supporting
responsible forestry
FSC
www.fsc.org   FSC® C018179

For my grandmother:
Je raconterai toujours tes histoires avec une joie
reconnaissante sur mes lèvres,
sachant que tu te promènes dans tes bois éternels,
volant des roses dans le ciel.

Consider ye the work of Almighty God:
for who can make straight that
which He hath made crooked?

– Ecclesiastes 7:13

January 21st, 1998

Flora Riddell was sixteen years old on the day she died. The town of Nectar had been sepulchred in snow. Stores were twined in fairy lights. And townsfolk were still wishing each other *happy new year*, despite the bleak imminence of February.

. . . A potentially damaging cloud is hanging over the White House today; CNN has confirmed that Whitewater counsel, Kenneth Starr, has been granted permission to expand his investigation . . .

In the kitchen, the TV was blaring. Flora was swishing her feet at the island, its wood dented from years of wistful daydream kicks. She ignored the news – which only deepened the dread in her gut – and tried instead to concentrate on sifting flour.

Esther Riddell was bouncing little Dolly on her hip. 'Ed, I *understand* money doesn't grow on trees,' she shouted over the TV into the phone. 'I happen to understand almost everything you say – Flora, have you started on the flour yet?'

'*Yes*, Mom.'

'Don't sigh at me, sweetie – no, Ed. I'm talking to your child. You have the attention span of one apparently . . . Aw, it's a joke. Don't you always say I don't joke anymore . . . ?'

Dolly was gurgling happily at her big sister as she sank down her mother's hip. Even though the baby was too young to understand, it was to be a *Nightmare Before Christmas* birthday cake, Jack Skellington's face in vanilla cream.

'– I'm just *saying*, Ed, the interest rate isn't unreasonable.

Your investments worked out and this kitchen is no longer workable. I really do think I should call Milton Schneck . . .'

Flora sipped her Snapple and played a quiet game of peek-a-boo with Dolly. She didn't want to get flour in her hair but it was worth it to see her goofy, gorgeous grin.

The baby's little smile was one of the few things that gave Flora calm lately.

'That's because you just *eat* here,' Esther snorted. 'You're not stuck here all day – what's *wrong* with it? How long you got? Wood panelling everywhere, even the damn fridge. Curtains that'd look dated in that Italian volcano town, you know the one, yeah, Pompeii –'

. . . Starr will be looking into new allegations that President Clinton had an affair with a former White House intern, and then urged her to lie about it . . .

'Then there's the purple radish motif wallpaper. Why, Edward? Why does it *exist*? Nobody knows. But from now on, this is a no-radish-motif household – no, I'm not done.'

CNN White House correspondent John King is following the story and he joins us now from the White House – John? . . .

'No, no, no. The recessed lighting was *your* thing. Yes, it was. Yes, it was. And all these lights do is collect sow bug carcasses . . . Edward, for Chrissakes. You can see their *silhouettes* at night!' Esther tossed over the remote. 'Ugh, Flora, honey. Something *else*?'

Flora changed channels. A smirking man was making slut jokes about the intern. She had heard them before. At school. Summer camp. Now the White House. There had been a time when the thought of being shamed that way would've terrified Flora. Not anymore.

Not since Lester Lamb. Since the Testing Pool. Now, she understood what it was to have real problems.

The memory of his smell still lingered in her nose. At

night, she'd hear the gulp of the water, the car horn, the little pops of the bubbles that followed.

It had been days. Yet still no news. No knock at the door. No calls. *But a man like that vanishes out of the blue? A man with followers behind him? Gotta be a matter of time.*

With a shaky breath, Flora hit the *mute* button.

'Oh, Ed. It's always *later, later, later.* Speaking of, when are you back tonight? I've got Bleeding Lamb in an hour, emergency meeting –' opening the fridge, Esther swore.

Flora's heart started thumping now. *This might actually work.*

'Flora, honey?'

'Yes, Mom?'

'I need you to run to Food-O-Rama – I could've *sworn* I got eggs. Oh well, you know the ones I like. And another pound of white sugar. Party cups. Oh, a nectarine for Dolly. Take the Food-O-Friendo card, for what it's worth now. And hurry back, you're still grounded.'

'Sure, Mom.' Flora tried to sound casual.

'Money is in my purse. In fact, take the whole bag – *hello?* Ed, my church tonight? OK fine, see you soon. The sow bugs send their love.'

Esther hung up and blew a kiss but too late. Her eldest had already peeked one last boo at the door frame. Dolly was still laughing like it was the best thing in the world.

In the hall, Flora checked over her shoulder.

Coast clear, she snuck the bundle of pills hidden inside her shoe into her back pocket. Then, she grabbed her Sony Discman and crossed her chest with her mom's handbag strap. Studying the mirror, she wondered how the world saw her. Older than her age, she hoped. The baby face said otherwise. *What about someone with a secret? A dark secret?*

Outside, Snow Shoe Lane was a black slush. Bare trees were still tangled in coloured bulbs. Old banners for the Fest finale hadn't been taken down yet. The houses stood in the Dutch Colonial Revival style, clapboard teals and blues, always reminding Flora of *The Amityville Horror*.

She scanned the windows, then re-located the bundle of pills from her pocket into her mom's bag. That's when she saw it.

The paper. The same headed notepad paper from Bleeding Lamb Pentecostal.

On it, just a single line in black:

I KNOW WHAT YOU DID.

Instinctively, Flora put the note back and looked around again.

Did someone send this to Mom? Can't be. She never does anything wrong. Shit, maybe it's for me? *Do they know? But how would anyone know I'd have her bag?*

Whatever the truth, the note only churned the dread in her stomach harder. Flora slipped her earphones in and hit PLAY. Like always, 'Gypsy' by Fleetwood Mac came jangling into her ears. Taking a deep breath, she tried to force a better mood.

Flora hurried down Snow Shoe and turned on to Main Street. It was pretty in a once-upon-a-time way. Flower pots hanging from lampposts, fading post-war ads in brickwork, still pushing cream mascara and miracle mints. She turned right, under the dead Christmas wreaths hanging from traffic lights. On the bus stop for a route that no longer operated, an old poster for *Titanic* promised: *coming soon.*

She passed the creamery, the orthodontist, Dad's photography studio – southbound. As Flora walked, she kept her eyes peeled for Bleeding Lamb followers. But it was raining softly and there was hardly anyone around.

On the corner by Town Hall, the exception: a small group of Versammlung kids selling the last of the season's peach pies and dandelion wine from their wagon. They wore black, the girls in white aprons and *Kappen* on their heads. With their horses and unsmiling faces, they looked like lost pioneers from a history class video.

The girl with foliage hair and freckles called out now: 'Tasty pies.' Rebecca Frey's English was heavily accented. 'Strong wine. Good prices.'

A knowing look passed between them – a moment too long – until Flora shook her head. 'Next time, maybe.'

After a few blocks south, she turned on Kinzua Ave.

Little piles of snow clumped around dead lampposts. Weeds loomed out of empty lots all the way to the trailer park which Mom always threatened they'd have to move to whenever Dad had a bad year.

It was half-abandoned – broken TVs, couches, blown tyres – more junkyard than home. But Flora had reached Dakota's corner by now.

Feeling nauseous, she tried to figure out what she would say. *Just act natural . . . Yeah, right. Whatever that means.*

On a whim, Flora fumbled in her mom's bag for a pen. There was only the strange note for paper, though. *Screw it.* Flipping it, she scribbled:

Happy birthday, loser! Have a totally dope day.
PS Wherever ya go, I'll come with.

Stuffing the note into the bundle of pills, Flora took a breath and made the turning.

Dakota Finch was sitting on the steps of her trailer. She wore her grey half-zip fleece and beat-up skate shoes, looking glum – as always lately – just staring into space.

Flora stopped at the foot of the stairs and stood up tall, hoping there wasn't flour in her hair. 'Hey, loser.'

'Hey,' Dakota's tired reply revealed the broken front tooth she'd never explained.

'Hanging out?'

'Yep. Nice Discman.'

'Christmas present. Wanna listen?'

'Sure.'

Flora self-consciously buffed the earphones, then handed it over like a newborn. Dakota slipped one ear in and rolled her eyes. 'Stevie Nicks, huh. Big surprise.'

'Course,' Flora grinned. 'And when we get a cat, we'll be calling it Fleetwood Cat.'

'Loser.'

'Eat a dick.' She kicked a pebble. 'So, uh. How you feeling? Still sick?'

Dakota shrugged. 'Feeling better. Anyhow. Where you headed?'

'Food-O-Rama. Come.'

'Can't. Plans.'

'Oh, really. What's his name?'

'Very funny.'

Flora reached for something to fill the silence. 'Mom's trippin' cos it's my sister's birthday tomorrow. Needed eggs for the cake. So boring. Blah. You def don't wanna come?'

'Look.' Dakota took out the earphone. 'I'm leaving soon, anyway . . . Maybe hanging out isn't such a hot idea.'

'OK, firstly screw you. But secondly . . .' Flora tossed over the bundle of pills now. 'Didn't think I'd forget *your* birthday, did you? Finest molly in Catoonah County.'

'Jesus *Christ*.' Looking around, Dakota hid the bundle under her fleece.

She grinned. 'Don't you worry your purdy little self.'

'What the *fuck*, Flo? This is a *lot* of MDMA. Where did you get it?'

6

Flora ached to tell her about that night. The dread that had sat on her ever since. The strange notes she kept finding. But she knew that was impossible.

'I don't wanna talk about it. OK? Just take the stuff.'

'You didn't have to do this, you know that, right?' Dakota scooched down a step. 'If I want something, I get it myself.'

'We're friends, so, yeah. I did have to.'

'Flora, you gotta be more careful. There are all kinds of shitty people around here –'

'– You don't have to tell *me* that. Look, I don't have long. I just wanted to say happy birthday and give you that. Figured we could sell it, you need the extra cash right now.'

Dakota gave her a sad smile. 'What did I do to deserve a friend like you, huh?'

'Don't get mushy.' Flora returned the sad smile. 'Where will you go, anyway?'

'Got an uncle in Detroit. I'll figure it out from there.'

'I didn't know you had family out there.'

'Not a blood uncle.' Dakota sighed. 'Look, Flo. You always looked out for me and I won't forget that but . . .'

'But what?'

'I don't know, maybe it's time to call it. With us. Don't you think?'

'No, I don't think. Fuck that.' She sat down next to her. 'Look, let me just smooth out a few things here and then I'll come out to Detroit. We can work stuff out together.'

'Flora –'

'No, that's all there is to it. Cos I'm sure as hell not staying here by myself.'

Dakota puffed her cheeks. 'OK.'

'OK? That's all you've got to say?'

'I don't know what you wanna hear from me, Flo.'

Flora wanted to hear that she'd miss her when she left. She

7

wanted to hear that she sometimes thought about that one time they'd been dared to kiss in Seth Switzer's basement. She even wanted to confess she had secretly smashed her mom's eggs to come here. But those words took a heart she didn't have.

'Forget it. Just wanted to say happy birthday.' She stood. 'Whatever. See you around.'

'Yeah, you will.' Dakota suddenly smiled. 'Cos whatever happens, wherever we go, we'll always be best friends.'

'Right.' Flora grinned. 'Maybe we can hang tomorrow? That'd be phat.'

'OK. Don't forget your Discman.'

'You hang on to it for a bit. Oh, and there's a note in the bundle. Read it later.'

Flora left in a giddy daze and headed for the store.

Once again, Dakota had talked of ending their friendship. But then she hadn't ruled out Flora following her to Detroit. *Always best friends.* That's what she had said.

The elation of those words in her chest fought with the dread that had made its home of late in her stomach.

The rain picked up as Flora reached an empty Food-O-Rama parking lot. A sagging banner announced its permanent closure today. SHOP NOW OR FOREVER HOLD YOUR SAVINGS. As usual, the makeshift stall stood ten yards from the entrance. A fold-up table held stacks of books, protected by two precarious umbrellas. One of the books faced out, its black jacket depicting a Jacobean illustration of a bearded man smoking a pipe. In ancient font, the title read: *The Nectar Witch: Corruption. Curses. A Copycat Killer.* Next to it, a laminated card pleaded: *buy one, get two free!* Behind the stall, a tall, chubby man was waving. Swearing under her breath, Flora approached.

'Ah,' the working side of Ira Pike's face lit up. 'The luminous Miss Riddell.'

'Hey, Mr Pike.'

'We're out of class, you can just call me Ira.' He half-smiled. 'You good?'

On one side, Ira Pike was plain. But the other side of his face was sunken deep from when a show horse had stepped on him as a child. Or that was the story he told, anyway.

'Fine! Just late. How's business?'

He flipped his ponytail. 'Booming, as you can see.'

'Aw, I'm sorry.'

'You'd think Nectarites would want to learn about their past.' He picked up a copy of his book, the motion revealing an *X-Files* T-shirt. 'Their *true* past, anyhow, but –'

'– They're only interested in football and happy endings, right?'

'Exactly. Most of them have no clue there's someone out there, copying the deeds of a witch from three centuries ago. Sheep, Flora. They have no interest in what hides in the darkness, so long as their mouths are full of grass.'

'Sounds about right. Look, uh, I really gotta run, Mr Pike.'

'It's *Ira*. And not so fast.' He flipped open a copy of his book and scrawled a few lines inside. 'Take it. Something to keep the rain off your head.'

Thanking him, Flora stuffed the book into her mom's bag and hurried for the store. It was dead inside. She was so busy replaying the exchange with Dakota in her head, it took three loops to find eggs. She scolded herself for saying dumb things like *phat* and *trippin'*.

On the other hand, her bravery had made the conversation happen. *If I hadn't tricked Mom into sending me out for eggs, or gotten those pills in the first place – I never woulda seen that smile. God, I could die for that broke-tooth smile.*

'Welluh, in ze end, it's ow zey say,' she opened a carton and spoke to the eggs in a silly French accent. 'To make *une* omelette, you must break a few . . . eggs.'

9

Chuckling, Flora grabbed cups, sugar and a nectarine, then headed for checkout.

'Hey, honey.' The young blonde woman on the register beamed.

'How's things, Carmella?'

'Not so rotten. Last day. Then going to the movies. If Sam ever gets here, that is.'

'Late, as usual, huh. What's playing?'

'Some Denzel Washington movie about the devil. How's Mrs Riddell?'

'Fine, you know. Worrying about big stuff like curtains. Whether or not our Food-O-Friendo points carry over.'

'Apparently, Market Basket said they'll honour them when they open. If they ever open. But, uh . . .' She adjusted her butterfly clips. 'How's the dreamy *Mr* Riddell?'

'Gross. He's good. Hey, Carm. You know the French word for *eggs*?'

'No idea, baby.'

The announcement for the store closure in five played, followed by the national anthem. Flora said goodbye to Carmella and collected her points. Hefting the grocery bag on her hip, she hurried for the exit. The doors whispered open.

Outside, Ira Pike had packed up and left. It was raining hard by now, the light almost gone. Darkness came so early up on this mountain.

For no reason, a sadness settled over Flora. Somehow, she knew Dakota would not wait for her in Detroit. She pictured all the things she'd never do with her. Dances. Movies. Vacations. This town, this body – it all reminded her of what would never be.

I got bigger problems anyhow, she scolded herself. *Cos sooner or later, someone'll knock on the door about Lester Lamb. Then my dumb feelings won't matter one lick.*

Yet despite her dread, on the horizon – in the last sunlight beyond the rain – birch trees flashed bright silver. And above them, a brave dusk fought the dark.

Or maybe nobody will knock. Maybe the world will just forget about him . . .

Something about those defiant colours filled Flora with an inexplicable hope for the future. Made her picture a day when things *could* be different. When she lived in a big city, far away. When she might be driven somewhere in a car and do things that she'd never tell anyone. And where Lester Lamb would never be able to touch her world again.

Flora ran into the rain, shrieking, clutching the groceries to her chest.

To save time, Flora had decided to cut through the old industrial quarter. She was outside the abandoned sugar mill when a cherry-red Camaro pulled up alongside her.

The window slid down. Sam Salinas wore a lumberjack shirt, rolled up to the biceps. His face was hard but his smile warm. Except for the green of his tattoos and dark hair, he was butterscotch, baked by years of sunlight through truck windshields.

'Whatcha doing out here, angel?'

'Hey, Sam. Just headed home.'

'Hop in. Rain's getting heavy.'

'Aren't you late for Carmella?'

'There is that.' He glanced at his watch and mimed a hanging noose.

'S'OK. I'll walk.'

'Suit yourself, baby.' Sam winked and the Camaro roared away.

Flora weighed up the rest of the route home: a quarter-hour, more or less. She'd already taken too long and Mom would flip. But she was shivering.

Twisting her body through the torn chainlink fence, Flora batted her way through weeds to the abandoned mill. It lay there like a sunken battleship in a sea of pine trees. Wind wooed through broken windows. Crows cawed from the old wooden sign.

CATOONAH COUNTY SUGAR MILL
CO – *The Beating Heart of Nectar!*

Giving the crows the finger, she sheltered under an awning. Rain lashed old iron, the blood-smell mixing in with soaked concrete.

But in that loud shush of a coming storm, Flora froze now. She'd heard something.

Music?

Squinting through the downpour, she saw a Merlot-red Subaru. It was parked in an old employee lot, half-hidden by shadows, windows hazed with condensation.

What is that doing here?

Unable to stop herself, Flora drifted towards it, gripping the grocery bag to her chest. The radio was playing inside the car. She knew the song: 'We Belong Together' by Ritchie Valens. But by now she was close enough to hear the grunting over it. Words caught in Flora's throat. She couldn't breathe.

Still, she inched closer.

On the back seat of the car, fluffy toys grinned up at her wildly. In the front, there were two people.

Cupping her shaking hands, Flora peered through the

glass. She saw the female hunched over, head in the man's lap, bobbing up and down. And now she saw his face too, twisting in pleasure.

Flora's scream ripped the crows up into the churning night sky.

Fifteen Years Later

ZERO

Attention all units: please be on the lookout for a 2010 Ford Taurus, bone-white. No plate info, possible damage on rear fender. Last sighted heading southbound on Kennedy and Plum. Male subject, surname: Maloney, given: Ivan. 6'1, 200 lbs. Scarring on chin. Charges outstanding of sexual assault relating to a minor. Suspect is likely travelling with an at-risk fourteen-year-old male subject.

Behind the wheel, Detective Dakota Finch swore. She was tired, hungry, way above this in the chain of command. But a white Ford Taurus had just jumped a STOP sign in front of her and all units meant *all.*

'Dispatch –' She grabbed the radio mic. 'This is 611. Finch, Homicide. BOLO Taurus possibly sighted heading eastbound on Potawatomi and Plum. In-state plate is: MAL048. I am now effectuating pursuit.'

MAL048. Potawatomi and Plum. Copy, 611.

Finch popped peach-coloured pills and accelerated. Twenty mg of Visprozan in her blood, she sailed past the Detroit nightlife – a murky coral of working girls and fentanyl freaks, castaway eyes everywhere. But Finch's eyes were that of a hunter – fixed on her prey.

On Cherry, she caught sight of the Taurus again. Bone-white. 2010. Suspiciously slow-moving now. Yet there was no damage on the rear fender. *Could be the wrong guy?*

Either way, she wouldn't pull him over just yet. Cherry

gave out on to the freeway offramp and that would leave her wide open to rear-end collision.

Instead, she followed the Taurus another few blocks. When the road levelled out, he turned on to Duquesne – an empty cannula of concrete, junk and dead industry where the road widened into three lanes.

Finch lit him up now, turning the street disco-blue.

No reaction.

She hit the airhorn to really get his attention.

A few seconds passed.

Finally, brake lights. A right signal – blinking.

The Taurus pulled over by an abandoned strip club. No traffic in either direction. No witnesses. Only darkness.

Did he choose this place on purpose?

Only one way to find out . . .

Finch pulled in behind and flipped on her high-beams to blind him. 'Long-ass time since I did one of these . . .' she picked up the mic. '611, I'm at Cherry and Duquesne by the old Boob Bungalow. Confirm: Taurus has stopped.'

611. Cherry and Duquesne, copy.

Door open, the cold stung her face. Steel trains squealed far away. The Detroit River was a cold knife in the distance. Above it, plumes of factory smoke billowed high like the city had been torpedoed.

Finch closed her door softly – no point in announcing herself. The camera on her body armour was running. Her gun was loaded. And the high-beams provided cover if the driver was tracking her movements in his rear-view. Still, her heart thudded.

She remembered her academy instructor's words: *The day you think it's just another traffic stop is the day you cop a bullet to the brain.*

Reaching the rear of the Taurus, Finch took a deep breath.

She checked the trunk. It was locked firmly. The back seat was empty too.

Stopping just behind the B pillar, she saw the driver's window was already open, breath corkscrewing out. His hands were on the wheel.

A good sign. *Or a sign this isn't his first rodeo.*

'Sir,' she called out, hand on weapon. 'Are you Ivan Maloney?'

'Yes,' he spoke clearly.

'My name is Detective Finch and I pulled you over tonight because you ran a STOP sign a few blocks back. I'm going to need you to step out. Slowly. Hands showing.'

Maloney got out, hands up, no expression on his scarred face. In one hand he held a key fob, in the other his wallet. 6'1 and 200 lbs checked out. His hair was combed, his shirt pressed. He could've been a Bible salesman, except for the scars.

611, confirming you are 10-4?

'Dispatch. Stop in progress. Stand by.'

Maloney waved his wallet. 'Would you like my licence, Officer?'

'*Detective*, I said. What's in the trunk?'

He frowned. 'But you're meant to ask for my papers.'

'And you're meant to answer my questions. The trunk.'

'Just my things . . .' He lowered his hands.

'Woah.' Finch unholstered her gun and levelled it at him. 'Hands back up. Do it.'

'You want to see?' He licked his lips. 'But I see *you*. The abyss inside you.'

'Hands fucking *up*. Right. Now.'

'Have you ever cavorted in your own darkness? From your eyes, I think you have. It is the only form of beauty in this chasm.'

'We're done with the dollar-store Schopenhauer –' She

flipped off her safety. 'Interlock your fingers behind your head and kneel slowly.'

'There's no darkness in this trunk. Only light.' His mincemeat lips formed a smile. 'The darkness is out *here*. And you're in it, with me. You live in it . . .'

'I gave you a command. Last chance, dickhead.'

'You did.' He smirked. 'See for yourself.'

611, come in.

'Dispatch, hold on one second –'

The man hit the key fob and the trunk swung open. Finch glimpsed a muddy tarp, shovels, a bag of quick lime. And blood.

But that was the split-second he had needed. Maloney was already running. Past the dead strip club. Towards the bushes and the industrial park beyond them.

'Dispatch –' Finch gasped. '10-13. We got a runner. Positive ID. Possible 09-01.'

Copy, 611. Possible homicide. Sending the cavalry.

Finch's ragged breath showed on the air. But she felt no fear now. Only hunger. The old, canine hunger to hunt the snake – to rip it apart.

The chemical plant loomed up ahead, belching white from its smoke stacks up into the night, the churn and pump of America's nocturnal needs a metallic requiem. Somewhere close by, a freight train roared through a level crossing, its signal clanging in panic, the death rattle of an industry.

Finch reached the chainlink fence. She scaled it too fast and landed too hard. Maloney rushed her from behind, fists wild. He landed one on her chin and bottom lip before she fired.

The round hit the man in the kneecap. He buckled.

Finch fell back against the fence and hunched forwards

to get her breath back. Except for that, there was silence. Maloney was blinking rapidly, turning pale.

'The boy?' she grunted. 'Where is he?'

Now his pain subsumed the shock, he began to scream for God. And something inside her gave way. Unable to think of any reasons not to, she turned off her bodycam.

'Please.' He mewled. 'I need help . . .'

'Is the boy dead?' Finch took her collapsible nightstick from her belt. 'Answer me.'

'God, please.'

'You killed him, didn't you?'

'The heart that cannot love . . .' Maloney closed his eyes. 'Must with fury hate.'

'On that –' She snapped out the nightstick, now long and black. 'We agree.'

Finch paced through her old warehouse apartment. She kept the lights off, glowering in a cocktail of darkness and peroxide streetlight. In the sink, takeout cartons were piled up. Banker boxes overflowed with casefiles. Her divorce papers were pinned to the fridge with a Chinese takeout magnet. And her nightstick was on the kitchen table – now clean.

She necked another 15 mg of Visprozan. Without that drowsy, warm disconnect, she was lost.

Out the window, Finch could see Detroit. Smoke stacks. Long-dead factories. Empty rails like cold veins. It all stretched out, a mangy dog under a blanket of darkness.

And right on cue, a familiar car pulled up by the DEAD END sign on her street.

Click, click, click.

Finch went over to the intercom.

Time to face the music.

'Yeah?'

'*It's me.*'

She buzzed Lieutenant Bill Moreno in and listened to his footsteps get louder.

He brushed past her, heading straight to the kitchen.

Moreno tossed a takeout box on the counter, then sat down by the nightstick, as if it hadn't split a man's head open like a tangerine a few hours ago.

Moreno was late-fifties, a lanky man of slow movements and quick eyes. His skin was the colour of ganache, except for the cheeks, where anger had given him a cherry-shine.

Finch went to him. *Click, click, click.* 'Boss.'

'Got you some bánh mì. You forget to eat, Dakota.'

'Well, *gracias*. But I'm assuming you're not here out of nutritional concern.'

'No shit. I could afford to lose a guy in Traffic. Goddamn it, I could lose ten. But I've only got so many brains around here and I happen to need yours.'

'He drove *right past me*, Bill. What was I meant to do?'

'No sass from you, girl. Not tonight.'

'Listen, I know you're angry –'

'*Angry*? Try something a little more excessive. You're good at that.'

Finch shrugged. 'He attacked me. I feared for my life.'

'How many creeps are you gonna break until you kill one? This isn't Gotham fucking City, Dakota. Jesus, you were already on your second warning.'

'And in your day, those warnings would've been medals, right?'

'For someone so smart, you can be really goddamn dense.' Shaking his head, he went to the coffee machine. There he poured two cups. 'You know the city is itching to burn cops and that was *before* the riots. You know it, yet you pulled this shit.'

'Bill, I told you, he drove straight past me.'

'Yeah? Well, I just got off the phone with Internal Affairs. Sounds like they've got you on violation of bodycam protocol and excessive force to the point of criminality. That Maloney asshole is on life support. You better pray he doesn't croak.'

Finch sipped her coffee. 'Should I lie and say I'm sorry?'

'Not to him, to *me*. Because IA want you, Dakota. You understand what this means, right? The City is saying you're a murderer.'

'So, Maloney is the victim. Tell that to the boy he buried in a shallow grave tonight.'

'You're not judge and jury.'

'*Someone* would be. They'd put on a tie to stumble over laws they didn't understand and Maloney would be out in fifteen. Ten, if he pretended to hear voices and –'

'That's the *law*, kid. What you did tonight is the opposite.' He set his cup down a little too hard, then took a breath. 'Guess I was stupid enough to come here expecting *sorry*.'

'Bill.' She went to him again. 'What I am sorry for is putting you through shit. You don't deserve that. But let's skip to the point. He ran a light. Fled the scene. And attacked me, having killed a child no less. I defended myself.'

'You turned off your bodycam.'

'Battery died. Or I slipped. Whatever. There'll be pageantry and opinion pieces, OK. But in the end, the facts are the facts. So, if you came for *sorry*, you got it. If you came to fire me, then –'

'Nope.' He sighed. 'You don't shoot your fastest horse cos he bucks.'

'Great. So, let me get some sleep and I'll get back to my caseload. Any chop, we'll weather it.'

'You can't stay on Homicide.'

'. . . You're fucking *demoting* me?'

'Protecting you. Small town up in the mountains a few hours away. They just copped a Doe and it's a little out of their league. Real fresh, discovered half an hour ago. Your old neck of the woods, in fact. Nectar.'

'Bill –'

'No, they asked for help. You're helping, or you're out. That's it.' Moreno went to the door. 'Flight leaves in three hours, so start packing. You can sleep on the plane. And for God's sake, get that glass from out of your boots. Damn clicking is driving me crazy.'

The door slammed and Finch glared at it.

Finding the Sugar Man had been the reason why she'd become a cop in the first place, all those years ago, when something like that seemed possible. For so long, she'd obsessed over hunting him. Dreamt about it.

But he had never resurfaced.

Down the years, slowly but surely, her early intentions drifted out of view as the machinations of Detroit Homicide – and her own broken life – had replaced them.

Returning to Nectar now, all these years later . . . Dakota couldn't determine her feelings. And that troubled her. She was only ever relentlessly clear about what she wanted.

'Shit,' she sighed. The only thing relentlessly clear to her now was that she wanted a solid half-hour of shut-eye.

Sitting on the edge of her mattress, she rested her boot on her knee to unlace.

That's when she realized it hadn't been glass in her soles.

With a pencil, she dug out two teeth, tossed them out the window, then got into bed.

Before closing her eyes, she glanced at her side table. Flora's old Discman was caked in a layer of dust.

Reaching under her shirt, Finch ran her fingers along the word carved into her ribs: *SILENCE*. For years, it had just been shiny white scar tissue, the skin dormant. But now it itched, as if the past sensed her return.

She understood what she felt now. Dread.

ONE

It was a regional flight, more of a little sky bus than a plane. By the time it reached cruising altitude, it'd be starting its descent. *Same as my ass*, Finch thought.

The cabin shook violently. A storm was building in the distance, thunder rolling like a child's skull in the trunk of a car.

Chewing on her cold bánh mì, she looked out of the window. A thousand Rust Belt towns glowed weakly in the darkness. Beyond them, through seething thunderheads, the Catoonah Mountains emerged – a broken spine in a shallow grave.

The pilot announced their descent, wishing all disembarking passengers a spook-tacular Halloween. Balling up the bánh mì wrapper, Finch heard a little crunch. She salvaged a Wisdom Wafer from the wrapper and wondered what was wrong with *fortune cookie*.

From the wafer, she pulled out a little slip of paper:

No man ever steps in the same river twice. For it is not the same river and he is not the same man – **Heraclitus**

Catoonah County Airport was just a lonely hangar in a nowhere field. The single billboard asked for her God-given American vote. *Tired of bad eggs? Vote for Melvin Neeley.*

It was silent here except for a scorned wind through pine trees. Above, the moon was the last coal in a long-dead fire.

'Not in Kansas anymore . . .' Finch whispered to herself.

Headlights cut through the darkness.

She turned to see a Nectar Police cruiser in the shadows. Its passenger door clunked open. The sheriff was in his thirties, burly, podunk grin with sandy hair in need of a cut.

'You must be Detective Finch. Welcome to Nectar. I'm Jesse Sullivan.' He tipped his hat cowboy-style. 'Mayor Cochran is waiting for you.'

Finch put her suitcase in the trunk and climbed in. 'He'll always be *Sheriff* to me.'

'Yeah, I heard you was local.' He pulled away from the kerb. 'You know him?'

'We've had dealings.'

'Well, seeing as you and me is basically colleagues, you can call me Jesse.'

They drove higher up the mountain along Route 6, a carpet of sugar maple and hemlock below. Despite it being late October, up here, trees were plump with snow.

As the road levelled out, then sank into the next valley, things started to twist into focus for Finch. Fields strewn with old cannons. Dairy farms. Orchards.

In her mind, she heard Flora's voice now. *All that civil war postcard crap, happy pioneers, blah, blah, blah. What about all the women they drowned? What about all the indigenous folks they kicked out? Or worse.*

The brief smile on her lips was cauterized by the billboards.

**BURR CUSTOM – SLAUGHTER
& MEAT PROCESSING**
Poultry • Pork • Exotics – USDA approved

<u>**ED RIDDELL STUDIO**</u>
Photoshoots / Portraits / Weddings /
Authentic Moments
For memories done well, come to Ed Riddell!

Finch looked away.

'How was the journey, Detective?' Sullivan eyed her in the mirror.

'Highly glamorous.'

'So, Detroit PD, huh? Can only imagine your caseload. Hell, I'd pay to see that on TV –' The engine sputtered now and he slapped the dashboard. 'Piece of junk. You know, the siren broke my first week. I was close to shouting *woo-woo-woo* out the window –'

Sullivan slammed the brakes. A doe bolted across the road, chased by a man with a compound bow. He was gaunt, in tattered camouflage, his hair long, his black beard bushy.

'Dammit, Ray!' Sullivan shouted. 'What did we say about night hunting?'

The man looked up at them. He locked wild eyes with Finch. A cigarette bobbed on his lips as he mumbled to himself for a second. Then he ran into the woods after the doe, towards Lake Sweetness, something familiar to Finch lingering after him in his wake.

'Happy Halloween, huh? That's Roadkill Ray.' Sullivan shook his head. 'Resident loon. But I guess you knew that.'

She shrugged. 'I left this place a long time ago.'

'Lucky.' He tossed her a bashful grin. 'How long you been a cop anyway?'

'Jesse, the car is old but it doesn't run on air. It'll still work if you stop talking.'

'Don't bite your tongue.' He laughed. 'I like that. Around here we paddle up and down a river of bullshit. Small-town cops never stop campaigning for re-election, as you know. Makes me more politician than lawman. Last week, guy complains cos I don't smile at him. I'm not kidding. Now I smile my ass off all day, like I'm some game-show assistant.'

Sullivan glanced over to see if she had cracked a smile. She had not.

Welcome to NECTAR
Est. 1867
Everything's just peachy in Nectar!
Home of the Hornets

VOTE TO RE-ELECT
★MAYOR QUAYLE COCHRAN★

GETTING RESULTS &
PROUDLY SERVING YOU
FUNDRAISER 6PM – SOLD OUT
STEAK FRY! GRAPE PIE! FALL PUNCH!

THE NECTAR HERITAGE FEST
IS BACK!
Embrace what makes you, YOU.
8AM–LATE | Military half price |
Kids go FREE

At the red light, Finch took in most of Nectar's Main in one scan: Merle's Diner. The old photography studio that had belonged to Flora's dad – long since sold up. Stickers for the

Nectar Hornets or Rick Santorum. And everywhere, Halloween decorations.

This place was a backwater town clutching on to the interstate like it would fall into the abyss otherwise. It had been pretty, once. Desirable. But the years had run it down. New roads had been built, sapping its relevance. Kids had grown and left. That included Finch.

Familiarity to her was a sickness in the pit of her stomach.

She took a breath before looking up at the letterboard outside the Lutheran church – unchanged all these years later.

BRING FLORA HOME

Nectar's Sheriff's Department was a quaint redbrick building, the town's train station once upon a time. The interior resembled a branch of a collapsed Reagan-era bank. Scuffed desks. Frayed carpet. Out-of-date maps on the walls.

Finch entered at sunrise.

On the large whiteboard in the bullpen, mugshots had been stuck up – all young women. Accompanying them, a few naked dead bodies. Around the whiteboard, a handful of patrolmen were laughing, one of them wearing a werewolf mask.

–*And so, the Mexican says: no, señor, me no emotional, only el pepper spray gets me every time.*

Guffaws.

–*Hey, Kucharski. You ever do the day shift? It's called work, you'd love it.*

–*Screw you guys, two written warnings tonight for expired licences. Two. Count 'em.*

Finch didn't recognize this new generation. But that cop smell hadn't changed in fifteen years. Microwaved food, sweaty pits, bleach losing its nightly battle. The stink, their pitch, this place – all of it brought her back to '98, back to Flora's disappearance.

Finch glanced at Interview Room B, a woozy, unwanted déjà vu. *Dakota, think carefully. It's very important, honey. Can you remember anything else? Anything at all?*

Over and over, they made her re-live that day.

At the time, she felt if she could just give them one little thing, they would catch the killer and give peace to the Riddells.

The disappointment in their faces had been clear. As if she didn't already know it was her fault. But she had told them everything she could. Every single thing.

Except one.

'Gentlemen,' Jesse Sullivan announced. 'Eyes this way.'

In their groan, Finch immediately understood that these men did not respect him.

'Now, as you know, Mayor Cochran called in out-of-county help for our Jane Doe. This is Detective Dakota Finch, seconded from Detroit. She has significant experience in Homicide. Some of you may know her, she grew up right here in Nectar. That being said, with the first Fest since 1998 upon us, you all know how important it is we get a result here and quickly. So, please extend Detective Finch every courtesy.'

They all turned to look at her, a half-dozen curious eyes. A half-dozen white-bread, button-up, all-you-can-eat carvery eyes. They took in the bruises on her unsmiling face, the looseness of her Detroit Homicide polo, the tattoo on her forearm of a sleeping woman's face, mouth closed, flies buzzing around it. Finch knew they were wondering how something so City could come from this place.

She gave a non-committal nod and received a few grunts.

Sullivan smiled at her now. 'Just gonna check on the mayor real quick. One sec?'

The bullpen went back to its jokes.

—Hey, Skaggs, you hear there's gonna be genealogy at Heritage Fest?

—So?

—So, maybe it'll turn out you're Italian. Would explain why you're so fucking short.

—That's low, Kucharski. You know my growth was stunted as a kid. Your mother gave me a cookie every time I fucked her.

As Finch passed them, the laughter fell quiet, their eyes locked on her.

'The fuck you looking at?' she spat.

Sniggers.

Finch marched into Sullivan's office and closed the door a little too hard.

Mayor Quayle Cochran looked up at her.

He was diminutive, red-faced. William H. Macy in a good suit and a bad moustache. 'Dakota.' He offered his hand with a *Fox News* smile. 'Long time. Glad you're here.'

'Yeah, well –' Finch brushed past him. 'Not much choice.'

Cochran sat down at Sullivan's desk. On it, a Steelers helmet signed by Rocky Bleier and a piece of concrete from the North Tower in a commemorative case. 'You met the boys?'

'Charming group.'

'They're good workers, a little boisterous. Anyhow, you need some coffee or –'

'You copped a dead body. Let's just get started.'

'OK.' Cochran sighed. 'Elephant in the room? We know Flora Riddell was personal to you. And that investigation didn't go as . . . it *could've*. We were pretty hard on you –'

'Doesn't matter.'

'Sure. Well. Lieutenant Moreno says you're his best. Your

record speaks for itself. I just want you to know, whatever you need, we'll make it happen.'

'Let's get this straight, Quayle. I don't wanna be here. And you don't want me here, either. So, the quicker we start.'

'Understood.'

'Good. Now, what do you know about your Jane Doe?'

'The shape she's in?' Sullivan grimaced. 'Nobody *can* tell much about her.'

TWO

Speedy's Mountain Truck Plaza was the busiest truck stop in five counties. Built on the site of an old logging operation, it was just outside of town, pushing up against the Fairgrounds. With Fest re-opening in just a few days, this dead body was about to be very visible. *No wonder Cochran is sweating blood over it.*

Finch knew this Jane Doe would be the only topic of conversation today in Nectar. And it wouldn't take long until a name was whispered: *the Sugar Man.*

It had been years since Finch had thought about him. Enough time had passed for the Discman by her bed to come to be just an object. But now, the memory of her old obsession broke through, like a weighed-down bloated body, finally surfacing. Though he had only ever been a shadow, the Sugar Man cast it long across Nectar.

Some said he had just been a man caught in a moment of madness. Others imagined him as a monster that lived to drink the last tears of children. Finch knew the reality would be unremarkable. She couldn't help but wonder, as she had so many times, if he was still here in Nectar, hiding in the skin of an every-man – secretly enjoying the legend he'd created. Or, if he was a million miles from here, having taken what he needed from Nectar, a satisfied bee, flying away forever.

Route 6 curved out of Nectar and along Lakeshore Drive.

A faded billboard showed the missing preacher, Lester Lamb, both as he was, and an age-progressed man:

MISSING, SINCE JANUARY 1998
LESTER LAEL LAMB – MAN OF GOD
If you know something, PLEASE
call Nectar Sheriff's Office

As it had so many times down the years, Lamb's disappearance nagged at Finch – so close to Flora being found dead. In a town where not much had happened since the 1600s, it was hard to reconcile a vanishing and a murder within a few days of each other. *Could his disappearance link to her death? Flora's mom was a Bleeding Lamb follower. Was that the connection? What about the note Flora had given her on the group's headed paper?*

Dead ends. Dead ends.

Sullivan's police cruiser pulled up to Speedy's Mountain Truck Plaza. There were two entrances. Two separate worlds divided by a chainlink fence. One for regular drivers who needed gas, restrooms, food. The other was for truckers.

From every corner of the country, an endlessness of men, carrying thousands of miles of solitude on their backs. And through them flowed the great river of American commerce: meat, bleach, car parts, milk, molasses, *Don't Tread On Me* baseball hats, fertilizer. Speedy's sustained that ecosystem and provided a secondary one around it: dealers, pimps, sex workers.

Entering, Sullivan drove past endless rigs, row after row, like a moveable warehouse with no roof. Many truckers still had signs up from the night before, rejecting any 'services'.

The police perimeter came into view. Tim Burr, leaning on

his stack of chest-high pancakes, leered down. Someone had slashed the Speedy's mascot with graffiti years ago:

VOTE YES ON AMENDMENT 4. UNIONIZE NOW. RIGHTS FOR DRIVERS. FUCK QUAYLE COCHRAN!

A large military surplus tent had been set up behind the police perimeter. It was marked with the words Nectar PD Mobile Command Center.

Inside, Finch changed into a tear-resistant forensic suit, shoe covers and nitrile gloves.

When she emerged, Sullivan pointed. 'Past the fence, down the hill. Just follow the flares. There's a small pond there –'

'I know the one.'

Finch headed for the gap in the fence. She climbed through carefully, then down a short, slushy verge through the wood, flanked by spent flares.

At the bottom, the Testing Pool, an ugly pond, encircled by pines. Finch felt a splinter of memory slip into her skin – Flora treading water here in the summer. Hugging herself as they trudged through the wood in the winter. In the years since Finch had left, a memorial bench had been set up for Flora. It had been built by the water's edge, without any kind of consideration for paths or access or whether anyone would ever want to linger in this lonely place. Its small plaque read: *Bud on earth, bloom in heaven.*

Breathing hard, head now swimming from the Visprozan, she gripped it for balance.

Finch felt punch-drunk with familiarity. So often, she'd returned to this place in nightmares. But under that cold, sad rain, she realized she had underestimated what she'd felt last night back in Detroit. It wasn't dread. It was fear.

Get it together, Dakota.

Taking a resolute breath, Finch opened her eyes. The pond was pitiful. A lot smaller than she remembered it. Across the water stood a sad blue tarp, like some abandoned fortune-teller's tent.

She went to it. Inside, the smell of mud and trapped rain.

Jane Doe was facing the horizon, lips almost touching the water. But there was only a lower half of her head. The upper half, the face, had been destroyed. In its place, a fondue of meat, blood and bone.

Extensive injury. Finch crouched down over it. *Shotgun, highly likely.*

From the blood spatter, she could see where the killer had fired from. But there were no footsteps in the mud, maybe washed away by the rain. If there had been signs of a struggle in the immediate area, they were gone, too.

Finch thought back to her training. *Shine a flashlight around your crime scene. New shadows can reveal evidence.*

Circling the area with her flashlight, she tried to illuminate some trace of a killer – the spent shotgun shells, condoms, cigarette butts, weapons, anything rich in DNA.

But there was only mud.

She turned her attention to Jane Doe. The slender body was unclothed, shoulders and back flour-white. The choppy red hair was the only colour on her, as if fall itself grew from her scalp. It had been cut recently. But poorly. *Who are you?*

She considered the positioning of the body.

It wasn't visible from the truck stop, unless you were right up at the fence, but it couldn't be considered well-hidden – especially not in daylight. If the killer had been hiding his work, he'd been half-hearted about it.

He wasn't trying to hide you . . . Or didn't have time. But then why bring you here?

Finch guessed Jane Doe was in her mid-twenties or early thirties, despite the missing face. Except for the shotgun damage, her skin held no obvious blemishes.

Hang on a second . . .

Finch gently rotated the girl's chin to look into what had been her face, careful not to cause any further damage to the decimated tissue. Though it had been destroyed from the nose upwards, she could make something out. What was left of Jane Doe's freckled mouth was open, ashen. With a slight droop. And there was not a single tooth inside it.

'. . . Weird.'

But now, tracking her flashlight lower, Finch saw it.

On the Doe's throat, a necklace of red marks.

And under her fingernails, blood. Shreds of skin.

'. . . He strangled you, you fought him . . . but he shot you *after* death. Why?'

With gloved hands, Finch examined every remaining inch of the body, searching for any trace of the killer. She felt bones beneath cold flesh. She searched wrists, genitals, thighs, mouth; any part a man might hunger for.

But for the face, all that stood out was Jane Doe's throat – a single concentration of violence, redness flocking into purple.

Somewhere nearby, a soft cracking sound.

Finch snapped towards it, scanning the treeline, hand on holster.

Animal? Snow from a branch?

The figure of a man emerged through the grey mess of the wood.

It's him. He's back.

'Detective Finch?' A well-upholstered man came into view.

Secretly exhaling, she removed her hand from the gun. 'Yeah. Who wants to know?'

'Hanlon Hopkin, coroner.' His blue eyes crinkled in the

smile as he smoothed down his badger's beard. 'You from Pittsburgh? Erie?'

'Detroit.'

'Ah. Go Wolverines.' He laughed and offered a gloved hand.

'Glad to know you, Hanlon.'

Hopkin pointed to the body. 'Real mess, huh?'

'Yeah.'

'Mayor Cochran sent me down here in case you needed a second opinion.'

'I'm usually OK with just mine.'

He laughed. 'I respect that. But if I go right back up, I look like a dunce. Maybe, seeing as I'm here . . . ?'

She shrugged. 'I see massive tissue damage, two shots. I'd bet on a shotgun. From colouration I'd say damage was post-mortem. There's wadding in those wounds.'

'Ballistics will take a while for the gauge but it looks like the shots came from within ten feet, give or take. Wadding looks normal enough. I don't see any shells left behind.'

'Yeah. So, he's not a total dummy.'

Hopkin nodded. 'I'd need to give her a proper look back at Olmstead, but my guess? The wadding was store-bought, common usage. Could've picked them up from Walmart.'

'Then, he could be anyone.' Finch went back to the body and crouched down over it again. 'No skin discolouration, ring indentations, jewellery. No teeth present, let alone dental work. No tattoos. *She* could be anyone, too. Absence of saliva, vomit and lung purge. No maggot mass. Found unclothed but no apparent sexual injury. And she looks fresh to me.'

Hanlon nodded. 'I see it the same way. Maybe a few hours.'

'Talk to me about the injuries.'

'Well, ignoring the shotgun, no significant corporal damage beyond the fatal injuries to the neck area. On that front, clear horizontal fractures of the thyroid cartilage, the hyoid bone. Expected bleeding; aural and oral. Despite the facial damage, we can see clear swelling and protrusion – she bit her own tongue. As you say, no teeth. From the gum damage, it looks sloppy. This guy wasn't a dentist. Looks like a home instrument. So, he wasn't rushing. Now, given the fingernail marks on her throat, I'd say the killer strangled her from behind. I'll send *her* bloodied nails for testing, of course. If he's on the database, this'll be over fast. Upshot? She fought like hell to live. But death is consistent with manual strangulation.'

'Any thoughts about *him*?'

'Not much. Likely a strong man. Almost certainly displaying scratch wounds on his hands, forearms, or even knees. He took the time to collect the destroyed parts of her head that could've identified her. Not a single tooth here. Maybe he kept them back. Maybe not.'

'Something's bothering me . . . There's a struggle, right? But no signs of one here.'

'Just the gunshots. So, she's already dead? He brings her here to destroy her face?'

'Right. That could make sense. Using a shotgun in your living room is messy. So, he's meticulous enough to transport her here, destroy her face, collect her teeth . . . but then he leaves her out on display? Almost carelessly? That bothers me . . . Hm. Maybe he wanted her found . . . but not identified?'

'Could be. Either way, he's likely a man able to keep his head in the face of carnage.'

'Appreciate it, Doc.' Finch stood. 'How long in the game?'

'Class of '88.' He gave a little salute.

'So, you oversaw Flora's autopsy?'

He looked at her for a long time before nodding.

'Then you know what I'm going to ask next.'

'*Do you think this could be the same killer?*'

'Well?'

'And my answer is I don't know. But I would guess not. There's no ligature here. Flora was found clothed, Doe was not. Plus, she's a lot older. A decade, or more. Only thing they share is location, gender, race . . .'

'You don't think it's *him*, then?'

'Look, this *could* be the Sugar Man. It'd make the locals happy. After all, they love a ghost story. Though if it *is*, then his methods have changed considerably and there would be a reason for that. But then that's your field.'

'You bet your ass.' Finch considered the horizon. 'One last point, Doc. No link was ever found between the Sugar Man, Flora, or any of the missing girls down the decades. Yet here, he destroyed Jane Doe's face. You think he was doing this to hide her ID?'

'Maybe. Or maybe those eyes had seen something the killer just couldn't live with.'

THREE

Back at the Nectar Mobile Command Center, Sullivan was smoking a roll-up. At a fold-up camping table, Cochran was nursing a coffee. He wore a brown leather bomber jacket over his shirt and tie, the messaging clear: *man of action*. The mere sight of him pissed Finch off.

'Jane Doe is ready for transport –' She marched in. 'But I want mats underneath her, can't lose any forensic material.'

'I'll see to it.' Sullivan nodded. 'What do you make of her, Detective? We've had our share of problems around here but someone getting blown away by a shotgun –'

'First off, she was strangled before the shotgun damage. Clear marks around her neck. There are no signs of a struggle down there but she has skin and blood under her nails – almost certainly a souvenir from her killer. I want it matched against all DNA samples collected in 1998.'

Cochran hoisted a bushy eyebrow. 'For the Flora Riddell murder? Those was early days, we only collected two: Sam Salinas and Ira Pike.'

'Whatever. Let's run it and see.'

Sullivan crushed his roll-up under his foot and whistled. 'A girl strangled, a few yards away from where Flora was found. Mayor, you think folks are gonna start talking about –'

'Don't you say that fuckin' name, Jesse.'

'But he's right,' Finch said. 'People will say the Sugar Man *is* back, true or not.'

'Goddamn it.' The mayor puffed out his cheeks. 'The amount of work we put into resurrecting Fest, into getting funding from Burr Group. They were very open about looking at other locations.'

'That's your problem, not mine.'

'Yeah.' Cochran grunted. 'So. What's the play?'

'First things first, the Testing Pool gets cut off. Nobody in or out. Now –' Finch went to the whiteboard. When she was done scribbling, in the centre of the board were the words *JANE DOE*. Radiating out from them, a series of bullet points.

A. SEARCH OF AREA.
B. MURDER SITE OR BODY DEPO ONLY?
C. CCTV?
D. WITNESSES.
E. VICTIM ID.
F. KNOWN OFFENDERS IN AREA, POIs, OTHER RELEVANT CRIMES.

'First one is easy. We need the entire area around the water to be subjected to a fingertip search. Smokes, cans, condoms, whatever. The killer most likely left *some* trace, however small. I want it found.'

Sullivan nodded. 'I'm on that. We've got out-of-county help coming and all our auxiliaries have been called up.'

'Good. I also want divers in the water. Here *and* Lake Sweetness.'

The mayor shook his head. 'We don't have those kinds of resources.'

'This is a piss puddle and you're telling me you don't have a goddamn mop? I don't care about your budget, find the divers.'

Cochran rubbed his eyes. 'I'll see what can be done.'

'You do that. Now, B. Where was Jane Doe murdered? Is that the crime scene itself down there? Or just the body deposition site?'

'No signs of struggle, like you say.' Sullivan shrugged. 'But then it's been raining.'

'That's also why A matters.' Finch returned to the white-board and tapped it. 'Jesse, what about CCTV?'

'Speedy's hasn't had a working system in years.'

'Who found the Doe?'

'A trucker by the name of Larry Hurford. Parked up right by the rear fence around 2AM and there was no body. An hour later, he comes back to his truck and bingo.'

'Doesn't give the killer much of a head start, then. What's Larry's deal?'

'Seventy years old. Diabetes on legs. But good-hearted. Old crow ain't killing anyone.'

'And he's *definite* about his timings?'

'Yeah. Paid for gas at 2AM. His meal receipt is at 2:58AM on his way out.'

'Then that's our disposal window, 2 to 3AM. Let's find video in town. Doorbells, dashcam, anything. I wanna see vehicles in that window, maybe we can tie one to Speedy's.'

'Done.'

'OK. Next, D. Witnesses. I'm guessing nothing?'

Two blank nods.

'Well, that's a short one. E. Who the hell is Doe?'

'No reports of anyone missing in Nectar. We got a few at-risk females in town, bad domestic situations, but they're all accounted for. We double-checked the Missing Persons Bureau already, no matches in county. And like you said, few identifying features on her.'

'All right, get on to all halfway houses, orphanages, rehabs.

Anything in surrounding counties, the state. See if they had any girls recently up and vanish.'

'You got it.'

Cochran tugged anxiously on his moustache. 'Let's say Doe *ain't* from here or anywhere close. What if it was just a nocturnal transaction gone wrong? Could be she crossed the wrong trucker.'

Finch shrugged. 'Possible. But she was healthy. Maybe Hopkin's autopsy will say otherwise, but I saw no clear signs of drug abuse, the associated markers.'

'She was nude, strangled. Don't that point to anger or something sexually driven?'

'Maybe.' Finch started pacing again. 'Or *personal*. Most women are killed by men they know. Someone close to them. *Could've* been a transaction gone wrong. But nor can we rule out that our guy lived around Jane Doe. That he knew her. Watched her. Wanted her. And *because* there was a link between them, he destroyed her face. To cut that thread.'

'But if that's true, she ain't from around here and he ain't either. We'd know about her by now, someone woulda reported her missing.'

'Maybe. Unless she's prone to going missing. Let's jump to F. Jesse, get your boys to question every single sex worker – in town and all the surrounding truck stops – is anyone missing? Any bad johns around? Anyone give them the creeps? The girls will know regulars, vehicles. Maybe one ties to Speedy's. And if we are covering our bases, this *is* a truck stop. Talk to local haulage companies, see if they have any workers with timetable anomalies in the last couple of days, anyone with a criminal record. And while we're at it, how about a list of all recently released violent offenders in the state. Or maybe any reports of a stolen shotgun.'

Sullivan nodded. 'I'll put the boys to work.'

Finch turned to the whiteboard. 'The killer. I gotta say, he bothers me. And I'm not easily bothered.'

Cochran shrugged. 'To me he seems like a garden-variety pissant.'

'No, too little here makes sense. Nectar is surrounded by caves, creeks, mines. A lot of places to hide a body. Yet *this* is half-assed. Or, at least it *looks* that way. Why?'

Cochran shook his head. 'I hear hooves and you're saying *zebras*. It looks half-assed because it was. He didn't plan this mess. Maybe it spins outta control in his rig a few feet away. A slap becomes a punch, which then becomes hands around the neck. Just happened.'

'Maybe. But whoever did this? He made *choices*. No mud on her feet, so he carried her body fifty-plus yards from up here down to that water. Could've left her on the ground in the parking lot. He didn't. That's a choice.'

'Now hold on, Dakota –'

'He destroyed her face. That's another. Why does he do that if she's just an out-of-town sex worker? Then he left her nude. Another choice. Stopped her being ID'd but left the door wide open on finding her. Another. On and on they go. I don't know who he is but he *is* talking to us through these choices. Now, to be honest with you, I don't really give a shit if you close this or not. But I'm telling you, you catch him by listening to him, not assuming.'

Sullivan scratched his beard. 'You think he chose this place to lead us somewhere?'

'Maybe Cochran is right. Maybe the killer is dumb and he just makes bad choices. But then, either he never heard the name *Flora Riddell*, or he has, and he knows if he gives us two and two, we'll make four.'

'You're saying you think it's the Sugar Man.'

'Or someone who wants us to think it is.'

Cochran sighed. 'Look, I know how people here talk. And I know the Sugar Man being unresolved means any time blood is spilled, his name gets spoke. But I see nothing down there that merits him being in the conversation.'

Finch shrugged. 'Maybe. But he *took* her down there, Quayle. Now, either the murder happened up here in the truck stop and he simply carried her out of view. Or he has a kill site away from here. Means of transportation. And he *chose* this place. So, I see three options. One: convenience, or lack of choice. Two: framing. He wants us to hear your zebras.'

Cochran pinched the bridge of his nose. '– I don't think I'm gonna like three.'

'Three: the Testing Pool is significant to *him*.'

Cochran shook his head. 'But she doesn't fit his profile. Our Doe is a grown woman, nude, physically completely different from Flora – who was ligature by the way, we've got manual here. Plus, the shotgun thing. And that's ignoring the lack of sugar at the scene.'

'That assumes he has a fixed script. It's been fifteen years. Tastes change.'

'Why would he come back? Why now? Why her?'

'No idea. It doesn't remove the possibility.'

'We have no time for this.' Cochran clucked his tongue. 'Heritage Fest is here.'

All of Nectar PD and a handful of auxiliary cops ambled around in the turret light outside. Most of them had never seen a murder. Still, they nodded for the benefit of the few folks gathered at the perimeter. For each other.

Finch pushed her way through to the front and gave Jesse Sullivan the nod. Down by the water she had felt fear. But now she began to feel the rush of the hunt again. *Go time.*

'Gentlemen, eyes this way,' Sullivan shouted. 'I will be

assigning tasks individually in a minute. But, as you know, Detective Finch here is going to run Jane Doe. So, do her the courtesy of listening up and let's find this SOB.'

'I don't need courtesy. Just silence.' Finch tapped the Kevlar on her chest for attention like she didn't already have it from every man present. 'My instructions are simple: the truck stop closes right now. Take names and plates. I want to know who every single driver parked up here is. Anyone who came in and out in the last forty-eight hours. Regular cars, too, not just truckers. If Jane Doe drove, her car could still be here. Canvass the diner. The gift store. I wanna know if anyone saw anything suspicious. Arguments, whatever, you know the deal. Go door to door, nearest residents, and spread out from there. Contact credit card providers, too. Who got gas here? Who ate here? Who bought a fuckin' snow globe? I want *names*. I bet the killer is hiding in those names, purchases, choices. So, we start by tying him to 'em. I want a list and I want it to be big.'

One of the auxiliaries cut in. 'I *bet* she wants it big.'

With a sigh, Finch beckoned. 'You. Yeah, *you.*'

A tall, grinning man stepped forward. He was in his thirties with a ten-dollar haircut and a box-beard to hide the chins. Finch hadn't seen Blevins McConnell since high school but she could've read his whole life in a glance anyhow. Popular at school. On the team. Achieved zero after it. *Nothing else in this world except police would give him power.*

'What's your rank?'

'You know me, Dakota, we used to –'

'*Who* you are is irrelevant, prick. And it's *ma'am*. Now, I asked your rank.'

'Reserve Officer.'

'Do we have a problem here, Reserve Officer?'

'No, ma'am.'

48

'But?'

He shrugged. 'Just that you arrive outta nowhere, giving orders like Stonewall Jackson. A little weird is all.'

'Why?'

'Just cos of, uh, your past reputation.'

'For what?'

Still smiling, he looked around for back-up. 'Being a good-time girl.'

'And you don't like good times, McConnell?'

'Look, it was just a joke, I –'

'On the giving-out-orders thing, heavy weighs the crown and all that. But someone has to do it. Not you, though, right? You're just a Reserve Officer. Here to make up the numbers. To do as you're told.'

The man lost his smile. Finch knew that expression by heart. Ten thousand men before him who'd wanted to slap the mouth off her. Some had.

'Look, Dakota, I was just –'

'It's *ma'am* or *Detective Finch*. And you were just joking, yeah. But I run manhunts. Just like this one. Which you are currently *interceding* in. You mentioned my reputation at school? Well, since yours was for being dumb as shit: *interceding* is just a fancy word for *fucking with*. So, here's how this goes. You delay me again, McConnell, and you're fucking fired. Trust me when I say: I will dedicate myself to that outcome. Same goes for any man here. Now, that would be a fair result but I'm not a fair person. My reputation is for good times, right? My good time wouldn't end at termination. So, for example, once you, McConnell, were no longer a Reserve Officer and just a sad, day-drinking fuck, I would be very happy to arrange for an unexpected home visit from a desperate scumbag who wants to be in my good graces. Are we clear?'

'Yes, ma'am.' McConnell spoke to his boots. 'I apologize.'

'Good. I take it everyone else here now understands the meaning of *interceded*. And since I know my instructions were clear, let's hop the fuck to it.'

Sullivan started barking names and making different lines for different tasks. Finch checked her watch. She hadn't slept properly in twenty hours.

'Hey, Jesse. I gotta find a motel.'

'Take my ride.' He tossed her the keys to the cruiser. 'Where will you stay? Most of the nice places are already booked up for Fest.'

'I'll try the shitty ones over the road. I need to crash for an hour or two.'

'Good idea.' He grinned. 'Wouldn't wanna see you when you're cranky.'

FOUR

Motels clustered on the land across from Speedy's truck stop like a black eye. Finch checked into the Friendly Motel for a week, signing the guest book *Elizabeth Taylor*. In the parking lot, a telephone-pole repair truck was covered in Mitt Romney stickers. Even the can of kerosene tied to the back insisted: *BELIEVE IN AMERICA*.

Room 202 was a box of scuzzy green carpet and faded nowhere-landscapes on pinewood walls. Unzipping her small suitcase, Finch immediately decided she couldn't be bothered with hanging up clothes. Instead, from the folds of a sweater, she fished out Flora's old Discman. As she had so many times, she gently rotated it and the battery cover came away. From inside, she took out the yellowed, folded page – torn from a Bleeding Lamb Pentecostal notepad.

Happy birthday, loser! Have a totally dope day.
PS Wherever ya go, I'll come with.

Turning it over, she stuck the note on the wall and read the block capitals she knew by heart:

I KNOW WHAT YOU DID.

Was that for you or for me, Flo?
Out the window, Finch could see the woods. As she

closed her eyes, she pictured the spot, through that sad little maze of syringes, condoms and abandoned furniture, where Flora's body had been found. Where the world had been cleaved in two.

Finch woke at dusk. On the streets of Nectar, there was hushed uproar. On street corners, in church parking lots, townsfolk were straining for small talk, desperate to pretend that this was just a regular day. That the text messages hadn't flashed all around the county before the sun had even risen. That their hometown was not, once again, a hunting ground.

Finch stopped at Nectar PD, marched in, and casually pulled the Flora Riddell casefile. Slipping it beneath her Kevlar, she got back in the cruiser and made the short drive to Main Street.

Merle's Diner was an unintentional throwback. Chessboard vinyl flooring, plastic creeping plants, a jukebox, and, for some reason, licence plates from around the world lining the walls. Up at the counter, in the booths, even between the waitresses – the word was out.

– *It's the heartless man, he's back, I know it.*

– *Oh, Irma. Nobody knows that. Probably not even the authorities yet.*

– *He's been biding his time all these years but a leopard don't change its spots. Pure evil. To kill a child and then eat a nectarine after? That's the devil himself. We been lost ever since Reverend Lamb left us. No compass. That's why the Sugar Man has come back.*

– *Now, Irma. You know he didn't* leave *us. He ascended. He's waiting for us.*

Shaking her head as she passed them, Finch took the back booth. The waitress came and poured coffee without asking. 'What can I fix for ya, hon?'

'Just the coffee.'

When she was gone, Finch took a breath.

Opening Flora's casefile was a sleeping bear. Her mind knew

there was way too much against *him* being back. But she couldn't ignore the nagging feeling any longer.

Finch took out Flora's evil-eye necklace from an envelope. It was broken, though the lobster claw clasp still worked. Its gold plating had faded down the years, revealing the cheap metal beneath. Looking around, she put it on, hiding it beneath her armour. Then she started to flip through the pages of the casefile.

In Detroit, they were stored electronically – behind layers of passwords, permissions. But this was a mess of tatty transcripts, phone and bank data, hardly legible arrest records, observations on persons of interest, a faded coroner's report – on and on it went.

Under height and weight, Flora's characteristics: *black hair, green eyes, a star-shaped birthmark at the back of her neck.*

Beneath, the general narrative began:

Victim went missing early evening of Jan 21st, 1998, aged 16. Last confirmed sighting at the Food-O-Rama on Maple Ave approx. 5pm. Victim found 4 days after disappearance behind Speedy's Mountain Truck Plaza. Manner of death was via strap of mother's handbag. No foreign 'DNA' found on body or in vicinity. Notable lack of evidence at scene; common store-bought sugar coating facial area, matching the receipt from victim's grocery purchases. A nectarine very close to the body displaying bitemarks. Dental signature returned no matches on criminal database. Killer believed to have large hands given indentations but a small mouth. Victim was found holding imitation gold 'evil eye' star necklace. [This detail intentionally kept out of media reporting]. Victim was also in possession of book with an inscription by her high school teacher.

*Victim was from a well-liked and respected family
who had no prior dealings with Nectar PD. Father,
Edward Riddell. Photographer. Owns studio on Main.
Had been out of town that day on a photography job
in Kane, PA. Returned around 5pm to care for infant
child. At that time, mother, Esther Riddell, left the
family home to attend her place of worship, Bleeding
Lamb Pentecostal. Phone logs and multiple witnesses
support their alibis. They could offer no known
enemies that might have wanted to harm the victim,
nor were they aware of any threats against her.*

Arrests

*Samuel Salinas – an anonymous witness placed victim
speaking to a male in a vehicle in the Old Industrial
District. This was subsequently identified as Samuel
Salinas who was arrested. Subject later released on
back of exculpatory findings.*

*Ira Pike – Seen talking to victim outside Food-O-Rama
prior to disappearance. Male subject was both victim's
high school teacher and made an inscription in book
found by the body on day of the murder. Arrested 1
week after body recovered but released due to lack of
evidence.*

Finch put the papers away and sipped her coffee with a
grimace. She glanced at the two old women at the counter.
They feared a devil, a Sugar Man. But even now, fifteen years
on, it wasn't known whether Flora's killer had been a moment-
ary madness or a monster. The press had latched on to the
spilled sugar and given him the moniker. Fable spread quicker
than fact. It wasn't known whether there even *was* a Sugar Man.
Whether the disappeared girls down the years had any kind of

connection, or whether they were simply disparate tragedies that happened to be from the same state. Then again, half of all homicides went unsolved. Secret monsters did exist. They mowed lawns, bought groceries, smiled at neighbours.

Looking at the two old ladies, Finch wondered again if the reverend's disappearance could have been connected to Flora Riddell's death. *Maybe she saw something she shouldn't have. And maybe one of his followers took care of it. Maybe Lamb is hiding in a Panamanian jungle right now.*

Opening the casefile again, Finch took out an old Polaroid. It was faded. She saw herself in it. And, next to her, Flora was mid-scowl, whereas she was laughing – the carefree kind that didn't yet have reasons to temper it.

Finch vaguely remembered the moment it was snapped – Flora's dad making a silly joke. *Brrr-itos. Get it? Brrrr. Cold.* Stomach twisting, she put them away.

Then paused.

Finch took the Polaroid out again and peered at it. In the background, a familiar girl. Messy, dark hair, green eyeshadow, freckles. *A friend of Flora's?*

Flipping the photo, she recognized Flora's handwriting. *Me, D and Alana on Day 1.*

'Alana *Wells* . . .' Finch mumbled to herself. 'That was her name.'

A building curiosity in her gut, Finch pulled up the details on the other murdered girls in surrounding counties. All unknown to each other, all murdered in different ways, no evident similarity beyond being under the age of twenty and female.

Vicky Bracco, 1985. Josie Bell, '88. Sasha Ducharme, '90. Henrietta Nowak, '93.

'Alana isn't on the list . . .'

Finch necked her coffee, then went to the counter. Merle

Boswell came out the back, his old face twisting into recognition. 'I'll be darned. Dakota Finch?'

'Mr Boswell. Been a hundred years, huh.'

'Well, look at you. I heard you was law enforcement and here you is.'

'Living the dream.' She handed over her money.

'No, ma'am. You don't pay here.'

'That's kind but I'd like to.'

''Fraid that's my decision, young lady.' He solemnly motioned up to the framed photo of Taylor on the wall, next to the urn containing his ashes.

'I heard about his illness. I'm sorry.'

'I know my son really cared for you in life, Dakota.'

'Yeah.' Finch pocketed her money thinking that, in life, the only person Taylor ever cared about was in that framed photo.

Back in the cruiser, she took out her cell and called Bill Moreno.

Ahh, Dakota. How's the country air?

'Pungent. Wish you were here.'

He laughed, deep and sonorous. *Listen, kid. IA haven't made a decision yet on the charges. Too early to say if that's a good sign. You get any press contacting you?*

'A few voicemails, but I deleted.'

OK, good.

'Listen, Bill. Seeing as you have me up here playing *Little House on the Prairie*, I figure you could do me a favour?'

Only you would ask for favours while you're on your last chance.

'Your guy in Records. Could he find someone for me? It's just one name, Bill.'

Go on.

'Alana Wells. Spent time in Catoonah County. Would be my age.'

This to do with your Jane Doe up in the hills?

'Could be.'

I'll talk to my guy. Meantime, try not to rock the boat too much.

Darkfall. Finch stopped on Kinzua and whispered to herself, *Time to rock the boat.*

The trailer park where she'd grown up had never been Shangri-La but today it was half-derelict. There was an ammonia tinge to the air. Several trailers showed the telltale signs of meth dens. Windows open, despite the cold. Baby monitors outside doors. Yards strewn with bottles of anti-freeze, duct-taped rubber hoses, blackened gloves.

Finch felt nothing. It never felt like home back then. *Sure as shit doesn't now.*

Walking through the past, she saw her old home, long-abandoned after her mother's death. The broken stoop where she used to sit. The outside shower where men would leer at her.

Closing her eyes, Finch recalled a swamp of shady men down the years who'd stared. Commented. Touched. And this trailer park drew them like moths to a bare bulb.

She recalled mentioning the shitty people hanging around Nectar, around Fest. Flora's response had never left her: *you don't have to tell* me *that.*

Finch shook her head now. *What did you mean by that, Flo? I was so caught up in my own shit, I never stopped to think you might have had your own.*

Opening her eyes, she looked at the last, decrepit trailer. Ira Pike had spoken to Flora not long before her death. Gave her a gift. He was a sleeping dog worth kicking.

Finch knocked on the trailer door and it shuddered in its rusted hinges. She knocked again. After half a minute, half a face emerged in the crack.

Ira Pike's face was red, his skin waxy. The sunken half

seemed even more sunken these days, somehow. Years of drinking had given his voice a slow control despite the drunkenness. 'The hell are you?'

'You don't remember me?'

'I don't remember much of much if I can help it.'

'Police, Mr Pike.' She tapped her badge on her belt. 'Can I come in?'

With a grunt, he swung the door open and went back to his kitchenette to pour a slug of vodka into an egg cup. Weeds grew out of the carpet. There was a dead wasp's nest in the corner of the trailer. Snowflakes blew in freely through a hole in the roof. The only order in this place was on the shelves. Everywhere Finch looked, stacks of books and old newspaper clippings. Newspaper reviews of his own book, curling away from the wall like toenails.

'You really don't recognize me, huh?'

'Nectar PD all look the same to me.'

'I'm not Nectar.' Again, she tapped her badge.

Pike squinted. 'Detroit. So, what? They're bird shit and you're caviar?'

'Something like that.' The field out back was a mess — trash bags, junk, debris. Plenty of room to burn and bury. 'That your land, Mr Pike?'

'My own personal utopia, yeah. What's this all about?'

'Was hoping you could give me a little of your time.'

'Nobody can give time, only lose it. *Tempus edax rerum.*'

'Nice.' Finch nodded, wondering what the Latin was for *tedious asshole*. 'But I don't think you ever got round to teaching us dead languages.'

Pike narrowed his drunk eyes now. '. . . I know you.'

'That's right, teach. You remember me, huh? And Flora? Thick as thieves, we were.'

Looking away, he refilled his cup. 'I've been over that a thousand times.'

'Not with *me*.' Finch sat across from him and let her presence weigh. 'You taught us about heroes in your class. Monte Cristo. Odysseus. You believe in heroes, Mr Pike?'

He leaned back from her. 'No.'

'No. Me neither. You ever seen a dead body?'

'What?'

'It's not a trick question.'

'No. Why, what is this?'

'I have. Green as shit, that first time. Only a few years out of your classroom, in fact. I was a rookie, responding to an RTA. I see a shoe on the road, right? Next to this car wreck. I can see the driver inside, eyes open. Figure he's still alive. For some reason, I picked up the shoe for him. But it wasn't empty. Big mistake. Now, I always give em' a little kick first.'

'. . . What do you want from me?'

'A week after that, I get an emergency call on the radio from Dispatch. Reports of an at-risk child on Cherrywood Drive, father has lost control. Dispatch have the kid on the phone, they can hear the sound of a metal bat, beating the life out of Mom. I reach the address within ten minutes, ready to save the day. Except nobody's home. I double-check the address. I'm on Cherrywood *Road* not Drive. By the time cops arrived, the whole family were dead.'

'I think it would be best if you left now.'

Finch pulled up a stool and sat right in front, boxing him in. 'See, Ira, I looked at those crime scene photos. I deserved that. You know what it's like to see a broken child? Six years old? The thing you can't get over is how small they are. Dead eyes don't shine. Like fish in a bucket. Cloudy. You look into them and it changes you. Your brain says *OK, this is the world,*

I guess. Because you're right, Ira. Ain't no fucking heroes. Ain't no fucking role models.' She held up a photocopy of his inscription. '*To Flora, don't forget me when you get where you're going. Ira.* Signed and dated. You remember that?'

'Please.' Pike spoke shakily. 'Leave.'

'Why'd you do that, Ira? Maybe you felt something for her, hm?'

'No.'

'Come on, *Mr Pike*. We all remember you. You were real good. Gave us a lot of attention. Especially the girls, right? And you were close with Flora, weren't you?'

'You were closer. What does that prove?'

'Your alibi is weak.'

'People who live alone tend to have that problem. Now, I was a *good* teacher. I never . . . If you had anything on me, I'd be in jail already. So, just get out.'

'I could shoot you in your fucked-up face right now. I'd say you went for a knife and they'd believe me. Who would care? You think you'll be remembered by the world, *teach*? Maybe for your little book with no author photo, huh? By your five loser readers?'

'Why?' he whispered. 'Why are you doing this to me?'

'Now don't start blubbing, I just got one more question. Where were you this morning between 2 and 3AM?'

'What?'

'You heard me.'

'Here, where else would I be?'

'Thank you for your cooperation.' Finch stood and went to the door. She left it ajar, as she always liked to do, as though she could march back in whenever she felt like it.

It was near pitch black by the time she got back to her motel.

As she made her way towards her room, the elderly clerk waved at her. 'I know you from somewhere, don't I?'

'I grew up here.'

'So, this is home.'

'A home*town*.'

'Hometowns are bittersweet. Like biting into a tangerine with a worm inside.'

Finch didn't have a reply. She skipped up the steps to her room and took off her Kevlar. Her chest was tight, her abdomen cramping. *Need to top up my prescription. Wait, did the old man say tangerine or nectarine? Whatever, doesn't matter.*

As she closed the curtain, she noticed something out the window.

Across from the motel, standing just away from a cone of streetlight, stood a slim, bearded man. He was motionless, as though waiting for a bus, looking straight ahead.

Watching?

With a shrug, Finch latched the door, slipped her gun under the pillow, and sank into oblivion again.

FIVE

In her dream, Dakota was lying on the clinic bed. She felt the crinkle of tissue-roll beneath her and listened to the distant clamour of protestors outside. The medical trolley squeaked as it was pushed towards her now.

Did they offer you something to eat on your way in, Dakota?
She nodded.
But you didn't eat, did you? It's very important that you didn't.

Finch woke in the dark and knuckled a tear away. The same nightmare. The same one as always. Sharp little fragments of memory, like walking over glass in the fog.

Get up. Time to go.

She had six voice messages from journalists seeking comment about the Maloney thing. She deleted them. Along with the single text from Jesse: *meet at town hall, 1 hour.*

Groaning, she forced herself up, her sore eyes fixing on the note on the wall:

I KNOW WHAT YOU DID.

The lightbulb in her room didn't work, though she could've sworn it had the night before. She made a phone call to reception and asked for a replacement, then prepared her things for the day ahead in weak grey dawn light.

In the bathroom, she took off her tanktop and panties.

The mirror showed a tangle of brown hair above a dog-weary face. The patchwork of taut abdominals she had slacked off on lately. And a ripening bruise on her chin.

She showered, averting her eyes as she cleaned her left side, leaving the word cut into her ribcage 'til last:

SILENCE

She put on her uniform, her body armour. Finch was good at what she did. It was just the rest she was bad at. Her now-ex-husband had accepted that long ago. She didn't have friendships. She didn't have family. She wasn't even really a person. Finch was a process. A scalpel to slice through artifice, exposing the truth beneath. That was her living. Her purpose.

Finch reached Old Town Hall at sunrise. It was a bugle reveille of clapboard, Doric columns, and pleated red, white and blues. Cochran's office was on the ground floor at the rear. Inside, his books on criminology were showcased prominently, photographs of him posing with the Republican Party top brass. His old sheriff's badge was framed on the wall, dates of service engraved in a plaque of thanks. Above his sandalwood desk, a chunky gold crucifix.

'Found God, Quayle?'

'Without the Evangelical vote, you don't get far.' He bit into a bagel, cream cheese splattering his tie. 'Wan' won? Only got onion-poppyseed left.'

In that moment, Jesse Sullivan entered. 'Morning, Detective.'

'Where are we at, Jesse?'

'No early breaks. But Hanlon is doing the autopsy today.'

'What about the ground search?'

'Turned up nothing. Same goes for the dogs.'

'CCTV?'

'So far, zero. We're still appealing for it but folk ain't partial around here. In terms of haulage companies, we're still going through lists. For now, a few employees with records but nothing concerning. We're digging into timetable anomalies. As for recently released violent offenders, we got a couple of bad eggs in-state. But nowhere near Catoonah at the time.'

'And no recent missing person reports?'

'Nope. Not around here, anyway. Likely, she's from far away. Or foreign.'

'Yeah, Jesse. But she got here *somehow*.'

'To that, none of the cars in the local area are un-accounted for.'

'Well, shit.'

'What concerns me –' Cochran smoothed cream cheese out of his moustache. 'Is not who she is, but who killed her.'

'Right, but the former leads to the latter, doesn't it?'

'Listen.' He tapped the framed poster on the wall behind him depicting the new Heritage Fest 2013. 'The asshole who killed Flora took the whole town down with him. We were hanging by a thread. Now, it's been fifteen years, it took a *lot* to bring Fest back home.'

'I told you, I deal in murder. I could give a rat's shit about this town or your legacy.'

'I'm aware of that. But you were brought here to get a result.'

'No, I'm here as a favour. Now, my directions were clear. If your boys can't execute, that's not my fault – no offence, Jesse.'

'None taken.'

Sighing, Mayor Cochran smoothed back his eggshell-white hair. 'All right, Dakota. Look. I know you don't like me. I know you don't like this place. But there are a lot of people here. Lives. We need Fest to be a success. We need the Burr

Group on our side. Not to mention the elections next week. That's the reality of it. You gotta close this and fast.'

'I've come here to do my job. I'll do it. Just don't start thinking I care.' She jutted her chin at the poster on the wall now depicting townsfolk in jeans and hoodies linking arms with smiling Versammlungsvolk. 'And I've just thought of something. Has anyone checked in with the colony? We need to see if Versammlung is missing anybody.'

Cochran baulked. 'That wouldn't be possible. Those people don't leave their village. They live in isolation. You know this.'

'And we both know there are exceptions for those who are under eighteen.'

'Jane Doe isn't under the age of eighteen. Anyhow, this is a homicide. For a killer to have even seen her, assuming she's from Versammlung, he'd have to be *inside* that village.'

'Right. And that does raise a possibility. How hard did you scrutinize the men in that colony after Flora's murder? Before you say anything, I *know* it's unlikely. I know they're pacifists. But it could explain why the killer was never found fifteen years ago.'

'Dakota. Get real.'

'Anyone can lie,' she shrugged. 'Anyone can put their hands around a throat.'

'But not anyone can fire a shotgun. Plus, if Doe was from Versammlung and the killer was too, how would he get her all the way out here? Horse and cart?'

'I can't answer that. But we need to cross everything off our list.'

'We don't bother them, they don't bother us.' Cochran sighed. 'I don't like this.'

'There's not a lot to like here. On that, we agree.'

*

Finch stopped the cruiser on a well-heeled, residential cul-de-sac off Main. The cars parked at perfect intervals, the white fences, the star-spangled banners – Snow Shoe Lane was an exercise in American perfection.

Yet Flora's house was a simple old brick foursquare. It seemed smaller now, somehow. Faded. Finch felt a wave of drowsiness crest inside, her mouth suddenly dry. The Visprozan was doing its job but she would run out soon.

Need to pass by the drug store.

Taking a breath, she got out of the car. The two-chime doorbell stirred old memories, the quick thunder of Flora's footsteps down the stairs. Her breathless grin. *Hey, loser.*

The door opened, trilling joyously as though announcing a customer. Edward Riddell wore browline spectacles and a blue Icelandic sweater. His beard was grey now but his eyes were still glum sea-green. '. . . Dakota?'

'Hi, Ed.' She could barely stand to look at that face. 'Sorry to turn up out the blue.'

'No, I just . . .' A conflicted laugh. 'I'm just a bit surprised, that's all.'

'I wish this were social, but –' She tapped her police badge.

'Oh,' he lost his smile. 'Come in, come in.'

Finch passed him into the sickeningly familiar hallway. In her memory, it had always been neat. Now it was a Tetris of moving boxes, piles of folders, packing paper scraps.

The thermostat was up way high. Flora's shoes were no longer lined up by the door. Esther's crucifixes and Pentecostal images were gone. Dolly's nursery was now a mini photography studio. But the smell hadn't changed. Each family had its own smell. And Finch had adopted this one.

She nodded up at the old store bell from the studio on Main. 'You kept it. That jangle is really clear in my memory.'

'Yeah.' He shook his head at himself. 'When I sold up, I couldn't stand to lose it.'

Ed led her to the kitchen and Finch sat in the counter chair she always chose as a kid. Before her, the fruit bowl was brimming. He set coffee to brew and stood across the island from her. They said nothing for a while, filling in blanks for all the long years between them.

Finch noticed the indentation in the wood island, Flora's old scuff marks. Her doodles on the counter. She'd been dead now almost as long as she had lived.

'How long has it been?' he asked.

'Do you actually want an answer?'

'No, I don't.' Laughing, he poured out two cups. 'I'm an old man now.'

'No, you're not.' Finch smiled. 'Seems like you're doing good.'

'Financially, I was for a long time.' He shrugged. 'The rest . . . you know about.'

She looked away and scanned the clutter. Rolls of scotch tape, pliers by the faucet, a couple of exacto knives. 'So. You're leaving?'

'Yes, actually. Years ago, I got an offer on the house. Said yes. Even took down Flora's photos. In the end, I couldn't. But recently, another came in. This time, it felt right.'

'How come?'

'I've wanted to sell up for years. Esther isn't coming out of that place anytime soon. I needed to make some changes for so long. I just finally quit my whining and made them. And now, I'm actually seeing some light. Took a long time but I'm seeing it.'

'I'm real glad, Ed.' She noticed the empty wine bottles lined up on the counter next to a small stack of photo albums. 'Celebrating with a lucky lady?'

'Lady?'

He tracked her gaze to the bottles. 'Oh. Well. She's a big reason for that light.' He laughed again, looser now. 'It's my daughter. She came over the other night.'

'Dolores? You patched things up? Last time we spoke, you were out of contact.'

'She didn't have an easy time growing up in all *this*. I think it was pretty lonely. I wasn't there for her. Not nearly enough. She went to live with her grandmother years ago. So much wasted time . . . But yeah. I talked to some people, got some help, you know. She came over and we opened up and it was . . . warm and hopeful. She even talked about co-habiting.'

'She'd come back to Nectar?'

'No. I'd move out to the city. We'd get a bigger place.'

'Well, I'm happy to hear that, Ed. Really.'

'And yes, if you're wondering, I did give her a little wine. Don't arrest me.'

When the smile passed, Finch pursed her lips. 'Listen, I know my being here tugs at old wounds. But I've been sent from Detroit to work a case. I can't get into details, I just wanted you to hear it from me rather than get a shock later.'

'Well, whatever it is, I think it's great you're here. They're going to need you.'

'Thanks, Ed.' She stood. 'And for the coffee. Beats Merle's.'

'Easily done.' He accompanied her to the door. 'You know, it really is good to see you made it. Your dream.'

'Detroit PD isn't the FBI.' She turned to face him. 'But it beats collecting garbage at Fest, right?'

'I'm proud of you, Dakota. I know Flora would be too.' He put a hand on her shoulder. 'And for the record? The past wasn't all bad. I hope you remember that.'

December 26th, 1997

Flora threw on the long grey denim skirt that she had picked out weeks ago and her favourite sweater. It was a big fuzzy brown mess but wearing it felt like a sip of hot chocolate, even if Mom called it *the hairball*. Checking her cola gloss, then lacing up her bovver boots, Flora glanced at her desk. Her class assignment lay untouched under last month's *dELiA*s*. The holidays had come and gone and she should've started on it. But the idea of the new semester was a substitute teacher that nobody was taking seriously yet. Besides, she was *late*.

Downstairs, in the front room, the TV was blaring. Dad's face was buried in the huge business section of the paper, mumbling to himself. Dolly was asleep on his chest. At his feet, a mound of puzzle books, ciphers, company brochures.

. . . Stocks retreated from early gains to end lower, hurt by weakness in computing issues and concerns that economic turmoil in Asia could damage US corporate profits . . .

'Dad, have you seen my scarf?'

'No, honey. Which one?'

'*My* scarf. It's purple. I only have one scarf, Dad.'

'Sorry, Flower Power. Have you asked your –'

'– No, she has not.' Esther huffed into the room, snatched the remote away and turned the business news way down. 'It's probably in the car. Ed, why don't you just drive her? You're headed that way yourself.'

'Yeah, but not for a while.'

'It's her first day of work.'

'I know that.'

'You just want to screw around with your little stocks.'

'We all have our hobbies. I don't crap on your church. Besides, these *little stocks* –'

'Save it, Mr Night School. I don't care.'

'You'll change your tune the day I strike oil.'

'And I'll be changing it the day you strike *out*. Why couldn't you take an interest in something free? We don't have money to lose.'

'I'm *aware* of our finances, honey. You have faith for other things. Try a little in me.'

'How can I put faith in a lottery, Edward?'

'Because not everyone is picking their numbers blind.' He took back the remote and turned the volume back up.

Esther sighed. 'Flora, you need me to run you to the fairground?'

'It's OK, Mom. I'm meeting Dakota anyhow.'

'Then get a move on. You'll be late.' Esther went back to the kitchen.

'I *know*.'

'Hey, Flower Power?' Ed called.

'Yeah?'

'You'll kick ass today. See you out there.' With a wink, he returned his olive eyes to the stock ticker on the bottom of the screen.

. . . Your 3PM recap, now. The Dow Jones Industrial Average fell for a fifth time in six sessions, losing 70.25 points, to 8,899.95, its first close below 8,900 since last April . . .

Flora left her home and hurried through the cold streets of Nectar. Reaching Main, she looped her dad's scarf tighter around her neck and grimaced on the sharp wind. Passing the offices of *The Catoonah Republican*, today's headline – for once – caught her eye.

FOOD-O-RAMA TO CLOSE DOWN IN NEW YEAR

Well, that's just great. Now we'll have to get groceries in McKinstry or Andover and that'll be all Mom talks about for the next millennium.
Underneath the headline, there was a piece talking about the recent appeal from Town Hall for Nectarites to not strap dead elk to their cars. *Outgoing mayor's 'polite request for use of tarp' during tourist season leaves townsfolk indignant – electoral wipeout looms.*
Hugging herself against the cold, Flora tried to picture herself as a journalist one day. Not in a shitty town like Nectar but in a real city. She didn't really know how it worked but she liked the idea of taking photographs in nature. Or maybe writing about bands for some cool magazine. Whoever she would become, Flora refused to worry about dumb little things, the way Mom did. Life could take her anywhere – her stomach flipped thinking about it. It was just the waiting-to-find-out part that sucked.
Still, Skunk Anansie was playing the Electric Factory in Philly soon and Flora would die before missing out. If Heritage Fest had to be the usual yawn parade of bunting and lame-o accordion music, at least she'd make a little cash in the meantime.
Beyond Main Street, Lake Sweetness was tea-coloured today, its grey beaches empty. Nectar had been built around its southern shore – first settled by the Catoonah peoples, then displaced by English pilgrims, only to be replaced themselves by German ones. For a minute in time, after coal had been discovered, people swarmed in. Ventricles of railroad along

with them. Grand hotels sprouted up around the lake. Even a casino at one time.

But the moment passed, the mines were picked clean. Today, Nectar's population hovered around a thousand. Her railroads sang melodies no more. And the hotels that still stood were clinging to life as senior-living homes.

Outside Merle's Diner, Dakota Finch had her hands stuffed in her pockets, Godzilla-stomping a paper cup. She wore brown Dickies carpenter pants, beat-up skate shoes, and her usual grey half-zip fleece. There was a new red mark on her face.

'Hey, loser,' Flora said.

'Hey, dickface.'

'Shall we?'

'First, Wawa.'

The girls entered the convenience store; Shania Twain was playing. Greeting the clerk, they went to the chiller. At the window, Ira Pike was fussing with his book, pretending he hadn't been looking at the dirty magazine shelf. Flora waved but he pretended not to see that either. Dakota picked out her bottle of Beachside Blast Fruitopia and motioned jacking it off. Shaking her head, Flora picked Cherry Vanilla Groove. They paid and left.

Dakota looked over her shoulder. 'Man, Pike is such a creep.'

'Come on, he'll *hear* you.'

'He can't lip-read, can he? Not with one eye.'

'Harsh. Anyway, he's harmless enough.'

'Harmless? The guy's obsessed with black magic. He'll probably cut up those porno mags into pentagrams and whack off thinking about you tonight.'

'OK, Finch. *Gross.*' Flora wrinkled her nose. 'But I'll say this. His book isn't bad.'

'As a sleeping aid, *maybe*. Anyway, who gives a shit about witches or pilgrims?'

'Well, I'm not saying I give a *shit*. But at least he's telling the truth of this place. All that civil war postcard crap, happy pioneers, blah, blah, blah. What about all the women they drowned? What about all the indigenous folks they kicked out? Or worse?'

'Nerd.' With a disguised grimace, Dakota put the Fruitopia bottle to her red cheek.

Flora wanted to ask about it but understood there was no point.

Everybody knew that Mrs Finch was 'having a hard time'. That Caldwell Finch would come home to his family, now and then, to make a go of it, only to jump back in his truck a few days later and roar away.

The marks on Dakota's face first showed up a year ago.

Flora hated to think of her suffering. It was wrong but she knew it was a pain her friend could live with. What really upset her, deep down, was that Dakota never spoke a word of it. Never let her in. It felt like, if one door was locked inside her, then they all were.

Around the time those marks showed up is when Flora's feelings had started to change. Her curious longing had become a desperate obsession. By now, her logic was a bank hostage but her heart the gunman, screaming *get down, don't look at me*.

They walked along Lakeshore Drive, the ring road around Lake Sweetness. In gaps between hemlock trees, vacation cabins stood empty. Boats along wooden docks were tarped and still. A honking van sped past now, leering boys hanging out the windows.

Dakota rolled her eyes. 'How much you wanna bet those out-of-town assholes will be working with us?'

For no reason, Flora blushed. She had always felt a paralysing fear that people would notice her friendship with Dakota. Or that it would be taken for something it wasn't. But then that fear always collided with the crushing truth that there would never be a reason to.

By now, they were passing groups of kids their age. Cars were backed up. Parents were dropping off, then pulling a U-turn to escape the traffic.

The County Fairgrounds sat on the northern banks of the lake. It was a vast green, stretching all the way to the woodland – through which, ordinarily, the hiss and grumble of the truck stop was distantly audible.

Not tonight. Tonight, 'What is Love' by Haddaway was thudding over the buzz of the growing crowd. The entrance turnstiles were all open.

The usual county sign had been covered up with a new one, which carried a little horse and carriage logo:

WILLKOMMEN TO THE 106ᵀᴴ NECTAR HERITAGE FEST!
[Proudly sponsored by The Burr Group]

'This is gonna suck,' Dakota said.

'Yeah,' Flora lied. She had to admit, she felt excitement as they joined the mass of kids pouring in. *Gotta be at least a couple hundred of us.* 'Not too late to blow this off.'

'I wish. I need the money.' Dakota scowled as she scanned faces. 'You think Taylor will show up?'

'Taylor Boswell?'

'Yup.'

'No idea.'

They passed through the turnstiles.

Everywhere Flora looked, she saw American and German flags knotted together. Most of the stalls were ready for business, selling everything from tater tots to *Don't Tread On Me* patches. Fried dough clashed with the smell of fresh lemonade. In the distance, the Ferris wheel revolved slowly, its gondolas empty.

'So.' Flora had to raise her voice over the hiss and clank of the test rides. 'Taylor – why'd you ask about him?'

'Eh, it's nothing.'

'OK.' Flora's throat knotted.

But now Dakota side-bumped her. 'Hey, look at all these fucking yokels. And you thought *we* lived in the ass-end of nowhere.'

'Yeah.' Flora forced laughter.

'Speaking of which, check out the freaks lost in time.'

Off to one side – a small gathering of Versammlung kids around a horse and carriage. They kept their eyes on the ground as they worked, unloading boxes of dandelion wine. Flora only knew what they taught her in school: the Versammlungsvolk and the Amish weren't the same thing. They didn't like their photograph being taken. And they spoke only old German.

'Kinda feel sorry for them,' Flora said. 'They look scared.'

'Because they think the devil is out here waiting to grab them.'

'But I don't get it. Why are they here? I thought their whole thing was isolation?'

'From the looks of it, *they* don't get it, either.'

The girls followed the crowd to the main pavilion. Above it, a giant vinyl banner read:

★ **VOTE TO ELECT QUAYLE**
COCHRAN FOR MAYOR ★

The field was a chaotic hubbub of kids, three hundred self-conscious glances. Braying boy laughter, shrieking girls. Flora took it all in, the desperation to be seen, unseen, to fit in.

'Goddamn bootcamp,' Dakota said.

She was right. The whole scene, Flora thought, looked like a rag-tag platoon, bound for some distant war.

Now a small man with ratty features emerged from the portacabin behind the pavilion, trotted up to the stage. He had a thinning mullet, puffy face, and a soul patch on his chin.

'I'm Parsons Rigney.' He tapped the mic hard and the field fell silent. 'Which, for all you first-timers, means I'm God. We open in two hours, so your beaks shut now. You've all had your training. Stick to it. Two breaks per night, twenty minutes, then ten. Coordinate with your detail manager. Pay in cash is at the end of the week. You mess up, you're gone, you get zip. Questions?'

He scanned the crowd scornfully.

'Good. Because that was a trick question. You got nothing to ask. You know your jobs, just do 'em. Oh, last thing: this is the first year where we'll have collaborating guests from Versammlung itself. You treat those kids like angels or you answer to me. That's it. And remember, dammit, folks are here to have fun. So, smile. Help people out. And your *Fest Helper* sash stays on at all times. Clear?'

An adolescent groan in the affirmative.

As they all dispersed, Dakota gave Flora her *what-an-asshole* eyebrow hoist. Neither of the girls noticed the gaze of Ira Pike off to the side. His one working eye followed them until they were swallowed by the crowd.

SIX

Finch walked through the industrial outskirts at dusk, hands stuffed in her body armour. As a kid, her dad had spoken of a time when Nectar had droned and churned loudly day and night, what his parents had called the *good days*. But now it was boarded up – silent except for the sound of freight trains galumphing to other towns that still had a use for them.

This mountain range was made up of hundreds of places like this. Snow-globe towns, home to generations of simple folk, picked up and rattled by conflicting corporate interests. One fine day, the mill, plant or mine was plucked out of their lives and then consequences snowed down: pink slips, debt, malignant disease.

Men in suits would visit from time to time, promising to bring back steel, bring back coal, bring back the good old days at the low, low price of their American vote. It disgusted Finch – that never-ending belief in a system that never deserved it. The blind faith that where they were vomited out into the world was the best place for them to live and die. Not that she was some world explorer, she'd only made it as far as Hawaii. But that was far enough for her. When all this shit was over, she'd find some cabin to hole up in and drink herself into a Pacific sundown.

The parking lot for the Mangy Moose was huge. It had to be on account of its clientele. Immediately, Finch recognized the dark-green Freightliner Columbia parked at the back. She'd pulled the licence from the DMV, for one thing. But if there was any doubt who it belonged to, the side of the cab was emblazoned with the name *Carmella*.

Finch entered the Mangy Moose along with a few truckers – salmon upstream. When her father had first started driving trucks, she'd still been in diapers. It was meant to be temporary. But Caldwell Finch intended a lot of things that had never come to pass.

She remembered him hating the CB radio lingo of these men, even in person – the lonely patter they shared. But whenever she travelled with him, she loved being able to understand that secret code, the language of adventure. It warmed her to know that these men, even though usually unacquainted, still cared for each other: *westbound, four-wheeler in the ditch, mile marker 28, bears all over it.*

It was like he was part of a fraternity, its only requirement a rig and solitude. But thoughts of her father pissed her off. Still, that was a useful emotion for the present.

Sam Salinas was in his booth at the back, flirting with the waitress. Finch slipped into the booth behind them.

'He told you that?' Sam laughed. 'The *reason* they call him Veggie Boo is because he used to be a vegetarian Buddhist. Until his wife left him. Now, he's just Slim Godless.'

Chastity Cochran laughed until her manager passed by. 'Sam, let her do her job.'

'I wasn't bothering the girl. Was I bothering you, sweetheart?'

'No, sir. One of the perks around here is the witty conversating.'

'Oh, I agree. For example: what do you call an honest dispatcher?'

'The mute button. You told me that one last week.'

'Well *excuse* me for trying to entertain.'

'You're a goof, Sam Salinas.' She laughed, her tongue curling out of her mouth, and took the pencil from behind her hoop earring. 'I gotta get back, what'll it be?'

'A pitcher of Milwaukee champagne and a kielbasa sub.'

'Beer and sausage, you got it.'

When she left, Finch slid into Sam's booth. His eyes were still on Chastity's swishing ponytail, her bouncing hoops.

'Sounds like the girl's got a crush on you.'

'Nah, she's just a kid.'

'Yeah?' Finch winked. 'Tell that to *her*.'

'And you are?' Salinas sized her up now, taking in the bruise on the chin, the coldness of the smile. 'I'll be damned. Dakota? Last time I seen you, you were just a kid . . .'

She flashed her Detroit PD badge. 'All grown up now.'

'You gotta be kidding me.'

'You're the one with the jokes.'

Salinas searched her eyes but they were thorn bushes. 'What do you want?'

'Pick your brains is all. How you been, Sam? I see you're still doing the same thing.'

'We can't all achieve our lofty goals.' Chastity Cochran returned with the pitcher of beer and left with an uncertain look. Salinas poured himself a glass, then licked the suds from his lip. 'Pick my brains over what, exactly?'

'My charming small talk had about run out anyway.' She slapped down a photograph of Flora on the table.

'I should've known.' He looked away.

'Sam, I know you've spoken to Nectar PD before –'

'– ten thousand times, yeah. And *I* know I don't have to talk to you.'

'Just a few questions is all.'

'Like what?'

'As it happens, I'm looking for a shotgun. You ever own one, Sam?'

'You really think I'm stupid? You didn't come here for Flora. You came here for that broad they found dead over at Speedy's.'

'We're just talking, Sam. That's all.'

'No. In '98, Cochran tried to burn me for Flora. If he thinks he gets another bite at the cherry, he's dumber than he looks. You bet your ass I'll fight him. Or you. Or anyone else.'

'Where were you in the early hours last night between 2 and 3AM?'

'Get fucked.' Salinas picked up his pitcher and moved to another booth.

Back at the motel, Finch paused in the lobby. Under faded brochures for tours and activities, she noticed something. The illustrated face of a bearded man smoking a pipe. Fishing it out, it was the jacket for *The Nectar Witch: Corruption. Curses. A Copycat Killer.*

'By Ira Pike . . .' She turned to the old clerk on reception. 'Hey, this yours?'

He gave a Gallic shrug.

'Gonna borrow it.'

'*Mi casa es tu casa.*'

'*Su.* When you don't know someone, it's *su.*'

Back in Room 202, the lightbulb still wasn't working. Finch showered, ordered pizza, and ate in the dark. Then she necked 15 mg washed down with Diet Coke. Before closing the curtain, she glanced outside. The watching man by the streetlamp was nowhere to be seen.

Finch got into her polyurethane bed, blood afloat on Visprozan. Head swimming, she pictured Sam Salinas encircling Jane Doe's throat with his hands. Those hands fit a lot better than Ira Pike's, in her mind.

All of Nectar knew about Sam's temper.

Down the years, they'd seen it in Carmella's face. On the rainy days when she'd wear sunglasses. Could it be that he had killed Flora after all and simply gotten lucky in '98? Then, drunk and careless, rolled the dice again with Doe?

And while I'm at it, maybe Sam has been out here all along, smiling and joking his way through life, winking and grinning, while strangling girls in the dark. Vicky Bracco, '85. Josie Bell, '88. Sasha Ducharme, '90. Henrietta Nowak, '93. And now Jane Doe.

Then again, there are a lot of differences. Flora was found. So was Doe. The other girls all just vanished. Nobody knows where they are. Buried under concrete, in some abandoned factory. Down a dead mineshaft nearby. Or burned to ash and taken by the wind.

On a whim, Finch reached for her phone and dialled Jesse Sullivan.

Detective?

'Jesse . . .' she murmured groggily. 'Need a favour.'

Shoot.

'I had a run-in tonight with Sam Salinas. He's not Nectar PD's biggest fan.'

That has been brought to my attention before. You OK?

'Dandy. He drives for Burr Heavy Haul still, right?'

Correct.

'So, let's use his employer, or lean on Carmella if we have to. I want to know what his alibi was on the night of the murder.'

Roger that. But why Sam?

'Just a hunch.' Finch hung up and tossed the phone into the darkness. In a shard of moonlight, she could see Flora's old note on the wall:

I KNOW WHAT YOU DID.

December 26th, 1997

Fest was in full swing. 'I Like to Move It' by Reel 2 Real was blaring. Ghost-train fog mixed in with the Virginia Slims smoke. Despite the winter bite, thousands of flabby moms were packed into Dirndlkleid and milkmaid dresses, thousands of flabby dads in pilgrim hats with fake beards attached. Embarrassed kids trailed behind them. Everywhere, smiles and stolen kisses. Neon-lit black eyes and teddy bear prizes. Distant screams and laughter. Lives lived.

But Flora was on garbage detail.

Sulkily, she stabbed trash with her nabber, then dumped it into a polyethene sack. She'd brought her Discman but it was pointless; it kept skipping each time she bent down. With her backpack, she had a method for keeping the Discman stable but it was at home.

The crowd went wild as a troupe of Schuhplattler dancers were welcomed on the Pavilion stage. Flora fought her way through the bodies and ended up by the port-a-potties in the space behind the Pavilion. Taking out her earphones, she huffed her bangs out of her face. A crushed can of RC Cola twinkled between two potties. Squeezing her way into the narrow space, Flora stabbed it.

That's when, through the gap, she spied Sheriff Quayle Cochran. He was a short, solid man, with greying hair and a painter's brush moustache.

'Pastor, I don't know what to tell you. I ain't mayor, yet. And even if I was, what could I possibly do? They're just kids.'

'They're muddying the waters.' Lester Lamb towered over him. His three-piece suit was a fir-green tonight. He finger-combed the jet-black and greying pompadour on his square head. 'Nectar is my pasture and I lead my flock. I don't welcome zealous wolves.'

'This is America, Lester. Folks believe whatever they want. Now, you know I honour your church. Heck, the wife sits in your front row. But with all respect, Nectar has one draw each year and that's Fest. It is the lifeblood of our economy.'

'My followers are integral to your *economy*.' He jabbed Cochran in the chest, gold rings catching the distant neon. 'And don't use the word *lifeblood* around me again.'

'OK, but you get my meaning. Fest pays homage to our past here. Like it or not, that past goes back to Versammlung. Now, for the first time, they've allowed their kids out here to sell wares. The public love it. So, I can't stop it. Not without a good reason, Pastor.'

'They are proselytizing.'

'They're selling pie. They ain't preaching to nobody.'

'Why are they here, then? They don't need money. Why the sudden change?'

'What do you want me to do?'

'Nothing, Quayle. Do nothing, like always. But when I lead my flock away from Nectar, just remember why it happened.' Lester Lamb adjusted his bolo tie, then stormed off.

Flora slipped out of the gap before she was spotted – and walked straight into her area manager. Devin Rigney was a potato-print of his father, only acne-scarred and twice his size. 'What's your name?'

'Flora Riddell.'

'You wanna tell me what you were doing just now, Riddell?'

'I, uh . . .' She chewed her lips and tasted cola gloss.

'Don't matter. I just don't wanna catch you slacking again, you hear?'

'Yes.'

'Good. Else I'll have you cleaning the port-a-potties for the whole winter.'

Scowling, he adjusted his *Fest Manager* sash then walked off. Flora angrily speared an empty beer can.

'Welcome to the first day of the rest of your life.' A girl with a frizzy mop of dark hair was standing there. Her voice had a crunchy, bored quality. With the oversized olive corduroy fleece and green eyeshadow, she looked like she'd just walked off the pages of *dELiA*s*.

'Right,' Flora said. 'Who woulda figured picking up garbage was so fun, huh?'

The girl laughed. 'First Fest?'

'Yeah.'

'Well, for future reference? Just ignore Trash Prince. I've lost count of the times he's threatened to fire me. All bark.'

'Trash Prince?'

'Devin Rigney. Manager's son. Total asshole. He walks around like he's in charge but he's on fifty cents more than us an hour.'

'Good to know. Thanks.'

'Alana Wells.'

'Flora Riddell.'

'Local?'

'Yep.'

'I'm from Danforth.'

'Whoa, that's a drive.'

'It was either this or being a mall elf.'

Now Flora laughed. 'You must really love our shitty town. I'd be the elf.'

'This job has its perks.'

Flora frowned. 'It does?'

The older girl bit her lip for a moment. Then she looked around and held open her jeans pocket. Inside, Flora saw a wad of fives and tens.

'Holy shitballs.'

The older girl winked. 'Tips, baby.'

'How?'

Alana sighed. 'All right. I'll tell you cos I like your sweater. First, introduce yourself. Maybe even with a fake name.' Her voice suddenly became girlish and bright. '*Thank you, I can take that trash from you. By the way, name is Cora, sir. Let me know if I can do anything to make your Fest experience more magical!*'

'Whoa. That's pretty good.'

'Or you could say some crap about letting you know if they have any questions. Or even drop some tips on them. *I'm not meant to say this but Collette's ribs are my favourite.*'

'I don't know if I can pull that off.'

'You'll get it. I prefer to circle around the food court where folks are paying cash not tokens – more chance of generosity.'

'But I'm meant to cover the Pavilion and restrooms.'

'You think anyone's keeping tabs? Now, always go for men. Always. Especially ones with sons around our age. It'll lead to some dumb joke about Junior being single but once you're *in* that joke, your chances of seeing green go way up. You'll wanna improve your make-up game, too. You're cute, so be cute in a way these assholes notice. Got it?'

'Yeah.' Flora blushed. 'Thanks.'

'Hey, loser.' Dakota approached now, hands in her pockets, eyebrow hoisted. 'Making friends with yokels?'

Alana took her in, then stabbed an empty hot-dog carton with her nabber. 'No offence taken by the way.'

'Whatever.' Dakota smirked. 'Come on, Riddell. Break time.'

'Good talking.' Flora smiled at the new girl who waved her nabber goodbye.

Dakota led the way, heading north through Fest. Flora followed. 'Pump Up the Jam' by Technotronic was blaring. Everywhere you looked, single words and short phrases:

PRIZES
PIG RACES
FRIED CHEESE
LAKE CRUISES
STRONGMAN GAMES

Dakota walked with a purpose, still scanning the crowd. She stopped from ride to ride – the Gravitron, Sinbad's Revenge, Starship 4000 – peering into the ticket booth each time.

'Who are you looking for? Taylor?'

'I refuse to do this damn job without a buzz on.' She marched towards the Tilt-A-Whirl ticket booth but was sent to the back of the line.

'Dakota, we don't have time for whatever this is.'

'Just quit being a little dork for two minutes.'

'I got *ten* minutes left of my break. I'm not getting fired day one.'

'No one's forcing you.'

Reluctantly, Flora joined her in line for the Tilt-A-Whirl, a rusty old monster around since first Fest. They passed puttering machinery and stinking tubes, listening to whirling screams over pneumatic hissing. It was getting colder but they were standing by the hot grease sizzle of the burger truck. This close, Flora could smell Dakota's sweat.

'Seriously, though.' She pushed it. 'Why you are you looking for Taylor Boswell?'

'He's got something for me.'

'What?'

'You really wanna know?'

'Yes.'

'This.' Dakota rummaged around in her pocket and when her hand came out, she was flipping the bird.

'You're a dick, Finch.'

By now, they were almost at the front of the line.

Seth Switzer was leaning on the railing above them, blowing a red Rain-Blo bubble. 'Evening, gals.'

'Switzer, you seen Boswell?'

'Nope. But I have seen *you*, milady. And you, Finch, are looking bomb tonight.'

'Been practising in the mirror?'

'Funny,' Seth screeched, his gangly body shuddering with fake laughter. 'For your *information*, my dad owns the ride.'

'Wow. Anywayyyyy, I'm looking for Boswell. You see him, you tell him.'

'Forget Taylor Boswell. Meet *me* after shift, I'll let you ride for free.'

'Really?' Dakota weighed it up theatrically. 'Oh, except I'd rather vomit and die.'

'If you're gonna be a bitch, I can send you to the back of the line.'

'I was leaving anyway, *Shitzer*.' She looped Flora's arm and they walked away.

A few in the line laughed. Others frowned at her language. But Dakota was oblivious. Flora glanced sidelong at her friend, wishing she could be more like her. Wishing she had that fiery freedom inside her belly too.

'Flower Power!' Dad was waving them over now.

Flora hissed as if her father's voice physically pained her. Head down, she shuffled over to his photography stall.

'Ladies. How's Fest treating you?'

'Majorly fun, Dad.'

'I can tell by your faces. The sashes are cute, though.'

'Ha-ha.' She groaned with embarrassment, the way he liked. Playing *sweet daddy dearest* usually increased the chances he'd shell out some cash.

Ed noticed the red mark on Dakota's face now. 'Everything OK, kiddo?'

'Fine.' She turned away. 'How's business, Mr Riddell?'

'Stall's quieter than a church mouse peeing on cotton.' He puffed out his cheeks. 'Folks having the time of their lives, nobody wants to immortalize it. There's a word for that. Probably in German, right? Anyhow. Feels like it'll snow later on tonight, huh.'

The girls looked at the floor, letting their silence do the talking. Reading it, Ed took out his wallet and handed over some money. 'I won't embarrass you any further. You ladies go get something to eat. Stay warm.'

'Thanks, Dad.'

'There's a Mexican food stall this year, try some brrr-itos. Get it? *Brrrr.* Cold.'

Dakota laughed as Flora groaned. In that moment, whip-fast, Ed Riddell raised his Polaroid and clicked.

'*Dad!*'

'Come on. I see cute smiles, I gotta snap 'em.'

A couple were checking the prices board so Ed put on his professional face. One last wink at Flora, then he mouthed the words *be safe*. As the girls walked away, Dakota wiggled her eyebrows. 'How much did ya get?'

'Fifteen buckaroos.'

'Dope. I'm parched.'

'Fruitopia?'

'I'm thinking something a little more . . . festive.' She nodded at the wooden wagon.

Off to one side, the Versammlung kids were working away, nodding politely to customers, but keeping their eyes on their clogs at all times.

'Wine? But they won't sell to us.'

'Just let me do the talking.' Dakota looped her arm again and they joined the short line. The Versammlungsvolk numbered around twelve. Most of them were younger kids, no older than fourteen. The three at the front of the wagon dealing with the public were older. The young men were around eighteen. The girl was around Flora's age.

'Tasty pies,' she called out in heavily accented English. 'Strong wine. Good prices. Authentic Versammlung product.'

Flora smiled at her. When the girl smiled back, she noted the clay-coloured freckles detonate across her cheeks. On her chest, a sticker read: *Rebecca Frey*. Like the other girls, she wore a long black work dress, a white apron, and a white *Kappe* on her head. Only a few strands of red hair were visible beneath it.

The largest of the group sat atop the wagon. He was oddly handsome, dark features, an axe resting on his thigh as he kept watch. His sticker read: *Eli Weaver*.

By now Flora and Dakota were at the head of the line.

'One pie. Or two?' The young man at the front of the wagon wore his red hair slicked back, his bulldog cheeks pink with razor burn. His limbs were slight but his body wide, like a little crow. Like the others, he wore black, though his garments were velvet. His sticker read: *Piety Schröder*.

'So,' Flora said. 'You picked the short straw, huh?'

'Straw?' Piety frowned.

'It means you're the unlucky ones that had to volunteer.'

'We hath been chosen for our Englisch tongue. Naught else. One pie. Or two?'

'You really put the pie in Piety, huh?'

'What?'

'Out here, we like a little conversation. A little friendliness before you go in for the hard sell.'

'Are my words unclear?'

'Just give me a bottle of your finest wine and we'll be outta your hair.'

Piety hoisted an eyebrow. 'Be it acceptable? That two girls should imbibe in public?'

Dakota laughed. 'Tell you what, *Little House on the Prairie*. When I come to your town, you can tell me what's acceptable. Until then, just do your job.'

Piety smiled coldly. 'And thou art of age? Twenty-one winters?'

'Duh. Obviously.'

'Thou look it not.'

On top of the wagon, Eli shrugged. 'Why would they lie?'

'Thank you for your view, Mr Weaver. But not all be as virtuous as thee.'

Next to him, Rebecca sighed. 'Piety, what difference does it make? We must away soon, anyhow. Just sell it and we can go.'

Piety responded curtly to her in his own language before facing Dakota again. 'Sorry. But it wast made plain to me that the sale of wine to children was not permitted. Lest thou hast the proper documentation, I wilt disobey not thy Englisch law.'

In the distance, fireworks popped distantly over the lake. The horse lifted its blinded head and whinnied.

Dakota shrugged. 'No need to get a hard-on, my virginal friend.'

The girls left the wagon and crossed over to the nearby food court. The Eagles were blaring 'One of These Nights'.

Diesel and fried chicken hung thick on the air. Kids on rides screamed as generators *bub-bub-bubbed.*

'Asshole, huh?' Flora shouted over the din. 'Anyway, I'm starved. You hungry?'

'I could eat a horse.'

They ordered pulled pork-loaded fries, jumbo dill pickles, and deep-fried Oreos. At the back of the food court, they watched an old biker in a bandana and bad tattoos kissing a woman half his age. Under his borrowed leather jacket, her T-shirt depicted a sausage dog in a Santa hat and read: *Dachshund through the snow.*

When Flora had finished her food, she wiped grease from her mouth and stood. 'I gotta take a leak, then I gotta get *back.*'

'Leave me some change.' Dakota burped. 'Want a frozen banana.'

Flora dumped out a few coins and went to the restroom. Wrinkling her nose, she hover-peed, then used the broken mirror to re-do her cola gloss. Something about that glittery gloss always made Flora feel better. As if it drew attention away from all the things that she did not like about herself.

Blowing a dumb kiss, she went back outside.

And what she saw twisted her heart.

Dakota was talking to Taylor Boswell behind the hot dog truck. They were standing close to each other. Close enough to share secrets.

SEVEN

Dakota.

Finch lurched awake, her throat noosed in the microfibre sheets of the Friendly Motel. She snapped the gun out from under her pillow, heart slamming, and scanned the room. Nothing in the bathroom, the closet. Opening the curtain an inch, she peeked out. It was still dark – a frozen haze hanging in the air, twinkling rime visible on every surface. But nobody watching, nobody by the streetlamp.

Still breathing hard, she puffed out her cheeks. *Fucking nightmares.*

Finch got into her uniform and put her hair up in a high bun. She didn't like her hair touching her collar, and she never used nail polish – old habits from the academy.

But at the door, she hesitated. *Screw it.* Two quick perfume sprays on her wrists.

Checking her gun and her Visprozan, Finch opened the door. Rippling above the grey, desolate Nectar landscape, a vein of nectarine dawn. *Maybe today will have something good in it.*

She closed the door and underfoot, it squelched. Lifting her boot, she saw a brown-pink severed cow's tongue.

Finch went to the Yum-Yum Donuts outside Nectar. It was a drive but it meant not having to see Merle Boswell. Staring off into the pollution-flossed valleys of Catoonah County, she bit open four donut holes and licked the jelly out. *What does the tongue mean? A warning? Someone came to my room in the middle of the night. It's not gonna be a welcome present, is it?*

Finch knocked on 14 Snow Shoe Lane holding two coffees. Ed Riddell opened up wearing a bathrobe, toothpaste foam still in his grey beard. There was a drop in his navel hair.

'Dakota.' He adjusted the robe around his body. 'Thought you were the paperboy.'

'Sorry, I know it's early.' She held up the coffees. 'Not from Merle's.'

'A woman of taste.'

'First time I've been called that.' She followed him inside. 'So, you're keeping the local newspaper alive, then?'

'I'm one of three subscribers. Folks in doomed trades have to stick together.' Again, he led her into the kitchen. 'One second.'

Ed went to the bathroom and she heard the sink. Then the hurried hiss of aftershave.

Finch unzipped her windbreaker. Again, the thermostat was up way high. She looked around the kitchen. On the fridge, there was a new photograph pinned with a banana magnet. A pretty teenaged girl with black hair and Flora's smile.

Walking back in, Ed caught her gazing at it. 'She's a beauty, ain't she?'

'Yeah. Really. Flora's echo.'

'We talked again about moving in together.' He gave a sleepy smile. 'I have my suspicions that me being well off sweetens the deal a little for her. Free rent and all that. But hey, I can't complain.'

'That's really wonderful.'

'Honestly, she's changed my life. So many years of . . .

nothing. Just silence. Then she walked back in and – like that – life. *Light.* Sorry, I know I'm corny.'

'I'd tell you if you were.'

'Calling out BS always was one of your fortes.' He smiled and held out his hand.

As she passed the coffee to him, the wool of his Icelandic sweater lightly grazed her wrist. 'You're not hot in here, Ed? It's like a sauna.'

'No, I think I'm coming down with something. Or it's just my age.' He grinned. 'Anyway, enough of me. What's up? Flattered though I am that you're here, I'm assuming it's not for my company.'

Finch put her cup down and looked into his eyes. 'I'm working a murder, Ed. The body was found down by the Testing Pool.'

'The pool?' He sagged back against the counter. '. . . Is it *him*?'

'We don't know. But there's nothing to indicate that.'

Ed closed his eyes. 'Jesus.'

'Listen to me. We don't know what we don't know. It's gonna be OK.'

Blinking, he regained his composure. 'Thank you. I . . . Uh, it's only that when you told me just now, I felt –'

'Like he's back, I know. I get it's scary but let's cross bridges when we come to 'em.'

'You're right.' He took a deep breath and attempted to calibrate himself to this new world. 'I'm glad you're running this, at least.'

Finch held his shoulder. 'You're OK, Ed.'

'Yeah.' He smiled weakly and cupped her hand for a moment. 'I just figured that this – *all this* – was closed. That it would never . . . you know. Re-open.'

'Like I say. There's nothing to indicate this has anything

to do with Flora right now. I'm not even meant to tell you. But I thought it was right for you to be prepared. Just in case.'

'I'm grateful. And listen, I'm not much help but whatever you need, I'm there.'

'I did actually wanna go over one or two things, just get my thoughts lined up.'

'Oh. Of course.'

'Was there ever anything in the investigation that you think Cochran missed? Leads he didn't go after?'

Ed tapped his lips. 'As I understand it, there *were* no leads. He questioned us. You. Me. Esther. The men that I'm sure you already know about. None of it went anywhere. I was told maybe the killer could make contact one day. What to do if he did. But that never happened.'

'So, the way you see it –' She took out her notepad. 'Cochran did all he could?'

He puffed out his cheeks. 'I'm just a photographer, Dakota. A dad. I wouldn't know how to qualify their work. Did they ever catch the guy? No. Did Cochran do everything he could? Yeah, I suppose he did.'

'What about the preliminary suspects. Ira Pike. Sam Salinas. Any contact ever?'

'No, never. Tell the truth, most people avoid me around here. Except for small talk.'

'Were there any suspicions around them you feel weren't looked into?'

'Let's see. Ira Pike . . . I think he's a strange guy but he was a good teacher. Though you'd know that better than me. At least, Flora liked him and I trusted her instincts. Sam Salinas? I don't know. I always heard rumours. He enjoyed female company a little too much. Violent. But do either of them have anything to do with Flora? No idea.'

'OK. Thank you. Listen, I'm gonna talk to Esther, too. I figured you should know.'

'That's fine.' Ed sighed. 'You won't get any answers. She's in the same place.'

'Gotta try.' Finch wrote down her number on the notepad and tore the page out. 'Look, if you remember anything, or if I shook something loose, call me.'

'Count on it.' He went with her to the door. 'So . . . is Flora's case being re-opened?'

'I'm here for Jane Doe. But so we're clear? Flora's case never closed. Not for me.'

The old stone sign was carved with the words *Catoonah County Psychiatric Hospital*. In this gentler, more understanding age, it no longer carried *For the Criminally Insane* beneath. Finch parked the cruiser in the horseshoe driveway and got out.

The building was in the Gothic Revival style, a dead sandstone giant carved into a furrow between the ribs of the Catoonah Mountains. The old clapboard clocktower above told her it was just after 9AM. The asylum, though crumbling, was still beautiful – erected back when a pleasant exterior was believed to pacify a lunatic interior.

Flashing her credentials, she was escorted by an orderly to a distant wing. The bleach stink twisted her stomach, though Finch suspected it was less to do with smell and more to do with who she was about to see. The dread weighed on her but there was no avoiding this. *Esther Riddell could've known something that Nectar PD had missed.*

'Normally, we require something signed by a judge.' The orderly glanced back at her. 'This about the murder?'

'Can't get into that.'

'Well, don't get your hopes up. She's pretty much

non-verbal. Wait here.' He knocked on Cell 901 and entered. A second later, he called Finch in.

Esther Riddell had been bound to a wheelchair, her body frail and small now. She was gazing listlessly out of a window to nowhere. Though different in colour, her eyes were the same shape as Flora's – only red-rimmed by years of silence. There were no sharp edges in this place, the floors wipe-easy vinyl, the window frosted. The cell was small and featureless, except for a simple desk and bed. Every inch of the walls was papered with simple sketches of a man, under an umbrella, only half his face visible.

'Mrs Riddell . . .' Keeping her distance, Finch crouched to her eye-line. 'Do you remember me? It's Dakota.'

No reaction. Finch knew the woman hated her, she always had – figuring her for a bad influence on Flora. Looking back, she probably wasn't wrong. But it was hard to see her so small now, so lifeless. 'I know this is going to be difficult for you. But we need to talk.'

No reaction.

Finch turned to the orderly. 'I got it from here.'

He left with a shrug.

When he was gone, Finch popped another Visprozan, then edged closer and lowered her voice. 'I'm here to talk to you about Flora. What happened to her.'

Esther closed her eyes.

Finch took out her notepad and pen, then nodded at the wall sketches. 'Why do you draw him? The man with the umbrella?'

No answer.

Being in this room, with this woman from her past, was unbearable. All the things Finch couldn't take back, the things she couldn't undo – this woman lived with them each day. She was trapped in them, prisoner to the *what ifs*. Looking into Esther's face was a fairground mirror of shame.

Closing her eyes, Finch willed the Visprozan to unfurl faster.

'You . . .' Her voice was a croak. 'Became a cop . . .'

Finch snapped her eyes open, chest thudding. 'Yes.' She spoke with the brightness of a parent encouraging a child's second word. 'You remember me, right?'

'*Does it make you happy . . .*' she whispered. '*Does it make you feel less alone . . .?*'

'I don't understand.'

'I want to see the water.'

'The water?'

'Very calming. Very calming. Flora loved that water.'

'Which water, Mrs Riddell?'

'I was on the phone that day . . .'

'That last day, right? When Flora left? I've seen the call logs.'

'I almost went with her . . . but I was too lazy to set up the stroller for Dolly . . . I drank wine instead . . .'

'I'm sorry, ma'am.' She didn't have words beyond that.

'I know you are . . .'

Finch shifted uncomfortably and sat on the edge of the desk. There she noticed a copy of Ira Pike's book: *The Nectar Witch: Corruption. Curses. A Copycat Killer.* 'Listen. I need to ask about the investigation into Flora. Your memories of that time.'

The broken woman shook her head. 'I want to see the water. Very calming.'

'Come on. You know *something* you're not saying.'

Esther pressed her eyes shut tight but Finch inched closer, close enough to whisper, 'Who is that on the wall?'

'The umbrella was dry . . .' she whispered. 'How could it be dry?'

That's when Finch's cell phone rang. Tossing her notepad and pen on the bed, she fumbled in her body armour. It was Jesse Sullivan.

'Yeah?'

Detective, it's me. I sent out a man to Versammlung like you asked. And you called it. They have a missing woman. Gone four days.

'. . . Holy shit.'

What do you wanna do?

'Let's meet at HQ . . . What was her name by the way. Doe?'

Rebecca. Rebecca Frey.

Finch's world carouselled. The phone was suddenly brick-heavy. She felt breakfast creep up her throat. 'You're sure –' Her voice was thick. 'Of the name?'

Yes, ma'am. I'll be there in five.

Finch hung up.

Whip-fast, Esther gripped her by the wrist, nails digging in, her eyes wide. 'I used to wish he had taken you instead.'

'Mrs Riddell. Please, let go –'

'– But not anymore. Now, I pray you have a child of your own one day, so you can feel what it is to have her ripped from you.'

Finch tried to pull away, suddenly panicking. 'I-I'm sorry.'

'IT SHOULD'VE BEEN YOU –'

Finch yelped as she stumbled back, her skin now torn. Esther was bucking in her chair, screaming from her guts. 'HE SHOULD HAVE KILLED YOU, IT SHOULD HAVE BEEN YOU, YOU LYING BITCH –'

The orderly was already pushing past her, unfazed by the outburst. Finch couldn't look away from Esther Riddell's eyes, wide and tortured by rage.

EIGHT

Finch made the short drive from the institute back to Nectar. Still shaking, she stopped by CVS where she topped up her prescription and bought supplies to clean herself up. Esther Riddell had raked her deep, her words still ringing in her ears.

She called me a liar. Why?

The question unsettled Finch. But the fact that there could have been any number of answers downright scared her.

In the Nectar PD parking lot, she swallowed another couple of Visprozan without water. She was racing past 60 mg a day now. Still, given her job, she knew she could talk her way up to a prescribable maximum of 90. Beyond that, she'd have to go underground.

Whatever. None of that matters now. Because Doe is Rebecca Frey. It was the three of us. And now two are dead. That can't be coincidence. Jesus, what is this?

Finch scanned the lot carefully before getting out of the car. Outside, the cold breeze on her exposed nape felt like the tickle of a man's breath. The dread she'd been nesting on since her arrival had hatched into full-on paranoia by now.

Nectar PD's bullpen was boisterous this morning, fat with auxiliaries and overtime. Tonight's Heritage Fest would have stalls offering online DNA ancestry analysis and the patrolmen were busy googling racist jokes for each other already.

Finch marched past them and into the sheriff's office. Sullivan was gazing out of the window. Cochran was pacing the whiteboard back and forth. Seeing her, he held up his palms. 'Now, Dakota. Before you go scorched earth, and I do realize this is a big break, at least *potentially*, I just want us to be mindful of relations with the colony.'

'I catch murderers, Quayle. I'm not the damn UN.'

'We have to *live* with them after this is all over.'

'Are you making a point? I'm not going in there with napalm.'

'You have to search for the killer inside that village, I get it. That's what I want too, if that's where he's at. But that whole goddamn colony is an apple cart.'

'Like I said, that isn't my –'

'– Problem, I know. Listen, they know you're coming. But you gotta remember, most of them have never even seen an outsider before – let alone you. No offence. I'm just asking for a little bit of calm. That's all.'

'Fine. I'll be goddamn Condoleezza Rice. Now can we get to the point?' She tapped the whiteboard at F – KNOWN OFFENDERS IN AREA, POIs, OTHER RELEVANT CRIMES. 'Versammlung is a closed society. Assuming their missing woman is our Doe, that would likely mean the killer was someone with access to their world *and* ours.'

Cochran shook his head. 'But we're still left with all the same unknowns. How did the killer transport her from there to here? How did he know how to use a shotgun? And that's ignoring that these are a non-violent people.'

'There are over 240 million drivers in this great nation, Quayle. How many you figure are stupid? Learning to drive a car isn't beyond the wit of man. Neither is firing a gun. Or getting access to one, for that matter.'

'You really think the killer is on the inside.'

'I told you. I think the killer put eyes on her. Watched her. Probably knew her. That would mean inside Versammlung, yes. But let's cover our bases. Jesse, how are you getting on with the haulage company employee search?'

'One or two fishy characters with weak-sauce alibis. But no smoking guns yet.'

'OK. Well let's narrow it. Find me guys who had access to Versammlung. That colony creates produce, tobacco. They need truckers. Men from the outside, who go inside.'

'On it.'

'We're also going to need a family member to formally identify the body.'

Cochran tugged anxiously on his moustache. 'The chamberlain knows. He won't allow photographs in there so he'll figure something out. Maybe a relative comes out here.'

'All right. Well. Diplomacy. Condoleezza Rice.'

'Maybe there's a quick resolution here.' The mayor sighed. 'On the other hand, a murder being tied to Versammlung is a problem.'

'Right. Tarnishes your bucolic image just before Fest. Now, if you'll excuse me, I'm gonna go find this son of a bitch.'

'You didn't even want to do this yesterday. Now, you're fired up. What changed?'

In her mind, Finch saw Flora and Rebecca lying on their backs, laughing up at the stars, their breath flocking together like a murmuration of birds.

She walked out without answering him.

Finch left Nectar along Lakeshore but on the rarely used eastern loop of Lake Sweetness. Its waters were verdigris today, with veins of gold sunlight breaking through across its surface. The narrow road rose up and Jumper's Bluff came into view – a jagged outcropping high above the rocks below, festooned in condolent bouquets and photos. As Finch zipped past in the cruiser, she saw a whirlwind of pink petals in the rearview.

The road wound back down and merged with Route 6.

Farms sprouted up, then subsided. After a few miles of dense forest, she saw the turn-off. It would've been impossible to see moving at speed but for police tape that had been tied around a couple of trees.

Finch took the turn and eased through the wood, tyres whining on mud. Once clear, she climbed a hill until it levelled out into wheat fields.

The land here nestled in a golden-green valley, hidden by mountains and thick wood. On either side of the mud path, a Mardi Gras of belladonna – six-feet tall, bell-shaped petals of violet, and berries black and bulbous as spider eyes.

And now, in the distance, Finch saw it properly for the first time. Versammlung was a wooden Eden in the gold, built out of the vertebrae of the forest. From inside it, a hymn rolled out across the field – hundreds of voices together as one, a strange, ancient German. She had the silly thought that it was sung in welcome. But Finch knew that these people did not welcome outsiders.

And now, as if to confirm it, a loud bell started clanging.

She slowed the cruiser to be as non-threatening as possible, then rolled to a halt at the thirty-foot-high timber colony wall. On the catwalk behind it, men were scurrying, shouting, pale faces peering down.

Leaving her gun on the dashboard, she took off her body armour. Then, Finch got out of the car. The loud tolling ceased, followed by a deep wooden creaking. Men heaved, the gate slowly lifted.

Versammlung was revealed.

December 29th, 1997

'Scatman' by Scatman John was pounding Fest. Next up would be 'Ride on Time', followed by 'Shy Guy'. Flora knew the playlist by heart by now. Her nabbing was fluent. Even the rats didn't bother her anymore.

She had bunched her hair and put on blue eyeshadow, finishing off with a flick of eyeliner. She was wearing a chunky Scandi sweater and a pleated plaid skirt from dELiA*s. It was meant to be over jeans but, on a whim, she'd plucked up enough courage for tights.

Still, all that work and I've made three crummy bucks. If I see that Alana chick, I'll tell her she's full of crap.

'Hey, loser.' Dakota stuffed her Fest helper sash in her back pocket.

'Hey,' Flora replied casually, despite her heart wanting to crawl up her throat.

'Break?'

'Can't right now.'

'All right.' They watched the number 2 train of the Raging Bronco teeter at the top of its lift hill, then the screaming plunge that followed. 'So. Ain't seen you in a while.'

'Yeah, you know.' Flora waved her nabber. 'Busy.'

'OK . . . Are we cool?'

'Sure. Why?'

'I don't know, you seem kinda bummed. Thought maybe I pissed you off.'

'Nope.' Flora's heart now wanted to crawl up her throat, out of her mouth, and into the palm of Dakota's hand. 'Everything's phat.'

'All right. Well, I'll catch you later –'

'– just, you know. The job drags. I go home, play *Streets of Rage*, then pass out.'

'Same. Except for *Streets of Rage*.'

Dakota maintained that SEGA was lame but Flora knew for a fact that she secretly loved it. In a drunken fury last year, Mrs Finch had thrown Dakota's Game Boy in the trash compactor and couldn't afford a Genesis.

'Anyway, how come you're dolled up? Planning to pop your cherry behind the Gravitron?'

Flora blushed and laughed at the same time. That one-two punch was Dakota Finch in a nutshell. 'One: eat a dick. Two: *you're* the one obsessed with Taylor Boswell.'

'Taylor?' She smirked. 'You actually think I give a shit about him?'

'Well.' Flora could taste bile and hope. 'Don't you?'

'Not even one little church mouse shit.'

'But I *saw* you with him the other night.'

'So?'

'So, you weren't getting a frozen banana. Maybe cos you wanted a Boswell banana.'

Now Dakota grinned wolfishly. 'You're such a kid, *Flower Power*.'

'Yeah. But I *am* a kid. And you are too.'

'Maybe. But I don't look like one, unlike *some* people . . .'

'Harsh.'

'I'm just messing with you.'

'Taylor is like five years older than us. So, seriously, what's going on?'

'You're as needy as that Switzer asshole, you know that, right?'

'And you're holding out on me.'

Glycerine smoke danced bright green around them.

Dakota looked deep into her friend's eyes. Then, sighing, lifted up her windbreaker.

First, Flora saw the tiny blonde hairs that ran up her navel, picked out by the laser-light. And now, hidden inside the fanny pack, she saw a shiny metallic cartridge.

'The hell is that?'

'Silver bullet.' Dakota winked. 'Kills werewolves. Now, let's go.'

'*Dakota.*'

'You're taking a break. Not robbing a bank. Come on, Cola Lips.'

Sighing, Flora un-sashed herself and followed her friend. 'Where now?'

'To smooth out that dickwad selling pies.'

'He's just gonna say no again.'

'Will he?' With a wink, Dakota flashed an Oregon driver's licence.

'*Crystal Fernández*? Looks fake as shit.'

'*Sí* but he *es muy estúpido*,' Dakota replied in a cheesy Spanish accent.

'Finch, he's gonna rat to Parsons Rigney.'

'Kindly remove the stick from your *culo*? For one second? That pie kid barely knows what the fuck a car is. Let alone what a licence looks like in the great State of Oregon. Now, come on, that dandelion wine is meant to be tasty.'

'Dakota. I don't have time.'

'Tay-steeeeee!'

'Their wagon is clear on the other side of Fest. I only get ten minutes.'

'Chillax, all right? We'll cut through by the Pentecostals.

One sip and you'll be back stabbing trash before you can say *Rigney smells like buttholes*.'

As she always did, Flora sighed her consent.

The girls weaved through revellers in milkmaid costumes and fake Amish beard-hat combos. Wood shavings thickened the air from the chainsaw carving stalls. The Barenaked Ladies were singing in favour of vanilla as a flavour.

In the distance, the glassy blackness of the lake was lacerated by glittering shards from Christmas tree reflections. Booze-cruise boats went in slow, pointless circles.

Dakota led them away from Lake Sweetness, away from the main concourse. There, in a neighbouring field, stood a great circus tent lit up with bulbs. Beneath it, a little crowd was swaying. Hands in the air, their murmur could be heard under the Fest music. Above the tent, in stark black, the words BLEEDING LAMB MINISTRY were emblazoned.

Lester Lamb was at the front, telling his followers why misery and confusion had cleaved them from their true path. His quiff was grey at the roots, deep chestnut in the lock. Tonight, he wore a mustard velvet three-piece. The plastic collection bowl being passed around was shaped like an angel.

'You have *thought* about other places. More *fruitful* lives. Much *happier* days. But your *fear* and your *sin* anchor you in these *dark* waters. That's why you don't move on from here. You seek a path of *light* . . . But you're mired in *dark*.' He swept a gold-ringed finger across the crowd. 'Your heart knows it's wrong. And that ain't to say that folk ain't good here cos I'm seeing a lot of pure hearts here tonight, a lot of good hearts . . .'

Dakota rolled her eyes and skirted the tent.

They cut through the wood behind and soon reached the fence on the other side of Fest. In the distance, the Pavilion was blaring with a Backstreet Boys tribute act. The girls were about to hop the fence when they heard the shout.

Fierce. Sharp. Scared. A single word.

No.

Dakota frowned. 'Hey, wasn't that the pie girl?'

'Who?'

'You know.' Dakota lowered her voice. 'Red hair. Amish.'

'They're not Amish.'

'Whatever, little Ms GPA. You know who.'

A second shout came.

'Yeah, that's her.'

Squinting through the dark thicket, they saw Rebecca Frey now – deep in the middle of some kind of altercation with Devin Rigney.

'We should go,' Flora whispered.

'Wait.'

Devin was holding the girl off with one hand, cradling a bottle of dandelion wine in the other – a drunk, woozy smile across his acne-scarred face. 'I'm just saying, *Fräulein*. If you ain't got a fair permit, you can't be selling this stuff. Regulations.'

Rebecca's *Kappe* had come loose, her face flushed deep. She was shouting in old German. Flora only caught the words *Kriminell* and *Fettsack*.

'Screw it,' Dakota whispered.

'Finch, goddamn it,' Flora hissed. 'Don't –'

'That being said . . .' In the clearing, Devin reached out to stroke the girl's hair. 'I think we could come to some sort of –'

Rebecca slapped his hand away. 'I am leaving.'

'We're not done,' Devin leered. 'You better come back here or I'll –'

'You'll what?' Dakota stepped into the light.

He spun around, a dog caught with its snout in the turkey. 'Take a hike, tomboy. Can't you see I'm in the middle of –'

'– yeah, I see.'

He smirked. 'Hey, I know you. You work for me. You wanna get fired tonight?'

'No, I work for your dumb father, asshole. And that's not the question. The question is: do you wanna get *arrested*?'

Devin's smirk faded. 'What you say, bitch?'

'Oh, I'm a bitch, all right. Enough of a bitch to go to Sheriff Cochran right now and tell him you're harassing young girls. Particularly, one from Versammlung. Figure he won't appreciate that none too much.'

'Maybe you misunderstood.' His face darkened, Babybel lips peeling back. 'Why don't you gals go back to your shift. No harm done.'

Dakota turned to Rebecca. 'You OK?'

Rebecca nodded, then snatched the bottle of wine from Devin's hands.

Stepping away, he opened his large palms. 'So, no misunderstandings here, right?'

'None. Seeing as you gave us the rest of the night off and all.'

Devin spat, then with hard, angry eyes, left. The three girls watched him walk away, through the wood, back towards the neon cavalcade.

They stood there in silence until, finally, the Versammlung girl spoke. '*Danke.*'

Dakota shrugged. 'No biggie.'

'Pardon?'

'Like, you're welcome.'

'I see. But I must ask. Why help me?'

'Dunno. Maybe because you vouched for us at your wagon the other night. Or maybe because that guy is an asshole.'

The girl frowned at that last word but held out the bottle of wine. 'For you.'

'Thanks. What was your name again?'

'Rebecca Dorothea Maria Ida Frey.'

'Wow, OK. Well, I'm Dakota. And this here is my friend, Flora.'

Flora nodded.

'Hello.' Rebecca's timid smile was a freckled peony-bloom.

'Tell you what, *Becky*, why don't you come hang with us?'

'*Hang*?' she gestured a rope around her neck.

'No, hang *out*. Like, fun.'

'I cannot. Mine wagon . . .'

'Your friends are there, right?'

'Aye. This man, Mr Rigney –'

'– The asshole.'

'The *asshole*, well, he said he needed to speak with me.'

'So, your people will think you're still busy, it's fine. Plus, you just got the night off.'

'Off?'

'Look, you're coming with us. Come on, just a little while.'

Rebecca Frey pulled her cape around her body and nodded.

Dakota headed for the dark wood. Flora followed. Then, cautiously, the Versammlung girl. None saw Devin Rigney glaring at them through the fence with drunk, angry eyes.

The girls had made their way away from Fest, crunching over dead leaves. At last, they came to the Testing Pool, a muddy little offshoot from Lake Sweetness. The grumble of rigs could be heard from Speedy's Mountain Truck Plaza, separated only by a cluster of pines.

Dakota made a blanket out of an old newspaper and sat. Then Flora. Rebecca bunched up her work dress and did the same.

'Aren't you cold with those clothes?' Flora asked.

She bobbed her shoulders under her cape. 'Versammlungs-volk be hardy to the cold.'

Dakota bit the cork out of the wine bottle. 'This'll warm you up.'

'Thou art *not* of wine age?'

'No. But see, this right here, Becky, is what we call a *secret*.' She drank deeply and passed the bottle.

Flora took it and lifted it to her mouth. She smelled flowers and mud, and felt a distant foreboding in her gut. But she wasn't about to look like a kid so she drank, grimaced, then croaked *not bad*.

'So, thy people do not believe . . .' Rebecca frowned. 'That a secret is a sin?'

'Nope. Now, come on.' Dakota winked. 'Jesus won't care about a few sips.'

The Versammlung girl held the bottle in her hands and weighed it against her soul. Then, with a deep breath, drank.

'Aye –' She sputtered. '*Not bad*.'

For the first time, they laughed together.

After a few sips, they were looser. Flora asked Rebecca about her village, her rules. She answered with a nervous smile, enjoying their bewilderment. She nodded *yes*, she would be married soon – to Piety Schröder. No, it had not been her choice but the very notion of choosing a husband seemed to amuse her. Dakota hid her grimace behind the wine bottle.

'How come you were picked to represent your village?'

'For I hath the most Englisch tongue. My father is village clerk. He hath the greatest learnings, save for our chamberlain.'

'How about school?' Flora asked. 'Do you go?'

'Nay. Not since last year. And thou?'

Rebecca now listened, wide-eyed, as Flora spoke of her school, university after that, of making choices for herself.

By now, the dandelion wine was almost gone.

'S'weird . . .' Flora slurred. 'You come into our world some-times but we never go into yours. Even though your village has . . . always been there. But out of sight. Kinda like some distant relative in a photo album.'

'Photo?'

Dakota laughed. 'You're talking to an alien, Riddell.'

A light snow started to fall.

Despite the cold, Flora's cheeks burned, her head so light it wouldn't have sunk in water. Far away, she could hear one of her mom's favourite songs playing – Fern Kinney's 'Together We Are Beautiful'.

But she didn't want to think about Mom. Home. The real world. She was happy in this dirty little wood, adrift on dandelion wine. With the new girl. With Dakota Finch.

Every so often, Flora looked away from her. In that moonlight, she swore she'd never seen anyone more sickeningly beautiful.

Dakota drip-dropped the last of the dandelion wine into her mouth, burped, and threw the bottle into the dark. 'Hey, Becky. What does *Fettsack* mean?'

Rebecca chewed her lips in thought. 'It is meaning . . . *very large*?'

'So, you were calling Devin a fatso crook?'

'Jah, fatso.' She smiled. 'And your word for him was ass . . . ?'

'– hole, yeah. *Asshole*. You know.' Dakota made a ring with her fingers.

Rebecca's laugh was childlike, shocked and delighted. Wine in their blood, they were all belly-laughing by now, grinning like carousel horses.

'Wait.' Dakota shushed them. 'You hear that?'

Two figures emerged from the wood across the Testing Pool – a man and a woman. The girls ducked down behind a dead log to watch.

Checking over his shoulder, the man unbuckled his belt.

Rebecca whispered. 'Do they mean to . . . ?'

'Becky, hush.'

Flora worried distantly that their breath would be visible on the dark but the wine made it hard to care.

The woman was facing away, hands propped up against a tree now. 'It's OK, honey.'

'I *know* it's OK . . .' the man grumbled from behind her. 'It's just damn cold is all.'

Dakota held up a forefinger in front of Flora's face, then curled it downwards limply. They buried their faces in their hands to hide the snorting.

'Hey!' the man shouted. 'Who's there?'

The girls rolled on to their backs to get lower behind the log.

'Buncha fucking comedians, huh?'

'Forget it, babe,' the woman said. 'Let's just go.'

Dakota put her forearm to her mouth and let rip the biggest raspberry-fart Flora had ever heard. Their laughter came in squeals now.

'Fucking kids,' the man muttered as they walked away.

When the couple was gone and the laughter subsided, the girls just looked up at the moon. Snowflakes landed on their faces as little kisses.

'That man and woman,' Rebecca whispered. 'Were they going to . . . ?'

Dakota marvelled. 'You really are green, huh?'

'Green?'

'Yeah. Like a baby. No life experience. You know what? Screw it –' Dakota went into her fanny pack and held up the small silver tube.

'What is it?' Flora asked.

'It's called whipped cream. I was gonna do this alone but you two *clearly* need a little life experience.'

'Shit, Dakota. You're HUFFING now?'

'*Relax*, loser.' She took out her folding knife and dug a

small hole in the top of the tube. 'The fried cheese will do you more damage than a little laughing gas.'

'What is it?' Rebecca eyed it curiously as gas hissed out.

'Just trust me.' Dakota took out a packet of balloons from her fanny pack and eased one over the leaking tube. When full, she pinched it shut and handed it over. Then another.

They watched as Dakota filled hers, held the neck of the balloon to her lips and breathed in deep. A moment, then she leaned back against the log with a dreamy smile.

Flora held the balloon to her lips. She was shaking but exhilarated to be doing something she knew would send her parents ballistic. Closing her eyes, she huffed deep. There was a vague sweetness on her tongue. At first, nothing else. But then her lungs tingled, her belly twisted, and the floating began. Instead of lying in the snow by a stinking pond, Flora felt like she was soaking in a silver bath as it filled with warmth and joy.

'Dakota?' she murmured.

'Mm.'

'What you said to Devin . . . That was pretty dope.'

'Aw, Riddell. Ya mushy lil' loser.'

'Fuck you, huff head.'

'I feel strange . . .' Rebecca murmured. 'Dost thou think God will be angered by my brooking thy traditions?'

'Nah.' Dakota closed her eyes. 'Plus, who's gonna know?'

'God sees all.'

Dakota brushed dead leaves and snow from the mud between them. With her folding knife, she carved out a little plot and scooped in the empty laughing gas pellets. She buried them, then wiped her hands against her pants. 'There. Now nobody'll ever know.'

The girls looked up at the glow-worm galaxy.

For the first time in her life, Flora felt like she actually had a place in it, like she was actually living. This friendship, this shared warmth, this love – she hoped it would last forever.

'Becky,' Dakota whispered.

'Jah?'

'You should hang out with us again.'

'OK . . . asshole.'

They laughed until their faces ached. Flora closed her eyes, her head swimming in the elation of a real human experience. Just a few hours ago, she never would've done something like this. Now here she was.

And it was as simple as Dakota Finch's *trust me*.

NINE

Versammlung was laid out in a horseshoe, some sixty timber houses – a bakery, a forge, a school. There was a large hall-like building off to one side, ringed by hemlock trees. The smell of smoke and manure was thick in the air, hens *buck-buck-bucking*.

But the villagers had fallen silent at the sight of the police-woman, mouths hanging open. Some Versammlungsvolk closed their eyes and began to pray. Others hurried their children indoors.

Finch had always imagined being in this place would feel like a glorified theme park. But now that she was here, now that she was looking at them, hearing them, smelling them – it was like waking up inside a Brothers Grimm tale.

She stood in the middle of a mud clearing. A group of watchmen wordlessly gathered around her. Almost all of them were red-headed, many with facial disfigurements. They wore black slacks, work shirts, straw hats. In their eyes, curiosity and fear.

A huge dead poplar tree stood at the end of the village. Around it, a rudimentary timber church had been built – roofs, turrets, but no walls, open to the elements. Finch had learned about the Versammlungsbaum in school, the sacred tree that had given life to this colony. To her eye, though, it was just a dead tree.

One of the watchmen spoke a curt phrase to her now.

Finch didn't understand it. Still, she felt no fear, only the vague awareness that she was seeing something most people never would. She couldn't help but imagine herself as a wildlife photographer in a deep rainforest.

'*Ich bin Dakota Finch*,' she said. 'Uh. *Polizei. Nectar.*'

No reply. But a single word came from beyond them.

Zurücktreten.

They parted for a wiry man in his fifties. His eyes were deep blue, his long beard was burgundy at the jawline, tiger-orange at his chest. He wore more ornate clothes: a doublet and breeches of black velvet, a wide-brimmed hat, smock and garters of white linen.

'Thou art come –' His English was clear but heavily accented. 'In representation of American law?'

'That's right.'

'A woman, no less.'

'I'm a senior detective assigned from Detroit PD. My name is Dakota Finch.'

'Ichabod Weaver. I am Chamberlain of Versammlung.'

'Sir, I was told that a family member of the missing woman would be available to speak with me?'

'I am not soft to it . . .' Ichabod tugged at his beard for a moment, then beckoned to his side without breaking eye contact. 'But yes, I see no other way.'

A young girl stood next to him now, around fourteen. Her hair was black as her dress. In her arms, she held a faceless doll. Despite the obvious differences – she had freckles and very pale skin – her eyes were like hand-me-downs from Flora, the same borrowed green.

'Sir, I was expecting a parent. Or adult relative. Time is very important. I assumed Mayor Cochran explained to you that the identification process would involve –'

'Perhaps Mayor Cochran might've explained to *you* that any adult in this Assembly cannot leave. It is forbidden. Except to youth. Therefore, the sister will go, despite my ill view of it. In this way our laws and thine may be kept. 'Tis is my decision. That is all.'

As Finch drove back to Nectar, the girl surveyed the land intently. She whispered to her faceless doll as they went. *Englisch houses, grey and box-like, no need of timber. Roads as smooth as butter. And carriages upon them, horseless, shiny and quick as brook trout.*

'What are you doing?'

'Committing to memory thy world.'

'Weird. But OK.'

'What is *weird*?'

'It means strange. You speak good English for a Versammlung girl.'

'All my winters hath I spoken thy tongue. Father taught me, as he taught my sister.'

'How come he speaks it?'

'He was a teacher. Though no longer is it taught . . . Thy land. Tis so vast. *Colourful.*'

'Trust me, it's a shitshow out here, kid. Uh, that means like very bad.'

'Oft, the chamberlain doth speak of this . . . Yet thy world provokes wonder in me. Curiosity is sinful to mine people. To thine?'

'Not even sin is sinful to us.' Finch glanced sidelong at her. 'What's your name?'

'Elesheva Maria Jutta Frey.'

'Slow. Ellie-shayba?'

'Elesheva. *El-eh-sheh-VA.*'

'Well, I'm just gonna go with *Eva*. My name is Detective Dakota Finch.'

'*Da-ko-ta* . . .' She half-smirked. 'An inquisitor-woman.'

'That's right.'

'Art thou married?'

'No. Now, we need to talk about what we're about to do, OK?'

'O.K.'

'You don't space it out like that. It's not O.K. It's just, OK.'

'OK.'

'You got it. Now, pay attention –'

'– What be that machine?'

'That's a radio. For music.'

'Why?'

'So you can listen to it while you're driving.'

'Why?'

'Driving can be boring and music is nice. People like music.'

'Then it is as Papa sayeth. The heathens think loveliness of consequence.'

'Yep. I guess we do. Now, look –'

'That!' She pressed her face to the window. 'Is it truly a sky carriage?'

'What, the plane? Yeah, that's true.'

'I *knew* it. Samaritan Yoder told me it was impossible. But wait, how do they float?'

'It's like one of your buggies but much, much bigger and instead of horses it has, uh, *machines* inside that make it go really fast.'

'But how does it *float*?'

'It goes so fast that gravity doesn't – you know what, kid. I don't know *how* it works, only that it does.'

'Weird.'

'Look, I'm just your ride. Not your camp counsellor.'

'Thou hast travelled in a plane?'

'Sure.'

'Verily?'

'Most folks have flown before. To us that's normal.'

'What be the most beautiful place thou hast travelled?'

'I don't know.'

'Thou hast seen only feculent places?'

'No. I don't know, Miloli'i Beach, maybe.'

'Where?'

'Kauai. Green cliffs, golden sand, Mai Tais. Water so blue it hurts.'

'Where?'

'West. Far away.'

The girl tried to imagine this. 'How many miles?'

'Too many to count. Across the land, across the ocean.'

'How does the plane know where to go?'

'Listen, uh, Eva. We're gonna be going through town soon –'

'Nectar?'

'Yes. I'm sure you've heard about it. Modern-day Sodom.'

The girl's eyes widened. 'Verily?'

'No, that's a joke. Forget it. Listen, we're headed to the hospital. We need to talk about how it works when we get there, OK?'

'OK.'

'When we arrive, we're going downstairs. We'll be in a room next door to a dead body. You understand what that means, right?'

'Yes, *Da-ko-tah*. I understand.'

'You won't have to see the body itself. I'll show you photographs.'

'Photo –'

'Like pictures. But very, very accurate pictures. Same as a reflection.'

'I understand. And thou dost think this dead body be my sister.'

'I think . . . there is a chance.'

'Well, it cannot be. I think it shall be one of *thy* people.'

Elesheva shrugged. 'My sister sometimes left Versammlung for a day. She will return.'

Finch looked at the girl again. She said nothing. This wasn't her business.

Parking outside Olmstead G. Holmes General, Finch and the girl approached the entrance. Elesheva walked just behind her, her pace slowing whenever she saw something to marvel at. At the reception desk, the girl laughed at the bing-bong announcement.

Finch flashed her badge and was pointed towards the elevators.

'Listen, Eva, this could be painful. But you have to try your best. If you recognize anything in those pictures, you tell me. It's very important. It'll only take a minute or two.'

'As I spake it. I understand.' Elesheva flinched when the elevator started its descent.

'Don't worry,' Finch whispered. 'Just like the car. But automatic up and down.'

The doors slid open and the disinfectant smell made the girl retch. ''Tis crooked.'

'It's OK, this way.'

Hanlon Hopkin was waiting in the side office.

'Come in.' He got out of his chair.

Elesheva drifted towards it and sat.

Without pause, she tore open the small envelope in front of her. The girl closed her eyes for a moment, then started going through the photos. None of them depicted Rebecca's face. Instead, they showed what they could: hands, arms, freckle sprays.

By the fourth image, she stopped, put them away, then nodded once. 'It is her . . . my sister. Rebecca Dorothea Maria Ida Frey.'

'Then let's get out of here.' Finch opened the door. 'Thanks, Hanlon.'

'No, I want to see her.'

'Eva —'

'She is my sister. And I wish to see her. No photo trickery.'

'Kid, it's really not a good idea.'

'Thy ideas disinterest me. I saw no face, so I do not know –'

'– Because there *was* no face, Eva. I'm sorry. But you can't see her.'

Jaw wobbling, she looked at her clogs. When she spoke again, her voice was small. 'Her hand, then. Just her hand. Please.'

Hopkin shrugged. 'No objections.'

'Kid, are you sure?'

A single nod.

Hopkin led them to the coolers. The metallic slider roared open, then came the purring rip of the body bag. Carefully, gently, he eased out Rebecca's pale hand. In death, it had curled a little, as if wishing to be held.

Trembling violently, the girl reached out and took her dead sister's hand. She spoke to her in that old, forgotten language. Finch could make out the words *meine geliebte Schwester*.

But now Elesheva paused.

With a frown, she glanced down. A puddle of urine was forming between her legs. 'Oh. I am sorry, I –'

'It's OK, sweetheart.' Hopkin pointed. 'There's a bathroom over there. *Detective?*'

Finch snapped out of it. 'Jesus. All right, Eva? Come with me.'

She led her to the bathroom where the girl sobbed in the stall alone. Finch pressed her eyes shut, desperately trying not to recall the past. 'Eva, listen. Once you've cleaned up, we can go back home, OK? We'll get out of here.'

The girl was still howling.

'I'm gonna give you some privacy for a minute, OK? I'll just be right outside the bathroom. When you're ready, we'll go.'

In the hall, Finch massaged her temples. 'Sorry, Hanlon.'

'Don't be, she's just a kid. Not the worst clean-up job I've ever seen by a long shot. How is she?'

'Not great.'

'Does she want some water? I've got a refrigerator in my office.'

'I'll check – Eva?'

In the bathroom the stall was empty. The window giving out to street level was open.

January 7th, 1998

Dusk. Rebecca Frey sat alone behind the Gravitron, picking at her jar of beans. The greasy stink stuck in the back of her throat and the metallic grind was deafening, but she liked it there. It afforded her a view of Fest, while nobody noticed her.

How fascinating the Englisch are. Grotesque yet beautiful. They dress as their pilgrim ancestors, about which they are ignorant. How lost yet knowing. All treasures and comforts afforded to them, but they lack the very Love of God. Everything. In the end, nothing.

Rebecca set her jar of beans aside. Her father had lovingly made them but the trouble in her heart robbed her appetite. It had been that way since last summer. What she had seen was unspeakable. Yet, secretly, she returned to it – whenever she could.

Wild grape blossom had been sweet on the air that day, fruit to be made into jellies. After many faintings in the working fields from the heat, the Council had granted a reprieve to stay indoors past the afterlunch.

That afternoon, the land had stood empty. She walked through the hemlock forest, chatting happily away to herself, stopping every so often to share a lick of honeysuckle with her old hymn doll.

Occasionally, she would pull the cord at its back and the heavy brass mechanism inside would tinkle a tune of worship. It was silly but it was her lifelong comfort.

Through little winking gaps in the blackberry bushes, she watched pollen float by like angels. Touch-me-nots bobbed pink in meadows. Brook stones slept smooth as baby noses.

By the time she had reached the other end of the wood, Rebecca's ardent copper hair beneath her *Kappe* had come free in wet coils.

Panting, she found shade by some mossy stones.

Above, *Sperling* and *Blaukehlchen* sang the song of summer. In the field before her, a placid bee floated back to Versammlung, its work finished for the day.

That's when she saw him.

In the middle of the field, Eli Weaver was sitting back against a large rock. His eyelashes were black fishing lures, his features a rare dark. Not for nothing did the village call him *Eli Black*. He was yawning, his sleeves rolled up. He had been so still in the long grass, she had not noticed him – as though another chirping *Grille*.

Rebecca could not look away as he took out a wood pigeon from his pack. He thrust his hand inside its body, his fingers fluent. From her hiding place, she watched, pressing the hymn doll to her stomach.

Despite his youth – eighteen winters – he was already considered the finest woodsman in Versammlung. His carcass baskets always brimmed, no matter the weather. Some of the children even sketched him in their prayer books. Mothers would smile as they tore up the pictures – vanity was sin, even for Eli Black.

Rebecca watched him brush away the scraps of food inside the bird. Now he forced his fingers under the oesophagus, and tore it in two. When the unfixing was done, he rubbed his long and bloody fingers together, making a little ball of feathers.

In that moment, she knew. It was as if he had made a ball

of her heart. As clear as the word of God resounded in her mind, she knew she had fallen in love with Eli Black.

Rebecca had always been sweet on him, though she could not explain it.

It was the way a cat chose the lap of one sister, ignoring the other. Or the way morning glories would refuse a well-tended bed only to bloom wildly from the roof of a dead barn. It simply was.

With Eli, it had been that way since she could remember.

Yet in that moment, she knew it was no longer sweetness. It was love. And she dreaded to think what else.

Eli placed the broken pigeon atop his pile, then lay back against the rock and covered his face with a straw hat. The sweat on his tanned forearms gleamed. He undid his work shirt to the waist.

Rebecca's breath caught. She had never seen a man's navel before. The amount of hair shocked her. Her face burned; she could barely fill her lungs. *Why dost the Lord give me this need for Eli, only to have him marry another?*

Rebecca had never questioned God before. Her head was whirling. But her eyes remained fixed on Eli.

He shrugged off his suspenders, pulled down his broadfall trousers and pulled free his marriage part. As he touched it, Rebecca began to tremble violently. *How could this be Eli? Good, dutiful Eli?*

'God punish me . . .' she had whispered, begging her eyelids to close. But they refused. She had looked and looked and looked. Rebecca could not unsee. She still could not.

Screams from the Raging Bronco lurched her into the present.

Thou art soon to be married yet thy thoughts are rotten with lust. God will damn thee.

Shaking, Rebecca reached into her pack. Just touching the

old, frayed woollen strands of her hymn doll's hair helped her breathe. Its featureless face was the only thing that brought her a little peace.

At her age, she knew such a silliness was not wife-proper. But it had been her lifelong habit and she could not stop it now.

Of all feelings, she thought as she hurried back to the wagon, *tis fear that makes us most childlike. No matter how many winters one hath lived.*

At the wagon, she put her pack away and smoothed down her dress. Piety Schröder looked at her sidelong.

'Didst thou become lost again?'

'I took my supper is all.'

'Well, this gentleman needs his.' He nodded at a man in a false beard and a pilgrim hat. *'One of each, please.'*

From the wagon store, she took out one of the pre-wrapped peach pies and a bottle of dandelion wine. There were no young ones to help anymore. The Council had decided that she, Eli and Piety could get by alone, thereby shielding the children from further corruption.

Piety pocketed the money, then recorded it with small, precise strokes in the ledger.

'Where is Eli Black?' she asked casually.

'I hath sent Mr Weaver for his break.'

'Thou wast alone?'

'Aye, given thy lateness, I thought it only fair on him.' He slapped the ledger shut, then drummed his inky fingers on its leather jacket. *'Dost thou not see, Rebecca? Thou art soon to be mine wife. If I say* one-quarter hour *and thou dost luxuriate in almost half of one, how now am I perceived?'*

'Nobody doth perceive thee out here.'

'A mockery thou dost make of me, even if it is only simple Eli as witness.'

'*I am sorry.*'

Sighing, he reached out as if to cup her cheek. Thinking better of it, he patted Gracie on the muzzle instead. The old horse nickered.

'*My love, I want thy apology not. But –*' He looked at his clogs. '*Thou ought be more . . .* mine. *Heed my word. That ought be thy happy purpose.*'

Rebecca nodded faintly, then busied herself with the wine stock.

When she looked up, she saw Devin Rigney in the crowd.

Had he just been looking at her?

Smoke machines belched. Knotted German and US flags writhed in a cold wind. 'Push the Feeling On' by Nightcrawlers was thudding while fat fathers bopped their heads and kids groaned. A mascot dressed as Tim Burr handed out flyers for Speedy's Diner.

Flora was in the employee hut. It stank of feet and hormones. She threw her sash and nabber in her locker, then punched out. Devin Rigney pointedly looked at his watch but said nothing. She'd been late for shift tonight – another flare-up between Mom and Dad – but it seemed like the truce in the wood the other night with Rigney still stood.

Flora hadn't seen Dakota in several days. Now, she was hurrying through Fest, desperately scanning faces. Something was going on with her, she could feel it. Dakota had been spaced lately. And dressing differently, too, trading on her looks – tank tops and hoop earrings. Flora didn't like it. Especially given all the out-of-town creepos floating around.

Flora reached the Raging Bronco but it was some other kid working the ticket booth tonight. She tried the food court but, again, no Dakota. Finally, she walked the stalls by the waterfront. The tips flowed more freely but her friend was nowhere to be seen.

Lake Sweetness was a grey floss tonight. A few of the employees Flora recognized were loading up a small party boat at an old wooden dock. Dakota was standing there, arms folded against the cold. Her make-up, which lately she'd taken such an interest in, was uncompromisingly beautiful. She wore the big Tommy puffer jacket that had mysteriously appeared around her body lately. Under it, a tank top even tinier than the mini skirt. Her bare legs were taut with gooseflesh.

Flora saw the way nearby eyes lingered on them. *Not on my watch.*

She hurried through the crowd and cut off towards the dock. A group of girls in heavy make-up that Flora didn't know were now standing by the boat too. Awkwardly, she pushed her way past them until she reached Dakota.

'Hey, loser.'

'Hey, Flora.'

'You're going out on the water?'

'Uh-huh.'

'I was thinking maybe I could – shit, you got your tummy button pierced?'

'Cute, huh?'

'Uh, yeah . . . Anyway. So.'

'So.'

'I was thinking maybe I could –'

'Look, tonight is gonna be a . . . different crowd.'

'I don't care. I'm cool. I can be cool.'

With a wry smile, Dakota shook her head. 'Cool, huh?'

'It's just a fuckin' party, right? I'll do my own thing.'

Taylor Boswell clanked down the dock now, blasting snot out of one nostril. He draped an arm over Dakota's shoulder. 'Ready, Finch? The boys are waiting.'

'Can't wait.'

'Cut the sarcasm. Wiggle your butt.'

'Not without my plus-one.'

'*Her?* She's a little young, ain't she?'

'She's my friend, Tay. And she's old enough to sit on a boat.'

Taylor looked Flora up and down. 'I don't get it, babe. What am I meant to say?'

'That she's with me.'

'Hot bitches come free. Everyone else, it's forty bucks. It's an exclusive operation.'

'Exclusive?' She laughed. 'OK, Drexl Spivey. Just let her on the fucking boat.'

'My rep matters.'

'Your dad runs a diner. I think you're safe.'

'I'm driving a brand-new Range Rover before twenty-five. I'm a businessman.'

'You got the Range from the son of a proctologist that owed you money, Taylor.'

'Look, whatever. She can't come without paying. Not my party, not my rules.'

Dakota turned to her friend. 'I'm sorry, Flo.'

'I'll get the money!'

Taylor Boswell shrugged. 'Well, we're almost loaded. You better hurry.'

Flora ran back towards Fest. She had almost reached her father's stall when Ira Pike snagged her by the wrist. 'Ah, the sagacious Miss Riddell!'

Flora awkwardly shook him off. 'Hey, Mr Pike.'

'It's *Ira.*' He smiled, the laser-light making his half-face sci-fi villainous.

'Right.' She smiled back through her panic. 'You, uh, taking a break?'

'Indeed. Observing the locals.' He snorted. 'In their natural habitat.'

'Sold many books?'

'Of course not. But, on that happy topic . . .' From inside his leather jacket, he took out a small white book. 'For you.'

'*If on a winter's night a traveler?*'

'A master work. Mr Calvino will steer you clear of adolescent silliness and elevate your already bright mind to new heights –'

'Look, teach, I appreciate it. But I really gotta go. Uh, hold it for me?'

'Oh. Well. OK, then.'

'Thanks. See you in class.'

Tonight, Ed Riddell's stall had a little line. Customers were going through the boxes of props, planning their poses. Sam Salinas was lining up with a young woman she didn't recognize. He was wearing a cowboy hat, the woman wore cat ears.

Flora waved as she passed. Sam stuck his tongue out playfully.

Dad had his stressed smile on, the one that people found charming but Mom hated. He was scribbling down an order slip as she slinked in behind the counter next to him.

'Give me fifteen minutes, folks.' Ed handed a couple their change and order number. 'I'll make you look as beautiful as you are.'

'Hey, Daddy.'

'What is it, Flower Power?' He spoke through his smile.

'How's it going?'

'Busy, as you can see. Open me up another Minox Mino Color 3, would you?'

She ripped open the box of film roll. 'How are things with your stocks?'

'Plummeting. Your mother's gonna kill me. Anyway, you

didn't come here to ask me about that. What do you want, kiddo?'

'Um, I was wondering if maybe I could ask for a little money?'

'Fine. Take a few bucks from the till.'

'Uh, I was thinking a little more? Forty?'

'*Forty*? Why?'

'Treat my friends.'

'To a toffee apple or a ski weekend? Jesus.'

Alana Wells passed the stall now. She wore a little gold pendant around her neck. It looked like an eye. Seeing them, she waved.

'Friend of yours?' Ed asked.

'Yeah. Kinda. Anyway, look. You know Dakota has nothing. But it's not just her. My other friend . . . Well, she's Assemblyfolk.'

Hoisting an eyebrow, Ed looked across Fest at the Versammlung wagon. *Tasty pies! Strong wine! Good prices!*

'You're pals with *them*?'

'Yeah. Sorta.'

They both watched Rebecca smile at a customer while she handed over their change. Above her on the wagon, Eli Black was making a joke.

'One friend your whole life and all of a sudden, you're Little Miss Popularity.' Ed sighed. 'Take whatever's in the till.'

'Daddy, you're the best.'

She pocketed $34 and turned to hurry away.

'Flora, hey.'

'Yes?'

'You be careful, you hear?' He cupped her cheek in dismissal.

'I will, Daddy.'

As she walked away, he became the showman again. 'OK, come on, folks! Capture the moment! Nights like these are special, y'all should keep 'em. For the kids. Grandkids. Heck, for the archaeologists. Step up. For memories done well, come to Ed Riddell!'

Flora was drenched in sweat by the time she made it back to the dock. She held up her money, doubling over to catch her breath.

Taylor Boswell laughed. 'You're short.'

Dakota zipped her jacket. 'Quit being an asshole, Tay.'

'Look, you wanna bring her? Fine. But she's short and I'm not spotting.'

'It's six bucks.'

'Then you pay the difference. We gotta go.'

'It's OK!' Flora shook her head. 'I'll get the six bucks!'

Taylor spat. 'Good thing for you I need to take a dump. Two minutes.'

Flora took Dakota by the shoulder. 'Wait for me.'

'Flo, keep your money. You're not even gonna have fun. *I'm* not gonna have fun if I'm worried about you. Let's just hang out some –'

'– other time? But you always dodge me. I'll get the money, just wait for me.'

'I'm leaving Nectar soon, anyhow.'

'Then we won't have many more nights like these. *Wait.*'

Dakota folded her arms over her chest. 'OK.'

Flora rushed back into the crowd, her mind whirring. *Go back to Dad? Right, because he'd be so thrilled and totally not suspicious that I needed more cash. Maybe I could steal it? Some fat clueless out-of-towner might give me a tip? Right, looking like a sweaty mess.*

Jesus, Flora. You got it bad.

The feeling of losing Dakota, of the little time they had together slipping through her fingers – it provoked such a sad desperation in her stomach she couldn't bear it.

'Shit. Money, money, money . . .'

In the distance, through the mass of bodies, smoke and games – Flora could see the parking lot. It was just a fenced-off field that gave out to Speedy's Mountain Truck Plaza. But she remembered now. Carmella would be starting her shift in the lot attendant booth.

Flora ran for it, her lungs wheezing on the cold, her legs shaking. She tried to think of some solid excuse. It had to be something that wouldn't get back to Mom. *Lost my purse? Nah, lame. I owe a drug cartel? Always with the pointless jokes. I'll just say Dad has run out of change at his stall. What if he finds out? Whatever, I'll deal.*

Flora was weaving between parked cars now, mirrors twinkling in the moonlight. In the distance, she could hear the Cardigans' 'Lovefool' playing, the metal clanking of rides, joyful screams. The frozen grass crunched beneath her hurried steps.

Thank God.

She could see Carmella up ahead in her booth. As she lifted her hand to wave, a car door shot open in front of her and a man got out. Lester Lamb put his hands in his pockets, gold rings swallowed in dark.

'Didn't your daddy ever tell you to mind dark places?' He smiled.

'Shit, you scared me.'

'No cursing, hon. But you know who I am. You got nothin' to fear. Ask your mom.'

'I do. But I'm in a rush.'

'You're in a rush to get *grown*. A few weeks ago, you was but a little girl. *Now* look at you. The Lord has done made you ripe. You'll make a fine wife one day.'

'Uh, OK.'

'Flora, I don't mean nothin' by it. Just calling 'em like I see 'em. But I did actually wanna talk to you about something. See, I notice the company you keep lately.'

'Mr Lamb – ?'

'– No, hold on. Listen, now. Them kids ain't evil . . . but they ain't on a path of light.'

'They're my –'

'– friends, I understand that. The young heart feels certainty like no other. But the young heart also makes mistakes, Flora. I just mean to look out for you is all.'

'Well. Thanks. Bye, Pastor.'

'God bless you, child. But before you go –' He took his holy book from the dashboard of his royal-blue car, then held it up to her face. 'I think you should kiss this.'

'What?'

'Receive the Light. It'd make your mother's heart soar. Heck, mine too.'

'No, thanks . . .' With a frown, she squeezed past him and hurried for the lot booth. Glancing over her shoulder, she saw him pat the hood of his Mercury Sable, then stride in the direction of the Bleeding Lamb tent.

Carmella beamed at Flora despite a yellowing black eye. Nobody said a thing about it. But then, nobody ever said anything in this town.

She handed over the six dollars without even asking for a reason.

Flora's whole body was soaked in sweat by the time she made it back to the dock. But the party boat was a little pixel of light in the black of Lake Sweetness.

She watched that light dwindle into nothing.

TEN

Outside the hospital, conifer trees swayed in a quiet rain. Beneath the glass canopy of the main entrance, people were smoking, eyes on the misted horizon, futures uncertain. Finch barged out of the automatic doors, her head on a swivel.

'Eva!'

The girl was nowhere to seen.

Finch turned to the smokers. 'Anybody see a teenage girl, five-two, black hair?'

Blank faces.

Finch clutched her temples.

Jesus Christ. She's just a kid. Not just a kid – but one without the first clue about this world. There were enough assholes around here to begin with, let alone now that Fest is in town and –

Squinting through the misty rain, she spotted her.

Elesheva was running towards the crowds. Towards Fest.

Dusk. The Catoonah County Heritage Fest was a free-for-all of bunting and accordion music. The crowd was still mostly families, but the tang of beer hung in the air. Axes thudded into targets. Tents offered free DNA and genealogy tests. *Introducing you to YOU! Look to the future, discover your past!*

Everywhere, the words: WELCOME BACK. WELCOME HOME.

Finch hurdled the turnstile showing her badge and

immediately was swallowed by the mass. Brain spinning with flashbacks, she snapped her head around.

'Eva!?'

Everywhere she looked, kids dressed in Versammlungs-volk costumes. A woman wearing a work dress and *Kappe* was giving a talk on her wooden stage:

VERSAMMLUNG: THE STORY OF NECTAR'S FIRST SETTLERS

'See, folks, the Assembly Tree is crucial to them –' She gestured to a papier-mâché tree behind her. 'It's beneath these branches that the forefathers, driven out from their homes across the ocean, first settled. Imagine, kids. No phones, no PlayStation. There weren't even any towns. They were just outcasts in a strange, empty land, dying of cold and hunger –'

Now a man in a fake grey beard stumbled on to the stage, followed by a dozen sad puppets dressed in rags. The children, sitting cross-legged, all laughed.

Finch skirted the show, then climbed up some bales of hay behind the stage to get a better view. Desperately, she scanned the crowd. But everywhere she looked: *Kappen*.

'After months of suffering, lost in these mountains, their leader found a beehive in the hollow of this dead tree . . .'

The actor slapped his forehead: *Eureka*.

'. . . And what did he find inside it?'

The kids all chorused: *honey!* From a hole in the papier-mâché tree, the actor pulled out golden ribbons and all the puppets jumped for joy.

'A miracle! What was it?!'

A miracle!

'Yay! Now his hungry followers would survive. On that day, the leader decided the search for a new paradise was over and named the colony Versammlung – *Assembly*. Ever since, his descendants have followed his faith, eating the honey each day.'

The crowd applauded and were herded towards her merch: novelty *Kappen*, fake beards, books on the history of the Versammlungsvolk.

Hopping down, Finch pushed into the bodies, towards the main pavilion. The crowd was clapping along with the Schuhplattler dancers on stage. Men in high socks sawed a log in time to the music, howling with Germanic jollity. Above it all, a vinyl banner read:

★ VOTE TO RE-ELECT MAYOR QUAYLE COCHRAN ★

The dancers finished to wild applause and the word *wunderbar* pronounced badly. Now a podium draped in the American flag was wheeled out. Mayor Cochran emerged. His wife and daughter stood behind him, both of them smiling without eyes. A few daring boos resounded until the national anthem drowned them out and everyone held their hearts and sang.

Finch was wedged in, no longer able to push forward. Instead, she struggled her way sidewards to a pole which she gingerly climbed for a better view.

On stage, Cochran shook hands with disabled veterans and thanked them for their service – automatically turning to smile for the photographer in the moment of handshake. Now he was at the lectern.

'Friends, thank you . . .' He tried to wrangle applause that had already died down. 'Now, I'd like to start by apologizing to my wife for not wearing the Lederhosen she tried so hard to find in my size . . .'

The audience laughed begrudgingly.

'No but really, I want to thank everybody for coming. I'm grateful to God for so many blessings today. Now, we all know that heritage is important. Understanding yesterday means understanding tomorrow.' He paused to look proudly at Chastity Cochran off to his side, who smiled bashfully. 'Heritage is family. And family is everything.'

Nectar cheered at this, as though anybody on that stage were suggesting otherwise.

'Now, without further ado, Miss Germany-USA, if you'd kindly do the honours?'

A woman in too much make-up and not enough Dirndl-kleid snipped the ribbon, then blew a kiss.

'Nectarites, after fifteen long years, Heritage Fest has come home! She is open! And remember – Election Day is Tuesday! Everyone, go out and vote! God bless America!'

The crowd began to disperse.

And now, a glimpse of black hair and pine-green eyes.

'Eva!' Finch gingerly climbed back down the pole. 'Suspicious Minds' began to play and she had to fight her way through the dancing crowd.

Reaching the food stalls, Finch stopped to catch her breath. She was panting, her head swimming. 'Where are you, kid!'

A few curious glances. No Eva.

Finch felt a rising panic. *The girl just had a freak-out. She's fine . . . Unless, he is back. No. No, quit that bullshit, keep your head.*

In the eating area, people were talking about what a great day it had been, about finally taking that trip to Europe, about the dead body in the truck stop.

But now, Finch saw her again. The girl was standing between an axe-throwing stall and a taco stall.

Relief. Followed by realization.

Something's off.

Elesheva was facing away, towards the perimeter fence. A man was kneeling in front of her, talking. He reached out for her hand.

As he did, a smile emerged in his long beard – a Venus flytrap smile.

Drawing her gun, Finch broke into a sprint. 'Police! Move!'

Pushing her way through revellers, she hurdled wooden picnic tables. She couldn't make out his face. Fifty yards away, she could only see a spindly man with dark hair. His finger was pointing away from the Fest, motioning towards the wood.

'Eva, get away from him!'

The girl turned and glanced back at Finch curiously.

The man bolted. He moved fast – vaulting the fence – then making for the wood.

'You!' she raised her gun and Nectarites screamed. 'Freeze!'

But with his head down, he poured on the speed. Finch reached the girl as the bearded man reached the treeline.

'Eva,' she wheezed. 'The fuck was that?'

'He said he was a friend.'

Finch grabbed her by the shoulders and shook. 'Listen to me, goddamn it. You don't understand this place. He could've hurt you. You've had the worst day of your life, I get it, but you can't –'

'– Do not touch me.' Elesheva pushed her away, her small body shaking with rage.

Finch slumped back against the fence, exhausted, feeling like she was going to throw up. 'Listen, Eva . . . I'm sorry about your sister. I really am.'

'I care not for thy sorrow.' The girl met her eyes in tears – in anger. 'Thy job is to find the one that killed her?'

'Yes.' Finch scanned the wood for the man but, by now, he had disappeared. The trees were as still as closed lips. 'I'll do whatever I have to, to find him.'

'Then, I wilt help thee.' Elesheva wiped away her tears. ''Til my last drop of blood.'

ELEVEN

In Room 202 of the Friendly Motel, Finch was trying to read Pike's book. Across from her, Elesheva Frey pressed her nose to the television. The nature documentary was making her gasp. She was washed, now wearing the oversized Detroit PD hoodie, her own clothes hanging up to dry.

'Come on, Eva. Finish your food. Then it's time to skedaddle.'

'But hast thou ever seen such a large spider?'

'It's not actually that big. They've just zoomed in.'

'Zoomed in?'

'Yeah, it's this nifty trick they do with cameras.'

'Nifty?'

'Like, good. You know, neat. Enjoyable.'

'And what this word: *skedaddle*?'

Finch laughed. 'To leave. Go.'

'Weird.'

'Yeah, you've got that one down. Now eat your pizza.'

'Piece of ah?'

'*Pizza* – that circle thing in the box.'

Eyes locked on the screen, Elesheva absently bit into the pizza. Then, with a retch, threw the slice across the room. ''Tis feculent.'

'Then don't eat it. Jesus, kid.'

The girl picked off the mushrooms from the pizza, collected them in her palm, and went back to her spot. 'I wish for more *Kaffee*.'

'I thought you said it was crooked.'

'Aye. Yet I crave more.'

'None left.'

'Dakota, I wish to be closer to the creature.' She waved the remote. 'I wish to *zoom*.'

'No, they zoom, you don't zoom. That only controls the volume and the channels.'

'Channels? I canst look upon other creatures?'

'Sure. Not just animals. Stories. Places. People. Everything.'

'How many of these *channels*?'

'I don't know. A lot.'

The girl changed the channel. As a travel show turned her face blue, she gave a Promethean smile. *Where America ends, Polynesia begins, in an azure paradise of unique beauty. 137 islands, endless discovery, Hawaii will delight your eyes and capture your heart.*

'That's the place I was talking about, Eva.'

The girl shook her head. '. . . How can such creation be possible?'

'See those little green things? Those are sea turtles. Baby ones.'

'Thou hast looked upon them?'

'Sure. I even got a keychain. Here.' Finch put her book down and pulled off a rubber Kauai keychain depicting a cartoonish sea turtle, then tossed it over. 'For you.'

'Beautiful.' Elesheva held it up to the light, then licked the grease on her lips. 'I will look upon them one day.'

'You know what? I bet you will. But we gotta go now.'

'Verily –' Elesheva put the remaining mushrooms in her mouth. 'This TV is a wonder.'

Finch threw the girl's wet clothes into a laundry bag and handed it to her. Then, checking her gun, looked out the spyhole.

'That is thy *spitzhacke*, yes?'

'My what?'

Eva replied with a cleaving motion.

'Oh, axe? Kinda, I guess. This is a gun.'

'It cuts swine? Beast?'

'Yep.'

'*High and mighty be His right hand. For He is a revenger of wrath upon evil.*'

'I've been called worse. Wait here.' Finch slipped out and scanned the parking lot below. The woods across the street. There was no one under the streetlamp. But the bushes behind it were bobbing.

Her ringtone made her flinch. 'Cochran?'

Dakota. Is the girl with you?

'Yep. We're at the motel.'

What the hell is she doing there?

'Long story. We had a . . . misunderstanding.'

I'm being told she ran off.

'She's a kid. When she found out her sister was murdered, she freaked. It involved clean-up. Wasn't gonna send her home like that. But I'm taking her now.'

Don't bother. I just got word from a pissed-off Chamberlain Weaver. Their gates are closed until dawn. So, the girl stays with you. He hung up.

Elesheva stood next to Finch on the walkway now, peering at the sodium vapour of the streetlamp. In the darkness, Nectar was a glow-worm cluster.

'Apparently, your village gates are closed.'

'Aye. The devil walketh most freely at night.'

'OK. Well. You got room for dessert?'

'What is dessert?'

The ice-cream parlour waitress gave Finch a strange smile as she set down another extra-large cup of coffee on their table.

144

That was understandable. *The cop and the colony kid. Guess we do make a strange pair.*

'Nay, the rule is not only for age. Versammlungsvolk art baptized just afore their marriage, usually at seventeen or eighteen winters. After baptism, they are forever bound to the Versammlungsbaum. Leaving the colony thereafter would be a terrible sin.'

'That's why only kids sell pies and wine.'

'Aye. Though the practice was stopped many years ago.' The girl lay back in the booth, half-comatose. 'I wilt admit, Dakota Finch. Though Englisch food be feculent, peach-choco and peanut sundaes art a fine thing.'

'Not bad for your first ice cream.'

'Perhaps I wilt order another.'

'You'll have to add the word *lactose-intolerant* to your lexicon.'

Elesheva burped, then dumped a small mountain of sugar in her coffee. 'If I had been born Englisch as thee, I wouldst keep a shop selling only *Kaffee* and peach-choco sundaes.'

'It's a niche, I'll give you that.' Finch's smile faded. 'Listen, kid. I know it's raw. But we're going to have to talk about your sister. You said you wanted to help.'

'Yes.' She bit into the glacé cherry. 'Until my last drop of blood.'

'You mentioned she sometimes left the colony?'

'Aye. Sometimes my sister walked alone. Long hours. Beyond our walls, I think.'

'Did she tell you where she went? If she was seeing anyone?'

'Who would she see out here?'

'I'm asking you.'

'We are much removed in age but Rebecca is my world entire . . . or was.' The girl looked down at her melted sundae. 'Oft, I would ask her about her time out here. Fest. I did not think I would look upon it. Today, I had the strange thought — the *weird* thought — that perhaps I would see her there. It is stupid.'

'It's not stupid.'

'My sister loved most thy music. She would always say that. *The melodies of the Englisch are writ in God's abode, even if they know it not.*'

Finch went into her back pocket and fished out a quarter. 'Here.'

Elesheva frowned. 'Money? For ice cream?'

'No.' She led the girl to the other side of the parlour. In a forgotten corner stood an old Select-O-Matic jukebox. 'You've only got one. Choose wisely, kid.'

'Choose?'

'Those are all songs.'

'But there are so many.'

'You want me to pick?'

'Aye.'

Finch punched in the numbers and the Select-O-Matic went through its beautiful, clunking dance. A warm, muffled crackling, and then music.

'It's by a band called Fleetwood Mac. The title is "Gypsy".'

At once Elesheva was enraptured by the alchemy of instruments, melodies. She barely had time to divine them before the woman's voice filled the parlour.

'. . . Who is she?'

'Stevie Nicks.'

Never before had words trapped the girl's heart in such a fashion — such warmth, such *beauty*. She closed her eyes as the sweet miracle-voice broke her already broken heart.

'What is her meaning?'

'The song? It's kinda like a story. About being alone. About feeling love for a person who's gone. About being afraid but unafraid at the same time.'

'My sister –' Elesheva whispered, her eyes closed. 'She was right.'

When it finished, the girl sleeved away the tear.

Finch went to settle up, pretending not to notice. Outside, they paused at the cruiser.

''Tis strange. I hath never feared being alone afore her death.'

'I wish I could tell you that goes away.'

'Thou hast lost a sister?'

'In a way.'

They looked up at the night sky. It churned grey as television static.

TWELVE

In the colony square, women were twining posies for the children's hair, their smiles catching the dawn. Youths stomped flowers into jam with their feet. Ponies were having their hair braided. A pregnant woman broke snails out of their shells into a vat of honey soup, while another sliced the pigeon meat.

When the gates opened and Finch entered Versammlung, again every soul stopped to face her. Some of the elders muttered curses at her, crossed themselves. There was a strange, filmic silence until the voice of Ichabod Weaver was heard, barking orders.

He approached now, shaming onlookers back to their tasks, away from their windows with a mere glance.

'Elesheva,' he said flatly. 'Be thy sister with the Lord?'

The girl gave a single nod.

'Condolences. Now, return to thy father. And remove that foreign clothing at once.'

'Yes, sir.'

She gave Finch a look she couldn't read, then hurried away, still clutching the laundry bag and her faceless doll.

'Detective.' Ichabod considered her. 'Is there cause for inquisition?'

'Yes. Very much so.'

'We'll talk in the fields.'

The walk through Versammlung was completed in fifty

paces. Every surface that was not coated in mud was sticky with honey or blood. Salted meat hung from porches, the only adornment on each house a single crucifix of wood and nail.

They came to the sacred poplar tree, to which the soul of each colonist was bound.

Ichabod hurried her past the ancient dead thing, as though something too delicate for a toddler. They cut through a wood, and then out to the golden land that lay north. There, men ploughed the fields like their lives depended on it. Pickaxes thudded into the earth. The withers of horses glistened in the brilliance of a winter sunrise finally breaking through cloud.

'Not many Englisch hath entered our colony.' Ichabod spoke over his shoulder, a cold civility in his words.

'Or seen your sacred tree. Where your first father found honey, right?'

'And proclaimed Assembly. *Versammlung*. Thou hast studied our ways in thy school, I see.' No hint of a smile on his white lips.

'I passed through Fest yesterday. Didn't see your people there.'

''Twas forbidden long ago. We were too open in the past. 'Tis how sin seeps in.'

'You still sell your stuff, though. Right? Produce?'

'Through an intermediary. Aye. Be this thy inquisition?'

'No. Just my curiosity.'

They climbed a hill to a small gathering of cherry trees. From up here, Finch saw men working far into the lambent distance. A vast carpet of tobacco crops, wheat, fruit groves. Ichabod could observe it all like a general.

Instead, he had stopped at a log shelter. Beneath it, two dozen beehives – the strong buzzing pleasant to the ear. All around them, little steel wood burners were lit, laid out next to the hives.

'Why the fires?'

'To keep them awake in the winter. Lest they hibernate.'

'Ichabod. Do your people know what's happened yet?'

'Just that there hath been a death. Adam Frey, the father, knoweth. And Elesheva, of course. The rest will be told tonight.'

With bare hands, he lifted the lids and inspected their golden worlds – one by one. 'Keeping bees, 'tis my duty.' He sealed the last hive with a caress. '*Gut, meine Lieben.*'

'You feel affection for them?'

'Perhaps.' He seemed taken aback by the question. 'Bees art pure, living only for their queen. No thought for themselves. For sin . . .'

'Like Versammlungsvolk?'

'Only our God differs.' An almost-smile. 'Tell me. Why art thou come here?'

'You spoke to Cochran, you know why. I need to know everything I can about Rebecca Frey. The more I know, the more it helps me to find the man that killed her.'

'We pray for it. But why seek him *here*? We are bound by God to do no harm.'

'We also have laws against murder.'

'Thy laws be adhered to less strictly, are they not? Near four hundred winters we hath lived here without murder. The man that killed her wilt not be found in Versammlung.'

'Mr Weaver, it's procedure. I start close to the victim's life, then work my way out.'

'No person here would hurt her. 'Tis impossible.'

'Well, in my experience, those closest to us are often the ones that hurt us.'

'And yet –' He faced her now for the first time, his eyes

a ferocious blue. 'Thy experience dost not encompass Versammlung.'

'Some things are universal, sir. Wherever there are people, there is violence.'

'We are taught to brook differing views.' He gave a thin smile. 'But respectfully, 'twas not upon these lands that Rebecca hath been found killed.'

'I'll explore all avenues. That includes Nectar. I'm only here to establish facts.'

'Very well. Then Adam Frey expects thee at his home.'

'I'll head over once we're done here.'

The men in the fields were stabbing the last of the crop leaves on collection spikes as they gathered them, a mechanical rhythm practised over lifetimes. Generations.

'For thy inquisition, what wouldst thou require from me?'

'Organizing. I need to speak with everyone that knew Rebecca.'

'Everyone?'

'Except for kids, yeah. *Everyone*. Especially those close to her.'

'But all here knew her in some way. Our population is vast, there are close to two *hundred* of us.'

'Sir, this is simple. Someone here could know something that can help me find the killer. Maybe even without realizing. So, I'll be asking them all about Rebecca, about recent events, maybe some uncomfortable questions. There is no avoiding this.'

'None here wilt becloud the truth. Thou art afforded full inquisition into our colony. I see if thou art denied today, more wouldst only come upon the morrow.'

'You're not wrong.'

'Then thy inquisition begins upon the morn.'

'I'll also need to search Rebecca's home for evidence.'

'Aye, *evidence*.' Ichabod nodded. 'I hath explained to Adam thy society be not founded on faith. He knows he must surrender to thy ways.'

'Thank you.'

'Miss Finch, my day is long, my tasks are many. Hath we concluded business?'

'I did have some questions for you. Does now work?'

'Very well.'

She took out her notepad and replacement pen from the motel, having lost hers somewhere. 'Where were you on the night of the thirtieth, morning of the thirty-first between 8PM and 4AM?'

'Asleep.' He licked his lips. 'As any other night.'

'Early to bed, no?'

'And to rise.'

'What did you do before that?'

'Afore that, I led prayer, dined with family. 'Twas an unremarkable day, I recall.'

'Rebecca – what was your relationship?'

'I am shepherd to Versammlung.' His tone was back to that of a tired parent regarding a new mess. 'I guide the daily search for goodness. My encounters with Rebecca were few: prayer, confession, or whence rarely I called upon her father.'

'And Rebecca was married, right?'

'Nay.'

Finch looked up. 'No?'

'She was betrothed. To my son, Jubilance – a good man.'

'I thought she was married?'

'Nay. Why?'

'Uh, her age, I guess. She's thirty, or so? From what I heard, girls here marry young.'

'She was engaged once before, many winters back. Piety Schröder.'

Finch saw his face in her mind. That winter. The lake. 'Well. Former partners can often be suspects in these cases.'

'Young hearts are raging rivers. Thou wouldst speak with him? Very well.'

Finch wanted to ask about Eli Black but couldn't figure out a way of dropping that name without showing her hand. *I'll come back to him.*

'I also need to talk to your son.'

'Of course. Jubilance hath the Englisch tongue.'

'Did Rebecca have any enemies, any bad blood?'

'Bad blood? There is none here.'

'Anyone who even disliked her? You're Christians, not robots.'

'Robots?'

'Never mind.'

'Nobody, to my knowing.' Bees zipped around him, softly rattling the early morning air. 'But such acrimonies would unlikely be openly discussed.'

'What role did Rebecca have in the village?'

'She worked the sweetness, like most of the women. Fruits. Jams. Dandelion wine.'

'You mentioned an intermediary for selling your products.'

'Aye. Our crops, fruits, milks, tobacco – we hath an arrangement with Burr Group. The percentage is reasonable. Be this connected in some way to Rebecca?'

'Not sure. How do they transport your produce? Truck?'

'Aye. Weekly, a large carriage comes to collect.'

'The same driver?'

'Usually. I wilt fathom his name for thee.'

'OK.' Finch put away her notebook. 'For tomorrow, I'm guessing nobody is going to be able to understand me?'

'Aye. Very few hath thy tongue.' He tugged his beard. 'Start with those tonight that do. For the rest, I shall think on a solution. The Frey homestead is west by that path yonder.'

'Thank you, Mr Weaver.' Finch turned to leave.

'Inquisitor. Why didst thou ask about the bees?'

'Oh, just my own curiosity again.'

'Then be careful. Curiosity, Frau Finch –' He put on his beekeeping mask. ''Tis the devil's most cherished music.'

THIRTEEN

The Frey house was on the other side of the working fields, through dense woodland, two miles west of Versammlung itself. It looked much the same as the other farms Finch had passed – three storeys, white wood siding, large barn, long porch. Some had doors painted blue. The Frey door had been blue also not so long ago. Now, it held a black ribbon.

Finch knocked. After a long while, Elesheva answered. Her eyes were puffy, lashes little black spikes. She said nothing, just stood to one side.

Inside, the house was a casket of wood and crochet. No photographs. No phone. No TV. Only a crucifix above the kitchen door. There was silence except for the grandfather clock in the hall – *snick-snick* – milk teeth rattling in a pocket.

In the kitchen, Finch heard a strange and constant metallic sound from below. Elesheva sat at the table, chartreuse eyes unwavering, as she wound the cord of her hymn doll. Now, the faceless thing tinkled its tune in the silence.

'How are you doing, Eva?'

'Papa wilt receive thee anon. He toils downstairs, cutting my sister's grave.'

'Would he mind if I searched your sister's room, then? Ichabod Weaver said your dad was aware of that.'

The girl shrugged and led the way upstairs. In Rebecca Frey's room, Finch felt for weak floorboards, opened drawers, checked behind them. She took down clocks and peered inside. She knocked on wooden panels hoping for hollowness, fondled pillows and unfolded garments, delving for secrets.

An hour passed. She found nothing.

Another passed as she searched the upper floor. Finding nothing there, either, she returned to Rebecca's bedroom.

Elesheva clutched her hymn doll as she watched. 'What dost thou seek?'

'I don't know. I want to understand your sister's life.'

'So thou canst better understand her death.'

'Yes.'

'It seems strange now. That I can love her but realize I knew little of her.'

'Like you said, there's an age gap. Besides, people live out lives in secret.' Finch prodded the faceless dolls sitting on the shelf. Went through every inch and seam and feather of Rebecca's bed.

'But a secret is a sin.'

'People sin, Eva.'

'Mother always said: *evil pursueth sinners but to the righteous good shall be repaid*. But then, what good hath been repaid to us?'

'Is your mother here?'

'She re-joined the Lord many winters back.'

'Sorry to hear it.' Finch paused by the bedside table. On it sat a leatherbound book marked with Rebecca's name in goldleaf. 'This a Bible?'

'My sister's *Schriften*.'

'Potato potahto.'

Inside, Finch found a small, glass frame that seemed to be detachable. Removing it and holding it up to the light, it held some sort of residue. Some text passages were hollowed out – almost like braille. She traced them with the tips of her fingers. They came back sticky.

'What is this?'

'This is how we read the verses, by licking the honey. 'Tis our way.'

'Why?'

'Goodness through sweetness. The passage is set by the Council afore each week's prayers and thereafter the *Schriften* is twined with the honey.'

'Weird.'

'To *you*.' The girl lowered her voice now. 'I wish to ask. Where didst my sister die?'

'We're not exactly sure yet. She was found in Nectar by a pond. Near my motel.'

Pain passed through Elesheva's face – clear as wind through a wheatfield. Finch was about to say something but stopped. Hidden in Leviticus, there was an old envelope. In scratchy, child-like handwriting, it was marked:

ATONEMENT.

Inside, Finch counted five $100 bills. 'Why would your sister have this money, Eva?'

'I know not. I hath never seen it.'

Finch turned back to the book and read out loud, '*An atonement shall be made afore the Lord: and any trespass shall be forgiven . . .*'

'How could she acquire Englisch money?'

'Possible she had it since 1998, I'll need to check the serials on them.'

'She had no need of money, I do not understand.'

'Ichabod mentioned a pick-up driver for your produce. Does he pay?'

'I am not sure. I think, perhaps, yes.'

'So, would your sister handle that money?'

'She works the sweetness only. It would be the duty of a man. Jubilance, perhaps.'

'What about this verse. Leviticus. Did it mean something special to her?'

'Not that I know. Nor hath it been preached on recently at the Versammlungsbaum. Ichabod may know.'

From downstairs, a deep voice called her name. Instantly, Elesheva jumped off the bed and went to the door. 'Papa is ready.'

Finch followed her to the kitchen.

Adam Frey was an enormous man, the seams on his black jacket struggling to contain him like nervous smiles. His beard wild red, his long hair curly brown, his eyes wilting begonias. He motioned to the seat opposite him and Finch took it. 'Afternoon, Mr Frey. I'm Detective Dakota Finch.'

No reply.

'I'm the "inquisitor" here on behalf of Nectar Sheriff's Department. I know that you were informed of your daughter's death. I want you to know we're very sorry for your loss. But I have a few questions at this time.'

Adam Frey held his palms out and puffed. A little sandstorm of stone billowed. When it had gone, he set out two glasses. Biting out the cork from a yellow bottle, he poured.

'*Honigwein.*' He spoke slowly, yet so deeply that it seemed as if the window panes rattled with his words. '*Du bist mein Gast, du wirst trinken.*'

Finch turned to the girl. 'I thought your father spoke English.'

'Aye. But you are an unmarried outside woman. He cannot speak to thee directly. Nor canst any man here. Only Ichabod. And even he hath struggled with it for –'

'– I need your father to answer.'

'I will translate. He invites you to drink, Inquisitor.'

With a shrug, Finch tasted spiced honey, rosemary, mud. It was sweet yet carried a medicinal bitterness.

Adam finished his glass in one swallow but watched until she had emptied hers too. Only then did he speak.

'My father wishes to know, when wilt Rebecca be returned to us?'

'Soon.' Finch tried to meet the man's eyes but he refused them. 'Sir, do you know why she would've been outside the village walls in the first place?'

A shake of the head.

'Had she ever done that before?'

'*Not since her youth, tendering as the others –*' Now Adam went on a rant, spitting words too quickly for Elesheva to translate. 'He-he says he never should have agreed to let Rebecca tender outside our walls all those winters ago. The root of this is there, he is sure.'

As Elesheva translated, she blinked rapidly and pushed her temples as if to find the words faster. A sweat soon broke out on her forehead despite the chill in the house.

'Ask him if Rebecca would have a reason to be outside a few days ago.'

'He says: *she was more than thirty winters of age, her business was her own.*'

'What about walks? Didn't she go on walks?'

Adam Frey looked at his daughter, then returned his eyes to Finch. 'He says: *no one may leave Versammlung. I know of no sin committed by Rebecca.*'

'Listen, tell him that I'm not accusing her of any sin, I'm not blaming her or you.'

'He wishes to know: *what of the man who killed her, what of him?*'

'We'll do everything to find him. When we do, he'll go to jail for a very long time.'

'Jail?'

'A place of punishment.'

'*I know the Lord will render punishment whether or not you find this man.*'

'Did Rebecca have enemies? Anyone who made threats? Anyone angry with her?'

'Nay.'

'Have you noticed anything strange here lately? Out of place? At all?'

Adam Frey shook his head.

'What about you, kid?'

'Me?'

'Yes, you.'

'What I think matters not. Mine father hath spoken.'

'Where was he on the night of the thirtieth and morning of the thirty-first between 8PM and 4AM?'

The girl translated. '*By that time my work had already concluded in the field. I came here, read my Schriften, dined, and slept.*'

'When did you last see Rebecca?'

'*The day she went missing. We bid each other good morning, she kissed my cheek. I suggested breakfast but she said she had duties to attend to.*'

'That didn't seem strange to you?'

'*Nay. We work to live here. As for her job, I do not know details. I work the crop.*'

'Did she ever talk of leaving here? For good – never coming back?'

He shook his head.

'She never showed unhappiness here? Never wanted to start a new life outside?'

'*There is no outside for us. Our people art bound to the Versammlungsbaum. Under its branches we find peace. Forever must we shun temptation. It leads only to corruption.*'

'So, Rebecca had no disagreements with anyone here. Even if small?'

'*She was much beloved by all.*'

'And she was engaged, right?'

'*Aye. Jubilance Weaver. To marry in the spring.*'

'What was their relationship like? Did they ever have any problems? It's very important. Even if something seemed trivial.'

Elesheva relayed this. Adam thought about it until he finally shook his head. '*Any disagreement would be their business. But I knew of none.*'

'Was there anyone *else* who liked her? Other suitors?'

'*Rebecca was a pure woman.*'

'I'm not suggesting otherwise. I just have to understand every aspect of her life. If there was a spurned suitor, for example, he could be a suspect.'

Adam's brow knitted. '*Here? There can be no violence here.*'

'I keep hearing that.' Finch rubbed her eyes. 'Rebecca was never engaged before?'

He grunted. '*You refer to Piety Schröder. Well. That was not to be.*'

'Why didn't they marry?'

'*I do not know.*'

'Wait, you don't *know*?'

'*It was an issue between he and the Council. Not I.*'

'Why didn't she marry someone else? She's past thirty winters, as you said.'

'*No man asked for her hand. Until Jubilance Weaver, this year. A good man, though I admit, he is younger than I would like.*'

'Why did nobody ask until him?'

'*Who can know the heart of men but God?*'

'Did Jubilance, or anyone else, ever give Rebecca gifts?'

'*I hath heard of "gifts". Thou art fond of them in thy world. But in our colony, the only gift is the word of the Lord. 'Tis the key to the door behind which paradise be found.*'

'What about money?' Finch held up the envelope

containing the $500. Adam Frey's eyes flicked down to the word **ATONEMENT**. 'This your daughter's, sir? Her handwriting?'

'*It . . . could be her hand, I know not. But she had no need of money.*'

'It was in her holy book, Mr Frey.'

The grandfather clock chimed. The huge man spoke a few sharp words with the girl, then went to the basement door and disappeared downstairs. 'He says he must finish the grave, the visit is over.'

'Well, I have to come back tomorrow anyway.'

'Tomorrow would be better,' Elesheva picked up her hymn doll.

They went to the front door.

There, Finch eyed the girl for a moment before lowering her voice. 'Eva, I know you people don't lie. But I get the feeling there's something you're not telling me. You know *something*. Maybe Rebecca told you a secret. Or maybe she met someone.'

The girl looked over her shoulder, pulled the doll's cord and the tinkling tune played.

Hiding her words in the tune – smart kid.

'My sister had a task to see to. That is all she would say. And she begged me that if Papa were to remark upon her absence, I was to soften him.'

'A white lie.'

'*Soften*, not lie.'

'Why was she was going outside Versammlung? What task?'

'I cannot say. That is all I know.'

'OK, kid. We'll talk more tomorrow.' She got halfway down the porch.

'I cannot unsee those images of my sister in my mind.'

'That's normal, Eva. I'm just sorry it had to be you.'

'Did she . . . suffer?'

'No,' Finch lied. 'She wouldn't have felt much pain.'

Grief twisted her face but she nodded, as if willing herself to accept this cold mercy. They held each other's eyes for a moment. Then Finch stepped off the porch, into the field.

When she was gone, the girl dropped to her knees, her mourning dress bunching up like black wedding cake. The doll fell from her hands and jolted into a lower, distorted pitch. Elesheva's wail was elemental.

January 12th, 1998

Flora was standing on the muddy banks of the Testing Pool. In the distance, fifty feet above the treeline, the new Tim Burr mascot leered at her – a bearded lumberjack holding a stack of pancakes. Closing her eyes, she thought back to last year.

It had been a dog-bite summer. The mountain valleys were already an infinitely folding scarf of fall gold and green. But down in Nectar, Dakota had wanted to go swimming that afternoon.

They had walked through the empty Fairgrounds, thighs scraped by wild flowers, cicadas rejoicing *wee-ohhh, wee-ohhh*. In the wood, a dark-eyed junco watched them as he sang his laughing song.

The egg stink of the Testing Pool mixed with the perfume of dead apples from a field nearby. Dakota kicked off her cut-off jeans, knotted her vest above her belly, and rushed in.

In the last year or two, Flora had gone from skinny to chubby. Her mother told her that was just her hips and breasts coming in, nothing to fret about, but then the boys in class started calling her *Jiggles*. So, Flora dressed baggy. She browsed men's aisles at Goodwill. And borrowed from Dakota, even if it meant putting up with her jokes.

Flora hardly ever showed her body. The thought of swimming with Dakota had excited her for days. But now the moment had arrived. And it was her turn.

'Get in here, loser.' Dakota was treading water. 'Feels amazing.'

'Isn't it radioactive?'

'Radioactive but refreshing.'

The mud between Flora's toes was warm jelly. Nausea fought with excitement as she took off her T-shirt and adjusted the new tankini she had stressed over all weekend.

'What do you want, wolf whistles? Get your cute tush in here.'

Shrieking, Flora rushed in, then a breathless plunge. Submerged in the cold murk, her heart hammered at Dakota's words. It had been a dumb joke but still. Those jokes were the vapours that kept her heart afloat.

That day, in the cool murky water, everything seemed simple.

Nothing was simple now.

Flora opened her eyes. The Testing Pool was half-frozen. And her friend had changed. Or maybe *she* had. Or maybe both.

Dakota emerged from the wood wearing waterproofs. She dropped a duffel bag and doubled over to catch her breath.

'Finch.'

'Hey, loser.' She wheezed little curlicues on the cold.

'Nice to see you wearing clothes for once.'

'Ha-ha. Just because I don't think *dELiA*s* is the word of God.'

'What's in the bag?'

'Stuff for Becky's bachelorette.' She took out a bottle of Appletini.

'Won't your mom miss it?'

'She'll just assume she already drank it.'

Dakota filled a pair of dollar-store cups marked: *bride to be!*

'Nice touch.' Flora gagged on the chemical flavour. 'Hey,

remember what we used to say about the logs at the bottom of the water?'

'That they were drowned witches.' One side of Dakota's mouth curled up. 'And they'd grab your ankles when nobody was looking and pull you down, down, down.'

'You'd be gone forever.'

'We were *odd*.' She topped up their cups. 'Speaking of, today is weirding me out.'

'How come?'

'It's Becky's fuckin' bachelorette, dude. Start of her new life and she's *seventeen*.'

'You sound jealous.'

'Of marrying Piety-whatever-the-fuck? *Hell* no. But at least she gets to start her life.'

'Ten kids with a dick bag? How much of a life is that?'

'But it's *some kind of life*, at least. Cos Nectar is nowhere and we're stuck here.'

Flora shrugged. 'You think Becky's coming?'

'Poor bastard would walk through a tornado to hang out. Only fun she gets.'

'How much do we get?'

'Fair point.'

Rebecca Frey now emerged from the wood, her cape wrapped around her. 'Forgive my lateness.'

Dakota started warbling 'Here Comes the Bride' before rolling her eyes. 'Just realized you got no clue what that music means.'

'*Music* be a strange word for what thy throat issued.'

'Way harsh.'

She grinned. 'What be this green wine?'

'*Apfel*, baby.' Dakota poured her a cup.

Rebecca winced. 'Most crooked.'

'You even notice the cups?'

166

'*Bride to be*. I cannot wait. Now, thou didst promise me a surprise.'

'The attitude on this girl is unbelievable.' Dakota shook her head. 'Come on.'

They downed their Appletini and followed her along the banks of the Testing Pool. Flora pictured them three hundred years ago, three young conspiring women in the woods, branded witches, accused of covenanting with the devil. She watched Rebecca's cape swishing and wondered how differently she was dressed to the first colonists.

'Hey,' Flora called from the rear. 'Did you guys know Nectar used to be called Neck Tear? It was for a native boy found ripped open by the water. Prolly a bear. But the colonists figured the flowers growing out of his bones to be a good omen from God. Creepy, huh?'

Nobody replied.

The Testing Pool behind them, they cut through the wood, coming out on to the broad banks of Lake Sweetness.

It was a milder afternoon today, a light rain over the grey water. In the distance, Fest glittered like a sea anemone in the deep.

Dakota led them to an old wooden jetty. At the end of it, she dropped the duffel bag into a moored rowboat. Crude pink letters had been painted on the side: *BECKY BRIDE*. On the bow, a dollar-store bridal veil had been attached.

'Surprise.'

'*Becky bride?*' Flora raised an eyebrow.

'Ran out of paint.' Dakota hopped in and loosened the oars. 'OK, Becky, climb in.'

'I hath never . . .'

'So, you're losing your b-card before your v-card, big deal.'

'What?'

'Just get in the boat, honey.'

167

Flora got in, chuckling. 'Hey, Finch. *Pier pressure.* Get it? *Pier.*'

'The spelling is different.'

'Well, I know that. Obviously, *I* know that.'

'And isn't this a jetty?'

'You ever hear the phrase *never let the details get in the way of a good story?*'

'Your jokes are worse than your dad's. Now, come on, Becky. It's freezing.'

Grumbling to herself, Rebecca got in the boat. 'What if we are seen?'

'We won't be. Chillax.' Dakota puffed into her hands, then started rowing.

At first the motion unsettled Rebecca. But the further they got from the shore, the more Fest shrank in the distance, the more she eased up.

Soon, a little smile crept along her lips.

Flora wondered if the girl was thinking to herself: *bet you never thought you'd end up on a boat with Englisch heathens.*

In the middle of Lake Sweetness stood a small islet. It was only some thirty yards long, a scrub of bent chestnut trees and brambles poking out of the water.

Dakota jumped out of the boat and dragged it ashore. The girls followed her as she batted her way through weeds and brambles.

And now they saw it. A half-fallen shack, lit up like Santa's grotto. Flora recognized the fairy lights, stolen from the Fest supply shed. A generator rattled and puttered, keeping the shack illuminated and warm. The walls were festooned in pink paper cut-outs and tinsel. There were old bean bags, a camping table heaving with Cheetos, Fruitopia. Countless Fest sashes had been turned inside out and tied together to form one large banner. In marker pen it read: *GETTING HITCHED.*

'What is this?' Rebecca whispered.

'It's your bachelorette party, *doofus*.' Dakota took the *Kappe* from her head.

'What are you doing?'

'Just trust me.' She replaced it with a dollar-store diadem, its plastic pearl letters spelling out *bride*, then draped out the attached veil over her long red locks. 'There you go.'

Flora started mixing the Fruitopia and Appletini while Dakota took out her supplies.

'Dakota, if that be woman paint, I-I cannot. 'Tis forbidden.'

'It's *make-up*, dork. And doesn't your rulebook only apply to your village?'

'Well, yes.'

'This is my island. Different rules. Now, sit still.'

Dakota set about applying the make-up from Claire's. Blue eyeshadow. Frosted lipstick. Inky black mascara that would flake in three seconds flat. Still, it didn't matter.

She got to work, her tongue curling in concentration.

At first, Rebecca flinched. But it didn't take long for her to go perfectly still, a kitten being licked by its mother. When it was done, Flora added the clip-on earrings and slipped on the scratchy pink tulle skirt around her waist.

They stood back to admire their work. 'The ugly duckling becomes a swan.'

Rebecca looked at herself in the mirror and gasped. 'Devilry.'

'It's called a make-over, honey.'

'I look like a woman from thy world.'

'A toast.' Flora lifted her cup of Fruito-pini. 'To the hottest chick in Versammlung.'

They drank, Dakota motioning to not stop until the cups were empty.

'Flora –' The bachelorette coughed. 'Thy mixture be crooked.'

Now the rain picked up so Dakota shut the shack door and blasted the warmth. The sound of the rain on the metal roof made Flora sad so she put on Skunk Anansie on the little tape player in the corner. They huddled around the heater, listening to the music and sipping the green concoction.

'I am . . . grateful to you,' Rebecca whispered. 'I thought there was no kindness here.'

Flora laughed softly. 'We're not all assholes.'

'*You* are.' Dakota threw a Cheeto at her.

Laughing, Rebecca thumbed the tears from her eyes. 'I know not why I weep.'

They went quiet as 'Hedonism' began to play. Flora normally shut her eyes to feel the song better. But now she watched Rebecca look out of the window, a bemused expression on her face, as though the music were a weather she had never seen before.

''Tis strange . . .' She spoke softly. 'At Fest, thy melodies be pleasant, yet no more than that. But in this, there is *beauty*. My heart bows to it as a sunflower to the light.'

'You're a fuckin' poet, Becky. And you're wasted making jam.' Dakota topped up their cups. 'Tell me something. Ever think about marrying another dude?'

'Another?' She laughed awkwardly. 'Who?'

'Dunno. Anyone.'

'Nay.'

'Why not?'

''Tis decided.'

'I'm asking if you've ever *thought* about anyone else.'

'Such a thought would be a secret. And a secret would be –'

'I know, a sin. But a secret is something you *keep* from others. Thoughts are different. They're just in our heads. Not sin, just ideas you haven't shared with anyone else.'

'In that case . . .' Rebecca smirked.

'No shit?'

'Jah. *Shit.*'

'OK, OK,' Flora shuffled closer. 'Spill.'

'No, it was but jest.'

'It damn well wasn't.'

'I cannot.'

'Yeah, you fuckin' *can.*' Dakota threw another Cheeto. 'On this island we share.'

'She's right.' Flora nodded. 'You can trust us, Becky.'

'It is only that –' She took a shaky breath. 'I hath . . . an admirer.'

'What do you mean? Like, not Piety?'

'Another. He – he watches me.'

'A peeping tom?'

Rebecca laughed. 'Nay. In Versammlung, we have such a man. Schlanker Hans. Exiled many winters ago, yet he lingers on the fringes, watching us.'

'Whatever. Tell us about the admirer.'

Rebecca shrugged. 'We hath spoken once or twice. The other night, he told me –'

A sharp knock at the door made her flinch.

Eli Black was standing there, soaked through, a worried look on his face. Rebecca went to him and addressed him in their language. '*Mr Weaver. How didst thou find me?*'

'*I saw thy name upon the vessel yonder. He would not listen.*' The tall boy sighed. '*He insisted –*'

'*Rebecca Frey!*' The shout came from beyond Eli.

Piety Schröder was propped against a tree, red-faced, shivering. '*What be the meaning of this?*'

'*Piety, thou art half-drowned.*'

'*I swam here, as a rat, fearing for thy soul. Now, answer me. What is this?*'

'*I am with my friends, that is all.*'

'*Ai! Look at thy face. Painted like one of* them.'

'*It is just a silliness.*'

'*Wash it off. There is nothing silly in thy whorish aspect.*'

Eli shook his head now. '*Mr Schröder, please —*'

'*Hush, sir. Address thine own wife.*' Piety turned back to her. '*Now, Rebecca, thou spake of gravely offending the Lord as a trifle.*'

'*And where, pray tell, dost the Schriften forbid friendship with the Englisch?*'

'*Speak not of scripture to* me.' He took her by the shoulder. '*Now, come. Thy* friends *wilt loan us the boat and —*'

Rebecca slapped him hard across the cheek. '*You dare touch me?*'

Holding his cheek, he blinked disbelieving eyes.

'*Once wed, I wilt do my duty. Until then, these are my friends, and thou, sir, hast issued much rudeness this day.*'

Piety shook his head. '*Rebecca —*'

'*God is all, that is true. But the rules of Versammlung do not carry beyond its walls.*'

'*That is not so.*'

'*Nay? Yet we speak the foreign tongue each day. Handle foreign money. Surround ourselves with sinners, lush on wine we made for their lips. There are exceptions. And I hath decided this be one.*'

The red mark on Piety's face deepened, slap or blush, Flora couldn't tell. There was only the sound of the rain, chests rising and falling.

'Boys,' Dakota poured two more cups of Fruito-pini. 'Come in outta that rain. *Mi casa es tu casa.*'

An hour had passed in an Appletini adolescent haze. Everyone was shouting over each other. Even Eli Black joined in now, having initially stayed at the door, scanning for boar that were not there. His axe slept in a stump outside.

Piety, who had only picked up the cup after Dakota called him a chicken, was by now loud and drunk.

'Relax, pie boy.' Dakota grinned. 'I'm not calling you a *Fettsack*. I'm just saying I don't think you have it in you.'

'Firstly, do not speak our language. Secondly, I swam here, did I not?'

'*Barely*. Besides, Fest is twice the distance.'

'Truly, thou dost not think I could reach that infernal bank?'

'And *back* again. No, I don't think you could.'

'Observe.' Piety started unbuttoning his shirt. Dakota wolf-whistled, Flora cackled.

'*No, Piety, please,*' Rebecca said. '*This is silliness.*'

'*Nay, woman.*' He tossed off his shirt, his pale torso gleaming white under the bare bulb. "*Tis not a silliness to put the heathens in their place and thy mind at peace.*'

'*What peace?*'

'*We are to marry.*'

'*That hath no bearing.*'

'*Forgive me but it does.*' He tensed the muscles in his arms, his pale, rash-riven body flexing as he posed. "*Tis true, I hath been sickly. But no longer. 'Tis an unfair trademark. See my strength, love. A fine husband I will make thee, my body is ready for fatherhood.*'

'*Piety, I judge thee not.*'

'*Judge me, woman.*' He marched out of the shack, slapping his way through the brambles, his skin tautening in the cold.

'*Thou wilt catch thy death.*'

Piety took a running jump into the water and came up grinning, hair plastered to his shoulders as red kelp. '*To the Fest and back! My lungs will barely notice it, wife!*'

Bellowing a war cry, he started swimming hard.

Dakota nudged Flora. 'Think he drowns halfway?'

'I think I gotta puke.'

'I'll be your clean-up crew.'

The two friends headed towards the treeline, leaving Rebecca and Eli alone. Together, they watched Piety shrinking in the distant water.

After a while, she glanced sidelong at him. *'Piety is a fool, is he not?'*

'He is as the Lord made,' Eli shrugged.

'And didst the Lord make thee half mute, sir?'

'I am watching.' He smirked sheepishly. *'In case of a drowning.'*

Laughing, she nodded to a sheltered part of the shore. *'Sit by me, Mr Weaver.'*

Eli did so and plucked a reed for no reason. *'Thy friends . . . are nice, even if they are not of our folk.'*

'Thou art horrified at my heathen ways.'

'Nay. I wondered where thou didst go to is all. But I wilt speak not of this.'

'I do not fret that, sir. Thou doth barely share a word with anyone, good or bad.'

'I am not one for talking.'

'Few occasions remain –' She looked daringly at him. *'To talk with me.'*

'I-I know not what to say, Miss Frey . . .'

'Whatever thou hast in thy mind.'

'I think . . . Piety Schröder is a fool and a poor husband he will make.'

'He is prideful.' She shrugged, trying not to sound hurt. *'But pure of heart.'*

'Aye. Forgive me. I am no man to judge any other.'

'Nay. I value thy thoughts. But what fortunate girl wilt soon call thee husband?'

'Fortunate?' He laughed. *'Forgiveness Schmücker.'*

'Oh. A nice girl. Comely. And, uh . . . dost thou love her?'

'*Not so much as she loves potatoes.*'

Rebecca's mouth hung open and then she burst into laughter. '*Mr Weaver.*'

Grinning, he tossed the reed into the water.

Piety was waving from the other bank in the distance.

Rebecca plucked a reed too. '*Thy devilish words gave me pleasure, sir. But thou didst not answer my question.*'

'*For thy question was a bramble bush.*' He met her eyes with oaky earnestness.

Rebecca could not understand how he could be a boy and a man at the same time. How fragility could be brute strength too. How she could speak normally yet feel at any moment she would die if she did not touch his mouth.

'*I intruded, sir. Forgive me.*'

'*I do not love her. But I must learn to. 'Tis my duty.*'

'*Eli, I . . .*' she whispered. '*Do not love Piety.*'

He locked eyes with her, his chest heaving. '*Truthfully?*'

'*Yes.*'

Pressing his eyes shut, he reached out and took her hand. They were both trembling. '*The truth is, Rebecca Frey, I am sweet on you. Always I hath been.*'

She wanted to purge, wanted to laugh with joy, wanted to thank God and curse God all at once. '*Truly?*'

'*Aye.*' He suddenly stood, his face stern. '*Forgive me. Thou art to be wed. I hath shamed thee and myself.*'

'*Nay, Eli. I feel the same. I hath always felt –*'

But Eli was already in the water, swimming hard for land.

FOURTEEN

The river had no name but was framed beautifully by golden larches. Across the water, vine maples swayed in the wind. A few weeks before, they would have formed a tapestry of flames. Now they were forlornly balding. Just as the young watchman had said, Finch found Piety Schröder beneath them, by the banks. He was sleeping, two empty bottles of dandelion wine at his side, his fish bucket empty. Next to him lay a crude wooden crutch.

The years had thinned Piety Schröder out, sickness sapping his fat away. The bulldog cheeks Finch remembered now sank beneath his red beard like stuck piano keys. Even from here she could see the bloody handkerchief he kept balled in the cuff of his work shirt.

Observing him, she tried to imagine his hands encircling Rebecca's throat. Physically, it made less sense than Ira Pike or, certainly, Sam Salinas. And both of them would've had no issues in accessing a shotgun, or the Testing Pool. But neither one of them had any way into Versammlung. So, an outside murderer relied on him finding Rebecca already beyond the walls of the colony. But what motive? Looking at Piety now, recalling his tantrums, his jealousies, the way he looked at Rebecca back at Fest – Finch couldn't help but feel his guilt.

How would he get a shotgun? No idea. But he's been outside Versammlung many, many times, he understands money, and he speaks English. Add in motive to that and what've we got? We got a nice, snug fit.

176

'Good afternoon,' she called brightly. 'You remember me, right, Piety?'

He snorted awake, then coughed and spat pink phlegm. 'Dakota? Why are you here?'

'You became a fisherman.' She tapped her Detroit PD badge. 'I became police.'

Laughing bitterly, he struggled up on to his crutch, one of his legs dangling. 'You? Police? The more the years pass, the more I see the Lord's humour is black.'

'Well, I won't take offence to that if you don't mind me pointing out that your fish bucket is empty.'

'I was a better teacher than fisherman. But why are you here?'

'You heard about the death, I'm assuming.' She watched him soak in that sentence but fired off another question to pull him in two directions. 'What happened to the leg?'

'A boar attack, many years ago. The bone break was bad.'

'Sorry to hear that.' She sat down by the riverbank. 'Fifteen years, Piety. We were kids. You remember that winter?'

'Those memories are dead petals to me.'

'You still friends with Eli?'

'We were never friends. And Eli is no longer with us.'

She looked up at him. 'What happened?'

'I have no idea. The Council would. Ask them.'

'I will.'

'I heard an outsider was coming in representation of American law.' He leaned back against the tree with an amused look on his face now. 'I have to say, I'm surprised it is you.'

'Because I'm a woman?'

'No, I know that women outside Versammlung undertake duties that would be forbidden here.'

'Why, then?'

'Because a law man that follows only their own path is not much of a law man.'

177

'Well, I prefer the term *detective*. You have a few minutes?'

'I know I don't have a choice.' He motioned to his fishing rod. 'As you know, I've been in your world many times. Seen your rules. We have many here in Versammlung, also. But in this place, they could all be melded into one single law: *submission*.'

'To God. Yeah, I'm seeing that.'

'To everything. Relinquish thyself to the many. Reject desire, embrace harmony, surrender to the holy book. *Surrender*, Dakota. Every moment here is for the purpose of it.'

'I did that once.' Finch plucked a reed for no reason. 'Surrender isn't something I'm ever going to do again.'

'Then perhaps that is why you seek the murderer.'

'My reason is no different from you fishing in this river.'

'I fish to eat.'

'Same as me.'

'But thy path is not chosen by a council. Of all those open to thee, why choose this one? Why do you seek the murderer – for truth?'

'And to stop him from hurting anyone else.'

'Then he will be punished by your American law. Perhaps, executed. Be that not simple vengeance?'

'Piety, my world has less of a problem with vengeance than yours.'

'But if you put a man to death, even a murderer, what does that make you?'

'Consequence.'

'That is how we differ most, I think. Not custom, nor faith. But by thy *acceptance* of filth. Of sin. It is expected. Tolerated. Thy very work is an admission of it.'

'You people really like to think about how different we are. Makes you feel good?'

'Dakota, you know I've walked amongst your kind. I do not

say these things to spite you. But consider this river. It meets your Buchanan River. Both hath run a long time alone. Across many palms of solitude, they hath come to understand, even love, their own way of flowing. But do you know what I saw at their confluence, Dakota? *Rage*. There are, perhaps, waters in this world which ought never meet.'

They watched the water for a time, gurgling as peacefully as a baby. 'It's true that your colony may be devout. But it is still made up of people. People sin, Piety. This is what I *do*. And I'm here because I think that whoever killed Rebecca was close to her.'

He snapped his head around to face her. '*Rebecca?*'

'Yes. She's dead. Why do you think I came to you?'

He slumped down the tree to the floor. '. . . My God.'

'I take it you didn't know.'

'Know?' He shook his head in disgust. 'How would *I* know?'

'Where were you on the night of the thirtieth going into the thirty-first between 8PM and 4AM?'

His shock seemed genuine. 'You mean to suggest *I* am the one that killed her?'

'I mean for you to answer the question.'

'I was here, fishing all day. 'Tis all the Council permits now. After, I went home.'

'Who saw you? Family?'

'I have no family. I live alone.'

'Why aren't you married?'

He snorted indignantly. '*Why?* I was once a good prospect, you remember. Later, I became a teacher at the Baumschule.' He nodded down at his leg. 'The Lord had other ideas.'

'Did anybody see you here that day? In the evening?'

'I don't know. Perhaps. I work alone. None here think much on Piety Schröder.'

'What time did you go home that evening?'

'At eventide. After prayers, I cooked a fish, then slept.'

'Talk to me about Rebecca. Were you friends?'

'Rebecca was not a part of my life.'

'But you lived in the same community, you both attended the same church.'

'Of course, I would see her face at a distance.'

'You didn't talk?'

'What we shared was in the past. I cut her out of my life as a rot many winters ago.'

'You were going to marry her. Why didn't you?'

'The truth is known by all here.' He smiled. 'But some things are perhaps *too* true.'

'Answer me straight.'

'Rebecca was sworn to me, yes.' He smiled wryly but Finch saw the pain beneath it. 'And then, one day, I was simply told that the union was broken. The Council promised a new match. But the months passed and life unfolded as it did. Today, I sit here before you, one of the few unmarried, childless men in Versammlung – a laughing stock.'

'Why did they call it off?'

'The Council do not explain themselves. Ask Ichabod Weaver.'

'When did you last see Rebecca?'

'As I spake it. Oft I saw her. But I looked *through* her, as though her face were just the fog on a sunrise of a day that did not matter.'

'And when did you last talk to her?'

'I could not say. Months. Winters, even.'

'So, when I ask around, and I will ask around, people are gonna tell me the same?'

He laughed. 'Much jangling thou wilt hear, I'm sure. Scandals such as our separation are juicy nectarines for the swine.'

'What did you say?'

'As I spake it. I've no doubt they will have their gossip.'

'What gossip?'

'*Behold, the harlot is with child by whoredom. Lo, Judah said, let her be burned.*'

'No more bullshit. What do you mean by that?'

'I mean nothing.'

'You're saying Rebecca was a harlot? That's why you didn't marry?'

'I'm just a crippled drunkard. I talk empty words.'

Finch got up and stood over him. 'Piety, you're gonna tell me what you know.'

'I know nothing of murder. I had no involvement.' He motioned to his crooked leg.

'You're happy she's dead, though.'

'I am not glad of Rebecca's death.'

'Yet you can't wipe that smile off your face. Why? Did her new life make you jealous? Her coming marriage hurt you? Why Jubilance and not you?'

Piety looked up at her, tears in his eyes but joy on his lips. 'Verily, the Lord's ways art mysterious.'

'Show me your arms.'

'I am not jealous of her.'

'Your arms, Piety.'

'She was never mine and one cannot feel a jealousy for that which one doth not own.'

'You're wrong about that. Now, show me your arms. Or we'll have a problem.'

'*I* am not the one whose envy thou ought probe, *Inquisitor*.' Piety Schröder rolled up his sleeves. No scratch marks. Just a canine grin.

FIFTEEN

Beneath the mulberry sunset, corn danced in the fields. The perfume of horse grease and dark flowers lingered. A weather vane changed direction. In her career, Finch had seen million-dollar inheritance murders on mahogany staircases. And she'd seen five-dollar murders on the street corner. But as she made for the dairy barns, she was thinking on the kind of murder born of white-hot, spasmodic rage. That's what Piety Schröder had suggested. And in her experience, she'd seen infidelity trigger it countless times.

Piety could've been projecting on this Jubilance guy. But then again, he was engaged to Rebecca years ago. Why kill her now? And how? Piety isn't going to have an easy time killing anyone in his current shape, much less transport a body away to Speedy's. And even if he could, how does he pull that off without anyone seeing him – either here or in Nectar?

So, let's try rage on for size with Mr Suitor, then.

Long shadows from wide-brimmed hats fell across the barns. Finch could hear voices, nearby, whispers unintelligible.

Inside the largest building, rows and rows of cows chained to timber poles. The men were clipping tails to rope, attaching udders to milking tubes.

'Jubilance Weaver?' she called.

They all looked away except a boy who pointed to the end of the barn. And there she saw him – sitting against a huge milk vat, Jubilance Weaver with his face in his hands.

He was in his twenties, pale to the point of albinism with

colourless hair. Finch knew he was going to be younger than Rebecca but she was struck by that pale baby face. Still, he was a large man, Adam's apple thick as a shovel. He looked up at her now, his pink eyes wet, his eyelashes white. It was as if God had wished a boy's face to appear on the body of a man.

'We need to talk, sir.'

'Not here.'

Finch followed him outside to an unseen patch of grass behind the giant grain silo. He took a nauseous breath, removed his hat and held it against his chest, as though to conceal his heart. 'These past days hath been . . . I cannot say *hell*. But –'

'I can only imagine, Mr Weaver. Unfortunately, I do have to ask some questions.'

'First, I beg to know, wilt thou find him – the evildoer?'

'That's why I'm here.'

'Very well.'

Finch took out her notebook and casually scribbled down: *first person not to reject idea killer could be found in Versammlung.* 'You were engaged to Rebecca.'

'Aye.' He eyed the pen suspiciously.

'Tell me more about that, please.'

He shrugged. 'Her father granted his blessing some moons past. The Council agreed. We were to be married on spring's first Thursday . . . I know not what else to say.'

'How would you describe your relationship with her?'

''Twas a normal courtship.'

'Were you having any problems?'

'Nay.'

'Mr Weaver, problems in relationships are normal.'

'We were engaged. We were not in a *relationship*. That is for . . .' He cleared his throat. 'Your people. Not ours. We hath marriage. Or not.'

'And did she return your feelings?'

'Return?'

'Did she love you, sir?'

'Love . . .' He puffed out his porcelain cheeks. 'It is true, women do not pick husbands here . . . But I believe that I dwelt in Rebecca's heart. Or, at least I hath never doubted it. Until thy question, now. Be it normal in thy Englisch unions for man and wife to feel no love?'

'Let's stay with *my* questions. What are your duties here?'

'I oversee many undertakings. Tobacco, milk, the sweetness. I manage the outside carriage collections. Schedule. Purse. I am trusted, for I speak thy Englisch tongue.'

'And you're the son of Ichabod. That can't hurt.'

'Hurt?'

'Never mind. Now, there's a driver who comes to collect, right? Burr Group.'

'Aye. But I know him not. The Council wouldst have his name.'

'Tell me about him.'

'We do not speak save for brief matters of undertaking.'

'You ever notice him looking at the girls? Ever say anything you didn't like?'

'Nay.'

'Did he ever talk to Rebecca? Any of the girls? Ever see him hand them something? Money, for example.'

'He never spoke with them, nor would the women of sweetness respond.'

'You mentioned the village purse? So, when he collects your produce, tobacco, all that – he pays you?'

'Aye. With thy money.'

'What happens to it?'

'I bring it at eventide to my father. He puts it in the village purse.'

'Mr Weaver, did you ever . . . hold on to any of that money yourself? Maybe a mix-up? Maybe you forgot to pass it on to your father one night? Something like that?'

His mouth fell open, aghast. 'Thou hast heard this said?'

'Just answer the question, please.'

'Never. And any suggestion otherwise be verily unkind.'

'OK. But I do have to stay with a delicate subject now. During my preliminary, uh, inquisition, there was some suggestion about Rebecca's reputation.'

'What reputation?'

'That she had a *past*.'

His fists bunched at his sides. 'Hast thou not a past? Or I? Or any soul here?'

'Mr Weaver, I'm here for *Rebecca*. To see justice is done for her. But I have to ask these things. Now, the word *harlot* was used. I'm just asking why. I'm not agreeing with it.'

'Much jangling hath occurred, I see.' The fists bunched hard enough for the skin to creak, whiter than white. 'I cannot say why this filth be said. Rebecca hath been naught but pious. If thou judge her not, then kindly slow thy tongue in future with loose ideas.'

'Sir, you need to be calm. I have to ask these questions. The more I know about her, the more chance I have of finding the man that killed her.'

'Forgive me.' Jubilance exhaled with a shudder, then held his translucent temples. ''Tis only that there be such wrath in my heart. I think of *him*, I think only of vengeance . . .'

'I do understand. But we have to continue. When did you last see her?'

'Some days ago, in the peach groves. Four, now? I have been sick with worry.'

'When you last saw her, tell me about that.'

'We were working. I waved. That is all.'

'You don't live together until marriage, I take it.'

'Aye.' Jubilance flinched at the village bell tolling now. 'Eventide prayer.'

'Where were you on the night of Rebecca's murder? The evening of the thirtieth, then early hours of the thirty-first?'

'Here. My schedule doth rarely diverge.'

'Take me through your whole day.'

'I rose long before dawn as my skin cannot bear harsh light. I oversaw the sweetness, the work of the women. There was no collection that day –' Blood started to trickle from his nose now, down his lip. 'During the day, I read the *Schriften* indoors. Then we had the meal. Mass. At eventide, I checked the tobacco yield. Finally, the milking.' He wiped the blood away with a rag, his sleeves riding up in the motion. 'After prayer, a simple dinner, then sleep. I cannot recall the times.'

But Finch's stomach turned. On his forearms, she had seen scratches. 'Mr Weaver, roll up your sleeves, please.'

'Inquisitor, I really must go. Prayer is –'

'Your sleeves. Roll them up now.'

Sighing, Jubilance obeyed.

Finch's stomach dropped. On his right forearm, she saw a patchwork of scratches.

''Tis from the roughness of the field plants and my petal knife. My skin is delicate. Oft I bear these little blemishes.' By now, the dairy men were emerging from the barns, heading for the village. Looking up, Jubilance saw them all staring at him. 'Please, I must go.' The pale young man walked away, his eyes cast down.

'Jubilance,' she called after him. 'We're not finished.'

But he hurried into the stream of villagers. Versammlung was illuminated by torches now, a small island of light in the descending pitch black. Beyond the dead Assembly Tree, the last of the dusk was threading across the horizon, a violet ribbon through an eiderdown of darkness. *Their lives revolve around that light, avoiding the darkness.*

Finch followed the tide, at a distance – watching. The entire community gathered under the roof of the tree-church. Two hundred of them, as Ichabod had said. Every soul faced forwards, eyes on their chamberlain as he took to his wooden pulpit.

She was shocked to see how many of them were displaying disfigurements: jutting jaws, severe underbite, fused limbs, albinism, cleft palate – what they called the Blight.

Ichabod raised his hands and eyes to heaven and Versammlung began to sing. As the hymn rose up, Finch felt eyes on her. Only one head in the crowd turned back to face her. Jubilance Weaver's eyes were red.

January 13th, 1998

Flora woke to a strange tapping sound. Her head was still distantly swimming from the drink earlier. Or yesterday, now. The clock read 1AM. *A dream? No, there it is again.*

She pulled back the curtain and flinched when she saw a face looking back at her. 'Jesus, you almost gave me a heart attack.'

Opening the window, Dakota flopped inside the room. 'You sleep like the dead.'

'Your lip is split.'

'No big deal.' She sleeved blood away from her mouth. 'How did you explain the puke stains?'

'I told Mom I'd had a bad oyster. Anyway, forget that. What happened?'

Dakota went into the little side bathroom and washed her face. 'Mom finally lost it.'

'The Appletini?'

Dakota laughed over the hiss of the tap. 'No. Doesn't matter. Look, can I stay here?'

'Obviously.'

'Thanks. Don't worry, it won't be long.' She got into the bed and sighed. 'Damn, this is comfy.'

'You gonna tell me what happened?'

'Nah,' she murmured, her eyes already closed. 'Just gotta find my dad.'

'You've been saying that for years.'

Flora got in next to her, facing away, and watched the shadow of rain rivulets snaking across the wall. Dakota rolled over and spooned her friend, rubbing her feet against hers for warmth. They stayed that way for a long time.

'Flora?'

'Yeah?'

'Talk.'

'About what?'

'Anything. Just don't wanna be in my own head.'

Flora talked about how the original Fleetwood Mac guitarist left in 1971 out of the blue to join a cult. And how Skin wrote 'Weak' when a former lover punched her in the face. And how during Apollo 17, Gene Cernan wrote his daughter's name on the moon in lunar dust because he loved her so much.

Then it changed. From the quaking, Flora knew Dakota was crying. She had never seen that before and it paralysed her with fear. She wanted to say it would be OK, that they could leave together, figure something out.

But now Dakota whispered it. 'I'm pregnant.'

At dawn, Dakota was standing by the exit of Speedy's Mountain Truck Plaza, beneath an empty billboard. The hills above Nectar were dead and white. Snow fell in needles. Her heart was broken. All was rust and grit and colourless here.

It took ten minutes to hitch a ride out of town. The first trucker munched on Polish sausages out of a jar, sneaking glances at her. At a red light outside McKinstry, he wiped his mouth. 'You're pretty but you're beat up.'

'Not your concern.'

'I just want to know if you're broken in or not. I'd pay more for a virgin.'

Dakota jumped out of the truck cab and ran.

Within five minutes, she hopped another ride.

To Dakota, this world was not alien. Her father was a trucker. Belly dumps, flat beds, low boys, tankers – if it moved on wheels, he could drive it.

When she was little, sometimes he'd take her out on the road with him. Dakota had seen half the country that way before the age of ten. Whole families living in a truck, school lessons taught on the hard shoulder. One time, in New Iberia, Louisiana, her father pointed to a young woman whose waters had just broken by the diesel pump. A few days later, not far from Evening Shade, Missouri, they passed a dead child being fished out of an irrigation ditch. The entire circle of life, right out on the interstate.

Her second ride passed uneventfully, the trucker listening to Bible radio, through Youngstown, Akron, Toledo, all the way to Detroit.

Dakota hopped out at a gas station on the outskirts of the city. In the bathroom, she saw spotting in her panties again. Already, her nipples were sore. And the smell of the burger truck outside turned her stomach. In that stinking stall, she broke down.

Oh Jesus, fuck. What am I gonna do? If he was here with me, he would tell me it would be OK. Even if it was a lie, I'd believe him.

But he'd been very clear. He wouldn't see her again until she had taken care of it.

Pull it together, Dakota. Just find Dad. He'll know what to do. Find him, it'll be OK.

When her breathing had returned to normal, she splashed her face and put on her waterproofs. Outside, it was raining hard.

She walked along Beaubien Boulevard, past a thousand dead factories, all the way into the city. With nowhere else to go, Dakota sat on the steps of a closed library.

It was cold. The kind that hurt lungs to breathe. The kind that made a runaway re-evaluate their choices.

But there *were* no other choices. Dakota couldn't take it anymore. The whispering in school hallways was constant. She had asked to transfer a hundred times but the papers went unsigned – Mom drinking all day, fighting all night. This was the only move to make. Still, in that cold, with the unwanted life growing inside her, Dakota felt her smallness, her lostness. A little paper boat on the ocean.

Closing her eyes, she rocked herself back and forth. 'You'll find him,' she whispered. 'You'll find him.'

Everything all right, honey?

Dakota lurched awake, blinking in torchlight. Jumping up to her feet, she ran. Right into the locked library gate. The man had her cornered. 'Get the fuck away from me!'

'Hey. You're OK.'

Dakota heard the buzzy murmur of a walkie-talkie. She turned. The cop's palms were outstretched, his big dog eyes worried. He looked gentle. Like someone's dad but not the kind who'd run away. The fur on his bomber jacket shivered in the wind.

'You're not from here, kid. So. Where you from?'

'. . . Far away.'

'I'm Officer Bill Moreno. What's your name?'

'Jane.'

'Jane, huh?' he smirked. 'OK, *Jane*. Why don't you jump in the car while I make some calls?'

'To who?'

'Around the neighbouring towns, see if anyone's missing a smartass.'

'Please don't.'

'It's my job.'

'Look, I'll leave, I'm not your problem.'

'Well, you're too young to be alone. Someone is gonna be worried about you.'

'Not me. Promise you that.'

Puffing out his cheeks, he looked at the floor. 'Where were you headed anyhow?'

'Find my dad.'

'Where?'

She had no answer.

'He left you. And you're gonna find him no matter what, huh?'

Dakota nodded.

'I don't know you, kid. But I do know that whatever answers you're looking for? Your dad isn't magically gonna have 'em.'

'You *don't* know me.'

Moreno sighed. 'What's his name?'

'Caldwell Finch.' Dakota spelled it out and he typed it in to his dashboard computer.

'Here we go. Catoonah County. Wife, Elizabeth Jo. Daughter, Dakota Melody.'

She nodded, hardly able to speak.

'He was booked a week ago in Cleveland for soliciting. Just promise me one thing –' He printed out the mugshot from the onboard computer and then handed her a fifty-dollar bill from his wallet. 'You be careful out there, Dakota Melody Finch.'

When Flora woke in the morning, Dakota was gone. If it wasn't for the pillow smelling like her, or for the splotches of dried blood in the sink, she would've figured it for a dream.

Mom was out for prayer meeting at Bleeding Lamb so Dad made her breakfast. Flora dissected her pancakes without any intention of eating them.

'How you feeling?' he asked.

'Fine.'

'Mom said you ate some bad food last night.'

'Oh. Yeah. I'm feeling better.'

He sat on the stool next to her at the kitchen island. 'I know it's a hard age, Flower. But you sure you're good?'

'Why do you keep asking?'

'I dunno, I guess you just seem more . . . teary.'

'Look, it's my period. Can we drop it?'

'Sorry.' Ed brightened. 'Hey, wanna hear about my stocks? Things are looking up.'

'I gotta get ready for work.'

That afternoon, there was no sign of Dakota at Fest. Flora took extra breaks to cry. *Pregnant. How could she be pregnant? With who?* Part of the pain was knowing – at last, definitively – that Dakota would never love her back, that she was someone else's and always would be. But what really hurt was that Dakota could get this deep with a man and tell her nothing.

Heading for the employee hut, Flora passed the Versammlung wagon. By now, those kids had gotten used to Fest, the commercial rhythms of the outside world. Flora understood now why the bachelorette party had to be yesterday.

Dakota knew she was leaving.

Up on the Pavilion stage, the different categories for Fest Queen 97–98 judgement were being announced – outfit, beauty and personality. Flora barged her way through the crowd, holding her nabber up like a bayonet until she reached the employee hut.

Inside, she didn't even register the stink anymore. Taking off her sash, she threw it in her locker and shut it with a satisfying slam. That's when she saw Devin Rigney opening Dakota's locker.

'Hey, hey. What's going on?'

'What does it look like? Finch is fired.'

'You can't.'

'No?' he sneered.

'Look, she's sick.'

'This is her second no-show. She shoulda been fired yesterday.' He emptied the contents of Dakota's locker into a garbage bag and shoved it into her arms.

In the corner of the hut, Flora hid herself in lost property. She could hear 'Barbie Girl' through the plywood walls. Dumping out the contents of the bag, she could smell a twist of Dakota. There were a few empty canisters of laughing gas inside. A bottle of deodorant. Some spare sneakers. And now, inside an envelope, a series of Polaroid insta-prints. Flora could tell they were taken the night of the boat party she never made.

In the photos, girls her age with older boys – men. Grins. Gropes. Sweat patches. Hair spray. Navels. Smiles. The smiles hurt. Alana Wells was there. Dakota too. Taylor Boswell in the background, selling molly.

In the last photo, he had his arm slinked around Dakota's shoulders, grinning. She was sticking her tongue out. In the pit of her stomach, Flora felt such a disgusted envy, she threw the photos in the trash can.

That's when she saw it. Written on the back of that last image in small, black scratched letters:

DON'T SAY ANYTHING. THIS MONEY IS TO GET IT SOLVED.

'It's *him*.' Flora booted the trashcan. 'He got her pregnant.'

SIXTEEN

Finch crossed the muddy Zentraler Platz, now lit by flaming torches, towards the main gate. Her body was exhausted but her mind wired. What she needed now was some takeout, a shower, a generous dose before sleep.

Reaching the main gate, she motioned to the watchmen on the catwalk above to open up. In reply, they pointed back towards the town square. One of the house doors had opened. It too held a black ribbon. Ichabod Weaver's house stood in the centre of Versammlung. Except for its position, it looked no different from any of the others. A tall woman with a stern, wrinkled face opened. She wore an apron over her black dress, spectacles and *Kappe*. The grey hair that showed was parted with absolute precision.

'Inquisitor.' She spoke in accented English with brusque politeness. 'I am Thomasina Weaver. Mother to Ichabod. He hath given word. Thou wilt stay here.'

'Stay?'

'Aye.'

'Let me get this straight. Ichabod Weaver wants me to stay here tonight?'

'Despite my distaste for it, yes.' She gave a snippy smile. 'Still, I bid thee welcome.' The kitchen looked identical to Adam Frey's. The Ten Commandments above the door. A heaving pantry. Ancient cooking apparatus.

'Sit, girl.' Thomasina went into the scullery and returned with a bowl of creamy gold soup. 'Honeyed snail.'

'That's . . . unique. What about you?'

'I hath already eaten.'

'And your family?'

'Men cannot dine here given thy presence. No matter. I shall tell you what Ichabod hath said. Given our number here in Versammlung, thy inquisition wilt take more than a day. Two, at least. As such, he requests that you stay here, amongst us. It is preferred. Thy conclusion wilt be hastened in this way.'

'Now, hold on –'

'However, whilst thou art a guest upon this land, thou wilt observe our ways. In order to lessen offence to the men, it is preferred if thou wouldst dress plain.'

Finch laughed. 'So, you want me to stay here and wear your clothes?'

'It is preferred.'

'You know what? I'll dress like a scarecrow if that's what it takes.'

'Save for the hat, that be close to thy aspect already.'

'That's the first joke I've heard here.'

'I intended no joke.'

'Well, I guess I'm grateful for your hospitality then, Mrs Weaver.'

''Twas not my choice.' Thomasina poured two glasses of *Honigwein*. 'Few families here wouldst suffer an outsider. Alas, my son hath seemingly more charity than sense.'

'Respectfully, I'm not here for fun, ma'am. My being here means you have an actual chance of catching a murderer. I'm guessing you folks would just sit around and pray.'

'The Lord rendereth recompense to His enemies, young lady. Prayer be no trifle.'

'If we wait for God to find the killer in *this* life, we'll be waiting a long time.'

'And what of thee, Inquisitor? Art thou not imperilled by the malefactor?'

'I'm not afraid of the devil.'

'Aye, thou hast no faith.' Thomasina sipped her wine. 'But I speak of the murderer.'

'I'm not afraid of him, either.'

'But if come ye too close upon his lair, wilt he not be provoked to rage?'

'Maybe.' Finch felt an icy tickle down her spine. She hid it with a spoonful of disgusting soup.

'And in that rage, in that lashing out, who wouldst protect thee?'

'Me.'

'I see.' The faintest smile possessed Thomasina's lips. She finished her wine, then stood. 'Upstairs. At the end of the hall. Goodnight.'

The clinic again. The crinkle of the tissue-roll beneath her on the bed. The distant clamour of protestors outside. A medical trolley squeaking as it was pushed towards her.

Did they offer you something to eat on your way in, Dakota?
She nodded.

But you didn't eat it, did you? It's very important that you didn't. That's how they get you. You eat, you can't have the anaesthesia. But you're gonna be OK, hon.

High above, she saw Tim Burr grinning down at her. The sound of the protestors had changed. There were no longer voices, just a solemn Versammlung hymn. And the scraping rhythm of the shovels. Dirt being dropped into the grave. Into her eyes. Into her mouth.

Choking her. *I look through her, as though her face were just the fog on a sunrise of a day that did not matter.*

Dakota looked up. Rebecca looked down at her, mouth dripping gore, a no-face smile.

Finch woke with a shout in a dark unadorned wooden bedroom. On the floorboards, the smell of vinegar, yeast in the air. There were no voices in this house. Feeling nauseous, she tried to get her breath back, her head throbbing.

It took Finch a moment to remember where she was. Sitting up, she realized just how woozy she felt. Her second realization was that her clothes were not on the chair where she'd left them last night.

Great. Now what? Guess I could just walk around with my tits out, give the village something to talk about for the next three thousand years.

Forcing herself out of bed, she stumbled and had to hold the frame in order to stay on her feet. *Gotta get control of my goddamn dosage.*

The door opened and Thomasina Weaver sailed in. 'Awake, at last. Praise be.'

'Fuck, don't you people knock?'

'Not in my own house. And that word wilt not stand.'

'Lady, I'm naked.'

Elesheva entered the room holding a dress, saw Finch, and suppressed her giggle.

'*Naked?*' Thomasina laughed. 'With such little hair down below, I barely noticed.'

'We call that *trimming*. Now, where are my clothes?'

'Here.'

The dress was black, made of scratchy cotton blend. It covered Finch's arms, and went down to her ankles – no pockets, no buttons, no adornments.

The girl helped her into it, then came a long fastening

process with pins. Thomasina helped, though she was less careful about pricking. When it was done, over the top went the work apron, the cape. Stockings. The shoes didn't fit so Finch kept her standard-issue police boots. Lastly, she pinned her hair back, and Elesheva helped her adjust the white *Kappe*.

'I feel like Bo Peep.'

'Who?'

'Never mind. It's just the bonnet is *a lot*.'

Thomasina nodded. 'Corinthians: *she who prays uncovered dishonours her head*.'

'Yeah, well, I dishonour mine all the time.'

'Finished.' Elesheva stepped back to regard her work.

'How do I look?'

'*Nifty*. But also, *weird*.'

'Laugh at me and I'll kick your ass. Mirror?'

Thomasina pointed to the bowl of water on the windowsill.

'Right. Humility.' Finch saw her own reflection. 'Talk about *plain clothes* police.'

Thomasina and the girl both frowned.

'*Plain clothes*. Get it? You people are plain and – you know what, don't worry.' Finch picked up her notepad and pen. 'Eva, do you know when the questioning starts?'

'They are already waiting.'

In the centre of Versammlung stood an enormous hall-like timber building, its roof thatched with reeds. Apart from the sacred poplar tree, it was the most prominent structure in the colony. Twenty men and women were already lined up outside, whispering.

They fell silent as Finch and Elesheva passed them.

At the entrance, Ichabod Weaver was waiting. Seeing Finch, dressed in traditional Versammlung clothing, amusement played upon his lips. 'Ah, Inquisitor Finch. Most proper dost thou look this day.'

'If I get wolf-whistled by your people, I won't be happy.'

For the first time, beneath his orange beard Ichabod smiled. 'My brothers and sisters stand ready to help thee as best they can. All knew Rebecca in some way.'

'Very good, Mr Weaver. You said you might have a solution for an interpreter?'

'Aye, she stands next to you.'

'Eva? No. She's a just a kid.'

'A moment, please.' Ichabod led her off to one side, smiling for the crowd, but his words solemn. 'Mark me, Dakota. There is nobody else.'

'A bunch of people here speak English.'

'A *handful*. The rest have but a single word or two. Most have nothing.'

'I *need* to question your people.'

'Correct. *You* need. Not I. I merely accommodate. Thou art an outsider. There is no one else here that will brook thy tongue, or thy sex.'

'Ichabod, she's just a kid.'

'Aye, and I sorrow for it, for she carries a burden already.'

'It's hard for anyone to talk about a dead woman in these circumstances. But in front of the kid sister? That could potentially affect their answers. This whole case.'

'I know it is not thy ideal circumstance. Nor ours. But I cannot allow the harmony of another to suffer in the way that Elesheva's already has. If thou knoweth of someone who would interpret from beyond these colony walls, we could talk on it.'

'There are one or two academics in the country that speak your language. But we're out of time as it is.'

'Then you know my solution. Accept or do not.'

Finch glared at him. Then she returned to the front of the hall. 'Eva, you're sure you're OK with this?'

She nodded. 'As I told thee. 'Til my last drop.'

As the watchman opened the old wooden doors, a strong, musty paper smell seeped out. Inside, Finch saw it was an archive of some kind – contracts, tobacco yields, records of birth, marriage and death. Shelves heaving with the minutiae of Versammlung life.

The watchman pointed to the narrow cherrywood staircase.

The upper floor was a kind of auditorium, with ancient oak bleachers on either side. Large lunette windows at the end let in a cold light. In the centre, a table had been set up for them. Two chairs on one side, a single chair at the other. A list of all those that knew Rebecca to be questioned, in the order they had been drawn from a hat.

Piety Schröder was there. Jubilance Weaver was about halfway down. All night and all morning, Finch had been thinking about the scratches on him. The wrath he'd spoken of in his heart. *Whatever, he'll get his turn soon enough. And who knows. By then, I might have a much better picture.*

The watchman lit the candles, signalled readiness, and took his place by the door. Finch took off her cape and placed her notebook on the table. Elesheva was pacing, muttering to herself.

'Eva, listen to me. If we're going to do this, you need to remember something. These are your people. Your family. You know them and they know you. Now, you might think it's not possible they could deceive you. But they can. Even here, *anyone* can lie. Trust me.'

'I am to distrust all others by trusting only thee?'

'Trust your instincts. Weigh them against what I'm saying. I'm not telling you everyone is a liar. But people do deceive – especially when they've done bad things.'

'OK.'

'OK. Ready?'

Taking a deep breath, the girl nodded. Finch gave the signal and so began the tide of villagers. Each one was announced by name as they entered.

Sanctuary Kaufmann was the first. She was a mousy, barefoot girl with an overbite. Her skittish eyes flicked up from the ground to Finch's notepad, then back down.

'Take a seat, miss.'

Elesheva translated and Sanctuary sat.

'My name is Dakota Finch and I need to ask some questions.'

She adjusted her *Kappe*, then nodded uncertainly, her eyes on Elesheva now.

'Miss Kaufmann, I want you to know that everything you say here is only for me.'

'*I do not understand.*'

Feeling ridiculous, Finch shifted in her dress. It was a cage of scratchy seams and sharp pins. 'I mean you can speak freely because nobody else will find out what you say.'

Sanctuary bobbed a shoulder. '*I wilt speak only the truth.*'

'Well, that's good. Let's start. How did you know Rebecca Frey?'

'*We both work upon the sweetness of Versammlung.*'

Finch watched her, unsure whether her apprehension was masking fear or just the unfamiliarity of this situation. 'Specifically.'

'*'Tis seasonal. Tending to the peach groves, strawberry fields, pies, dandelion wine. Of late, we sow currants and berries for they are –*'

'– I mean, were you friends? Did she ever share any worries with you? Problems?'

'*Friends? Aye. But no worries that I recall.*' Sanctuary pondered this. '*Well . . .*'

'Go on.'

'*She never spoke of it, 'twas but a feeling. But oft she seemed . . . alone. Or, distracted, perhaps. I wished to ask of it but she is much older than I and I felt it not my place.*'

'What about men? Did she ever mention anything there? Any problems?'

'*No. Though, that in itself I thought a little strange.*'

'Go on.'

'*Well, she was promised, like many of us. But she never spoke of him. Her life ahead. Us girls speak oft of the future. The house our husbands shall build. The family we wilt raise. Our lives. But not Rebecca. I always assumed it to be her age.*'

'Miss Kaufmann, you're definite that Rebecca never mentioned the man she was to marry? She never spoke about Jubilance Weaver?'

'*Perhaps he was mentioned. I cannot say, I hath known her all my winters. But I mean that it was a conversation that seemed to bring no joy in her.*'

'Do you know him?'

'*Of course. But much less than my knowing of Rebecca.*'

'What do you make of him?'

'*Make of him? I wilt not speak ill of my people.*'

'I'm not asking you to speak any which way. Just honestly, like you said.'

'*I-I know not what to say. He is a good man. The chamberlain's son.*'

'When did you last see her?'

'*Five days ago, perhaps. The morning after, she did not come upon the berry grove. That was when I heard that nobody had seen her that day.*'

'And how did she seem that last day? Or the days before that?'

'*As ever, I think.*'

'Sanctuary, it's really important. Even a minor change of

character or habit could actually lead me to the murderer. Think. Was there anything out of place at all?'

The girl closed her eyes to better recall but shook her head. '*Nay. She seemed distracted, as I hath said. But this was not out of character.*'

'Did you ever know her to handle money? English money.'

'*Money?*' she frowned. '*Nay. We hath no need of it. Rebecca never spoke of it.*'

'Last question: do you know anyone that envied her? Disliked her? Yearned for her?'

'*Again, I wouldst speak no ill of mine people.*' Sanctuary Kaufmann checked over her shoulder. '*But there is one. From the outside who comes . . . He looks at us. I do not know if it be yearning but I dislike the manner of his eyes.*'

'The delivery man? With the big truck?'

'*Aye, the Englisch carriage man.*'

Finch finished jotting down her notes. 'All right. Thank you, miss.'

Sanctuary stood, then paused. She whispered curtly to Elesheva, then left.

'What was that about?'

'She told me that she prays for my sister's soul. But that if I had kept my faith, the Lord would have not repaid me with such pain.'

'So much for not speaking ill of her own kind. Why did she say that?'

'It matters not.'

'Eva, these kinds of things could affect my questioning.'

'Very well. I hath felt doubt since winter last.'

'Doubt?'

'In my faith.'

'Oh.'

'My father says it is just that I am much taken with curiosity.

That it will pass soon, when I am old enough to marry.' She shrugged. 'It matters not. Let us finish the work.'

Finch gave the signal and the tide of villagers continued.

Each one gawped, first at Finch's pen and paper, and then at the girl translating for the outsider. Many of the folk had never heard the Englisch tongue before. Much less being spoken and interpreted by little Elesheva Frey.

Finch lost count somewhere after fifteen statements. The girl never once flagged, hesitated, or asked for a break. Several times, she pressed if an answer didn't satisfy her. Often, she clarified details and asked follow-ups without being prompted. One or two villagers seemed to hiss insults at her but she ignored them.

By midday, Finch had built a vague biography of the victim.

It wasn't one she recognized in her friend in 1998. Rebecca Frey had been cheeky. Curious. Smart. Not unlike her little sister.

But the Rebecca known to Versammlung was a silent woman who never spoke out of turn. Their Rebecca had loved the Lord and was described as a good young woman. Still, there was an elusive tone from the colonists. Some kind of feeling buried under their words. Maybe pity. Maybe dislike. But not one colonist spoke a single word more than needed.

Ichabod had given the order to cooperate and clearly his order stood. But the script stayed the same. Nobody knew anything. Nobody had seen anything. Nothing out of the ordinary. Some spoke of bad omens, *Luzifer* whispering under doors, windowsills, tempting them from the shadows. But nothing relevant to a murder. And not a single lead emerged, or even an inconsistency.

It was as if Versammlung all wanted to tell the same underwhelming fairy tale. *There once was a young woman with hair of copper, who went away one day, never to return.*

At 1PM, the watchman brought up some peach pie and burdock root tea.

Finch stood and stretched. 'What I wouldn't give to be on Miloli'i Beach right now.'

The girl said nothing, just chewed and silently looked out into space. When their break was over, another name was barked and Finch's notebook opened again.

January, 1998

Dakota paraded the mugshot of her father up and down the strip bars near Cleveland airport. She talked to anyone that would give her a minute. Nobody recognized the picture but most of the working girls were nice to her. Others told her to go home. Almost all made her swear to not talk to Moonlight Jack.

On the first night, she stayed in a motel paid for by an older runaway called Sapphire from Buttonwillow. She held Dakota in the dark and told her everything would be OK, that she would find her dad soon. Sapphire wasn't her real name but it would be her stage name because, she said, even if God had made her blue in life, he'd given her a voice to shine with. Then she quietly sang Del Shannon's 'Runaway' as a lullaby.

The next morning, Sapphire was gone. Dakota woke to fists on the door and escaped through the bathroom window.

The next night, she slept in rolled-up cardboard behind a Market Basket, listening to the soft whoosh of the I-90. After that, sleeping rough didn't seem so scary anymore.

She had the money he'd given her. But she was keeping it back to take care of things.

After a few days, Dakota came to know the streets. To know the girls. She learned their ways. Their language. Their survival tricks.

Dakota hardened inside. Understood that joy was only ever

a glint – a passing beauty seen from the window of a speeding truck. Understood that friendship never lasted long in this life. And that the fear inside her would never go away. It was part of her now. Like a bone. It was there for a reason.

Dakota quickly came to feel like she belonged to the city.

Like she was everyone's kid sister.

She wouldn't get into cars but the johns who only wanted to talk were allowed to park on the corner in full view of everyone. Dakota would drink strawberry milk and listen to them complain about their lives. Moonlight Jack didn't even take a cut from her.

One night, a plain insurance broker recognized the mugshot of Caldwell Finch. *Yeah, I know him. I've got his phone number.*

Dakota followed him a few blocks to a Holiday Inn parking lot. He whistled as he walked, hands in his pockets, loafers scuffing the floor.

'How do you know my dad?'

The man shrugged. 'We met a while back in Buffalo.'

He opened the trunk of his station wagon. 'Gimme a sec, it's around here somewhere. Caldwell . . . Caldwell . . . Got it.'

He held out a Chinese takeaway menu.

Dakota reached for it but he was already pushing her into the trunk, his thick hands encircling her throat. She punched and scratched but the crushing was instant. The pressure in her skull overflowed, blood in her ears thundered. His tongue came out of his mouth, curling up over his neat moustache. She went for his eyes, but he only slipped his thumbs up under her chin and pushed harder.

'Over soon, honey.' He shushed. 'Over soon.'

Dakota's vision blackened despite open eyes. The warm drowse of death slithered close. *What a strange thing to die like this.*

But then the man let go. Blinking, he hit the asphalt, a bullet hole in his temple.

Dakota breathed in smoke and blood particles. Moonlight Jack helped her to her feet, then dragged her over to his car. Only now did she realize her ears were ringing.

'Where do you come from?' He tossed the gun in a trash can and checked the rear-view continually. 'I'm taking you to the bus station.'

'Got no home . . .' she croaked.

'Well, you gotta go somewhere.'

Officer Bill Moreno opened his door. It took him a moment to recognize the kid looking up at him with the bruises and the marks around her neck. 'Dakota, right? Or was it Jane?'

'Hi.'

'How can I help you, citizen?'

'I was wondering if you know anyone who can help me find a person.'

'Detroit PD investigates crimes, kid. Not estranged dads.'

'He's missing.'

'Missing to *you*. Or actually missing? You'd have to fill out a report.'

'I got money.'

'Money for right now. How about next week?'

'Listen, you helped me once. You either will again or you won't.'

He sat down next to her on the stoop. 'You got guts, Dakota. But I think you got brains, too. And if you use them, you'll see this world is gonna eat you alive. Go home.'

'I got no home.'

'You do. It might not be much of one but it's better than out here.'

'I just need to find him.'

'Look, if he was any kind of father, you wouldn't have to search.'

She brushed an angry tear from her cheek. 'Well, screw you, Mr Happy Families.'

'Why don't I call social services –'

She stood. 'I'm gone.'

'Wait.' Bill Moreno sighed. 'If I help you, you gotta promise me something.'

'I can pay.'

'Pay me with your *word*. I'll make some calls, find him. And if it turns out your dad's not the solution to all your problems, you go the hell home. OK? *I swear, Bill.*'

'I swear, Bill.'

He held out his big hand and she shook it.

Flora searched for Dakota everywhere. When she wasn't searching for her friend, she was thinking about it. Sometimes, through the bodies at Fest, she would see a broke-tooth smile or a swish of brown hair that would make her heart thud.

Sometimes, over the jolly carousel calliope, under the rattle of the rollercoaster, Flora would swear she'd heard a bray of Dakota's laughter. Along school hallways, a brief tang of her perfume. The ghost of her fingerprints on the glass of the chiller at Wawa.

When Mrs Finch left her home, Flora would climb through the back window and slip inside Dakota's closet. Hugging those clothes, her fingers would come back rich with the scent of her.

A few days after Dakota disappeared, Flora ran away too.

She made it as far as Andover before changing her mind.

Back at home, nobody had even noticed her absence. Only Dolly grinned at her, wanting to play peek-a-boo.

In her bedroom, Flora put on Fleetwood Mac as loud as it

would go. Then she stuffed her face into the pillow Dakota had slept on, and cursed her own cowardice through angry sobs.

Lake Thunderbird, Oklahoma. The gas station was an island of bleached light in a sea of darkness. Trucks grumbled their way in and out like clockwork. Dakota listened to the wind in the reeds, mole crickets trilling their swamp song. It was 3 AM. She didn't know the date.

Her father's truck was parked crooked. A little boy was sitting close by. He wore a man's T-shirt like a dress, a pink belt around his waist – oblivious to everything but his toy car which he raced along the kerb.

Now a woman jumped out of the truck, spat into the gutter, and washed her mouth out with a Sprite bottle. The little boy waved at her. She did not wave back. The woman went to the next truck and knocked on the cab door.

Dakota had done whatever she had to in order to survive, to make it this far, telling herself that when she found her father, everything would be OK.

But now, looking at his truck, seeing this sad nocturnal exchange, she couldn't recall why she'd felt that way in the first place.

Closing her eyes, she tried to remember the name Flora wanted to give their cat when they left Nectar one day. Maybe if they had stayed together, things could've worked out. Or even been good.

But then *he* had walked into her life. She'd fallen for him hard and now 'good' was gone. That much she was sure of.

Opening her eyes, Dakota took a shaky breath. 'Fleetwood Cat.'

She went to her father's truck, climbed the metal steps to the cab and knocked on the window.

Caldwell Finch waved her away. 'Too late, baby. I'm empty.'

'It's me.'

His face fell. '. . . Dakota?'

'Surprise.'

He unlocked the door and she sat in the passenger seat just like when she was a kid. It smelled of diesel and truck-stop cologne. The radio was playing low. They stayed silent for a long while until he sighed.

'What do you want, Dakota?'

She shrugged. 'You're my dad.'

'Everything OK at home?'

'Swell.'

'You grew up.'

'That's meant to happen, I think.'

They listened to the Backstreet Boys sing 'As Long as You Love Me'.

'So, why you here? Something must be up.'

'I dunno. Nothing is happening in my life the way it should. It's like I'm on rails and I can't make a turn. Or something. Shit, I don't know, I just missed you, Dad.'

'You came all this way for that?'

'Yeah. No. I'm in trouble. Kinda.'

'You need money.'

'No. I didn't come for that.'

'I don't have much but – wait, are you turning tricks?'

'What?'

'Dakota, you're too young for that life.'

'You think I'm . . . ?' She kicked open the door. 'Asshole.'

'Hold on.' He reached for her but she slapped his hand away.

'Don't touch me.'

'Goddamn it, Dakota, stop.'

Leaning out of the truck, he lunged to pull her back in but grabbed a fistful of hair. In that moment, all the silent, impotent rage inside Dakota came surging out. She punched him in the face with everything she had. The smack was loud.

Clutching his eye socket, he punched her back.

Dakota fell out of the truck and smashed her mouth against the kerb. In the puddle of blood, she saw half her tooth.

'Shit, baby, I'm sorry.' Caldwell hurried down from the truck. 'I'm so sorry.'

'Forget it.'

'Listen, Kota, honey, I didn't mean that. I just reacted.'

She picked up her tooth and put it in her pocket. 'You're a loser. And we're fucking done.'

The call came through early in the morning. Ed Riddell's eyes were still on the financial forecast. He'd just done the calculations, the pen still shaky in his hand. The growth of Burr Publishing stock had been exponential, his original profit goals left in the dust. It was time to sell up. And sell *big*.

That's when the phone rang.

'Yello?'

'Hi. It's me. Dakota.'

'Oh. Hi, Dakota.'

'I, uh. I . . . think I need some help.'

'Hold on one second.' He took the phone to the kitchen where Flora was staring into space. 'It's for you.' He grinned. 'It's your buddy.'

All morning, the Riddells argued. Esther was dead against getting involved, Flora couldn't miss school.

'It should be her mother's business, Ed. Not ours. Besides, we've done so much for that girl as it is.'

He shrugged. 'Come on, Estie. She's alone. She's in the middle of nowhere.'

'What about your work?'

He smiled. 'You don't have to worry about that anymore.'

Flora had been watching them from the door. Esther glanced at her daughter now. With a sigh, she relented.

Ed made some calls, then packed a small bag. In tears of joy, Flora followed him to the car. She took his big, gloved hand on the wheel.

'Thank you, Daddy.'

'I know how much she means to you. I'll bring her home, Flower.'

SEVENTEEN

The elderly man was helped up the stairs of the auditorium. He was built like a scarecrow, driftwood hair, skin sour milk. At first, Finch had little interest until the watchman barked the name: *Atonement Löwe*. Finch flipped back in her notebook and read the notes from Rebecca's room search. *$500 in victim's bible in paper envelope. Marked 'Atonement'.*

'Your name is Atonement, sir?'

Elesheva translated his answer. '*As the watchman spake it, aye.*'

'How did you know Rebecca Frey?'

'*Barely. I do not often leave my cottage.*'

'But all the people on this list have some kind of connection.'

'*Jubilance Weaver is my kin. Perhaps this is why.*'

'Thomasina is your daughter?'

'*One of them, aye.*'

'Well, Jubilance was marrying Rebecca. You must have had some kind of opinion.'

'*I will be frank. I did not approve of the union. But that boy is headstrong. He loves not with his heart but his eyes. And his father dotes on him wickedly. Too much to deny him, it proved.*'

'Why didn't you want Jubilance to marry her?'

Eyeing the girl, the old man grunted. '*It is not personal.*'

'With respect, sir, it seems like not wanting her in your family is entirely personal.'

'*I hath no issue with the girl. Merely her reputation.*'

'Reputation?'

'*It is known by all.*'

'Not by me. I would ask you to be clear in your answers.'

'*Thou art fortunate to be here at all, much less pry into family matters. It is precisely because of thee and thy kind that corruption seeps into our colony. Be that clear enough?*'

'Did you ever give money to Rebecca?'

'*Money? I hath naught to give. Much less to that girl.*'

'Would she have any reason to give it to you?'

'*Nay. As I said, we knew each other not.*'

'Then why did I find money in an envelope marked with your name?'

He snorted. '*I could not say. Nor care.*'

'Mr Löwe, if you don't cooperate, I can have you removed from this place and taken to a police station outside where we will pick this up again.'

'*Dost thou see fear in me?*'

'Just answer my questions and we can all go back to normal. Why did you give Rebecca money?'

'*As I spake it, I did not.*'

'Did you like her? Trying to tempt her?'

'*Tempt?*' His breath caught, his eyes widening.

'You missed the sight of a young woman, is that it? Many years since you last saw a naked ass? Go ahead, Eva. Translate.'

Looking at the floor, the girl obeyed.

The old man started to tremble now, the confused smile on his face twisting into wrinkled anger. '*Lust? I am not the one guilty of that.*'

'No? Maybe, envy then? That why you didn't want her to marry Jubilance?'

'*Thou wouldst accuse me?*'

'You're the first person to not answer my questions, Mr

Löwe. You say Rebecca had a reputation but then you can't explain why. In my experience, people who talk about secrets are often hiding their own.'

Atonement Löwe stood, indignant. He spoke a few quietly furious words and the girl hissed at him right back. Now the watchman took the old man's arm and led him away.

'What did he say, Eva?'

'That he had only been trying to save my feelings by not calling my sister a jezebel but that he shouldn't have bothered. That Rebecca was a harlot and that to live sinfully was to tempt a bad death.'

'I'm sorry, kid.'

'He is an old fool.'

'Why do people say this kind of thing about your sister?'

'I hath heard it before in whisper. Papa says it is a stone hurled from a place of envy.'

'Is it the reason why her marriage with Piety didn't move forward?'

'I know not.'

'A lot of talk in this place.' Finch closed her notebook. 'But nobody *says* anything.'

It was 3PM when Ichabod Weaver took his turn, like any other colonist. He clapped the watchman guarding the stairs on the shoulder on a job well done, then sat down, giving the girl a little nod.

'Thank you for coming, Ichabod. I know you have a lot to do.'

'As do we all. How goes thy work?'

'As far as logistics, pretty well. I appreciate you setting this up.'

'As I said, we pray thou wilt uncover the serpent.'

'I will.' Finch flipped through her notebook. 'Let's get

started. We spoke a little about the produce collection from Burr Group. Any word on that driver's name?'

'It should come today or on the morrow.'

'And your son oversees that process, right?'

'Aye.'

'So, the driver picks up the produce, the tobacco, whatever – then he pays Jubilance in cash.'

'Yes. Then he passes that on to me after eventide prayer. The money goes into the village purse. That money is kept for dealing with thy government, emergencies.'

'Any reason why he would give Rebecca money?'

Ichabod frowned. 'None come to mind.'

'All right. Maybe you can help me with this verse. *An atonement shall be made afore the Lord: and any trespass shall be forgiven.*'

'Leviticus. It concerns bringing a flawless ram to thy chamberlain as an offering of compensation for thy sin. The chamberlain wouldst then make atonement before the Lord. But what significance hath this?'

Finch held up the envelope marked ATONEMENT which she'd placed inside an evidence bag. 'Is that your son's handwriting?'

'I-I do not think so. But why –'

'It contains five hundred dollars, sir.'

'Jubilance would not take money from the colony. I cannot accept that.'

'You understand that when I leave this place, we will run tests on the envelope. If your son handled it, we will know.'

Ichabod shook his head in disbelief. 'It would be in vain. Moreover, that money –'

'– Right now, it's evidence. You'll get it back.' Finch flipped back in her notebook. 'The day of the thirtieth, sir. You saw your son?'

'Of course.'

'Talk me through that day.'

'We rise early in my household. Earlier than many others in the colony. Jubilance's skin does not handle the sunlight well. He went to work in the sweetness, as always. I went about my duties. At lunch, we all ate together.'

'Jubilance was there?'

'Yes. After the meal, he stayed in his room, reading the *Schriften*, as ever.'

'When did you see him next?'

'At Mass, I think. The eventide. Then he went to check on the tobacco, the milking. After that, dinner with extended family. Then sleep, as I told you.'

'How did he seem?'

'As ever. Good spirits. He is much fond of his uncle Albrecht, who visited that night. We all laughed.'

Finch flipped forward in her notebook. 'Talk to me about Piety Schröder.'

He shrugged. 'A sad case with little to say. He hath been dogged by ill health all his life. After the boar attack, he was much changed.'

'How?'

'Once, he had been a respected, diligent man. He was trusted as the village teacher. It was known that oft he was lush on dandelion wine. But there was whisper that he would go outside colony walls to further feed the habit.'

'Piety was buying harder liquor?'

'He hath been exposed to corruption during those tendering days fifteen winters back. Alas, his habit overtook him. He was removed from the school and given fishing duties.'

'Why did you send those kids out in the first place? I've never understood that.'

He cleared his throat. 'Versammlung hath long been hounded by thy government's levy. There was much debate on it but, in the end, it was decided that year to go in a new direction in order to swell our purse. Now, with the wisdom of winters, we see the cost was too great. It is perhaps unsurprising that all three that went outside hath all suffered.'

'Piety's marriage to Rebecca was called off. By the Council. That's you, right?'

'The Council is chamberlain and two trusted eldermen. Fifteen winters back, 'twas my father, who is with the Lord now. If thou wouldst ask the reason for the break of this union, I do not know it.'

'Come on, Ichabod. Half the people I spoke to had to bite their tongues before the word *harlot* or *jezebel* would slip out. Rebecca had an affair, right? She loved someone else.'

'People jangle, Inquisitor. I can tell you only that Rebecca was a good woman.'

'I'm not saying she wasn't. But I need to know her past to understand her end.'

'As I spake it. Rebecca was no harlot.'

'Versammlung disagrees. Atonement, too. Nobody wanted to marry her until now.'

Ichabod shifted in his chair. 'I hath only respect for Mr Löwe. But he sees the world as he sees it.'

'He was against Jubilance marrying her. Were you?'

'My son is a man. He makes his own choices. As Council, we only deny a union if there be good reason.'

'So, there had to be one fifteen years ago. Piety was told there was.'

'Again, I know not. Perhaps he hides a change of heart. It has been seen before. Or perhaps his health affected the decision. I do not know. But it ill becomes to speculate. And I only say all this to defend Rebecca's name.'

'Just so I'm clear, you had no issue with your son marrying her.'

'My feelings matter not. I love my son, I respect his choice.'

'You're dodging my question.'

'I have answered it.'

'Did you ever clash with Jubilance about it?'

'We do not *clash*.'

'Disagree, then.'

'He carries the Blight, as thou hast seen. Her advanced winters gave me pause; I did not want their children to be afflicted. But it was not against *Rebecca*. I honour my colony as best I can, each soul I love as my own.'

'What about Eli Black?'

Eva turned to look at Finch.

Ichabod's eyebrows hoisted too. 'How dost thou know of him?'

'One or two people mentioned the name.'

'Well, that would be strange.'

'Why?'

'He was sick. I lost my brother many winters ago. My heart hath not healed.'

'Wait . . . Eli was your brother?'

'Yes. I am the oldest, he was the youngest.'

Before Finch could go on, the watchman whispered something to Ichabod.

He stood. 'Inquisitor, I am needed. It relates to the funeral arrangements.'

Elesheva looked at the floor.

'Understood,' Finch shut her notebook. ' Thank you for your time.'

4PM. The fruit grove was silent. Frozen. Peach trees were bare as stag antlers, filing off into the distance. It was the girl who saw Piety Schröder first – asleep in a hollow beneath one.

'Eva. Wait for me back there.'

'Why?'

'Just do it, please.'

The girl made a face but did as she was told. Then Finch nudged Piety with her foot.

'Rise and shine.'

He gasped awake, reaching for a wine bottle that was not there. 'Hardly recognized you,' he grunted.

'You like my dress?'

'You make a very fine wolf in sheep's clothing.'

'Why didn't you come to the auditorium today, Piety?'

'I told all that I know.'

'I'll be the judge of that.'

'So mighty are you? The colony trembles when you pass. Yet we both know what you are.'

'And what exactly is that? A harlot? Like Rebecca? Or is that just another way of making yourself feel better when a woman doesn't think you're special?'

His smile died. 'It is easy to step on me.'

'Piety, listen to me. I don't give a shit about you one way or another. I'm here for the truth. That's it. Now, this colony hasn't seen a murder in centuries. Everybody tells me that Rebecca had a good heart. So, why the fuck do they act like they don't want me to know a single thing? It doesn't add up.'

'You suggest I am involved.' He held up his crutch. 'Such mighty inquisition you make yet you are blind to the –'

Finch booted the crutch out of his hand and stood over him. 'You *know* something. And I swear to fuck, you think your life is bad now? I'll have you on Obstruction and you'll be getting gang-raped in County lock-up faster than you can say *Hail Mary*.'

Despite rapid breaths, his eyes were defiant. 'You have rules. You can't hurt me.'

'You were right –' Finch planted her heavy boot on his kneecap and twisted. 'Stepping on you *is* easy.'

Piety screeched out in pain and tried to crawl away.

'You think I'm fucking around?' She crouched over him. 'I never liked you, Piety. You watched Rebecca like a hawk in '98. Back then, I thought you were a controlling piece of shit. And I think you're still trying to control her now because you're sore she passed you over for someone else. That's it, right? Who – Eli?'

'Get off me.'

Another stomp-twist, his screech now a squeal. 'Talk and I'll stop. It was Eli, wasn't it? You found out they had a thing. You went to the Council to cry about it.'

'This is madness.'

'I saw the way she looked at him, Piety. *Desire.* The kind you see in a woman's eyes when her whole soul is soaked with it. The kind you'll never understand or cause.'

Lips peeling back, Piety grabbed her by the *Kappe* but Finch batted his hands away. 'Now I got you on assaulting an officer, dickhead. So talk. Now.'

He began to sob but Elesheva's voice silenced them.

'Dakota.' The girl was standing there, tears in her eyes.

'Hold on –'

'You lied . . . You asked me to trust you but you lied to me.'

'Eva, I know it looks that way but this is complicated –'

'You knew my sister before . . . Yet you looked upon her dead body and said nothing.'

Finch released Piety and he hobbled off.

She went to Elesheva.

But the girl slapped her in the face and marched away, back towards Versammlung.

EIGHTEEN

Beyond the walls of Versammlung, Finch smoked a cigarette watching day wed the dusk. Once again, she was adrift on her own thoughts. It disconcerted her to realize, distantly, that she felt less safe on the other side of the village walls.

Get it together. You're not here to play Little House on the Prairie.

Rebecca Frey had, it seemed, lived a simple life, with no enemies. Yet, fairly or not, she also had a reputation. Unexplained money hidden away. And a bitter ex. Then there was the matter of Jubilance Weaver. A man, it seemed, with a temper. A man who lived amongst pacifists, but clenched his fists until white.

Finch's phone rang and she answered distantly. It was Sullivan. 'Hey, Jesse.'

Ah, Detective. How's the plain life?

'Thrilling. What have we got?'

Sadly, not much. Mayor's press conference didn't lead to anything and the fingertip searches gave us zero. I was just calling to say Hanlon has released the body.

'I'll let Weaver know.'

How about at your end. Anything?

'Actually, maybe. Two things. The girl had money in her room. Five hundred bucks.'

Damn. That's a pretty penny for an Assembly girl. Where'd she get that? Outside?

'I'm still trying to find out. Gonna need you to run some serial numbers on the bills.'

Done. What was the other thing?

'We got at least two horses in this race. Firstly, the ex, Piety Schröder. A drunk, full of bitterness, and he volunteered at Fest back in '98.'

So, he knows the outside world. Could've got a gun?

'Possible. On the flip side, he can barely walk. Likely not overpowering anyone.'

OK. Horse Two?

'The husband-to-be. Turns out, Rebecca was getting married to a Jubilance Weaver. The young man has a temper and get this: scratch marks on his arms.

I'll be damned. Just like Hanlon said.

'Maintains he got 'em working in the field. He has delicate skin.'

Alibi?

'His dad vouched for it. I spoke to a few family members and acquaintances who saw him either working in the field or at home during lunch and dinner.'

He has a temper. How?

'The way he reacted to my questioning. Grief can look a lot of different ways, but I saw a rare aggression in him. And Hanlon said we're looking for a large man with scratch marks. Jubilance fits like a glove.'

Yeah, that doesn't look great.

'There's one more but I just wanna say something out loud that's been bugging me. Ichabod Weaver.'

Oh boy. The mayor is gonna love that.

'I'm not casting any stones. Hell, I have no proof against him, or anyone. But Ichabod fits physically and even if I saw no scratches on him, it's possible he heals fast.'

Why the bug, though?

'Motive. He didn't want his son to marry Rebecca. Damaged goods, apparently.'

Still, seems a little extreme.

'To us. But our way of seeing the world is not the same as theirs, Jesse.'

Hm . . . Who's the last horse?

'The delivery driver who collects the produce. Works for Burr Group. A few folks complained about him.'

A man with access to their world and ours.

'Exactly. And the means to move a dead body. Then again, the way they treat outsiders, maybe it's unsurprising his name came up.'

Let me look into it. Stay in touch. An awkward pause. *Be safe, Detective.*

Rebecca Frey's body arrived under cover of first darkness. Ichabod Weaver had agreed the meeting in the wheat sea outside the colony. The watchmen unzipped her from the body bag and carefully placed her inside the coffin that Adam had spent all day wreathing in white carnations – the only frivolity he would ever show his child.

Then the watchmen loaded the coffin into a black wagon and slowly, sombrely drove it home.

Versammlung entire had gathered in Zentraler Platz, the only sound to be heard the flames of their torches, smacking like lips. Adam Frey and Elesheva were waiting by the Versammlungs-baum. It jutted out from the land as a vast, grey bone.

Father and daughter joined behind the wagon. Then came Ichabod Weaver, Jubilance and Thomasina in the procession. Then the rest of the village, their black suits and dresses fitting for this day, funnelling into a black plume behind Rebecca – as if in death she had struck oil.

As Finch followed at a distance, she went over her thoughts. *Rebecca got that money from somewhere. Not that old crow Atonement Löwe – an asshole but a truthful one with no scratches on his arms or hands.*

So, who, then?

And what for?

Does the money connect to her supposedly being a jezebel? Or going outside?

Either way, I gotta get a name from Ichabod for that delivery driver. Could be just a man who stares too much. But he's also one with access to both Versammlung and the outside world, like Jesse says – and that ties in nicely with the crime scene.

Still. For all that, nothing here so far connects to Flora. Or the Sugar Man.

Versammlung's cemetery was a mile beyond the village, north of the sacred dead tree. Row after row of lopsided gravestones, no adornment, merely names, dates and lifespans – humility before God, even in death.

Adam Frey led his daughter to her final resting place with his big hand on the horse's neck, the nag's shoes clopping on the path. Versammlung kept its eyes on the floor. Mothers shushed their babies. The night sky was turtle-dove.

Watchmen lowered the coffin into the earth – no ceremony, no words. As Rebecca descended, Adam kept his eyes on the horizon instead, his tears blurring the stars.

By his side, Elesheva looked up at her father. Finch wondered if she had seen him cry before. Many clapped his shoulders, expressed their condolences to him. Nobody said anything to the girl.

Finch looked across the plot and saw Jubilance Weaver. Fists trembling at his sides, his pink eyes fixed on the words carved into the gravestone – *Here lies Rebecca Frey*. No other words were needed. More would be vanity.

Jubilance's nose started to bleed now, little red carnations blooming in the cotton of his shirt. He didn't seem to notice.

Finch scanned the congregation. She looked for telltale signs – guilt or fear. But nobody met her eyes, except for some of the elder folk who cast her dirty looks.

By the time the watchmen were smoothing down the flat soil with the backs of their shovels, the congregation started to disperse. Finch was about to follow when a slight movement caught her eye.

The shadows were undulating. Or were they?

Finch was certain there had been movement – a figure? In the distance, at the treeline, she saw him. Half a face was peeking out. Watching. Wild hair, wild beard.

And then he was gone.

After the funeral, the townsfolk returned to Versammlung, speaking quietly amongst themselves. Ichabod Weaver pulled alongside Finch and asked her for a minute. She nodded and he led her into the wood, away from prying eyes.

They stood in a moonlit clearing. Ichabod meticulously packed his limestone pipe three times before striking a match, then he touched the flame to the top layer of the tobacco. His face flared red for a moment, then darkness, the sounds of his pipe wet and crackling.

'Hast thou found the serpent yet, Dakota?'

'No, I haven't.'

'I told thee, the killer wilt be found not in Versammlung.'

'You did. But then the job isn't finished yet.'

In the darkness, he might've smiled. 'On the matter of the Englisch carriage man. An answer comes upon the morrow, that is what the company hath told me.'

'Thank you.'

'Well, I bid thee goodnight.'

'Who was that at the funeral tonight? Guy with a beard, watching us from the forest.'

'That is a child's tale. Schlanker Hans. Always, he watches and follows.'

'No, this was a real person, Ichabod. I saw him.'

'He is but a hermit with a bedevilled mind. He watches us sometimes as he hath done for years. But to no harm. Children fear him. Some parents use him as a warning.'

'A warning?'

'Mind thy duties and thy prayers lest Schlanker Hans take thee away in the night.'

Finch realized now: *these people have their own Sugar Man, too.*

Back in her room at the Weaver household, Finch saw Thomasina sat at the kitchen table, eating pigeon soup. The woman glared at her. *Ichabod must have told her about my line of questioning today.* Saying nothing, Finch went upstairs to her room.

She had just kicked off her boots when her cell phone rang. It was Hanlon Hopkin.

'Hey, Doc. I can't speak too long.'

Yes, I heard you're in Versammlung. This won't take a moment. The click of opening spectacles. *My work is finished, as you know. Toxicology gave us nothing much, though there was some kind of strange substance on her lips which we figured was honey and it was. The only other thing I can tell you? The victim was not pregnant at the time of her death. But at some stage in her life, she has given birth.*

'. . . You're sure about that?'

Positive.

Finch hung up, her head spinning. 'You had a baby at some point. *That's* why they call you a harlot . . . But is that why he killed you?'

*

Finch heard the girl before she saw her. In the darkness of the field, the metal tinkle of the hymn doll guided her way. Elesheva was sitting on her porch, expressionless. She didn't look up as she sat down beside her.

A long silence passed until Finch took out a cigarette. Turning away from the cold wind, she protected her flame.

'How easily thou dost conjure fire.'

'Technology is pretty nifty. But hey, on the other hand, your soul is saved.'

'Not mine.'

Finch laughed softly, then cleared her throat. 'Eva, I'd like to talk to you.'

'Inquiry be thy strength. Not talk.'

'Look, this thing with your sister . . . You deserved to know. It was a long time ago, all right? We were just kids. And that was a hard time for me –'

'Be it not a hard time for me? Thou hast asked for trust yet given none in return.'

'Yes, I know I should've told you about knowing Rebecca –'

'Inquisition is over.' The girl went for the front door. 'Goodbye.'

'There were three of us.'

Elesheva paused.

'Your sister. Me. Flora. And she was . . . taken away.'

'Taken away?'

'Murdered. Years ago, when I wasn't much older than you. Flora was my best friend. She was friends with Rebecca, too. She disappeared. They found her in the same place as your sister.'

The girl turned to search her eyes. 'Why tell me this?'

'You needed someone to be there for you but I was too scared. The truth is, you remind me of me. And I've been trying to avoid being me all my life. But you're right, I did ask for your trust without giving it back. So, from here on in, that changes. If you want.'

'Why?'

'Because when I was in your boat, I needed someone real bad. I got nothing.'

Elesheva searched the darkness of the field as she mulled this over. 'The one that killed your friend. That is why thou hast returned. To find that serpent.'

'Maybe. Look, Eva. I know you're learning the world. I can only imagine how hard and bewildering all this must be for you, let alone with what happened to Rebecca.'

'And, so? Thou art my friend now?' She teared up. 'I hath no friendship left. I hath only wrath. What use be a friend to wrath? Or a friend who will leave me in this place?'

Finch scooched closer. 'Kid, you're smart. Really smart. But you're wrong here.'

'Thou art wrong, I hath no one, *no one —*'

'Hey, come on.' Finch went to her, arms out.

'Don't touch me.' Sobbing, Elesheva pushed her away. 'Thou art a *liar.*'

But Finch enveloped the girl in a hug, despite the squeals. 'I know, honey, I know.'

Soon, there was only the swaying rhythm of an adult and the gentle *shhhh.*

When it was done, Finch curled the girl's bangs out of her face. 'When I found out Flora was dead, it felt like my heart was being crushed. You know what I told myself? *I'm alone now, I don't have anyone.* But I was wrong, too. You will connect with other people. And nobody will ever take away your love for your sister or hers for you. But one thing I know for sure? If you hold on to that wrath, it'll only keep your wounds open longer.'

Elesheva pulled away, her eyes flytrap-green. 'When does it stop?'

'It won't. Not really. You just . . . learn to carry it.'

The girl held up her doll and considered its facelessness. 'The wrath gives my pain, my fear, somewhere to live.'

'I know. But it'll rot you. I'm a shitty person, Eva. I've got no advice for anyone. Except this. These days will overwhelm you. But you'll get through. And Rebecca will always love you. So, you hold on to that, get back on your feet in time. That's all there is.'

The girl took off her *Kappe* and wiped her eyes with it. 'OK.'

'OK,' Finch sighed. 'I should go. Thomasina will give my dinner to the dogs.'

She was halfway down the stairs when the girl spoke again. 'The man that spoke to me at the fair . . . I saw him here tonight in the shadows.'

'I think I saw him too.' Exhaling, Finch scanned the darkness. 'Eva, how do you feel about going outside again?'

'Why?'

'Because I think it's time you learned how to defend yourself.'

January 17th, 1998

It had taken her hours, but at last Rebecca Frey slipped away
from the wagon. Tonight was the final night of Fest and sales
were good. Piety Schröder was revelling in his assumed role as
leader. Soon, he would be head of her household, too.

Heart thudding, she weaved through the crowd, checking
over her shoulder. Some story would have to be conjured.
Perhaps an illness.

At first, she had prepared excuses in advance. But as time
passed, she became more desperate and cared less. Sometimes, the thought of Piety enraged her. Others, it filled her
with guilt. She knew he was the future – her only future – and
that the sooner she submitted to this, the sooner she would
find peace. Yet she could not extinguish the mad hope in her
heart. Even a few moments with Eli felt like breaking the
surface in an underwater world.

Rebecca stood behind the usual stall, chewing her nails,
lost between self-pity and excitement. But now Eli took her
by the wrist and pulled her into the wood.

'*I didn't know if you'd come,*' she whispered through giggles.

'*I wouldst suffer one thousand Appletinis to come here.*'

'*I don't have long.*'

His smile told her he knew she had as long as he chose.
'*Then we must hurry. I wish to show you something.*'

Eli led her through the forest and soon they were trudging
uphill, away from Fest.

When they finally came to the top, they sat on an outcropping. High above Lake Sweetness, Nectar was bright in the distance. The wind was strong up here and she fought to hold her *Kappe* in place. As she gasped at the view, Eli playfully tugged it down over her eyes and she laughed.

The Englisch had made roads vast, houses vast. But what delighted her most were the lights – quilting out over the land, twinkling happily. The last of the sun melted into the ocean, as a torn plum. Rebecca's heart swelled as she took it all in.

On the lake, a large white boat sailed in circles. She knew it had no destination, no purpose other than the pleasure of its passengers, lush with wine and merriment.

The music from Fest floated up to them. Eli Black offered his hand and she took it. Palms together, they danced upon that outcropping, on borrowed music, on borrowed time, laughing at a world where things had been made only for loveliness. In those few moments of unthinking joy, Rebecca laughed as freely as she ever had.

In the glory of the setting sun, and the stippling of stars in the darkness above it, she felt as if she did not have to exist in what had happened. Or what would. Merely in what was presently so. Until, the sadness inside her reared up.

She broke off from him to sit back on the rock.

'*What is it?*'

'*I am free and imprisoned all at once.*'

'*We both are.*'

They watched the lake wed the night, the stars spinning, as though all creation were just a maple seed whirling through God's darkness.

'*Rebecca, I brought you here . . .*' He exhaled. '*Because of Forgiveness Schmücker.*'

'*What of her?*'

'*Thou knoweth the tongue she hath. It never ceases. She makes plans. The dimensions to which our house must be built. Emmanuel for a boy. Elesheva if a girl —*'

'*I do not wish to know these things.*'

'*Just look —*' From his pocket, he pulled out a handkerchief — dark with dried blood.

'*What is this?*'

'*Forgiveness suffers the coughing blight.*'

'*. . . Eli, I do not understand.*'

He stepped into her space and softened his voice. '*She may not have long left.*'

'*But that is awful.*'

'*Yes but . . .*' He whispered in her ear, '*It is God's will.*'

Rebecca shook her head, her stomach twisting with guilty revulsion. '*Will? I cannot understand it.*'

'*'Tis not our place to understand.*'

'*Aye, merely to suffer.*' Rebecca pushed past him, tears brimming. '*Goodbye, Eli.*'

'*Where are you going?*'

'*I don't know. This is wrong.*'

He reached for her but she was already heading down the hill.

The secret sweetness she had carried for him all these years started as a dahlia bud. But it had grown monstrously until becoming a tangled maze in which she had lost herself. She could no longer parse her own feelings, her own wishes. One day, jubilant light warmed her heart. The next, a foul sinfulness sickened it.

How canst I delight in the mortal fever of an innocent girl — one I hath known all my days? How could God put such love in me only for it to fester poisonously?

Several furlongs passed until Rebecca realized that she

could no longer hear the Fest. She had no sense of how long she'd been; measuring time in Eli's company was counting raindrops on a window pane. But Piety would be angry and full of questions.

By now, it was almost completely dark. She would not yet concede she was lost but it was true that she had never been to this part of the wood. In fact, without Dakota or Flora, or without the hunter's eye of Eli, she hadn't once walked this place alone.

'*Lord,*' she whispered. '*Guide me, light my way back.*'

After going in ever-darker circles in the wood, she finally found a path. She laughed with relief when she saw the dim glimmer of the Testing Pool. Not far beyond it stood Fest, with all its life and light. She would endeavour to virtue. To silence. To duty. It felt safe to submit to that future.

Rebecca passed the pool. In the distance, Lake Sweetness shone in the interstices of the forest as shards of black glass. She reached the small wood before the fence where she had argued with Devin Rigney. Fest thudded loud as a laughing heart. Its lights warmed her face. A man's hand clamped over her mouth and dragged her back. She felt the prickle of stubble at her ear.

'Come on, honey. Hush now, you know me.'

She bit into his palm and kicked – her clog finding shin.

She screamed between his fingers, too confused to know the right English word.

'Little bitch –' The man clamped her mouth again, his smell strange. 'You've been giving me the eyes for weeks.'

He dragged her away from the fence, back to the Testing Pool, down to the ground. Now, he was trying to pry open her thighs with his knees. She dug her heels into the mud, a bug trying to burrow for safety. As Rebecca screamed for her father, his earlobe slipped into her mouth. She bit down hard and tasted his blood.

Shouting out, the man straddled her and cocked back his fist. In the snapshot-moment before the punch, the moon revealed his face – fragmentarily silver, as a coin.

Rebecca's heart stopped. '. . . It's you.'

Flora thundered down the stairs and marched into the kitchen where her mother was going through a curtain samples book. The girl stood there, chest rising and falling, waiting for an explanation. 'So, what? You're not going to say anything?'

Esther Riddell carried on flipping pages. 'I made a decision, Flora.'

'She's my *best friend*, Mom. My only friend.'

'That's not true. Anyhow, that girl is no good. She can't stay here.'

Flora started pacing the kitchen. 'That's crazy. She has nowhere else to go.'

'She has a home.'

'With a mother who is a violent drunk and a mess.'

In reply, Esther opened her handbag and took out a handful of empty laughing-gas pellets. 'I found these in your room. This is not acceptable. You are a *child*, Flora.'

'You don't know anything about me,' she spluttered.

'I'm sorry your friend is from a broken home.' Esther dropped the pellets in the trash compactor and shouted over the noise. 'But you are not. You understand me? You are *not*.'

'Cos we're so perfect? And you're such an angel?'

'I know you hate me right now. You feel I'm just trying to ruin your fun –'

'You think this is about *fun*?'

'I'm doing this because I love you.'

'If you loved me, you'd listen to me. But you only listen to that fucking preacher.'

'Watch your mouth.'

'She had nowhere else to go, Mom. And you just kicked her out on the street.'

'You're a *child* and there are things happening here you do not understand –'

'– So, if I'm a child, what's she?'

'Not our problem.'

'Some Christian you are, huh?'

'Honey, listen. That girl has a spell over you. But she's trash. You'll see one day.'

'Trash?' Flora ripped the sample book from her hands and hurled it across the room. '*You're* trash. And I'm going.'

Next door, Dolly started crying. 'Flora, I'm calling your father right now. You're out of control.'

'Yeah?' She snorted. 'Good luck with that. It's the last night of Fest. You think he's gonna miss the biggest payday of the year to come give me a lecture?'

'And since when are you so concerned about family finances?'

'I don't know, since when are you? I don't see you working a job. The house is always a pigsty. All you do is pray with those losers, speaking in tongues.'

'Flora. Watch your mouth.'

'Does it make you happy, to listen to his bullshit? Maybe it makes you feel less alone? Cos we can all see you can't stand being here. Around me, or Dad. Even Dolly –'

For the first time, Esther slapped her daughter hard across the cheek.

Flora turned slowly back to look her mother in the eyes. '*I'm* out of control?'

'Honey, I'm sorry.'

'I'm late for work.' She marched away.

'Baby, let's talk –'

'Fuck you.' The kitchen door slammed behind her.

'Flora! You *will not* see that girl again!'

NINETEEN

Finch made her way through Speedy's truck stop. At the police cordon, Reserve Officer Blevins McConnell nodded at her respectfully, even if he gave a strange look to her Versammlung dress first, and then the girl.

He had nothing to report so Finch sent him to the diner for a half-hour break. Then she made her way down the muddy verge. Elesheva traced her footprints down, dodging used condoms and syringes, the cycle of pleasure and sorrow turning a world she did not comprehend.

Across the Testing Pool, a sad little mist played. Sounds from the truck stop filtered down through the trees – back-up beepers, idling diesel engines and, beyond that, the distant shushing of Route 6. The world beyond the walls of Versammlung was so loud. Finch realized now, she missed the silence.

'Where did you find her?' Elesheva whispered.

Finch pointed at the exact spot by the water's edge where Rebecca's body had been found. The girl went to it and dropped to her knees. Shaking with rage, she delved her fingers into the snowy mud. Then she brought a handful of earth to her mouth and swallowed.

Finch understood. *Keeping something of her sister with her.*

She realized how weak she felt. Inside Versammlung, she'd hardly touched the Visprozan. Now, she was paying for it.

Elesheva stood and nodded. She was ready.

They went to Flora's commemorative bench a few yards away. There, Finch took her knife from her boot and she began to dig in the frosted earth underneath the bench.

'Flora . . .' the girl whispered. 'Your friend.'

Finch didn't answer. It didn't take long to reach the cookie tin wrapped in cellophane.

'Take it, Evie. It's yours.'

Brushing off filth, the girl prized open the lid. Inside, there was a short-barrelled pistol with a wooden handle.

Together, they set up old bottles on a dead trunk, angling the cell phone light to see the target properly.

'First things first, kid. You have the power of God in your hand. Understand?'

'Yes.'

'You treat it like it's always loaded. It's always dangerous. You never point it in the direction of something you don't mean to shoot at. And you keep your finger off the trigger until you're ready to fire. You with me so far?'

'Aye.'

'Good. Because I'm trusting you with this.'

For the next twenty minutes, Finch taught her the basics. Loading. Handling. Firing. Elesheva got the hang of it surprisingly fast.

'Now, if it comes to it, you'll be able to defend yourself, at least. Let's just hope it doesn't come to that.'

'I would not mind –' An old wine bottle on the logs exploded. '– if it did.'

'Evie. Tell me about the man you saw.'

'Several times hath I seen him before. In shadow, at a distance.'

'Men don't stare for nothing. What did he say to you at Fest?'

'That he was a friend. I-I don't recall exactly, I was upset.'

'He spoke to you for a reason.'

'I do not know. You think he is the one that killed my sister?'

'It's possible,' Finch noted her subject change. 'No idea. He could just be a weirdo.'

Un-squinting, the girl looked at her. 'What is it? Why do you look at me so?'

'There's something else you should know, Evie. I got a call from a doctor tonight. At some point in her life, your sister was pregnant. Were you aware?'

Numbly, the girl returned her gaze to the empty bottles. '. . . No.'

'That's why people called her a jezebel, isn't it? She had an affair. That's why her marriage to Piety was called off. Because she got pregnant.'

'She hever told me . . .' Elesheva spoke softly, distantly – her eyes glazing over. 'Sometimes, it was as if she wanted to tell me a secret . . . But she never did.'

'You know what? I think inquisition isn't over.'

'You suspect Jubilance Weaver?'

'He had scratch marks on his arms. Was engaged to your sister. Reacted angrily to my questions. Could all be nothing. Or something.'

'But where is the baby?'

'I don't know. That could be part of the reason why your sister was killed.'

Elesheva's face hardened. 'Well, then.' She closed one eye and fired – another bottle exploding. 'Let us cast our eye upon him.'

Daybreak washed the acreage cherry-plum. Enormous tobacco leaves bowed to the weak morning sun, giving up their sweet tea perfume. Elesheva led the way, past the field hands. These men all suffered the Blight – fingers fused together, lips torn, an eye that had never opened. Finch greeted them as they passed but they kept their silence.

'They can't say good morning?'

''Tis *my* presence they ignore, Dakota. Not thine.'

'Because you doubt your faith.'

'To them, I doubt life itself.' She shrugged. '*Whatever.*'

Jubilance Weaver was hidden in tall tobacco plants, the air around him sweet with leather and tea. His translucent eyelids were closed, a slight smile upon colourless lips, enjoying the soft light.

Finch watched as he cut out the tobacco flowers with a curved knife, little pink heads swiftly decapitated, a masterful motion. His rolled-up sleeves revealed strong arms, the scratches half-healing.

'Morning, Mr Weaver.'

Hearing her voice, the large man stood up straight but didn't turn for a moment, as if hoping he'd imagined it. 'Inquisitor.'

'Why do you cut the flowers out?'

'For favourable growth. This darkens. Enriches. 'Tis more desirable to thy people.'

'And you just throw the flowers away? But they're beautiful.'

'Beauty hath little virtue and will oft draw evil.' Jubilance stacked another full basket of beheaded flowers on a large wooden cart. 'My knife affords them function.'

'You didn't come to talk with me when you were meant to, Mr Weaver.'

'Aye.'

'I won't be avoided.'

'To speak plain, Inquisitor, I hath struggled with thy intrusion here. But it is as Papa sayeth.' With a sharp glance at the girl, he wiped the blade on his thigh then pushed his cart towards the barn. '*The Lord calls upon imperfect vessels.*'

'Imperfect?' Elesheva spat. 'And who judges perfection, Jubilance? Thee?'

'It seems,' he stopped his cart to snarl at her, 'thou hast found thy tongue amongst the heathens. So easily thou dost betray us in thy Godlessness.'

'Hey.' Finch stepped into his space.

'She should learn her place.'

'You raise your voice at her again, you'll be learning yours.'

A squall of scarlet spread across his cheeks but he shrugged. 'Ask what you will.'

'Here's my question, Mr Weaver. See, we have a special doctor in Nectar who learns truths from dead bodies. And he told me that the killer is a powerful man. A powerful man with scratches on his arms, his hands. Now, I've seen near-on every man in Versammlung and the only one who comes close to that description is you. Can you explain that?'

'It is for me to explain why thou hast heard *man* and *scratches* in the same breath and come unhesitatingly upon the name *Jubilance Weaver*?'

'You were one of the few people who didn't attend my interview.'

'As I spake it, I hath struggled in my grief. I hath struggled to wake in the mornings. Much less brook the judgement of a heathen. Be this so hard to fathom?'

'Normally, the innocent partner of a murder victim is the *first* one through the door. They *want* me to do my work. They don't struggle with intrusion.'

'Clearly, our worlds diverge.'

'But I don't think they do. Not totally. See, there are four main motives for murder, Mr Weaver. Loot, love, loathing, lust. And unfortunately for you, they could all apply here.'

He stopped his cart again. 'Thou dost accuse me?'

'Let's start with loot. You're the only one with access to

money in this village other than your father. In Rebecca's room, I found five hundred dollars. Where else would she get that?'

The other men in the field glanced up at them through the plants, under hat brims.

'I know not.' He lowered his voice. 'Rebecca had no need of money.'

'It was kept in an envelope in her holy book, next to a verse: *An atonement shall be made before the Lord, and any trespass shall be forgiven.* Atonement for what, sir?'

'Again, thou dost invite me to the abode of empty speculation.' Shaking his head, he picked up his cart and continued towards the barn. 'I know *not*.'

'Was there something you had to atone for, Jubilance?'

'No. I gave Rebecca only love.'

'We'll come back to loot. Let's move on to love.'

'Thou wouldst turn my sweetness for her against me?'

'Maybe you did that yourself. Tell me the truth, Jubilance. It bothered you, didn't it?'

'What?'

'Her reputation. Maybe not at first. You were delighted to be matched with such a beauty. Let's face it, she was beautiful, you are not. And then . . . the gossip started to sting. The laughter behind your back. You knew she had betrayed Piety once. Why not you, too?'

'That is false.'

'And you knew you'd be the only man in Versammlung not marrying a virgin.'

'Please!' he caught himself and lowered his volume. 'I beg, do not use such words.'

'Come on, that had to cut you up. That Rebecca had carried another man's child —'

'Stop.' Breathing hard through his nose, he bunched his fists at his sides again.

'*You* stop. Stop the lying. Your love turned to loathing, didn't it?'

'Against *him* –' Jubilance dropped his cart. 'Wrath be a sin, aye. But it is *not* guilt.'

'I think your love for Rebecca became rotten with jealousy. Maybe you didn't mean to kill her. Maybe it was just a moment of rage. But out it spilled all the same. I know there is anger in you; I see it now, I saw it on day one. You said it yourself. *Such wrath in my heart.*'

'Nay,' bewildered tears brimmed. 'I never hurt her.'

'Would you hurt me if there was no consequence? I see rage in your eyes right now.'

'I loathe thee, I admit. But this is trickery, I am not violent.' Wiping away his tears, he picked up his cart and entered the drying barn, its ceiling a canopy of tobacco leaves. 'I *never* hurt Rebecca.'

'OK.' Finch turned to the girl, who was red in the face. 'What does that leave us with, Evie?'

'Lust.'

'Ah, yes. How about it, Jube? If not loot, not love, not loathing, what about lust?'

He upended the cart, his flowers forming a pretty pink burial mound. 'Stop thy torment.' He spoke weakly. 'Please.'

Finch picked up a dead flower head and breathed in. 'If there's wrath in your heart, is there lust in there too? I'm betting there is. You're a red-blooded man, right?'

'No,' Jubilance whispered.

'He lies.' Elesheva shook her head. 'I see the weight of them sitting on him now.'

'She sees it, my friend. She's just a kid. I see it, too. I see how exhausted you are. Probably haven't slept in days, huh? You're not gonna get out of this just by saying you did nothing. Confess, now. Let the weight off, Jubilance.'

Closing his eyes, he slumped to his knees amid the pink petals. The desperate rays of reborn sun turned him semi-opaque, his skin just sheet-ice over a lake of vein and bone.

'All right,' he gagged on the words. 'It's true. I-I took some.'

'You took some money?'

'Yes.' Now the tears came.

'Did Rebecca ask for that money?'

'Yes . . . and God help me, I did it.'

'Why, Jubilance? *Why* did she need that money?'

'I know not.' Sobbing, he threw his petal knife away, dawn catching its curved blade. 'She said only that she needed it. She begged me. But God as my witness, I never hurt her.'

Long shadows fell across them now.

Finch turned to see a horrified Ichabod Weaver filling the doorframe. 'Inquisitor . . . Thou art called for.'

'I'm not done here.'

'My son will say no more.'

'Your son will talk until his tongue falls off. If you try to stop this, I will return to this place with everything I have at my disposal and burn you down.'

Ichabod shook his head in disbelief. 'Lord help us, you are mad.'

'He is confessing.'

'He has made the mistake of thinking he was helping. No more.'

'I believed you, Ichabod. But you didn't tell me about her pregnancy. That's why your piece of shit son was paying her off. That's what he was atoning for.'

'No.'

'It's the only thing that fits here. You lied to me. And what did you people do with that baby? Drown it? Leave it in the woods for the animals to –'

247

'Enough,' he shouted. 'There never *was* a baby. That is the end of it. Now, I am here to tell thee that thy people are coming.'

Finch realized now, the village bell was tolling distantly. 'I'll deal with them. But I'm not finished with Jubilance. I want his DNA and fingerprints.'

Ichabod shook his head. 'I know enough of thy law to politely decline his submission to any test. If there is *evidence* of his wrongdoing, speak it plain. If thou wouldst arrest him, do so now. If not, thou wilt leave immediately.'

Finch smiled through her anger. 'I'll be returning here, Ichabod. Count on it.'

'We will see.'

Finch brushed past him but he gripped her by the forearm, a little too hard. 'Get the fuck off me before I –'

Ichabod took out a scrap of paper from his work shirt and handed it to her. Then he let her go.

Head still swirling with adrenaline, Finch headed for the colony gate.

The walls were empty this morning, except for two watchmen. She motioned for them to open up, glancing over at the auditorium. Now she saw the rest of them. They were all carrying large white banker boxes to and fro.

The boxes were marked *Catoonah County Voter Services*.

As the gate was opened, Finch took out the paper Ichabod had given her. Unfolding it, she read two words:

Samuel Salinas

January 17th, 1998

Corona's 'Rhythm of the Night' was thudding through Fest as Flora scanned the happy faces. Under her big winter coat, her stomach knotted with dread so hard she could barely breathe. With nowhere else to stay, Dakota would have to go back home to her mother. After that, it wouldn't be long until she hit the road again. Twice as fast now she was pregnant.

Flora and Dakota had always been best friends, always had a good thing. For as long as she could remember, Dakota had wanted to leave town. That had always scared Flora but she knew that, if it came to it, she would follow her friend anywhere.

Until that piece of shit ruined it all. He doesn't get away with doing that. I'll make the son of a bitch pay.

Pushing deeper into the crowd, Flora reached the stalls and games area. She ignored her father, who waved, and headed instead for the back of the fair, searching in the usual spots Dakota might be found. Instinctively she knew she wouldn't be there but she didn't know where else to search.

Piety Schröder beckoned her over to the Versammlung wagon. Though he and Eli were doing good business tonight, his face was pale. 'Hast thou seen Rebecca?'

'No, why?'

He held his temples. 'I am concerned. Gravely.'

'She's probably on break and lost track of time.'

'For more than an hour?'

Flora exchanged an unseen glance with Eli, who then looked away. 'Well, I'll keep an eye out for her.'

Piety nodded his thanks.

She hurried away from the wagon, through Fest, towards Lake Sweetness. On the pleasure dock, only one or two boats were still moored. The water was awash with coloured lamps, drunken laughter across its surface, all awaiting the Fest firework finale.

Lost in the irrelevant happiness of others for a moment, it took Flora a second to realize she recognized one of the boys from the party night photos.

'Hey,' she said casually. 'You're a friend of Tay, right?'

'So?'

'I'm a client.'

'Client, huh? OK. Taylor was in the parking lot when I saw him.'

Leaving the dock behind, Flora cut past the empty Bleeding Lamb Pentecostal tent and made for the parking lot. Even though the silver Range Rover was parked at the back of the lot in the shadows, it wasn't hard to spot.

Flora knocked on the window of the passenger side.

Frowning, Taylor lowered the window a crack. 'Jiggles, what do you want?'

'Molly.'

'You'll need more than pocket money to score.'

She answered by flashing a wad of rolled-up twenties. 'Come on, man. It's cold.'

The door clunked open now and she climbed in.

It smelled of his aftershave. Flora wondered if Dakota liked his smell. If this is what she was breathing in when he pushed himself inside her, when he impregnated her. She shut the car door a little too hard.

'All right, what are you after?'

'Molly. Like I said.'

'Yeah, but I got CK1, I got sky, I got Medusa, phoenix, Nixon, bareback, nirvana –'

'Is it your baby?'

'What?'

'Did you get Dakota pregnant?'

He searched her eyes for a long time. 'You're telling me she's –'

'Don't act like you don't know. Was it you?'

Taylor reached across and slapped her face. Instinctively, Flora held her raw cheek. He'd hit a lot harder than her mother had.

'If she's in some shit, that's her business. It has nothing to do with me. You hear me, Riddell? I swear to God, if I find out that you're spreading this around –'

'You're a piece of shit, you know that?'

'I just told you. It ain't nothin' to do with me.'

'Who, then? You pimp her out?'

'Not my style. And who knows? Who cares? Just another party girl that got left holding the bag.'

Rage swam in Flora's blood like dandelion wine. He had hurt her, taken her love away, belittled Dakota. In that moment, she wished Taylor Boswell dead. But the wish also shocked her, revulsion turning her stomach. That wasn't who she was. Or who she would ever be.

'You know, Taylor, one day, I'll be far away from here. And I won't ever think about you again.' Flora went to open the door.

'Nuh-uh,' he hit the auto-lock. 'You don't get to waste my time, little girl.'

'Let me out.'

'You come in here to make a transaction, you're gonna make it.'

'Just let me the hell out, Taylor.'

'You wanted molly.'

'Fine. Give me one tab.'

'Deal. Open your shirt.'

Flora's breath caught. His pupils were tiny, his face red. She understood now; she had jumped into the dark of a testing pool without knowing what lay beneath the surface.

'Taylor, I think you should let me out.'

'You wanted to come here and be a grown-up. This is your way out.'

'I won't do it.'

'Yeah, you will.'

'I'd rather die before –'

'No, you wouldn't,' he pulled his jacket to one side, revealing the black gleam of a gun butt.

Her stomach coiled with fear.

'Just fucking do it. Then you can go home.'

Trembling violently, she began to unbutton her shirt.

'Come on. Ain't got all day.'

As Flora looked out of the tinted windows, her numb fingers fumbled her shirt open. In that dimmed world, somehow it felt like this had all happened before.

'Holy shit, that *bra*. You look like a fuckin' grandma.' He snorted. 'Nobody's ever gonna screw you, Jiggles. But I bet you'll make damn good pierogis, huh?'

The words hurt, despite their stupidity. The fact this idiot could hurt her that way filled Flora with shame. 'Let me out now.'

'You're not done yet.' He unzipped his jeans and pulled out his penis. 'Dropped a few Medusas earlier so you're gonna have to work for this.'

Before she could move for the horror, he was pulling her down into his lap. One hand shoved her head down, the other squeezed her nape, as she felt the flaccid thing on her chin.

The cell phone on his dashboard beeped.

By dealer reflex, he held her down and looked at the screen. Flora snatched out the gun from his waistband and lurched back into the passenger seat.

'Whoa, Flora. Relax. We're just goofing.'

'Goofing?' she wept rage. 'You piece of shit.'

'Listen, I fucked up. I didn't mean to horse you that hard, all right?'

'I'm going to the sheriff right now.'

His pupils eclipsed with fear. 'You don't need to do that. Hey, look.' Holding up one palm, he slowly reached under his seat with the other hand and took out a large bag stuffed with packs of multi-coloured pills. 'Everything I got. Take it, OK?'

'The doors.'

'Sure, sure.'

He switched off the locks and Flora shunted outside still holding the gun. Head swivelling, tears down her face, she shoved the bag in her shirt, then buttoned it up wrong. Nobody paid any mind as she ran through the lot – just another over-excited kid.

Flora crashed back into the bodies, her head spinning in the noise and lights. Stumbling through the pandemonium of final night, she didn't know where she was going.

Without meaning to, she ended up in the employee hut. The harsh lights gave her a new urgent focus.

Flora tossed the gun in the trash, hid the bag of pills in her locker, then tried to clean her face up. But Devin Rigney was glaring so she picked up her nabber and left.

Outside, she tried to stab garbage but ended up vomiting against the fence. Sobbing, it took her a long time to get her breath back.

That's when she heard a girl's scream. One scream amid thousands.

But this one was familiar.

Close.

At the edge of the Testing Pool, Rebecca Frey clutched her own wrists. She could still feel his grip on them. In that numb drowse, her mind floated above her body, only her lips moving in whispered prayer. *Angel of God, my guardian dear, to whom God's love commits me here. Ever this day, be at my side, to light and guard and rule and guide.*

She heard approaching footsteps from the wood, crunching through dead leaves and snow. The thought that *he* had returned swam above her but, somehow, she did not care.

Yet it was not the admirer who emerged.

It was one of the men she had seen around Fest. The chamberlain of the false God.

Lester Lamb lit a cigarette and webbed the moon with his smoke. Only then did he notice her.

'You made me jump, girl . . . Say, you OK?'

Rebecca had no reply as he approached.

'Don't be frightened. I'm just asking if you're all right.'

She was not frightened. Only numb and nauseous. She spoke drowsily. 'Thou art the preacher from under yonder canopy . . .'

'My God.' He saw her properly now – dress bunched up, face swollen, nose bloodied. 'You're hurt. What happened?'

'He said if I screamed, he would kill my parents.'

'Who? Who said this to you?'

'. . . I cannot say.'

'You need a hospital, OK? I'm just gonna get my car, don't move.'

Flora staggered through the wood, calling Rebecca's name. She knew it had been real – the scream – yet now she doubted everything. Distantly, she remembered Piety searching for her. Had that been real, too? Maybe not. Maybe Rebecca was back at home right now. Maybe Taylor Boswell had never touched her. Maybe Dakota had never run away at all.

Emerging into the clearing, Flora saw the Testing Pool was lit up. Tears blurring her vision, it took her a moment to understand what she was seeing: a car parked in the small clearing just above the water. The glare of its brake lights turning the pool warm pink. And a large man loading something into the back seats.

Flora saw legs now, a skirt bunched up, a glimpse of bloodied pubic hair. One foot was bare. From the other, a wooden clog fell off and rolled down the muddy verge.

In her kaleidoscope mind's eye, Flora saw Rebecca's white body being lowered into a shallow grave, a snowfall of quick-lime falling. Except now, the face was Dakota's and the belly was swollen. Except now, from within the darkness, a half-born baby was screaming.

The beehive inside Flora broke open – rage, pain, rejection, heartbreak – built up over years. She felt herself let go and rushed the man, dark furies under her breath. The nabber made a dull *thunk* as it punched in between his ribs twice, then between his shoulder blades.

Puzzled, Lester Lamb turned. He tried to reach for the blade stuck inside him but now the pain unfurled across his face.

Flora pushed past him to drag Rebecca out of the car. In her friend's face, there was bewilderment.

'Becky, we gotta go, right now –'

Moaning, Lamb grabbed Flora by the throat.

She dug her nails into his hand. Bodies locking, they rolled down the muddy verge. The nabber had come free, its blade now gleaming with blood.

Flora reached for it as he held her back by the ankle. 'Wait. You don't understand —'

But Flora was driven by righteous rage.

With her free leg, she kicked out. Twice, her boot hit him in the face but he wouldn't let go. And now his weight and strength started to tell. Lamb dragged her back towards him, trying to shift his weight on top of her.

'Flora, listen to me. I was helping her —'

She scratched and bit and punched, but he would not budge. In that suffocating panic, Flora knew that he was a liar. That he had attacked her friend. And that, if she let him, he would kill them both.

'Flora . . .' He grunted. 'I can't let you go. I can't let you go —'

She screamed out for help and the world responded with fireworks. Distant little pops of joy in the night sky above Lake Sweetness.

'Please, I'm trying to help —' Lamb covered her mouth with his palm. The smell of lemon cologne clashed with the stink of the air. Exhaust snaked above him in the night, now sparkling and rippling multi-coloured.

Flora closed her eyes as she struggled, screaming into his soft hand. Her fingers raked in the mud. And now touched something half-buried. It was cold. Smooth. Hard.

An empty wine bottle.

They had shared it weeks ago. Lifetimes ago. Dakota had thrown it into the darkness. And now, it was in Flora's hand — lit up pink by fireworks.

She smashed it into his face.

Lamb rolled off her. Spitting out blood, he blinked, his nose at a strange angle.

Flora hit him again. The neck of the bottle slurped into his eye socket.

He spoke the name of God, then twitched, then fell still.

256

Flora scrambled away from him, chest heaving.

Instantly, she felt the weight of what she had just done. Reality sat on her hard. Her stomach twisted violently, heart convulsing in her chest.

In that shock, she didn't hear Rebecca was shouting her name.

'We must go –' She was clutching her head in panic. 'We must go now.'

'Let me think, let me think. We can't just leave him like this . . .'

Rebecca went to her and held her face. 'Flora. We have to go.'

'No. The body. They'll find him.'

They both looked at Lester Lamb.

It seemed as though Rebecca wanted to say something. But she didn't have the words for it in her own language, let alone another. Instead, she merely hurried over to the corpse and started dragging.

'What are you doing?'

'Help me, Flora.'

Together, they wrestled the body up the verge, and into the car. Flora could still feel the weight of him on her. Like a kid in a spinning tea cup, she saw herself bundle the body into the driver's seat, bottle still sickeningly deep in its head.

They fetched up his pack of smokes and threw it in the car, along with her bloodied nabber. Flora couldn't see anything else but she felt the sinking certainty she was missing something.

'Now what, now what?'

'Into the water.'

Flora took a deep, nauseated breath.

Reaching across, she fought her need to gag and tied the body in place behind the wheel with the seatbelt. For some reason, she set the hands on the wheel. Then she released the handbrake.

Gravity kicking in, the car inched forwards. On that muddy incline, the tyres started to whine. Then it was free.

Before Flora had a chance to consider her choices, the royal-blue Sable was picking up speed.

It crashed through the old wooden barrier.

A second of silence. Then the hard slap of speeding metal on water. It was a surreal image, the preacher's car afloat.

Then the car started to sink; its wipers flailed for help, alarm beeping. The panicking horn changed pitch as the pool gulped it down. Cartoon bubbles came now. *Bloop, bloop, bloop.* Underwater, the headlights of the car flickered, then died.

Now silence.

The girls stood there at the edge of the Testing Pool, both of them breathing hard. 'Becky . . .' Flora's voice was wet with bile. 'Listen to me. We never saw this man. And we never came to this place. Do you understand?'

'But —'

'— we *never* saw him. I know you don't lie but if you speak about this, we're both in deep, deep shit. Do you get what I'm saying? *Police.* They'll come for us.'

The fireworks had reached their rippling crescendo, the night sky now the colours of the American flag.

'The mouth is made for silence.'

Flora took her friend by the shoulders. 'We can't see each other again. Ever. Do you understand me? Go back to your village and live your life. Forget all this.'

A small nod.

The girls embraced.

Then they walked away in separate directions.

TWENTY

The gates of Versammlung fell shut, pounding the earth hard enough to raise the dead. Outside, Sullivan was sitting on the hood of his police cruiser, smoking a roll-up. Finch walked towards him, as if in a daze.

'Detective.' He smirked at her colony dress. 'Kind of suits you in a weird way.'

'Funny.'

'How was it in there?'

'A lot of closed lips.'

'Well, I've come because we got a break.'

'Same here. Two, actually.'

'Ladies first.'

'One. Jubilance. The husband-to-be. It always is. He lied to me, Jesse. He'd given the victim money before her death in an envelope marked *Atonement*.'

'No kidding? And Hanlon said she'd been pregnant before. Could be motive.'

'Secondly, the driver who comes here to pick up their produce? It's Sam Salinas.'

'You just gazumped my break.' Sullivan grinned. 'Obviously, we knew he worked for Burr Heavy Haul. What we didn't know? He rents a parking spot at Speedy's – *yards* from where the body was found.'

'*Ho-ly* shit.'

'You tied him close to Rebecca in life. And we got him close to her in death.'

Nectar. Civil war tours dawdled through the fields outside town. Out on Lake Sweetness, a troop of scouts were kayaking. And high above it, hikers twined the trails in the misted Catoonah Mountains.

But Town Hall was thronging for election day. Finch – now wearing her police gear again – had managed to bundle the mayor into his office for a minute.

'Dakota, I *heard* you. You ain't got a whole heap. This really ain't the moment –'

'Listen to me. Jubilance Weaver has anger. Scratches. Motive. Money. Speaks English. I can get him on probable cause, then prints, DNA, we nail that son of a bitch.'

'If I put this before a judge, they will weigh the evidence before signing any warrant. And at the moment, what you've got is a manual labourer displaying minor injuries and reluctance to talk about personal finance with his fiancée.'

'That's bullshit.'

'Call it what you want. Now, Dakota. I'm not ruling this guy out of anything. But you asked us to look into the truck man. Jesse did. Just listen to him.'

Sullivan cleared his throat. 'Burr Group love Salinas. Trusted contractor, sun shines out his ass. But then I ask about his hours on the night of the murder. Sam's truck is fitted with an ELD – Electronic Logging Device. Measures driving hours, alerts when to take a safety break. So, I ask the dispatcher to look at his log for the night of the murder –'

'– He turned it off?'

Sullivan wiggled his eyebrows. 'Bingo.'

Mayor Cochran leaned forward in his seat. 'If a Versammlung girl left that day, she had a reason. Why would anyone in her village talk her into coming out here? If they wanted to hurt her, why not use all that wilderness around them to hide her?'

'. . . But if Sam wanted her, he knew he couldn't get her alone in the colony.'

'You said she had money, right?'

'No,' Finch shook her head. 'Jubilance paid her.'

'For all we know, she's got cash hidden in every damn cuckoo clock in that colony. If she's willing to take payment from one asshole, what's another? Maybe she got used to that money coming in. Now, think about it. Who else did she know out here? Maybe things got out of hand. Maybe she pressed Sam for more than he had.'

'But, Quayle –'

'But *nothing*. I have listened to everything you've said about this Jubilance and what I hear is a scared young man who ain't processing his grief too good. But zero tangible evidence to put before my judge.'

Finch went to the window. 'I don't know.'

'Are you even thinking straight? I put a lot of faith in you. Now, I ain't judging but you've been seen taking medication –'

She snorted. 'Half this country is.'

'Half the country ain't running this damn investigation. Salinas was a POI in the Riddell case. Known to have a wandering eye. And now he's tied to Rebecca's colony, with a clear connection to the body depo. History of violence. Hell, the judge *will* sign for all that.'

Jesse nodded. 'Dawn raid? Won't know what hit him.'

Cochran smiled. 'The first promise kept of my new term: a safe community.'

Under her body armour, Finch thumbed the letters carved into her flesh. *SILENCE.*

*

Nightfall. The big green eighteen-wheeler was parked in a dark turnout, miles out of town. Sam Salinas was leaning against his rig, smoking. His eyes were on the abandoned depot for the dead sugar train in front of him. The forest had reclaimed it long ago, the branches around it as black veins.

Two hundred yards away, Finch was watching from the shadows. She had followed him all afternoon. The dread that had been building in her ever since she'd arrived was curling its fingers around her, an unwanted hug.

If Salinas killed Rebecca, how? Abduction from Versammlung would've been next to impossible. So, he must've talked her into meeting him outside. Money, maybe? She'd taken money before. And Eva said she had mentioned a task outside. Hanlon said the killer strangled her from behind. Would she turn her back? If so, she must've known him.

A car pulled in quietly next to the truck now. The door opened. Footsteps scrunched over gravel.

Finch saw a woman, her face hidden by the dark. Sam tossed his cigarette. She went to him as if to embrace. But his hand shot out and gripped her throat. He held her there, unflinching, then slammed her up against the truck. The woman croaked some inaudible words.

Finch pulled her gun. But already he had softened. He still held the woman by the throat but she was leaning into him, her mouth open.

Salinas enveloped her like an eclipse.

When the kiss was over, they walked towards the abandoned depot, hand in hand.

On the way back to the motel, Finch swallowed all the Visprozan she had left in the cruiser. By the time she reached Room 202, her vision was gently spiralling, her tongue felt like walnut shell. Fumbling for the key, she saw Sam's hands fitting around Rebecca's throat in her mind. And now Flora's too.

I was wrong about Jubilance. Salinas was right there. He always was.

Only now did she realize the strange sensation beneath her boot. Looking down, Finch saw another severed cow's tongue.

It made a sticky sound as she booted it away into the darkness.

Inside the room, Finch locked the door and scanned the street. Nobody watching. Nobody in the streetlight.

She turned on the TV and put a cold, hard pizza crust in her mouth that still held Elesheva's teeth nibbles in.

I'm Kristen Kowalski on the hour. Topping our KRQ 7 News tonight, Nectar decides: the grand prize? The mayor's seat in one of Catoonah County's big-ticket agricultural towns. Polls have already closed and the early news: the expected Melvin Neeley wave looks to be CRASHING into the breaker of the incumbent, Quayle Cochran.

Let's go to City Hall now where we have Dean Garduno with on-scene reporting. Dean, this is quite the turnaround, isn't it?

– Correct, Kristen. Despite lagging behind in the polls, pretty much since candidates announced their campaigns, Mayor Cochran, the former sheriff of Nectar, looks to have snatched the early lead. I'm hearing that's thanks to an unexpectedly large postal vote. To sum it up? A shock on our hands potentially here in Nectar tonight. With that, I'll throw it back to the studio, Kristen.

Finch picked up the book about the Nectar witch and collapsed on the bed. She couldn't get past the first few lines of her chapter. As her consciousness warmly whirlpooled, she heard the distant pop of fireworks.

TWENTY-ONE

The tactical entry team were ready. Given the risk of evidence flushing, Jesse Sullivan had ordered for water lines to be cut for the whole area. At 4:19AM, they breached. Sam Salinas was ordered to lie face-down and served with a warrant to search his home.

'Gentlemen!' Sullivan marched in like Napoleon. 'You know what I want. Search the drains. Garbage. Pipes. Are there burn pits in the garden? Soil disturbance? This is Easter and you are my bunnies.'

The search team fanned out and the suspect was bundled into a chair. Sullivan sat across from him with a smile, 'Rebecca Frey sends her regards.'

'This is a goddamn set-up, Jesse. You know it.'

'Keep singing that song.'

959, come in?

Sullivan went into the next room and lifted his shoulder radio. 'Right here, Glennis.'

959, just to let you know that the forensics boys searching the Salinas truck have found hairs. Long hairs. Red in colour.

'That's one big, happy copy. I owe you an oyster dinner, Glennis.'

Over and out and in your dreams, Jesse.

8AM. In the Nectar PD interview room, Finch stared into the eyes of Samuel Salinas. The suspect stared right back at her through cigarette smoke. Defiance or fear, she couldn't tell. *Maybe both.*

'Must be getting déjà vu in here, Sam.'

'Couldn't I say the same to you fuckers? This has been going on for fifteen years.' He glanced at the two-way mirror. 'Cochran has a hard-on for me the size of the Washington Monument. Always has. We both know why.'

'You rent parking at Speedy's. You pick up produce from Versammlung, take it on to Burr Group for distribution.'

'I do a bunch of jobs in a week. None of that is a secret.'

'What was the job on the night of the thirtieth?'

'Chems run out of state. Hydrogen peroxide. Agricultural grade. I just drive the shit.'

'Lay out the day for me. Gimme detail.'

'Most of the day, I was at home, resting. Had lunch with my wife, my boy. I picked up the chem load at a plant in Flicker-wood after that, drove it out of state.'

'What time did you get back to Nectar?'

'Late. I can't remember exactly. Had a drink at the Moose. Then, went home.'

'How long were you at the bar?'

'An hour or two. I don't remember.'

'The Moose closed up at 2AM. You live a few minutes' walk away.'

'Then I guess a few minutes after that.'

'Your wife will vouch to that?'

'The truth is, Carmella and I are separating. But yeah, she'll tell you what happened that night. Look, Dakota. We both know what this is. Quayle has hated me ever since she turned him down, even though he's twice her fuckin' age. He went after me for Flora in '98 and now he's going after me with this shit.'

'Your Electronic Logging Device. Ever turn it off?'

'Hm.' He stubbed out his smoke and she noted the pause. 'Sometimes, yeah. Look, it's against the rules but we all do it. If I hit my driving limit two miles from home, I'm not gonna pull over and take a nap.'

'What about on the night of the murder?'

He snorted. 'You really *are* trying to pin that dead girl on me too, huh?'

'Did you turn off your ELD on the night of the thirtieth going into the thirty-first?'

'No, I don't think so.'

'Did you know Rebecca Frey?'

'No. Never even heard the name.'

'We got a body, Sam. Once again, you're floating around in all the wrong places.'

'Those places are where I work. Can't help that.'

'So, this is all a frame-up job? You're a good guy but Cochran has it in for you?'

'You can sass me but that's exactly what this is.'

Finch held up a data log printout. 'You got back to Nectar at midnight that night. You *did* go to the bar. Testimony puts you there. But then things get messy. Witnesses have you leaving at 1 AM. Around the point you turn off your ELD. Why?'

A lip-twitch. 'Well, *if* I did that, no idea.'

'Seems strange to turn off a machine that tracks movement if you're not moving.'

'I was tired. I made a mistake. So what?'

'So, maybe you didn't want your employer to know you were still rolling. You're a contractor, Sam. You own your own rig. It would make no difference to Burr Group what you do in your own time, or where you go. Why turn off that machine, then? Unless, of course, you wanted to hide any record of your movements that night.'

'That's plain wrong.'

'Let's hope so. For your sake.'

'I don't need no hope. It's truth.'

'I got automotive forensics on your truck right now, running the numbers on your ELD, your odometer. They'll find out one way or another.'

'Why, though? Why would I do any of this?'

'My best guess? You got drunk that night. Angry. As you said, things aren't working out with Carmella. Maybe one thing was broken in your life, you figured you'd fix the other. So, you went to Versammlung. That's why the ELD was off. You went to meet Rebecca. Then, I think you killed her, took her to Speedy's and dumped her sometime after 2AM. When you were done, you cleaned up.'

'That's a goddamn lie.'

'Is the ELD lying? The witnesses? The man who found the body?'

'Look.' His glare was unwavering but his voice was not. 'I ain't perfect, OK? But that night, I never went to Versammlung. And I never killed anyone.'

'We got people on the farm saying you liked to look at the girls. And Rebecca was easy on the eye, huh? You introduced yourself. Started a flirtation. Only, maybe what started off as fun got a little too serious. But Versammlung girls don't just have *a little fun*, right? They play for keeps. And you were already on your last chance with Carmella. Did the girl want more money after the abortion? Or was she threatening to go to your wife? Either way, she backed you into a corner. No choice, huh, pal?'

Salinas closed his eyes. 'This is a fucking nightmare.'

'Oh, I bet it felt that way. You needed to shut her up, to protect yourself. You made threats, only she didn't scare. So, your hands ended up around her neck and then . . . well, then the moment for letting go just passed you by. Before you knew it, you were driving round with a corpse in your truck.

And you figured, the old dopes at Nectar PD? If I give 'em a body by the Testing Pool, they'll think the big bad wolf is back. The Sugar Man did it.'

He opened his eyes, hateful tears in them. 'I got nothing left to say.'

'You don't have to. Because everything else is talking for you. Your ELD. Your timeline. Your past. The red hairs in the cab. And soon, whoever I saw you with last night.'

'You followed me? Shoulda known.' He shook his head. 'I want a lawyer.'

'Where's the shotgun, Sam?'

'I don't know about any shotgun or abortion or whatever the hell you're talking about. I just want my lawyer. I'm finished here.'

'Yeah, you are.' Finch nodded at the two-way mirror. 'Jesse, read him his rights.'

She left the interview room and stepped into applause – the whole bullpen cheering. Hands clapped her back and shoulders.

–*Got the bastard at last.*

–*Let's hope he likes it raw and dry.*

–*We'll be on Dateline for this.*

In Sullivan's office, the mayor already had the bourbon bottle out. 'My golden girl.' He winked. 'You crucified the prick. And just as I take up my next term, too.'

'We still haven't proven a link between him and the victim.'

Cochran snorted. 'He told so many lies in there. They'll all stack up against him. And maybe not just for Rebecca, but Flora too.'

'Lies or not. All we've got is circumstantial.'

'Circumstantial evidence still counts. Who *else* could've done this, Dakota?'

'Point stands: I got some good hits in but he didn't go down.'

'The red hairs in his truck. The blood under Rebecca's nails. When it comes through, he'll go down and stay down.'

'Maybe. But, Quayle, if you approach this wrong, he walks free. You'd be back to square one, only now you look dumb. How does *that* sit at the next election?'

Sullivan entered the office now.

'Jesse.' The mayor smoothed down his moustache. 'She's not wrong. We have to be airtight sure about this bastard. I want searches of Sam's truck, home, phone – all of it – sped up. Let's do another fingertip spread of the depo site. He *is* guilty, we gotta make sure.'

'Done, Mayor.'

Cochran turned to Finch. 'I shouldn't have doubted you. Go get some rest.'

Finch drove to the Walgreens in Andover. In the parking lot, she called her doctor and gave her some cockamamie story about her luggage being lost. The doctor asked for the pharmacy address and called in the new prescription immediately. Finch walked out of the pharmacy with another thirty days of Visprozan and a bag of flaming-hot Cheetos for her breakfast.

As she got into the cruiser, her cell buzzed. It was Ed Riddell. 'Nice surprise.'

Hey, Dee. Listen, I was calling because –

'– You want to know if the rumours are true. And yeah. They are. We arrested Samuel Salinas for the murder of Rebecca Frey this morning.'

Jesus.

'Obviously, I'm just telling you. His name isn't out there yet.'

Of course. You can count on my silence.

'Appreciate that, Ed.'

I'm the one that appreciates it . . . It's just a lot to process. You think he could've . . .

'Rest assured; I'm going to be looking at him for Flora's murder, too. It could be that the present is the key to unlocking the past.'

God . . . OK. Good to know.

'Look after yourself, Ed. And Dolly.'

Finch hung up.

But as she started the engine, she paused.

Across the lot, she saw a black Escalade now. Chastity Cochran was behind the wheel, phone in hand, crying.

January 21st, 1998

Dakota Finch looked down at the Discman in her hands. She hit the OPEN button and the lid popped up. For no reason, she sniffed the new plastic scent. To her, it smelled of a childhood where parents loved you and protected you and bought you the stupid things you wanted.

She loved Flora, she was like her little sister. But sometimes, Dakota felt she was a whiny brat that only ever thought about what she wanted. It made Dakota want to break something she didn't have.

In her room, she hid the bundle of brightly coloured pills under a loose floorboard, along with the Discman. There was no telling what Mom would do if she found it. Either accuse her of stealing it, or try and pawn it herself.

She was about to place the floorboard back in when she saw the little note sticking out of the pills. Dakota fished it out:

Happy birthday, loser! Have a totally dope day.
PS Wherever ya go, I'll come with.

There was something on the other side, too. Frowning, she flipped it.

I KNOW WHAT YOU DID.

'Is that for me?'

That's when Dakota heard the car horn. Twice. Discreet. Like always.

She stood up too fast, the cramping in her stomach making her gasp. With a sick sigh, she whispered to herself, *It'll be OK.*

The Merlot-red Subaru parked at the end of the trailer park like always. Dakota got in and he looked at her with that usual sphinx smile. He was so beautiful, it always took her breath away. But in that breathlessness, Dakota felt revulsion too now. It was as though her body had learned to reject him, even if her heart was as yet unable.

Your weather now with KRQ 7 News meteorologist Tim Kester; clear tomorrow, around 30, highs of 35 with a little luck. Up next, a special bulletin on the White House scandal. But first, a little early evening emotion, Celine Dion with 'My Heart Will Go On . . .'

'Dakota. How are you feeling?'

'Better.'

'Good. It would have ruined your life.' Reaching out, he curled a strand of hair behind her ear. 'You did the right thing, but you already know that. Say it.'

'I did the right thing.'

'Attagirl. Tell you what, why don't we get you something to eat?'

'Not hungry. Thank you.'

'A soda, then. We'll go somewhere quiet, nobody in your business, and you can tell me how you've been feeling. Sound good?'

Parked outside the abandoned sugar mill, she sucked him in the car. He had said it would be better to go back to only sucking for a while – *until everything had settled, at least.*

The constant rain on the car roof sounded like mocking applause.

Dakota's motions were robotic, numb, feeling only a distant helpless disgust as she willed it to be over.

He grunted. 'You're doing real good, baby. Things have been tough on you lately . . .'

She paused, trying not to gag on the smell of his genitals – Vo5 shampoo and an odd, chemical scent beneath it.

'No, don't you stop. Just know that you've been a good girl.' He unlocked the glovebox. Glancing up, she saw a necklace inside, coiled as a golden snake.

'Don't stop, I said –'

But the gold darkened now as a shadow fell across it. From outside the car, a guttural scream.

He flinched out of Dakota's mouth. 'Oh, fuck. She saw us.'

'Who?'

'She fucking *saw* us.' He was struggling to buckle his belt now.

Dakota heard footsteps away from the car – fast wet splats. Through the rain-slick windshield, she couldn't see who.

'Listen to me. Whatever happens – *whatever* – you don't tell anyone about us. OK?'

'Of course not.'

'Swear it.'

'I swear it.'

'Good.' He kissed her on the forehead. 'I'm trusting you because I love you. You know that?'

'Yes.'

'Attagirl. Stay here, I'll be back soon.' Then he was gone.

The call came through at 9PM. Esther Riddell had sent her sixteen-year-old to the store but the kid never came back. She had driven through town searching, retracing her girl's route.

By midnight, Sheriff Quayle Cochran had sealed off Nectar

and set up roadblocks for miles around. The biggest manhunt in Catoonah County's history was mobilized. Officers went door to door. Helicopters were heard whupping overhead.

All that was found was some party cups rolling in the wind outside the old sugar mill. A few drops of blood in the concrete nearby.

The forests were searched, creeks, long-closed mines, every rig in Speedy's Mountain Truck Plaza. Questions were even asked at the wooden colony of Versammlung, miles out of town, where the devout lived in complete Christian isolation.

Still, no Flora Riddell.

Drawing a blank, Cochran started with the parents. He sat them down in their kitchen and spoke to them softly. The mother was broken, the father a grenade with no pin. Esther Riddell had been at home with the baby. Edward had been out of town photographing for a tractor catalogue.

He took Sheriff Cochran outside and placed a big hand on his shoulder. 'You have to find her, Quayle. She's out there, goddamn it – just a kid.'

'I know, friend. We are doing everything we can.'

'God as my witness, if someone has done something to her –'

'Don't talk that way, Ed. It's just a few hours, she'll turn up.'

After the parents, Nectar PD questioned Flora's friends. Next, neighbours and passing acquaintances. Then folks who worshipped at the mother's church. Then folks that knew her through Fest. That accounted for pretty much all of Nectar and a lot of out-of-towners besides.

Cochran and his men interviewed janitors, ride technicians, concession staff, game attendants, lifeguards, security guards, trash nabbers – hell, even the Tim Burr mascot who handed out leaflets for Speedy's Motor Diner.

Dakota Finch, the best friend, had seen Flora on the way

to the store. And Carmella over at Food-O-Rama said she had picked up groceries just fine.

Beyond that, only some vague talk of a large, dark-haired man with an umbrella in the area when she vanished.

There were zero other leads.

By day two, volunteer searches were organized. The kind-hearted came from Kane. McKinstry. Andover. Even as far away as Flickerwood.

On Main Street, Merle's Diner handed out free clam chowder and coffee for the searchers. Ed Riddell, who owned the photography studio next door, offered to buy snow boots for anyone who needed them.

He called Cochran day and night. *Anything I can do to help, Sheriff. Anything. You need funds, I'll sell the business, the house. Anything.*

For twenty years, a black letterboard outside the evangelical Lutheran church on the hill above Main had carried the words of Jeremiah: *YEA I HAVE LOVED THEE WITH AN EVERLASTING LOVE.* Yet overnight, the letters had been rearranged to form a plea:

BRING FLORA HOME

Pastors organized joint vigils. Men threw out suspicious names across the bar at the Mangy Moose. Women whispered theories over phone lines. Parents cried in the aisles of Wawa. Yet everyone was forced to live with the ugly truth. *A predator had come to prey on their town. Or maybe he was here right now, hiding in plain sight.*

All through Nectar, all through the county, Flora's face could be seen. Gas stations, laundromat windows, newspapers, phone booths. In the missing poster, her yearbook smile was timid, dimples half hidden by char-black hair.

By the third day, the story had gone national. News vans descended. The police told the parents not to give interviews but that didn't stop Nectarites from talking. Locals in diners shared their thoughts and prayers as they chewed on shoofly pie. Esther and Edward Riddell stayed by the phone all day in case a ransom demand came through.

None did.

Search parties expanded. Dogs came in from Pittsburgh. Scanning equipment from New York City. Even the Versammlungsvolk, despite their lack of English and complete rejection of the outside world, lent their horses to help with tough terrain.

A brief, sensational break came when an anonymous tip was given about Sam Salinas talking to Flora shortly before her disappearance. When traces of blood were found in the trunk of his car, he was arrested, only to be released when Carmella's movie alibi checked out and the blood turned out to be from a deer.

On the third night, the Nectar Hornets held a minute's silence before the fundraiser game. It had almost been cancelled, given the cold weather. But in the end, it was decided it would lift community spirits. Cheerleaders spelled out *Flora* with gold pompoms, their breath on the night air like a gathering of little ghosts.

On the fourth day, a call came through on the Flora Riddell hotline – an anonymous whispering woman. *I know who did it . . . I know who did it . . . He-he – oh God help me.*

The call was traced to a payphone an hour away, the lead went nowhere.

The final call came before dawn on the morning of the fifth day. A dog walker had made a discovery in the lonely woodland behind Speedy's Mountain Truck Plaza – not far from the sugar mill where the blood spots had been found.

Nectar patrolmen approached, guns drawn. In the distance, Tim Burr grinned down at them as though entertained. Cops crunched through snow in silence until they reached the Testing Pool. Nothing moved in that clearing except mist on the water.

It was Sheriff Cochran who saw the broken egg in the snow. A few yards on, another. Then the whole carton. Now her schoolbag, its contents spilled. A book had fallen open: *The Nectar Witch: Corruption. Curses. A Copycat Killer.* Its pages fluttered in the breeze. On the title page, an inscription:

To Flora,

Don't forget me when you get where you're going.

Ira

And there, finally, on the frozen banks of the pond, lay the body of Flora Riddell.

Removing their hats, patrolmen silently gathered around her. Her face was so pale she was almost translucent – except for her throat. There, the ligature marks from the strap of her mother's handbag looked like raspberry ripple. In the palm of her hand, there was a broken necklace – cheap gold, its pendant an evil eye inside a star.

'That necklace is ours,' Cochran said thickly. 'We keep it back. Nobody knows about it. Only us. And the killer.'

Patrolmen slapped Quayle Cochran on the back.

You'll get this sonuvabitch, Sheriff. You'll get him.

In the mud nearby, they found a half-eaten nectarine. $2.02 in loose change. And next to her head, a torn bag of sugar. Flora's face had been lightly coated, the granules pooling in her closed eyes, her closed lips.

TWENTY-TWO

Exhausted, Finch traipsed up the stairs to her motel room. She turned on the TV, already thinking about the shower and the day-long sleep she would treat herself to. The local news was about Cochran being elected mayor for another term.

That's right, Kristen. Quayle Cochran has been firmly in second place pretty much for this whole campaign. But the pollsters got it wrong and his camp is now claiming victory. As mentioned earlier, it looks as if a higher voter turnout confounded predictions, with the postal vote playing a big role. Mayor Cochran is expected to give a victory speech today . . .

Finch turned on the hot water faucet in the shower then paused at the little window. Through the frosted glass, down in the bush, she saw a pink-brown blur. She went to the room door and stood in the frame. There, she saw it – the fleshy curl of the cow's tongue.

Again, Finch stopped the cruiser on Kinzua. The trailer park looked the same this afternoon as before. Beer cans were snagged in the dead grass. Trying not to breathe in the ammonia, she passed the broken stoop that she sat on the last day that Flora had drawn breath on this earth. Somehow, it was harder to look at now than it was a week ago.

Finch knocked on the rusted door of the last trailer. Ira Pike answered through the door without opening. 'What do you want?'

'To talk.'

'I told you, I had nothing to do with Flora. Or this murder now.'

'That's not why I'm here. But I think you know why I am, Ira.'

After a moment, the door creaked open.

Finch followed him into the trailer and joined him at the table.

Ira turned down the volume on the TV and poured coffee liqueur into his cup of vodka. 'Want one?'

Finch shook her head. 'Nostrovia, though.'

'It's *na zdorovie.*'

'Ever the teacher, huh? And here I was, about to apologize to you.'

'No apology needed.' He lifted his cup.

'We arrested Salinas.'

'I heard. Did he do it?'

'Looks that way, yes.' Finch nodded at a stack of copies of *The Nectar Witch*. 'So, I read your book. Not exactly uplifting, Ira.'

He half-smiled now. 'In the next life, I'll write a romcom.'

'You're the one leaving the tongues for me. But not in warning. They were an appeal, weren't they? To change the direction of my investigation without talking to me directly.'

'Can you blame me?'

'No. I was hard on you when I had nothing on you. So . . . why try to help me at all?'

'Because you're the one chance at the truth this town has. And there were questions that were never answered. About Flora. About Nectar. And I believe they all lead back to the Nectar Historical Society.'

Finch sized him up, trying to decide if she was talking to a nutjob or not. Half his face was tinted blue now from the UFO conspiracy programme on the TV. 'What's your beef with them? They're just in charge of preserving historical stuff.'

'*Supposedly*. But then you read my book.'

'You think they're out here obsessed with the Neck Tear Witch. That they're tied to the disappearances of the girls around these mountains down the years, making – what? Satanic offerings? I'll be honest, you didn't really sell me, Ira.'

'If there had been a second edition, I would've. And they're not just obsessed with the witch. They *worship* him. They look into the evil eye, hoping to see him.'

'Eye?' A twist of memory, a bright glint in cloudy water – shark-fin quick.

'That evil eye is their secret symbol.'

'Symbol for what?'

'They believe the witch to be the devil incarnate. That he'll return one day.'

'So, you're saying the handful of retirees that meet for museum trips and bridge are actually out under a full moon, sacrificing kids? Ira, you must know how that sounds.'

'Evil hides in incredulity. And I'm not talking about the *members*. They're just puppets. I'm talking about the *inner circle*. The men of power. The real worshippers.'

'Who?'

'I have my suspicions. Though they went underground after '98, of course.'

'I see.' Finch stood. 'Well, when you have something that I can actually use, let me know. Try the phone, though.'

'Alana Wells.'

'. . . What?'

'She was involved with them. I'm sure of it. I was at Fest, you remember. Flora was friends with her. We know what happened to Flora. Whatever happened to Alana Wells? Just disappeared one day, nobody knew a thing.'

Back at the motel, Finch paced her room. So much stacked up against Salinas. Yet nothing sat right. Ever since leaving Versammlung. Ever since seeing Sam Salinas written down on the piece of paper. And ever since Ira Pike had mentioned the evil eye symbol.

It was as though she had a word on the tip of her tongue but all she could do was stutter. Finch felt she was close to an understanding. But it was hazing in and out of focus.

Again, she closed her eyes, forcing herself into the jumble of her memory.

There's a Mexican food stall this year, try some brrr-itos. Get it? Brrrr. Cold . . . Making friends with yokels? . . . And remember, dammit. Folks are here to have fun. So, smile. Help people out.

Finch overturned her table, kicked her suitcase, and screamed in futility.

But she saw something now.

In the clutter from the overturned table, the casefile had spilled its contents. Finch walked around it until the photograph was the right way up.

It was the Polaroid of her and Flora, taken a lifetime ago. *Come on. I see cute smiles, I gotta snap 'em.*

Finch had looked at this image a million times. But in grief, she'd only had eyes for Flora. Now, she looked beyond her soulmate. Beyond herself. And saw, in the background, Alana Wells. The photo was faded, the quality bad, but it was clear what was around her neck. A necklace with a star and eye pendant. *An evil eye?*

On her knees, she shuffled through the casefile.

Victim was found holding imitation gold 'evil eye' star necklace.

Now, she fished out the crime scene images, seeing Flora's lifeless body as she had so many times.

It had always been a hopelessly unchanging motion, never seeing anything new or useful. Until now.

In the palm of Flora's hand, there was a broken necklace – cheap gold, its pendant an evil eye.

Finch pinched the pendant on her collarbone now, holding it up to the light.

Jesus Christ. It's the same one Alana Wells was wearing.

February, 1998

Edward Riddell sat in the family car, his head on the steering wheel. He knew what was waiting for him inside. A house full of cops. A wife that couldn't look at him. And no Flora to kiss his cheek. *What am I gonna do? How can this have happened to me?*

As he absently listened to the car radio, Ed considered killing himself. The exacto knife was in his pocket. Two quick, expert cuts. Veins open, if he ran around the front lawn, his pumping heart would finish him faster. In his mind, he saw his own blood, so red in the dirty grey snow. Then it would all be over – the pain. The fear. The endless fatigue.

Midnight weather from KRQ 7 News meteorologist Tim Kester; a cold one tomorrow, dropping to around 20. Up next, we got the news. But first, a little witching-hour wistfulness with LeAnn Rimes and 'How Do I Live?'

Ed tossed the knife in his glovebox and got out of the car. He skirted the two Nectar PD cruisers parked in his driveway. Sliding his key into the door, he took a breath before opening. Inside, he was hit by the wail of the baby. The fuzzy radio chatter of the cops.

Like always, Ed laid his shoes neatly in the rack.

Controlling his breathing, he now entered the front room. The Nectar patrolmen all gave him respectful nods. Ed put his hand on his wife's trembling shoulder and kissed her crown. 'OK, hon?'

'Huh?'

'Dolly's crying. You didn't hear?'

Esther Riddell could only frown at him blankly, her eyes void.

'It's all right, Estie. I'll go.'

Ed fixed his smile before entering the baby's room. Dolly fell quiet the second he hefted her small, reassuring weight on his chest.

'See? It's OK, pooper. I got you now. Shall we take a walk?' As usual, he took her to the hallway mirror. 'Who is that, huh? Is that a beautiful little pooper? Is that a pretty little Dolly Doll Pooper?'

Laughing now, the baby pawed at her own reflection and Ed tried not to see how violent the resemblance to Flora was.

He rocked the baby gently and sang her old mountain-mine songs in that hallway, until her eyes lolled shut.

'OK, pooper,' he whispered. 'Pop needs to go talk to the silly ugly man now.'

Ed returned Dolly to her crib. Back at the hallway mirror, he met his own eyes. He was pale, exhausted, and his gingham shirt stuck to his sweating torso.

But it was almost hard to believe. Despite everything, he looked the same. Olive eyes, dark eyebrows, greying hair. It was the kind of face that helped sell photos. It might have been cars. It might have been houses. But those were lives he would never live. He was living this one. And, in this one, inside he was dead. Even if outside he looked like a sitcom dad.

Why carry on?

Rubbing away the sweat from his brow with a calloused hand, Ed recalled the knife in the glovebox.

No, Esther can barely function. How would Dolly survive?

Ashamed, he looked away.

In the kitchen, Sheriff Cochran was sitting at the island, his painter's brush moustache wet from hot chocolate. He had dripped on Flora's doodles on the counter.

'Ed, how you holding up?'

'I . . . honestly don't know how to answer that.'

'I understand.'

'You understand.'

'Well. As much as I can.'

'Any calls? Tips? Anything?'

'Nothing concrete, yet.'

'Look, I've been thinking.' Ed started pacing. 'You said it was strangulation, right? Well, how? Did he use his hands? I mean, you must be able to come up with a *list*, right? Creeps who *do* this kind of thing. Were any in the area? Or maybe fingerprints on her –'

'I'm sorry,' Cochran sighed. 'You got me sounding like a broken record here, Ed. But I can't give details of –'

'– an ongoing investigation, I know. But you gotta give me something. Just a hint. Or-or a sign that you people are out there *doing something.* Jesus, my wife is . . .'

Cochran held up his palms now. 'Ed. I know you're hurt. Every man here understands that what you and Esther are going through is just beyond. But you're gonna have to trust me. When I have something definitive, I will come to you.'

Ed looked out of the window, shaking his head. '*Beyond*, huh?'

'Now, uh. Just so I can get my ducks in a row. We gotta go over the day of the disappearance again.'

'Fine,' he rubbed his eyes. 'I was out of town during the day. Catalogue job. When I got home, Esther went out to church. She figured I knew Flora was due back any minute. But I didn't know.'

'When Esther got back, that's when you realized? When you went searching?'

'Yes. Obviously. What else would I do? What would you do?'

'I know it's frustrating to repeat stuff. But the ducks, the rows? They gotta be done.'

Ed sighed. 'Yes, I went searching for her.'

'In the car? Out the car? Did anybody see you?'

'Jesus, I don't know, Quayle. It was raining hard, I don't remember many people out; I didn't strike up any conversations, as you can imagine. But I did see cars. I was calling her name. Yeah, I drove but I also parked up and got out. Looked through her usual places. It was real difficult to see anything with the dark, the rain.'

'It was raining hard that night.' Cochran tugged his moustache. 'How *did* you see?'

'How do you think? I had an umbrella and I squinted. Look, I'm not gonna leave my kid out there because of bad weather.'

'I know. An umbrella might be noticeable is all. And I'm only asking if anybody saw you so we can clear exact timeframes and move on.'

'Move on?' Ed laughed bitterly. 'I know you're doing your job, Quayle, but I have answered this five times already. I searched for her for maybe an hour. I can't be sure. Esther searched too. After that, we called you.'

Cochran nodded. 'OK, Ed. I appreciate it.'

'You done trying to catch me out? Then go find the piece of shit that killed my child.'

Dakota Finch made her way down the muddy wooded path behind Speedy's, dodging the used condoms and syringes. She sat on the edge of the frozen water and drew her knees up to her chest. A week ago, they'd found Flora here. A small mound of flowers marked the exact spot where she had left this world. Ink from the sympathy cards had bled long in the rain, white petals blown across the dark ice.

As kids, the Testing Pool had always been Dakota and

Flora's place. Where they came to be alone. To share secrets. To creep each other out. To conspire.

Ever since she'd heard the news, she'd been wracking her brains. Who could have done this? Nectar was full of creeps. But to murder a kid and dump her here?

Flora had turned up with a bundle of MDMA. Where did she get it? Could that explain her murder? But nobody had come looking for it. Then there was Lester Lamb. He was still missing. Could his disappearance be linked to Flora? It didn't seem likely, either.

A few weeks back, Rebecca had mentioned a man watching her. An admirer. At the time, Dakota hadn't given it any thought. But what if it was *him* that had done this?

Ever since the moment she'd been told Flora had been found murdered, Dakota had wondered: *why not me?* It would have been easier if he had chosen her instead.

Cochran and out-of-state suits had been questioning Dakota non-stop. *Did Flora seem different? Was she unhappy? Did she mention a boy? Meeting someone? Did you see Sam Salinas at any point that day? Even for a second? What about Ira Pike? Did either of them seem upset or agitated?*

Sam was always a little overfriendly. Then again, half the men in Nectar were. Dakota didn't get why they were so interested in him. And Mr Pike was always a sleazy loser, even if he never came right out to say anything.

She just told the detectives what she had told them a dozen times already. *No*, she hadn't seen Sam or Ira that day. *No*, Flora hadn't seemed any different. And *yes*, she had stayed indoors all day. The lie turned her stomach, the weight of the dread sitting on her every thought. But she had promised.

In the aisles of Food-O-Rama, Carmella admitted to

Dakota in a whisper that the police had asked her pretty much the same questions.

Over and over, cops made Dakota re-live that day. *Can you remember anything else? Anything at all?*

But she had already told cops everything she knew.

Or everything about Flora, at least. That's all they needed to know.

The fear of them finding out her secret kept her awake at night. Her head would spin with all the ways it could go wrong for her.

But most of all, she feared losing him. Now that she'd had the procedure, he barely talked to her – one or two phone calls. It was as if she was just a teenage girl to him again.

Dakota rubbed her chest. It had hurt ever since she'd learned that her best friend was gone. A strange pain, like the trapped ache before crying. But no tears came. Her face was numb. The only thing she felt was dizzy and alone.

Realizing tomorrow was Monday, Dakota sighed. The thought of being back in that stinking school suffocated her. It wasn't like she had many friends there before. But now everyone avoided her. In the hallways, she caught people staring, whispering. The gossip was she knew the identity of the killer. Others said she was touched by death itself.

Remembering to breathe, Dakota dug her bare hands into the dirty snow just to feel something. She heard the sounds of the nearby truck stop and thought about climbing into a rig – any rig. Taking Route 6 all the way to the end. Far away from Nectar.

But she knew she couldn't leave this place.

Not without him.

Dakota got up and walked out across the Testing Pool. The ice groaned quietly, her footsteps sending out little pops and echoes in all directions. She headed for the middle of the lake. Looking down into the black-blue she saw tiny white bubbles, trapped in time. Deeper down, dead tree trunks were pale figures, arms outstretched, searching in the dark.

Dakota laid down and closed her eyes.

The cold beneath her body was overwhelming. Yet she felt weightless – a moth in a web.

She wished she could be a kid again. She wished Flora were still alive. And she wished her father would come home to tell her everything would be OK. Even if she was too old and too hurt to believe that anymore.

The ice creaked gently, a living, moving thing, trapped air pockets and shifting pressures making strange music.

Another creak.

Then another, sending out underwater moans.

The footsteps squeaked closer. A cold wind rose, then wooed.

'Hello, Dakota,' he said.

'Hi.' Reaching out her hand, she closed her eyes. This was the first time she was seeing him since Flora had disappeared.

Looking around, he laid down next to her on the ice. It yearned under his weight. Dakota nuzzled up to him reflexively, the way she knew he liked. The beating of his heart was loud and slow.

'We won't be able to keep doing this. You know that, right?'

She nodded softly against him.

'Maybe when things calm down . . .'

'I know,' she whispered. 'I just miss you.'

Ignoring that, he pointed up at the sky now. 'So many stars but people only ever look at the same few constellations. Which ones do you know, Dakota?'

A little shrug. 'Orion, I guess. The Big Dipper.'

'Give me your finger.' He took it and traced a shape in the

darkness. 'Do you see? *Monoceros.* That's Greek for *unicorn.* Special. Like you.'

'It's pretty.'

'Everybody looks at it but nobody really sees it. And it holds something very special. You know what a black hole is?'

She shook her head.

'It's a place of such overwhelming gravity that nothing can escape it. Not even light itself. It's not good or bad. It just is. It needs. It desires. And the light needs to give in. See? It's like us. I was made to need you. And you were made to be needed.'

He propped himself up on his elbow now to look into her eyes, the way he did. His face got slowly closer until their foreheads touched. 'I need to be able to trust you, Dakota. You understand that, don't you?'

'I understand.'

'If you want love, you have to give complete trust.'

'You can trust me.'

He slid his hand under her clothes and felt for her heartbeat. 'Did you tell the police anything about us? Anything at all?'

She shook her head, their noses touching.

'Say it.'

'I didn't tell them anything. I swear.'

'Your heart is beating wild.'

'Because of your hand.'

He searched her eyes, left, then right, until finally he nodded.

'I believe you. Make sure it stays that way.' He went into his pocket and handed her something wrapped in a sock. It was heavy. 'Listen to me carefully. If the police come for you, if you see lights and sirens? You use this.'

From inside the sock, she took out a short-barrelled pistol with a wooden handle. '. . . Use it?'

'Yes. On yourself. You have to be quick, though. Don't let them catch you.'

'But –'

'Oh, baby, no. You don't have to worry,' he pulled her head into his chest. 'Shhh, shhh, shhh. It's just like turning out a light. I'll be doing the same thing. And you know where we'll be going?'

'Where?' she mumbled into his chest.

'Monoceros. Together, in that black hole. Forever.'

'OK.'

'Not *OK*. Swear to me.'

'I swear I won't let them get me.'

'Good, baby. If you want my love, you know what I need, don't you? Say it.'

'Yes.'

'Say the word.'

'Silence,' Dakota whispered. 'You need silence.'

TWENTY-THREE

McKinstry was a picture-postcard college town, north of Nectar; all red brick and wrought-iron streetlights. The rival football team's mascot had been slung up at the college's main gates in a noose. Colourful flyers lined the walls selling cheap 'homemade' beer and obliquely worded QR codes to buy fake ID cards. The first few students back were taking selfies, playing frisbee.

Finch parked outside Admissions. As she got out of the cruiser, she couldn't help but picture Elesheva amongst them.

The university website had told her he'd be in the Lusk Building. The basement was a featureless warren of cramped classrooms and tiny offices. Finch knocked on the door marked: *SEMIOTICS*.

'Come.'

David Schultz had gained weight and lost hair since the academy but his face spread inside her a warmth. They'd been paired up early on and, though he lacked the cutthroat determination his cop father had wished for, Finch had appreciated his smarts from the jump.

'Holy shit. Dakota Finch.'

'And look at you, *Professor*. Shaping young hearts and minds.'

'Makes the crippling mortgage so worthwhile. Come in, come in.'

Finch sat across from him and saw her friend's characteristic clutter, amid the paper towers, a small Pittsburgh Steelers flag and a photograph of a slight woman with red hair.

'You made Detective.' He glanced at the rank on her badge. 'I never doubted you.'

'Yeah, Homicide. Detroit. *Speramus Meliora.*'

'Right. Aren't we all *hoping for better*?'

They took each other in, their presence an opened time capsule.

'I'm sorry we lost touch, Dakota. My heart wasn't in the police.'

'Don't be. I'm glad you found your path.'

'That's why you're here, I'm assuming.'

'How did you know?'

'All you ever did was ask for favours. I figure leopards, spots, you know.'

'Hey, Holiday Inn, Veterans Day. We're square.'

He laughed now. 'You always were a romantic.'

Finch passed him the photograph of the star necklace in Flora's dead hand. 'I need to know what the evil eye means.'

He looked down at it, losing his smile. 'Then, I'm guessing this is about a murder. Your friend we talked about all those years ago?'

'How did you know?'

'Photo is date-stamped 1998.' He put on his glasses and peered at it again. 'This was found in the victim's hand?'

'Yeah. Undetermined origin. Low-grade materials, though.'

'Look, I know cops usually want short, punchy answers. Two plus two, and all that.'

'You're gonna tell me I gotta take your class to understand you?'

'Crash course.' He grinned. 'Let's start at the start. Sign versus symbol. What's a sign?'

'A sign is like a picture telling you to do something.'

'A sign is something that *creates meaning.*'

'But isn't that anything?'

'True, not only signs are "signs". That's why we split into two camps. Denotation and connotation. Literal and implied. So, you're on a beach and you see a shark fin sign. Denotation – *shark* – connotation – *scary, danger, death.*'

'OK. I get it. So, my evil eye is a connoting sign.'

'Not necessarily. Signs are polysemic. They're capable of having several meanings across cultural contexts. A second ago, you just said the word *get*. I'll *get* beers. You acquire. I *get* seasick. You become. I *get* your point. You understand.'

'Polysemic. Right. So, you're telling me that without knowing where the evil eye sign came from, I can't know its meaning.'

'Well, here's the thing. It's not a sign.'

'So, it's a symbol?'

'Potentially. A sign thinks for you. *No entry. Stop. Watch your step.* The information is clear and, even if we associate things with them, the sign still instructs us. We don't need a lot of prior knowledge to understand.'

'Symbols represent stuff too but they require some know-ledge or context?'

'Yes. They invite you to think for yourself. To interpret. In Asia, if I see an infinity symbol on a map, it's telling me there's a temple. Whereas here, I'd likely understand that symbol as a swastika. Interpretation, of course, depends on where we are. Which brings us to cultural codes. Why does Disney open a park in Japan and it's a huge success but then sees far less success in France using the exact same practices, symbols?'

'Because the people interpret them differently.'

'Right. Dakota, I'm telling you all this because what you're calling the evil eye might not be considered *evil* at all, depend-ing on where it's from.' He opened up a reference book and flipped through until he stopped at a black-and-white photograph of a woman with misaligned eyes. 'This woman, suffering strabismus, was believed to possess *the evil eye*.'

'What does that actually mean?'

'It's a supernatural belief going back to prehistory – the Caribbean, Balkans, Asia, Latin America, rabbinic texts. Essentially, the idea that an evil look can cause misfortune or injury.' He flipped to an image of a downturned hand with an eye in its palm. 'The Hamsa is popular in North Africa, the Middle East, providing protection against the evil eye. However, the Egyptian Eye of Horus is a symbol of protection, fortune and health. On and on it goes, through time and cultures – take your pick.'

Finch peered at the photograph of Flora's necklace. She saw an eye embossed on a star, golden rays of light radiating. *Could be anything.*

'Shit. So, this was a wasted journey.'

'No offence taken.' He stood and shuffled through the books on his shelf. 'Dakota, you asked me what the evil eye meant. But it's not the evil eye. Your eye sits within a star.'

'Great, so it's a symbol my symbols guy has never seen.'

'Actually, it's not a symbol at all. It's a company logo.' He placed a colourful kids' book before her. 'Eye within a star.'

SEEING EYE 3D MAZE BOOK

[Second Edition]

Find out why everyone is talking about our MAZES that AMAZE!

Sure enough, in the corner, the logo of the publisher was identical to the pendant in Flora's hand – the eye over the star, light radiating out. 'Holy shit.'

'Burr Publishing. 3D puzzles. It was a whole craze in the 90s.'

'Yeah,' Finch replied distantly. 'I remember.'

He glanced up at the clock. 'Listen, I gotta go.'

'Hot date with a redhead?'

'Actually, an offer to re-join Kyoto University I have to talk the hot redhead into.'

'Japan? Whoa. Well, congrats.'

'Thanks,' he grabbed his jacket. 'I'll walk you out.'

They made their way out of the Lusk Building. It was a Romanesque fairy tale of arches, red bricks and stained-glass windows. In the sunset, they painted the campus in watercolours.

'Thanks again, Dave. Was good seeing you.'

'Yeah. You too. I hope I helped.'

'You did.' She turned away, then paused. 'You know, I never could solve those 3D puzzle things.'

'A secret image, hidden inside another.' He grinned. 'Every illusion is solvable. If you know how to look at it.'

TWENTY-FOUR

Finch made the drive back from McKinstry to Nectar, her head full of symbols and curses. The mountain road was silent at this late hour. Either side, woods so dark – infinitely black – dead trees made bone-white by her headlamps.

Speedy's Mountain Truck Plaza was mostly empty tonight. At the back, the police perimeter was still in place. An NPD auxiliary guarded it, his cold breath billowing out from beneath his hat. He seemed surprised to see Finch but said nothing as he waved her through.

She went down the muddy verge and came out by the Testing Pool. A thick mist sat jealously over the pond. The scene-guard tent was wilting.

She went to the commemorative bench, where Flora's body had been found fifteen years ago. Where Finch had buried the gun *he* had given her all those years ago. The gun which, two nights ago, she had dug up for Elesheva to protect herself with.

Circling the bench, Finch held up the photograph of Flora – handbag strap around her throat, sugar granules pooling in her eyelids, her lips, and the evil eye necklace in her hand. As Finch tried to recreate the exact position, she considered the symbol.

The necklace itself had been snapped back then. Maybe it wasn't a gift from a man? Maybe Ira is right for the wrong reason. Alana Wells hasn't been seen since 1998 – because her necklace was in the hand of a dead girl. Maybe there never was a Sugar Man and it was something between friends that went wrong. The molly?

Then again, how likely is it Alana killed anyone. Much less Flora.

Finch laid down in the position her friend was found, the photo of the eye pendant in the palm of her hand.

'An image . . .' Finch whispered. 'Hidden inside another.'

Movement.

Upside down, she saw him – across the water, peering at her from the trees. The wild man. The one from the funeral, Schlanker Hans. The one watching her from across the street. The one that had tried to lead Evie away from her at Fest.

Finch got to her feet cautiously, holding up her palms. 'You don't have to run.'

A moment between them – then he bolted.

He was in the wood instantly, only foliage bobbing where he'd been standing.

Scrambling through the mud, Finch drew her gun and gave chase.

Reaching his vantage point in the trees, she snapped her head from side to side and tried to listen over her heaving breath. There was only the distant rumbling of trucks. But she saw flattened grass going off north. Heart thudding, Finch followed. In the distance, she could hear little galloping footfalls.

Nectar. Flora. Rebecca. It had all been a hall of mirrors ever since she had returned. But now she realized, this man had watched her all the way. This man was hanging out at the place where both her friends had left this world.

Is it him – the Sugar Man?

Realizing the footfalls had fallen silent, Finch froze. Hand on her gun, she stalked forwards, concentrating on her breathing. She couldn't let him double-back on her.

From up here, through gaps in the trees, Route 6 was

visible, winding back towards Nectar. Eighteen-wheelers emerged through the mountain mist like ghost trains.

Now Finch saw him. He was standing with his back to her at the top of a leaf-blanketed ridge, his visible breath ragged on the night air. *He's scared too.*

'Sir,' she called. 'Don't run. We can just talk. First, go ahead and raise your hands.'

'You think you see . . .' He complied, his voice sad. 'But you're blind, Dakota.'

'We can talk, but meantime, I need your feet placed shoulder-width apart –' She drew handcuffs from her duty belt. 'Interlock your hands behind your head, then slowly go down to your knees –'

He was running again, down the embankment, a landslide of dead leaves after him.

Swearing, Finch pursued. She slipped down a muddy drop, tumbled, but came up with her gun out in front.

He was close. Her training told her that if she ran, her aim would bounce and any shots she had to take wouldn't be worth a damn.

But Finch didn't want to shoot.

She forced small, concise but rapid steps, *heel-to-toe*, letting her knees absorb the shock but keeping her upper body steady.

He used my name . . . You think you see . . . That's what he said. I know that voice.

She had emerged from the wood into an abandoned honeymoon lodge complex. Trees grew out of the tennis court. Outer walls had fallen away, exposing graffiti-slashed suites. Heart-shaped jacuzzis had collected snow and fallen leaves.

'You got no cause to run,' she called out to the emptiness. 'I just want to talk.'

No reply. But in the snow, she saw footprints. He'd peeled off the path, downhill. Finch traced them. They led back into a dense wood.

Which bottomed out to a vast cranberry bog.

The pools were entirely flooded, vivid red. Cutting through them, a narrow wooden walkway, off into the mist.

Three hundred yards up ahead, workers were shouting, their rakes in the air. Finch saw him just as the wild man looked over his shoulder.

I know that face. Rebecca's funeral? Fest. Outside my motel. Somewhere else, too.

She raised her gun but he had already slipped back into the mist.

Gonna lose him at this rate.

Holstering her gun, she broke into a sprint.

Soon gasping for air, Finch concentrated on keeping her balance on the slimy slats. She could hear his footsteps clank in the distance. But he had disappeared in the fog.

The walkway ended, bisecting left and right along the fringes of the cranberry marsh. There were no more footsteps. Just crows cawing.

Shit, which way?

A few yards ahead, she spotted something now. On the muddy embankment across from where the bog ended, flattened grass leading up to a wire boundary fence.

Finch jumped into the water, yelping at the cold, then waded to the embankment and clambered up to the boundary fence. In its metal wire, she saw the tiniest quiver.

Hopping it, she swatted through brambles, and emerged into greyness. Mist flossed over flatland playfully. But in the centre of the expanse stood a hulking structure. It was hangar-like, with a massive ventilation system, marked: *BURR POULTRY CO.*

Finch drew her gun again and approached cautiously. The steel door clanked open in the wind. She gagged now on the smell of shit, ammonia, and rotting.

Inside, it was dark, the stench overpowering. The clucking of hens was deafening. Finch could only make out murky shapes at first. She felt for a light switch but there was nothing. Just row after row of tiered battery poultry cages, thousands of vacant eyes blinking at her. One conveyor belt carried feed right under their beaks, another one ran beneath them, carrying away shit. Automated pipes from above sprayed some kind of liquid around, the chemical stink intensifying now.

'You can't run forever . . .' she called over the noise. 'And you don't have to, either.'

He has something to hide. Murder? Gut tells me no but I've been wrong before.

Finch took a breath, trying to slow her heart, control her fear.

Ignoring sensory overload, she eased down the first row marked *INSEMINATION*. All around her, panicked wings chopping and squawking, giving her position away.

With every step, Finch checked her shoulder, cleared corners, above the cages. She stalked slowly and methodically, despite her trembling hands.

'Who are you? I know you,' she shouted over the chaos. 'I can't let you leave here without talking to me.'

A screeching blur in her blind spot.

She whirled around and batted away the hen. In that same split-second, the fist smashed into her temple. Finch fell back against the cages, her vision blurring. Now spread-eagled in the shit, she felt the gun being prized from her hand.

'I did not want this.' The wild man's deep voice was almost regretful.

'I know you . . .' Finch's consciousness spiralled.

'You are chasing the wrong man.' With a sigh, he cracked the gun over her skull.

Blevins McConnell entered the sheriff's office at 9PM, holding the printouts sent over from the Computer Forensic Unit in Lancaster. Jesse Sullivan and Mayor Cochran were in deep, hushed conversation. Two serious expressions snapped around to face him.

'Sir, this just came through from CPU Forensics.'

'Leave it on my desk.'

McConnell cleared his throat. 'All respect, I think this is important, sir.'

With a sigh, Sullivan took the papers and shuffled through. 'Why am I looking at data from a washing machine, Blevins?'

'That's the wash cycle from Salinas's home washing machine.'

Sullivan paused. '. . . I'll be damned.'

Cochran grunted. 'What is it?'

'The last wash cycle Salinas does is at 3:09AM on the thirty-first. He's washing his clothes right after the dumping window.'

The mayor snatched the papers. 'Son of a bitch.' He chuckled. 'Jesse, call a press conference. I think it's time we formally announce this arrest.'

'We should confront Salinas with this. Shall I call Finch?'

'At this point, it's safer if you do it. We never should've called for outside help.'

11PM. The spire of the Lutheran church stuck out of the winter treeline like a white needle in a basket of brown yarn. The parking lot was packed, despite the late hour. Folk had left their cars on the hill all the way up from Main Street.

The pews were heaving with concerned Nectarites. In the first row, easily accessible for the press, the assembled families of the girls that had gone missing from around the state. The Braccos were, by now, elderly. Josie Bell's parents had passed away years ago. But the Ducharme family and the Nowaks were holding hands. Edward Riddell sat next to them.

Mayor Cochran thanked the crowd for placing their faith in him once again. Then, without further ado, announced the arrest of Samuel Salinas for the murder of Rebecca Dorothea Maria Ida Frey.

Over the uproar, someone shouted: *Is he the Sugar Man?*

Mayor Cochran paused for effect. *Investigations are ongoing.*

In the same moment, Sheriff Jesse Sullivan and McConnell were heading down into the basement lock-up of Nectar PD.

It was at the rear of the building, facing the old slaughter-house. The cold air carried the smell of blood down here. As he marched down the hall, Sullivan tried not to breathe in that iron and bleach stink.

Sam Salinas was in the last cell, sitting on the edge of a plastic mattress. The cameras were on. McConnell waited outside. Sullivan entered.

'Bad news, Sam.' The sheriff pursed his lips. 'Mayor won another term.'

'What a shock.'

Sullivan chuckled. 'Listen, Sam. We can call your lawyer. But it's late. I figure maybe we could just have a word amongst ourselves.'

'I told you. I got nothing left to say. We'll see it out in court.'

'I haven't come down here to make life difficult for you. The opposite. I've come here to give you a chance.'

'Right. You're so worried about saving my soul.'

'I won't BS you, Sam. You're in a bad spot. No denying that. But it doesn't mean you can't make things better than they are.'

'How?'

'I know it's not easy to admit a thing like this –'

'Get out of here, Jesse. You're wasting your time.'

'– I know it's not easy, I seen that all my career, Sam. But I swear to you, if you give me honesty here, I'll walk with you every step of the way and ensure you get fairness – that you are recognized for your courage.'

'Fairness?' He smiled wryly. 'You'll be my personal saviour, huh.'

'I can't promise anything concrete. But we can take certain things off the table.'

'Things? Like what? Potassium chloride?'

'I'm making you an *offer* here, Sam. Not talking miracles. Confession is all there is.'

'You want me to admit killing the colony girl and you'll give me, what? The chance of parole in the year 3000?'

'The colony girl. And we'll need to talk about Flora Riddell. Potentially think about the other abductions around Catoonah, maybe beyond.'

'Jesus Christ, are you for real?'

'I'm as real as it gets, my friend.'

'Yeah? Cos all I've heard you got against me is turning off my ELD. My attorney says that ain't enough for even losing my job.'

Sullivan sat next to Salinas on the bed now. '3:09AM on the thirty-first.'

'What?'

'You washed your clothes at 3:09AM. That's just after the body was dumped, Sam. There are female hairs found in your truck which I know will match up to the victim. We got witnesses left and right talking about your behaviours, your suspicious movements. And when the results from the blood under the nails of the girl come back, you're down the creek, amigo.

Now, they're due any moment. It would look good for you if you were willing to man up here before the definitive proof arrived. Juries look favourably on that kind of thing. So, you heard my offer, Sam. No more talking from me.'

Salinas looked up at the sheriff with defeated eyes, his voice small. 'I need to know something . . .'

'Whatever you need.' Sullivan licked his lips.

'You won't ever give up, will you?'

'In proving your guilt? Sam, I know you did these murders. I know it like I know the face of my own mother. I will follow you through the apocalypse to put you down. But you get to decide how it ends.'

'What about my wife?'

'You're not stupid. You know we can be soft on her. Or we can make life hell for her. Your son. Me personally? I'd prefer them not to get caught up in all this.'

The accused man closed his eyes. '. . . All right.'

'All right.'

'No choice, huh?'

'No choice, pal.'

Now he was standing. The sheriff went for his gun but too late. Salinas smashed him face-first into the wall with sickening force. Sullivan heard a pop from his nose and now his gun was pressed to his own temple.

'Zzsam –' Sullivan gagged on the taste of his own blood. 'This dun' help you –'

'Shut the fuck up.' Salinas pistol-whipped him, then bellowed, 'Door. Open. Now.'

The door buzzed open and he nudged Sullivan out, holding him close, gun fixed to his skull. An alarm began to wail, boots thundering down stairs. In just a few seconds, a swarm of beetle-blue flooded the lock-up, the guns of every patrolman in Nectar PD trained on the body of Sam Salinas.

'I've got nothing to lose. I see that now.' He spoke calmly. 'Jesse does.'

Come on, Sam. There's no way out of this.

'Yeah, there is. My way. Or me and Jesse buy the farm.'

Nobody's talking about that, Sam. Easy, now.

'I'm fucking talking about that. Now. Drop. The. Guns.'

Sullivan's eyes were rolling back in his head, his nose break was bad. The patrolmen looked at one another. Panic pin-balled around the room. Who had command here?

'I won't ask again.'

Hold on, Sam. You know we can't do that.

'Then you made your choice. See you in hell, Jesse.'

A deafening crack.

The patrolmen hit the floor.

The bullet breached the skull of Sam Salinas. His body spasmed, then he collapsed. Behind him stood Blevins Mc-Connell, his face wet from the fine pink mist of brain tissue.

2008

Dakota Finch sat in her Detroit PD cruiser. She observed the nocturnal rhythms of the city, waiting for the radio to crackle – a lioness, still in the bush. Yesterday, an insurance broker had snapped and driven into the river. Recovery workers on tugboats were shouting, a helicopter circled above.

Finch closed her eyes. The noise morphed into the shouts of the protestors in her memory. Ten years had passed. She'd lost her best friend. The only person she'd ever really loved. In that nightmare-fever of interrogations and guilt that followed, all she could do was disassociate. And so *this* was the moment she went back to instead. The clinic. Always.

She didn't want to go.

But like squeezing a bruise until it hurt because it felt good, her mind always returned to that day.

The clinic was on the outskirts of the city, between a pet hospital and a pizza parlour. The devout were on their knees outside, praying, chanting slogans about life and hell. The second they saw Dakota, they had encircled her, smiling as one, unblinking.

We've come here to help you, Mom. Don't take away the gift of life, Mom. A human child is not a choice, Mom.

One of them placed a brownie in her hand, the chocolate sweating in its plastic. *Here, eat this. You need to keep up your energy.* Dakota dropped it and ran for the clinic.

After an hour filling out forms and listening to a

county-mandated counsellor trying to talk her out of it, Dakota had been laid down on a medical bed.

She remembered the crinkle of the tissue roll beneath her and listening to the distant clamour of protestors outside. The medical trolley squeaked as it was pushed towards her.

Did they offer you a brownie on your way in, Dakota? But you didn't eat it, did you? It's very important that you didn't. That's how they get you. You eat, you can't have the anaesthesia. But you're gonna be OK, hon. In five minutes, you'll be done.

The IV made Dakota sleepy but she stayed awake.

As she felt the numbing agent spread through her cervix, she looked at a colourful diagram of the uterus on the pale green wall. Next to it, a framed poster of a sunrise read: *you deserve to choose your own future.*

After an hour, it was done.

As he wouldn't come into the clinic, a kind Guatemalan receptionist led Dakota from the recovery room out to his car. He said nothing, he just started the engine, and kept his eyes on the road. The clinic had been picked for its distance from Nectar.

They stopped at a motel in Niagara. He had promised to look after her but ended up spending most of the night in the casino.

The drive back the next day was long and slow, with frequent stops for her to clean up. When they finally reached Nectar, she got out of his car. He drove away without saying anything, knowing he could count on her silence.

After Flora's burial, Dakota died inside. She drifted from class to class, the rumours washing over her. At some point, she just walked out on her own life. Jumped in the first truck that came along. Ended up in Detroit, breaking into Bill Moreno's basement.

He found her three hours later, face-down, surrounded by pills and vomit.

Bill drove her to the hospital, where her stomach was pumped.

In the next days, he came to sit with her whenever off-duty. He brought puzzle books, crosswords, having noticed she had a knack for problem-solving.

After her release, Romina Moreno tried to talk to her about Jesus, about salvation. Dakota wasn't interested.

But she did appreciate their warmth. She started travelling back and forth between Nectar and Detroit.

In the mandated therapy sessions, she had nothing to say. Still, the Visprozan helped.

And then, one day, as Bill ignored his dinner, Dakota happened to ask what was bothering him. He had motioned to a casefile. *Mitchell Enlow – a landscaper whose wife just shot herself in the garden out of the blue.*

That night, with nothing else to do, Dakota took the casefile down to the basement and started reading. In the morning, she made phone calls. By sundown, she walked across the city, and straight into Bill Moreno's police department.

Ignoring the looks from other officers, she placed on his desk copies of the insurance policy taken out on Mrs Enlow.

The husband's testimony is that he didn't touch the body, right? Come on, Bill. Childhood sweethearts, mother of his child, but he doesn't check for a pulse? Makes no sense. So, I started digging. Turns out, insurers don't typically pay out for suicide until two years have passed. Big surprise, check the dates. Mrs Enlow's policy was coming up on its second birthday.

A slow grin spread across Moreno's face, wide as the Nile. *One of these days, Dakota Melody Finch, you'll be sitting where I am now.*

Mitchell Enlow was arrested for murder a few days later. Shortly after that, Dakota joined the Detroit PD Reserve Corps.

That same day, she decided. *No more tears. Only anger. Only the Sugar Man.*

309

TWENTY-FIVE

The clinic again. The crinkle of the tissue-roll beneath her on the bed. No, not the clinic. The Testing Pool. Not tissue-roll, the sad blue tarp of the police tent. High above, Tim Burr was grinning down. Silently screaming, Dakota floated towards the tent, unable to stop herself.

Inside, the riven body of Elesheva Frey, pale and broken, a handbag strap cutting into her throat. Her glassy, dead eyes rolled to meet Dakota's. Then her bloody mouth flapped open: *Thou art my friend now?*

Finch woke in a blue room. It took her a moment to understand where she was. Then she saw the scan of a brain on the TV screen in front of her. An intravenous stand. A privacy curtain hanging open. The clipboard at the foot of her bed read: *Olmstead G. Holmes General.*

Finch sat up, a wave of agony washed over her. It felt like fingers had wrapped around her brain and with every tiny movement they squeezed. But her head had been bandaged up at some point.

Groaning, Finch remembered now. The man. The chase. The hens.

I backed him into a corner. No witnesses. He could've killed me but he didn't. Why?

A knock and Jesse Sullivan entered. 'Impressive hole in your head, Detective.' He sat across from her, his nose taped up, his eye turning purple. 'Sorry, I didn't bring flowers.'

'For the best,' she croaked. 'People would start talking.'

He laughed. 'How are you feeling?'

'Wunderbar. How long have I been out?'

'About twelve hours. You're lucky you're still with us. The hell happened?'

'Saw a man snooping at the crime scene. I gave chase but he got the drop on me.'

'The cranberry workers gave a pretty clear description of him.'

'Yeah, I'm almost definite it was Roadkill Ray.'

'Thought so. Well, I've got an APB out. Most of our resources are still on Salinas but a couple of auxiliary guys are searching abandoned buildings for him. I'll let you know.'

'He could've killed me but he didn't. I think he's just scared, Jesse.'

'Scared? Look at your head. Can't have him running around. He's dangerous.'

'Speaking of, what happened to *you*?'

'That's why I came here, Dakota. Salinas is dead. I thought you should know.'

Through her pain, her numbness, Finch felt an immediate, deep disquiet. '. . . Dead?'

'He got loose during questioning last night. Suicide by cop, more or less.'

'How?'

'He made like he was gonna confess. I took my eye off the ball. Blevins managed to put him down.'

Finch said nothing. Despite herself, she had trusted Sullivan almost immediately. Yet this didn't sit right.

'Still.' His voice brightened. 'If there's one silver lining – you get to go home.'

She felt the strange urge to reply she already was home. 'He was going to confess?'

'Yeah.' Sullivan licked his lips.

'He said that?'

'I offered him a deal. No death penalty for the truth about Rebecca and Flora. He started saying *all right*. Next thing I know, he's got my gun and all hell breaks loose.'

Finch grunted. 'Maybe him saying *all right* meant you gave him no choice.'

In that moment, the door burst open. Cochran marched in – firecracker-red. 'I gotta hand it to you, Finch. You really know how to rain on a parade, huh?'

'I'm feeling much better. Thanks for your concern.'

'No, no. No more cuteness from you, girl. I've got a judge pissed off for wasting his time over the shit-thin warrant request for Jubilance Whatever-the-hell. I've got a missing Flora Riddell casefile and no prizes for guessing where that went. I've got cranberry waders saying they feared for their lives when you pulled a gun. I've got the Burr Group purging two hundred thousand dollars in bird stock due to possible infection, legal action obviously on the table. And the goddamn cherry on top in all of this? Your little stunt made the farming news.'

'Oh no. The *farming news*?'

'Always a smartass, even now.'

'Quayle, I gave pursuit of a male acting suspiciously at a live crime scene. The goddamn Burr Group have insurance and you can bitch about my work, but at least my suspect is still drawing breath.'

Cochran shrugged. 'Son of a bitch Salinas saved everyone a lot of time and money.'

'Right. And now your election is won, and he can't protest his innocence anymore.'

'I'm sick of your insinuations, Finch. Salinas was guilty. If he wasn't, tell it to the historians. Either way, the people of Nectar know the shoe fits. But don't act like you cared about the *case*. You're not a detective. You're a goddamned narcissist. Now this is closed. And you are on the next plane out of here.'

Finch packed her bag at the motel, paid up, then made the short drive to the airport. In the terminal building, which amounted to a few chairs and a vending machine, she paced – as if movement might somehow quell the frustration inside her.

In the cold light of day, the evidence against Salinas was thin. Finch had seen that from the second she'd stepped inside the interrogation room.

It was possible, of course, that she was wrong and that he was Rebecca's murderer. There was plenty not to like about him and, clearly, he was lying about *something*.

But the trip to McKinstry had given Finch one certainty. If Salinas was the one that murdered Rebecca, he almost certainly wasn't responsible for Flora.

Symbols, hidden meanings, magic eye puzzles – no way he had any interest in all of that. But now he's dead and the Rebecca Frey case is closed.

Or cold.

Same difference in this goddamned town.

Looking out across the runway, the billboard was still making promises about the election it had already lost: *Tired of bad eggs? Vote for Change – Melvin Neeley.*

'A dead end inside a dead end . . .' she muttered to herself.

Her gut told her Salinas hadn't killed Rebecca. Much less Flora. And whoever had was still out there, slurping clam chowder. Or maybe inside Versammlung, holding his hands up to God, under the soft rip-rip of the honeybees.

But Finch's body was broken, her brain sautéed in benzos, and she wanted to go home. *I did everything I could.*

At 4PM, a Cessna Grand Caravan 208 landed. The co-pilot checked off passenger names from his manifest, asked everyone's weight, then assigned seats accordingly.

Finch was last on. She looked out of the window as the plane began to taxi. The co-pilot shouted over the throttle.

We have three emergency exits: two at the front, one at the back. You'll find safety cards in your seat-backs. Fire extinguisher is to the left of the captain. In the event of a fire, please grab it, pull the pin, aim at the base of the fire, squeeze and sweep . . .

From here, Finch could see the lights of Fest twinkling. The end-of-season dance was coming up. Fest Queen 2013 would be chosen tonight.

Closing her eyes, Finch was back on that little dock, the cold of Lake Sweetness at her back. Her best friend was looking up at her desperately.

Look, tonight is gonna be . . . a different crowd.

I don't care. I can be cool. It's just a fuckin' party, right?

Finch's cell phone buzzed now. It was Hanlon Hopkin.

She ended the call and typed out a text message saying she was on a plane.

His reply came through immediately: *Spoke to my friend at the lab and the hairs found in the suspect's truck look to be a match for Rebecca Frey. The bad news: DNA results from under her fingernails came back. No match with Samuel Salinas.*

Stomach lurching, Finch immediately undid her seatbelt and held up her police badge. 'Stop the plane.'

On the humble fringes of Nectar, Carmella Salinas was shunting bags into the trunk of her car. Gone was the blonde hair, the butterfly clips, the smile. Now, Finch saw only pain and Celexa. Maybe Zoloft.

'Carmella,' she called. 'I was hoping to speak with you a minute.'

'You got some goddamn nerve.' She strapped her son into the backseat.

'I'm so sorry about Sam.'

Carmella shook her head. 'Quayle always hated him. But you?'

'Listen, last night had nothing to do with me. And what's more, I think there's a good chance he wasn't guilty of what they're saying.'

Carmella put her bags down to search her eyes. 'What do you want?'

'I just want to find out the truth.'

She curled her hair behind her ear. 'OK. Two minutes.'

'I know you answered this with Sullivan. But night of the thirtieth. Where was Sam?'

'Me and Sam are done. Have been for a while. I'm back with my parents in Kane.'

'You saw each other that day?'

'Yeah. I brought Noah over, we had lunch together. He had to work that night but Noah was sleepy so we just stayed here. Sam got home late, I remember that. The next morning, we argued. Then I left. Look, I'm only back here now for my stuff.'

'What did you argue about?'

'Same reason as always. His brain's too small, balls too big. I don't even care no more. What pissed me off is that he couldn't go one night without it. He lied, of course. Said he wasn't with anyone. He's a good father, he loves Noah. But I just won't have him growing up around a man like that . . . I guess now he won't.'

'When you argued, how did Sam seem?'

'Angry.' Carmella blew her bangs out of her face. 'How do people argue?'

'Did you notice any cuts on him? Scratches? Anything like that?'

'No. No blood on him either. Washing his clothes in the middle of the night would've been enough to know he was out with some little slut. But I could just see it in his eyes.'

'Down the years, did he ever say anything about Flora Riddell? The investigation?'

'No. Look, he used to beat me. But he got counselling. That stopped long ago.'

Finch moved closer, lowering her voice. 'Carmella, do you think he's capable of murder?'

'Listen, tell you the truth? I don't care. But I'll be back here with lawyers for wrongful death. Even if he was a fuck-up, this goddamn town took Noah's daddy away. Least it can do is put him through college.'

She took one last look at the house. Then she got in the car and drove away.

Finch went back to the cruiser, dialled the number for Nectar PD, and identified herself to Glennis.

Who shall I patch you through to, hon?

'Actually, I need you to check something. Sam Salinas. Did he make any calls from inside Nectar PD?'

Let me look at that for you, one sec . . . OK, yeah. He made a call to – huh, that's weird.

'What is it?'

He called the mayor's home phone.

'Glennis, you sure?'

Positive. But it didn't go through. Cut off the same minute he dialled. Only, then we received an incoming straight after from an unregistered Pennsylvania cell.

It clicked. Now Finch understood.

Darkfall. Finch pulled in at the Kwik Pump gas station and got out of her car. She approached the black Escalade, checking over her shoulder. A neon sign from the gas station window blinked at her:

THANK YOU FOR SUPPORTING THE LITTLE GUY

'Strawberry Wine' was playing low in the car, the pilot light off. Chastity Cochran kept her pink eyes dead ahead, hands on the wheel, like she'd drive off the second the conversation took a turn she didn't like.

'How did you know?' she sniffled, her voice thick.

Finch shrugged. 'It wasn't hard. You work where Sam drinks, for starters. Then, there's the way you looked at him. Plus, you fit the female figure I saw him with the other night. But the jail phone records just confirmed it. He called your home phone, Chastity. Who else would he want to talk to in that household?'

They were silent for a while. On the radio, Deana Carter was still singing about drifting away from her lover like leaves in the fall.

'I still can't believe he's gone . . . Like a dream I'm waiting to wake up from.'

'You'll wake up, kid. Soon enough. Only not the way you think.'

Chastity fixed her with a pissed-off side glance. 'You haven't told my dad about Sam so you must want something from me.'

'Just an answer. I already know he lied about everything to protect his affair with you – he knew Cochran would destroy him. He was with you on the night of the murder, wasn't he? That's why he washed his clothes. Sam had nothing to do with Rebecca's death.'

'He's a good man. He never hurt anyone.'

'Except for you.'

'We played rough but he would never hurt me for real.'

'What about the black eyes on Carmella down the years? His other girlfriends?'

'People talk shit but he's not like that. We loved each other.'

'You're old enough for it to feel real. But one day you'll realize you were just a kid.'

'I'm young, I get it. But I know what I know. And we had something real.'

'I don't care. Now, why did your dad have it in for Sam so badly? Carmella?'

Chastity laughed. 'Maybe it had something to do with that frump *once* upon a time.'

'Why, then? Tell me.'

'We talked a lot about leaving Nectar but Sam went back and forth. One day it was: *you're my girl, I want babies with you.* The next, it would be: *leave my old ass, go to school.*'

'Go on.'

'OK.' A shaky sigh. 'Sam has a lot of debt. He talked about it non-stop. *I'm busting my ass every day, while men like your father sit on their asses and rake it in.* So, one day, I got sick of it and just blurted it out. Said I knew a way we could get some money from him.'

'. . . You were blackmailing your father. With what?'

'He has a deal in place with the colonists. Mutually beneficial type thing.'

The ballot boxes I saw in Versammlung.

'Holy shit . . . Cochran buys their votes. *That's* how he pulled off the upset. But what's in it for Versammlung?'

'Something to do with their produce prices. He keeps them fixed in their favour –'

'– In exchange for enough votes to swing the mayoral

election. When Sam found out, he wanted cash in exchange for his silence. Goddamn it.' Finch opened the car door.

'Wait.'

'What is it?'

'I'm pregnant.'

'Shit,' Finch exhaled. '. . . You're sure?'

The girl nodded, then started to cry. 'I can't do this alone. What do I do?'

'Shit, I don't know, Chastity. You'll regret your choice either way. That's what life is. Picking an amount of regret that you can live with and then years of thinking you made the wrong call.'

TWENTY-SIX

Fest was in its final-night frenzy, a swarm of black pilgrim hats and novelty *Kappen*. Diesel was thick on the air, carousels spinning, rollercoaster cars rattling over tracks. 'Gangnam Style' was competing with the Schuhplattler dancers on the pavilion stage.

Above it, the banner read:

★ CONGRATULATIONS MAYOR COCHRAN ★

The dancers took their final bow and trotted off the stage. Now a campaign lackey was at the microphone, testing it out for the speech to come. Red, white and blue balloons were in a net above, ready to drop.

Finch made her way behind the pavilion where there was a small portacabin. Inside, Cochran was sitting at a desk, tapping his fountain pen on his lip, looking up at the gold crucifix on the wall.

Seeing her, he shook his head. 'I thought I made myself clear, Finch –'

'– Who planted the hairs in Sam's truck? I'm assuming it was Jesse.'

'What are you talking about?'

'Drop the act, Quayle. I talked to Hanlon. The hairs in that truck match Rebecca Frey. But the blood and skin under her fingernails don't match Sam Salinas.'

'Maybe he didn't attack her alone,' he spluttered. 'Or maybe she struggled with someone else before running into Salinas, who killed her.'

'Horse shit. I've just come from someone who would testify that she was with him at the time of the murders. Salinas was innocent and you know it.'

'Now, hold on a goddamned sec –'

'No, I see this for what it is. I know Salinas was blackmailing you. I know about your cosy little deal with Versammlung and their postal votes. If I had been listening, I would've heard you say it: *you don't get far without the Evangelical vote*. You needed Salinas handled but you also needed some separation. *That's* why you asked for outside help. Make it look like he had been arrested naturally. But all this underhand shit, just to win, Quayle?'

With a resigned sigh, Cochran glanced up at the crucifix on the wall. 'You never cared about this place, you couldn't understand.'

'I understand why Versammlung do this, they need to survive. But you? You'd betray everything you stand for just to win an election in a nothing town? By framing Salinas, the real killer stays free.'

'I thought he was the killer.'

'No. You *wanted* him to be the killer so you took the chance. And now a murderer gets a pass. And for what?'

'It wasn't just an election. Melv Neeley's campaign was just a few chimps on typewriters. But all the polls had me losing. He's a self-made man, standing up to the big companies. People trust him around here. People are dumb. He wanted to sell our Fest rights and we'd lose Burr Group forever. A whole generation of downturn just to make a point.'

'It's their right to be dumb, Quayle. You ought to be in cuffs.'

'That's why you're here, then?'

'I'm here to make a trade. You re-open the Rebecca Frey case. It belongs to me. I run it how I want or your little voting deal ends up at every news outlet on the Eastern Seaboard.'

Quayle Cochran blanched. 'You're going back into Versammlung.'

'Damn right I am. Jubilance Weaver has motive. And a whole lot of stink about him. So, get your judge to pull his pen out his ass right now because I want that court order.'

Finch held his eyes until the desk phone rang.

It was Jesse Sullivan. Cochran hit the speakerphone button.

Mayor? I'm down at the Testing Pool, disbanding the search teams like you asked.

Cochran pressed the button. 'I'm here with Finch. Go on.'

Finch? But I thought she —

'Just go ahead, I'm listening.'

It's the dive team, sir. They've found something. We have a situation.

'What do you mean?'

A body, sir. I think they've recovered a body.

In the nightmare, Elesheva Frey had been kneeling before the Versammlungsbaum, her hands clenched in prayer. Her sister was next to her whispering, *Fear thou not; for I am with thee. So sayeth the Lord.* But when she turned, Rebecca was not there.

Instead, a mound of pink tobacco petals. Jubilance Weaver's voice whispered to her now: *God as my witness, I never hurt her.*

She lurched awake with a shout. Her mouth was sore, like someone had stuffed their fingers down her throat while she slept. Heart still pounding, Elesheva got out of bed, not bothering to put on her sleeping *Kappe*.

She looked at her *Schriften* on the bedside table. She knew the verse her dead dream-sister had recited. It was not far from the one where she had hidden Englisch money.

But Elesheva had not opened the book in many moons now. She no longer believed that the Lord was with her.

She went to Rebecca's bed. But her sister's smell no longer clung to her sheets.

Elesheva descended the old walnut stairs, built generations ago by her kin. She had never met them but she knew that they had all lived the same way, held the same beliefs. Something about that made her feel sad. They had lived and died and never tasted a peach-choco sundae. Or heard Stevie Nicks. Or felt speed in an Englisch carriage on a smooth road.

But then those that had never tasted honey would never crave its sweetness. Perhaps it was not them *the Lord had cursed with curiosity. With doubt.*

She sat at the kitchen table and watched her chilly breath unfurl in the gloom. Starshine poured through the crack in the curtains, jars gleaming – jams, honeys, sweetened pears. The whole house creaked, a wooden ship sailing on a soft night current.

Elesheva could not stop thinking about what the man at the fair had said to her. *You are being lied to. When you are ready for the truth, seek me out.*

That could not have been coincidence. She did not recognize the man and yet he spoke her language fluently. Dakota Finch had implored her not to trust people. Especially men. And she was the closest thing to a friend Elesheva had ever known. Yet that man's eyes had held hers earnestly. And perhaps *he* knew where the serpent that had taken her sister hid.

Elesheva walked through the darkness, following Route 6. Each time a car approached, she slipped into the bush to stay unseen. The mud there was half-frozen, shining like glass in the moonlight.

In Dakota's car, the Englisch world had seemed only a few minutes away from Versammlung but it had taken her more than an hour until the lake came into view. Tonight, it was a peaceful cobalt. With no mist, she could see Fest twinkling in the distance, the warm glow of Nectar not far away.

It was some time after midnight when she reached the abandoned Nectar Honeymoon Lodge. Swimming pools once shaped as wedding bells now resembled dark blisters. The land here had been reclaimed by the woods. Through the tree gaps, cranberry bogs glinted below.

Elesheva stopped to get her breath back. Cold sweat ran down her back and her stomach growled. Her faceless doll looked up at her without eyes. *The strange man said he was your friend. What will you do if he is not where he said he would be?*

Hoping she had not misunderstood his directions, she entered the main building. The reception had been turned into a fire pit. Vending machines stood gutted. Wallpaper curled.

'Hello?'

Cobwebs shivered in the cold. She smelled dust and pigeon shit. Every step triggered echoes. Rainwater chortled through a large hole in the roof.

There was no life here.

Elesheva turned back, cursing her choice, when she heard a distant cough.

She followed the sound, through the door marked BOILER ROOM, and down several flights of stairs.

The flicker of candlelight across the wall beckoned her in. And there, in a basement den, she saw a man curled up in a makeshift bed.

He was bony, a tangle of long black hair down to the shoulders, beard past his chest. On the floor by his cot, Elesheva recognized Dakota's gun. She fumbled out her own weapon now but kept it at her side.

'*Do not make any sudden movements.*' She spoke in her own language, hardening her voice to sound older. '*You told me to come when I was ready for the truth.*'

The bony man rolled over to face her, a little smile beneath his beard. '*I promised you the truth . . .*' His cheekbones sank back. '*But it is a hard truth.*'

'*I'm ready.*'

1AM. The cruiser was moving at speed, sirens wailing. The turret lights washed blue the eskers of snow either side of the road. Finch cut through the dead industrial quarter.

A community news bulletin was blank, telling the truth. Weeds loomed out of lots. Buildings of spalling brick were once hardware stores here, pharmacies, five-and-tens. Now only a freight train passing through could be heard, honking laughter.

Her Visprozan should've kicked in by now. Or if it had, she hadn't noticed. Bad sign.

Finch parked at Speedy's, the search teams there all but packed up. Mobile lamps were being dissembled. Tracker dogs were barking from one of the out-of-state police trucks.

Getting out of the cruiser, she crossed the lot, her numb brain fumbling for answers. *A body in the Testing Pool. What goddamned body?*

At the fence, the sound was clear – a hydraulic hum.

We know what happened to Flora. Whatever happened to Alana Wells? Just disappeared one day, nobody knew a thing.

Finch's stomach dropped.

He strangled Flora here. But was Alana's body in the Testing Pool all along?

Down the muddy verge, through the sad wood, and now

the water before her. The divers were packing their equipment away. Beyond them, a recovery crew. The winch had already pulled the car out of the lake.

It was dangling there, just above the surface, helpless as a newborn.

The brown body was coated in zebra mussels, its wheels twisted, its windshield cloaked in a silty mud.

The car spun.

And behind the wheel, a human skeleton.

With no eyes, it looked at Finch.

With no face to hide it, a human skull smiled forever.

TWENTY-SEVEN

Down in the boiler room of the abandoned hotel, the bony man set about making a fire in some breeze blocks. Despite the shivering and coughing, there was a peaceful smile on his bony face.

'*This should warm thee soon.*'

'*I'm fine,*' Elesheva said. '*Thou art the one that seems fevered.*'

He shrugged. '"*Tis but a chill.*'

Gun still in her lap, the girl looked around his little den. She saw a buck skull fixed to the wall. A bed of foam and rags. A crucifix above it made out of driftwood. And towers of books everywhere. It was clear he had been here for a long time.

'*I know thy face from somewhere, sir. Who art thou?*'

'*I hath had many names.*' A wry smile. '*But I was Elijah Weaver once, son of Tobias. Known as Eli Black.*'

'*Then, Ichabod is thy older brother. I see the familiarity now, except for thy hair.*'

'*He is kin no more.*' From a decanter, Eli filled two cups. '*Whiskey. For the cold.*'

'*Thank you.*' The taste was crooked but the warmth was welcome. '*Thou art the one that watches us distantly, art thou not? Schlanker Hans?*'

'*There are a few of us lurking in those woods. Or were. I hath not seen a fellow exile in several winters.*'

'*There is more than one?*'

'*Yes, I am not the only sinner. We are but sad wretches pining for the past.*'

'*But why watch?*'

'*Habit, perhaps. A spirit haunting its old homestead.*'

Elesheva observed the man over the rim of her cup. '*Thy strength is the stuff of child's tale, Eli Black. The finest hunter in all of Versammlung, until thou wast torn apart by boars, of course.*'

'*As thou canst see, I am no Samson now. And it was but one goring.*'

'*Why wast thou exiled?*'

He shook his head. '*Thou art so much like thy mother.*'

'*You knew Joanna Frey?*'

'*'Twas not my meaning.*' He stoked the fire, seeming to regret his words. '*Forgive my rambling. Long hath I been alone.*'

'*Alone but free.*'

'*Be that what thou seeketh out here?*'

She shrugged. '*Oft did my sister speak of the outside. Secretly, I didst long to look upon it. To taste it. To travel it. Sometimes, I wouldst look up and see their planes in the sky. Even as a small child, I did not believe Luzifer would make such things only to confound us. That they were made by people ignorant of Versammlung, for it was their world, not ours.*'

'*Truly, it is filled with wonders. But it is no place for our kind.*'

'*Yet never did I feel as our kind.*' The girl plucked a twig from the fire and snapped it. '*And thou didst elude my question. Why wast thou exiled?*'

'*Aye, I promised thee the truth.*' Eli Black sighed. '*And my exile is woven into thy reason for being here. Seeds planted long afore thy birth.*'

'*Thou knoweth my sister.*'

'*Many winters ago, I tendered out here at the Englisch festival with Rebecca and Piety Schröder.*'

'*Yes. I know of this.*'

'*She was promised to him. But later accused of knowing a man outside of that bond.*'

'*I hath heard that jangling too. And she became pregnant with this other man.*'

'Yes.' He seemed surprised by her knowing. '*We were chosen for having the greatest Englisch tongue. My knowing was nowhere near as complete as Rebecca's or Piety's but the Council bade me watch over them, to keep them from devilry out here. And that was my intention. To protect her.*'

'*. . . But thou didst become soft on her.*'

'*And she to me. In that winter, we led each other through darkness. Shared pains and hopes, understood each other. We spoke of marriage, knowing it would never be blessed . . .*'

'*For she was already promised. Yet she broke that promise to lie with thee.*'

'*No.*' He nested the new-born fire in his hands, his face half in shadow now. '*Elesheva, the truth is that thy sister was violated.*'

Immediately, the girl stood, her chest heaving. '*You lie.*'

'*I am sorry but it is the truth. A truth that was buried.*'

She shook her already spinning head. '*That cannot be.*'

'*I wish it were not.*'

Elesheva closed her eyes and saw her sister in memory – laughing, scolding, planting a kiss upon her crown – Rebecca in fragments, a broken mirror of love.

She knew it was true. The pain in her heart was deep. So deep she wanted to burrow into the earth as an insect. '*Why?*' Her voice a trembling whisper now. '*Why was it buried?*'

'*Because her life in Versammlung would have been over. She was terrified. And so, a story was agreed upon. To protect her. To protect you.*'

'*And in turn, it protected the man that violated her,*' she spat. '*Who was he, Eli?*'

'*The Council also demanded a name from her.*' Regret rippling across his cheeks, he went to the slat window and stood in a jagged shard of moonlight. '*But she would never tell them. Or me. She never spoke that man's name.*'

'*So, thou didst take the blame for her pregnancy to hide the truth of her violation. This is the reason for thy exile.*'

'*I kept watch over Rebecca as best I could. From a distance. Loving her shadow.*'

'*What of the child?*'

'*The baby joined the Lord at birth. After that, Rebecca fell silent for a long time. For several years we did not see each other.*'

The girl looked into the fire, tears falling on her gun. '*Always, I felt my sister was . . . missing something. Now, I understand.*'

'*I know it was a heavy burden for her to carry.*'

'*But why did she not run away? Live with thee out here? She was already damned, why not be free, at least?*'

'*Because of* thee, *Elesheva. She loved thee more than anything. Of that, I am certain.*'

The girl's face screwed up in pain. He went to her, hands outstretched. In that moment, that movement, she realized that nobody knew where she was, alone with a man nobody knew. Something clicked. A memory – Dakota's words.

'*How?*' She raised the gun. '*How couldst thou know all this?*'
Eli froze. '*Know what?*'

'*Of her love for me. Thou wast exiled afore my birth.*'

'*Because she slipped out to visit me oft. Our love never dwindled. And always, she would speak of thee.*'

'*And when –*' She flicked off the safety as she was taught. '*– did you last see her?*'

'*The night afore her death.*' He took a step back.

'*And how do I know –*' She was aiming at his heart. '*That thou speaketh the truth? That thou are not the serpent that took her from me?*'

'*Lips lie.*' He took a deep breath. '*The heart does not. What dost thine sayeth?*'

The girl dug deep into his eyes. In them, she saw love. Pain. Solitude. But no fear. No secrets. '*That you loved her.*'

'*All my days.*'

She flicked the safety back on. '*I need the full truth now from you, Eli.*'

'*I will speak only truth to thee. That is why I bade thee come here.*'

'*I see now why she left Versammlung. It was to be with you. But lately, she spoke in passing of a task. Something that she had to take care of.*'

'*Aye. She told me, too. But would not say what. I have thought of it much in these last few days.*'

'*In what place didst the violation occur?*'

'*The Council would know. I never did.*'

'*Do you think her task is related to this?*'

'*I know not.*' He sat back down at the fire. '*She mentioned it several times but when I asked, she did not want to discuss it – only saying, once it was done, she would be happier.*'

Elesheva stood and went to the corner of the room.

Her chest tightened and the tears came, indignant sobs of helpless pain. She could not take her mind's eye from that broken mirror of Rebecca.

But then, without her choosing, the sobs evened out into one guttural cry. As when bees change pitch before attacking, her cry became a scream. She embraced the fury in her heart, cauterizing pain with vengeance.

'*Goodbye, Eli Black.*'

'*Thou wouldst return to Versammlung?*'

'*Aye, I wilt uncover him. Or give my last drop of blood in trying.*'

Finch drove across the Catoonah Mountains through the night. She needed sleep, her body was a wreck, but she couldn't just wait around for the morning plane.

Four hours later, she reached the Detroit Police Vehicle Impound. It was off Plum, not far from where she'd pulled over Ivan Maloney a little over a week ago. Back when the idea of the Sugar Man was still just a bad memory. And Rebecca Frey was still breathing.

She bought herself a terrible vending-machine coffee and greeted the one or two familiar faces still around at this time of night.

In vehicular forensics, she saw a technician poring over some papers. She held up her ID and he nodded.

'You're here for the Mercury Sable?'

'That's right. What have we got?'

'She's a '95.' He shrugged. 'Or was. Except for the water degradation, no major external damage on her beyond some light impact crumple around the bumper. Low-rise, consistent with a barrier.'

'Any fingerprints in there?'

'No prints or immediately apparent forensic evidence but given how long she was submerged, no shock there. Last time she pings anywhere was a speeding ticket late 1997, McKean County. She was registered to one Lester Lael Lamb. Any of that make sense?'

'Yeah. He was reported missing just after that. Ran a Pentecostal group in Nectar.'

'Well, that explains the trunk contents.'

He pointed to the steel table. On it, there were pamphlets relating to the inerrancy of the Bible. Christian early-learning books. And various stinking bags of donated clothes.

Finch snapped on a nitrile glove and carefully searched through the mound of objects but found nothing of note.

'Where is the car?'

'In the controlled room. It's not perfect but it's cold in there. Medical examiner is collecting the body in a few hours.'

The technician led her to a smaller forensic lab. The floor space was almost completely taken up by a plastic tarp. In its centre, Finch she saw the sunken car. Its doors were open, various numbered markers strewn on and inside it.

The rusted car body was now royal blue again in parts. The

zebra mussels had been mostly shaved off and the silty mud had been washed off.

Finch went to the driver's seat.

The skeleton was slumped away from her but still grinning, as though in on a joke it did not wish to share with her. Its limbs hung by the tiniest of threads. It wore a fir-green suit, gold rings. She could smell its vague scent – wet stones. What flesh was left on the skeleton had greyed like bread mould. Its hands and feet had been bagged in the hope that they might contain evidence but Finch could see that was pointless.

The technician crouched down on the passenger side.

'Car stopped a lot of the normal scavenging. Plus, the water is pretty cold up there, so your victim isn't in bad condition.'

'Victim?' Finch frowned. 'How do you know he didn't just fall asleep at the wheel?'

'You're kidding, right?'

'No.'

With a wolfish smile, he beckoned her over to his side.

Finch went to it and her heart twisted.

Protruding from the other side of the skull she had not seen was a broken bottle. The kind that would have once contained dandelion wine.

TWENTY-EIGHT

On the red vinyl surface of a Downtown Detroit diner table, sugar granules had been spilled. Finch swept them away, trying to ignore the clatter of plates and pre-dawn crowd mutterings. Her head was throbbing from where she'd been hit in the temple. Closing her eyes, she still saw Lamb's skeleton smirking at her.

His disappearance had always bothered Finch. Fumbling for an answer in the dark, her fingers had always encircled the same possibility. Lamb had molested Flora, then split. But had he been involved in Flora's death somehow before vanishing? One of his followers, maybe, was responsible while he put miles between him and any culpability?

Whichever way she'd looked at it, she had always assumed Lamb simply left. Sheriff Cochran, as he was back then, had always thought as much – that the preacher had just split for pastures new, the Assemblyfolk getting too much traction. Yet all along, Lamb had been in that water, wasting away.

When she first saw his skeleton, she imagined him overcome by the guilt of what he'd done to her, loading up on pills, and driving into the water next to where she'd died.

Now, Finch looked at it from another angle. All those years ago, on the day of her death, she had warned Flora not to get caught up with shitty people.

You don't have to tell me that.

That had always bothered Finch too. And there had been

something she didn't want to talk about – Flora was never like that. But what were the chances of Flora turning up with a packet of molly that big just after?

All right, Fest brought creeps and lowlifes with it each year. But except for the disappeared girls, Nectar had no crime like this.

What are the odds that Lester Lamb and Flora both ended up dead in the same town a few days apart?

Her cell phone buzzed now, a withheld number. Assuming it to be another journalist coming after her over the Ivan Maloney thing, she let it ring. But now her voicemail beeped.

Finch typed in her keycode and listened.

Detective Finch? I'm from R&I Division, Bill asked me to look into a record for you? Alana Madeline Wells. Date of birth, 3/3/80, Danforth, PA. Now living in Cleveland, OH. I'll send through the address now.

Elesheva Frey found him in the cemetery, crouching over the grave. Jubilance Weaver had laid a single pink flower on Rebecca's headstone and was silently praying as a muted sun rose. The girl stood over him, her shadow making him flinch.

'They were looking for you. I thought thee gone, child.'

'To thy misfortune, I am back. Back with many learnings made.'

'Let me mourn in peace.'

'But we are not finished, brother.'

'Thy little game,' he stood, his white face turning pink, *'be concluded, Elesheva. Thou wilt offer proper apology for wickedness or I will take a birch branch to thy –'*

She took out the gun from her dress.

Stopping in his tracks, he slowly raised his hands.

'I told thee, many learnings have I made. This gun makes all equal afore the Lord. Men, girls, it matters not. The greatest oak, the smallest paper shred – all burns in flame.'

'What do you want?'

'Proper apology *was thy phrase, was it not?*'

Jubilance searched the cold rage in her eyes. They were beyond caring. '*I swear it, child —*' His voice was quick with fear. '*I spoke truth to Finch, I hurt thy sister not and —*'

'*Thou spoke* some *truth. The rest, I shall weigh. Empty thy pockets.*'

Jubilance obeyed, a small rain of pink petals falling. His knife landed in the little heap, its curved blade catching the sunrise like fish scale.

'*Move back. Six paces. There, yes. Now, kneel.*'

Jubilance got down to his knees as she plucked up the knife. '*Elesheva, I know thou hast suffered much unkindness here —*'

'*Of the Inquisitor's list of motives, thou didst hide from lust. I looked into thine eyes as she spake that word. And thou didst lead her away from it with thy admission of stealing.*' She lifted the blade up before his face.

'*I spake all that I know.*'

Elesheva pushed the knife to his mouth.

He screamed and bucked as the blade slipped through the film of lip-skin but she held his head in place. '*Every lie you speak is paid in blood.*'

'*Please, I do not heal!*'

'*Nor I. Thy apology is not yet to my satisfaction, Jubilance.*'

'*I lamented thy sister, too. I swear this. Please, no more.*'

'*Thy lament is nothing to me. Now, we return to the subject.* Unless,' she held up the knife, the sun turning his blood honey wine-gold — his pain, somehow, strangely sweet to her.

Jubilance closed his eyes. '*It-it was just once. God help me, it was once . . . I-I desired her too fervently.*'

'*You wanted to lie with her. Speak it.*'

'*And she let me. I am damned but she let me.*'

'*In exchange for the Englisch money?*'

'*Yes. After that, we barely spoke again. But on God above, I never hurt her.*'

'*Why did she need it?*'

'*She would not say, I-I am not sure.*'

'*You were risking everything. You must have asked her why she needed it. Speak.*'

He held up a trembling hand, his voice childlike. '*If I tell you, you will cut me.*'

'*Jubilance, if you do not tell me, I will paint thy father's house in thy blood.*'

'*You,*' he whispered. '*It was to do with you.*'

'*. . . That is what she said?*'

'*Yes. She needed the money for thy father. She begged me for it. That's all I know.*'

Elesheva searched the man's terror and found truth in it.

As he started to sob into the earth, she flicked his blood from her hand. A single drop landed on her sister's grave.

Adam Frey ate his breakfast before sunrise. A simple meal of mourning; bread and honey. He slowly chewed his way through half a loaf, his beard twinkling. Between Joanna and his two daughters, there had always been voices in this house. Life. Now there was only silence except for the *snick-snack* of the grandfather clock.

But like a dream, the door creaked open. Then, the small stomp of Elesheva's clogs. Without a word, she entered the kitchen and sat at the table. Heart beating like a herd of wild horses, Adam sliced her some bread and criss-crossed it with honey.

She did not touch it.

'*I heard thy footsteps last night, Elesheva. Another nightmare?*'

'*Nay. I needed a walk to settle my mind is all.*' She poured herself a cup of burdock root tea. '*Dost thou recall what I asked ye as a child afore bed?*'

'*For my spitzhacke to be left outside in the tree stump at night.*' He laughed softly. '*To ward off evilcomers.*'

'*I wouldst look down upon it from the window. I remember Rebecca whispering: If the devil visits with thee, call for Father, he wilt come running with his axe.*'

'*Yes.*' He smiled sadly. '*Verily, she loved thee.*'

They looked out of the window and watched morning fog crest the alpine horizon, like slow, pale fingers over a dark back.

'*Papa. Know thee that thou hast my love always?*'

'*Yes,*' his face fell. '*Why?*'

'*There is much anger, much unknowing in me. It fills me as breath drawn into a lung. I want to know the truth but I fear I may speak an unkindness to thee.*'

He closed his eyes, a small nod. '*I knew this day wouldst come.*'

'*That Englisch money the Inquisitor showed thee. Thou knew of it?*'

'*Nay. I had never seen it before.*'

'*Then it is as I thought. You are not my father. Joanna was not my mother.*'

'*Elesheva, I know not what thou hast heard but —*'

'*The truth. For the first time. I know Rebecca was violated. But were that to be commonly known, her life here would have been over so a story was agreed upon. To protect her. Me. A story that half this village doubts. Yet I believed. Always. You made me believe it.*'

Adam Frey blinked. '*Whatever else hath gone before, I am thy father, Elesheva. And Joanna wast thou mother.*'

'*Enough.*' The girl smashed the table with her fist. 'Rebecca was my mother. And you don't know who my father was. But instead of finding out, you lied and lied.'

Bottom lip trembling, he went to the window. '*What choice did I have? How couldst I tell you a truth this black? Elesheva, if the village knew what had befallen her —*'

'*They wouldst have blamed her? Spoken of lust or sin or harlotry while never once wondering if there be a rapist in their midst? If that were the goal, thou didst fail, then.*'

'*Thou dost judge me deservedly. But . . . in that darkness, I saw no light.*'

'Who, *Papa? If she told anyone, she told thee. Who violated her?*'

'*I know not . . . Though it is my doing.*' The old man buried his face in his hands. '*She begged me, child. Begged me not to send her outside.*'

'*But thou didst follow thy duty. As all do here.*' Elesheva stood.

'*Stay. Please.*'

'*I cannot stay in a place I revile.*'

'*Versammlung is your home.*'

'*Home? I am a leper to these people.*'

'I *am thy people.*' When he opened his eyes, they were pink. '*Not them. I only ever tried to love thee.*'

'*But never truly forgetting who I was.* What *I was.*' She put her arms around his neck for a moment and kissed his cheek. '*I blame ye not for thy cowardice, Papa. I only wish thou hath lived thy life through love, not fear.*'

'*Elesheva. Leave not in anger.*'

'*Anger is what I am now.*'

TWENTY-NINE

Cleveland. Finch stopped on the corner of 66th and Bliss, across from a mint-green clapboard fixer-upper with an oak tree in the front yard. She forced herself not to remember this city. The Strip. Moonlight Jack. *Over soon, honey. Over soon.*

Instead, she sipped her coffee and watched for movement.

Sure enough, at 7:30AM, a man and a preteen boy left the house, loaded into a family minivan, and drove away.

Finch got out of the cruiser, skipped up the porch steps and pressed the bell. Alana Wells answered the door in athleisure, a HIIT workout blaring on the TV behind her. She'd aged well, her hair still frizzy, though her freckles had faded.

'Yes?'

'Alana Wells?' Finch asked the question despite knowing the answer. 'I'm with the Detroit Police Department.'

'Police? What is this about?'

'Nectar.'

Alana cocked her head. '. . . I know you, right?'

Finch took off her hat. 'Heritage Fest, 1998.'

'Jesus.'

When the small talk ran dry in the spacious kitchen, and after a few awkward sips of coffee, Finch produced the Polaroid Ed Riddell had taken all those years ago and slid it across the table. Alana Wells glanced down, then cleared her throat. 'It's blurry.'

'But you remember.'

'Yeah. I remember. You. Flora. The colony friend.' She sighed. 'Look, don't take this the wrong way, but I'm not big on nostalgia. So, whatever *this* is, I probably don't know anything –'

Finch silenced her with the magic-eye necklace from her pocket. It dangled from her fist, the way the sunken car had above the water.

Alana took it in, her whole life receding in the rotation of that small, golden thing. 'Look again at the photo. This was around your neck a few days before Flora was found dead with it in her hand. Why?'

Alana shook her head. 'It can't be the same one. I still have that piece of junk in a box somewhere. Maybe he gave her one, too.'

The tingling promise of the word *he*. 'Who, Alana? Who gave it to you?'

'I can't remember his name. But he promised me all kinda things. Said I could make it as a model. Said I had talent, wit. Then again, he also said the necklace was real gold.'

'What did he look like?'

'White guy. Tall. Mike? Bob? The name is gone. Nice face. I remember *that* clearly.'

Finch went into her pocket and unfolded photocopies from the casefile. Alana studied the faces of Ira Pike and Sam Salinas but shook her head.

'Was he from Nectar? Or an outsider?'

'From Nectar, I think? I wasn't so it's hard to tell.'

'Was he part of the Nectar Historical Society?'

'The what?'

'Apparently, some kind of cult obsessed with Nectar's history.'

'Oh, those guys. Yeah, I think he was connected to them.'

'Was that why you disappeared?'

'No. And *cult* is a strong word. To me, they were just losers who'd meet up to talk about pilgrims, witch trials, I don't know. I didn't pay too much attention, I was too busy getting paid. And I didn't disappear. My dad was military. He was rotated in '98, that's all. After he died, we came here.'

'Back up. *Who* paid you?'

Alana sighed, then lowered her voice. 'Listen, this can't get back to Pete, OK?'

'It won't.'

'*He* paid me. The guy who gave me the necklace. I didn't sleep with him but I did take off my clothes for him. He took a few pictures. Yeah, it was weird. And look, I'll admit, I had a crush on him. Looking back, he was a sick bastard, though.'

'Did he ever hurt you?'

'No.'

'You ever see him with other girls? Flora?'

'Don't think so. I mean, it was Fest. He would talk to everybody.'

'The Historical Society.'

'Right. He seemed friendly with them. And a preacher? A cop, maybe? It's fuzzy.'

'What did he do at Fest, what was his role?'

'Jesus, I can't remember. Maybe he worked for Parsons? I really don't know.'

Finch tried to control her frustration. 'Alana, it's very important that you remember a little more here. A name, or something identifying –'

The woman's expression shifted. '. . . You think this man killed Flora, don't you?'

'I can't answer that.'

Alana stood. 'I'm sorry. You need to leave.'

'Wait. Just a name. Or place. Something I can track –'

'I have a *life* here. A kid. Now, I answered your questions but I can't get caught up in some dark shit, all right?'

Finch tapped the Polaroid Ed had taken all those years ago. Alana's eyes took in Flora's embarrassed expression. Then, herself in the background. The magic-eye pendant around her neck.

'Please. His name.'

'I don't *know* his name. I would tell you if I did. Just go.'

Shaking her head, Finch collected the necklace and the Polaroid, then made for the front door but paused.

'You have a nice life here. Flora would've been happy.'

Alana hung her head, then called after her. '. . . Little star.'

Finch froze, her stomach twisting violently. 'What?'

'He called me Little Star. That's all I can remember. Or maybe it was *shooting star*. Something in Latin? I blocked out most of that time.'

Finch closed her eyes. '. . . He told you that you were special.'

'Yeah.' Alana frowned. 'How did you know?'

'Because men like him always do. You're lucky you left when you did.' Finch went to the front door and Alana followed.

'Now that I think of it, that night before I left, I saw your friend. The redhead colony girl? She went into the woods. I'd seen her do that before . . . That night, he followed her.'

Mind spinning, Finch thanked the woman, got back into the cruiser, and drove away at speed. She made it four blocks before she pulled over and broke into tears.

So many stars but people only ever look at the same few constellations. Which ones do you know, Dakota?

Fumbling for her Visprozan, she remembered his words as he traced the night sky with her finger.

Do you see? Special. Like you. Monoceros . . . Greek for unicorn.

'At last,' she whispered. 'I know who you are. And I'm coming for you.'

Elesheva breathed in a sweet tang of mud and rain. The forest floor was a sundae of dead leaves and snow. She had with her only her faceless doll and Dakota's gun. Cold stung her nose as she whisper-sang the words of Stevie Nicks.

When Elesheva reached the working fields, she could hear the Assembly Tree bell tolling for mass. It was always the same dejected sound, resounding only thrice – too many would be vanity. As the girl walked through her people, they stared at her. Some mouthed curses. Others prayed for her, for her dead sister. But nobody spoke.

She found Ichabod Weaver amid the cherry trees, softly lamenting to his bee hives. Each one had been taken by a sickness. The hive cells no longer shone with gold, now just black and empty. At his feet, piles of dead bees – their wings papery as autumn leaves.

Dropping the hive lid, he turned to face her. '*Elesheva Frey.*' He spoke her name as a regrettable if predictable inconvenience – as though the girl were made of rain.

'*Thy bees suffer the blight.*'

'*Some punishments the Lord maketh seemingly without cause.*'

'*Who can know the Lord's will.*'

'*Or thine. Why art thou returned?*'

'*To speak with you.*'

His cheekbones lifted beneath his beekeeper's mask. '*There is an order here. You do not merely speak with me. It is as these hives. Every bee hath its position. The cleaner. The warrior. The drone to mate. Each life hath a purpose. No bee may live without one, for it would die alone.*'

'*But thy hives are already dying.*'

'*The queen has died, that is all. She rules over everything so must be*

344

replaced. One will soon be sent to me from a cousin colony. She arrives in a block of candy and I place her inside. Still mourning the loss of their old queen, the hive wilt be enraged by her foreign presence. And so, they gorge upon that candy in an effort to purge her. But after three days of tasting the sweetness, they come to know her smell, understand her grace, her power. And once she is eaten free, she emerges as their new god. Through sweetness, they worship. As do we. The hives do good example make. Child, if only thou wouldst accept thy place, happiness would follow.'

'Ichabod, I don't see happiness here. I see drones. I see a prison.'

The mesh of his mask clouded his eyes. *'My watchmen tell me thou didst leave our walls last night. Art thou set upon living outside as a heathen?'*

'Am I not already treated as such here?'

'Thou never didst brook our ways. And now the devil's music thou hast heard. I see such pride in thee, Elesheva.'

''Twas doubt in mine heart before. Not pride.'

'Thou surrendereth not. This is why thou art shunned.'

'Wrong. I was shunned for fear these people would also begin to doubt. But it matters not. Dakota Finch weighed this place and found it unclean. I see it too now.'

'We do not live immaculately. But piously.' He took off his mask to reveal a sad smile. *'Child, doubt is not a sin. But to shut thy heart away from the Lord is grave. Every man, woman and child hast purpose here. What purpose canst thou have without faith?'*

'To find the one that killed my sister.'

'That is not thy place. There is no authority except from God, and by God authority be appointed.'

'But none can know the will of the Lord. So, who appointed thee?'

'Oh, Elesheva,' he laughed. *'The most wilful child, oft be the one that draws the most affection in a parent's heart.'*

'Parentage is the very thing I hath come to speak of.'

His lost his smile. *'Thou art bewitched by thine own bewilderment. I sorrow it.'*

'*Bewildered? Then what of these people, cowering before a dead tree?*'

Ichabod's face twisted into anger. '*Watch thy tongue, girl.*'

She took out the gun in reply. '*It is what is in my* hand *that should concern thee.*'

Between them, only the soft buzzing of the few remaining bees. '*. . . Thou wouldst threaten me?*'

'*I spoke with Eli Black.*'

'*So, my brother lives?*'

'*In a manner of speaking. But he is not my father. Nor is Adam Frey. Now, I want the truth from thee. For it, I will pay any price.*'

He faced the working fields far below. '*What truth?*'

'*You know it well. Neither one of us will leave this place until his name is spoken.*'

He exhaled. '*Thou walketh a path which I cannot follow.*'

'*There is a tongue in thy mouth, sir. Willing thou may not be. Able, thou art.*'

'*. . . God would curse me.*'

'*Ichabod, oft I hath heard thee speak of God's acts. Great miracles, mighty vengeances. And yet –*' The gunshot echoed in the misty morning, her bullet biting into the mud at his feet. '*This* is the power of God. In my hand. Now, give me what I am owed or I will levy it against thee.*'

Ichabod fell down on his back. He scrambled his way backwards until his shoulders hit against a hive.

Standing over him, Elesheva raised the gun. '*A name.*'

He searched her eyes, then closed his. '*. . . Rebecca told me she had been violated at the fair by one of the Englisch. I-I told her that she was not to blame, that a solution would be found. But I reminded her: the mouth is made for silence.*'

'*Why blame Eli Black for a crime he didst not commit, then? For so long thou hast vilified the Englisch – and yet, when my sister wast violated by them, thou didst protect an outsider at the cost of thy own brother. Why?*'

He chewed his lips, trying to find the right words. *'The Council did debate this. I do not want thee to think it was an easy consensus —'*

She pressed the gun to his forehead. *'Why?'*

'We needed him!' Ichabod yelped. *'We needed his business.'*

'Go on.'

'To survive. We need him still. Every year, our number dwindles. Sickness deepens. Crops spoil. Without his money, Versammlung will fall. His company, we rely on it as we rely on the sun.'

'Burr Group . . .' she whispered.

'The man that took it over afore all this. He is the one that violated her. To settle his sin, he gave us good terms. Water to a parched mouth. We could not say no.'

'And you put Versammlung before her.'

'Please, child. Understand me, I safeguard the colony. *Thy sister —'*

'She was not my sister.' Elesheva booted over one of the dead hives, covering him in golden filth. *'She was my mother. I see that now. So. For the last time. His name.'*

'Thou wouldst kill him?'

'With all my heart. It is why I am made. Fury from fury.'

'Then, you would destroy us. Child, think of Christ. Whosoever shall smite thee on thy right cheek, turn to him the other also.'

'I too can quote thy little book, Ichabod.' She held up her gun now, her voice guttural as a sermon. 'He beareth not the sword in vain. For He is a revenger of wrath upon evil; high and mighty be His right hand, and so let Vengeance be His name.'

THIRTY

Dusk. Twenty miles outside of Nectar, rain turned to hail. Finch blinked as she drove. The road undulated up ahead in her vision but she didn't know if that was the weather or the Visprozan. She'd lost track of her dosage long ago.

Taking a breath, she dialled Ed Riddell's number.

Dakota, hey. Good to hear from you.

'Ed. We need to talk.'

Always. But what's going on? You sound like you've been crying.

'I don't know how to say this.'

In your own time, your own words.

'I know who killed Flora. And it wasn't Sam.'

She heard his breathing change. Then him vomiting. Now a tap running. And the line went dead.

A minute later, he called back. *Sorry, I just . . . God. Are you sure?*

'Yes. The Sugar Man.'

Jesus Christ. Who was he?

'I wanted to talk to you in person before going public.'

. . . I never thought this day would come . . . I don't know how to feel.

'I can only imagine. Look, I'm outside Nectar on the 6. Headed to you.'

Good. Good. OK, Jesus. Well, I'm at home, I'll wait for you.

'Give me twenty.'

Thank you. And, Dakota? Be careful.

*

Elesheva Frey slipped into Room 202 of the Friendly Motel at darkfall. Finch had left the spare key on top of the doorframe. Her car wasn't in the lot outside. Inside, the lights were off. Locking the door behind her, she tossed her faceless doll on the bed and looked around the room. The knife was by a pizza box. Next to it, a candle. And some matches from the sundae parlour.

Picking up the knife, she went to the bathroom and began to chop at her hair with it. When she had whittled her black locks enough, she switched to nail scissors.

After twenty minutes, the sink looked like it held a small black feathery creature. Elesheva peered into the mirror. The girl who glared back at her was no longer her. And it delighted her raging heart.

Taking off her Versammlung dress, she put on the hooded garment belonging to Finch that she had worn before. The jeans were too loose but she remedied this with a belt. She put the gun in her waistband the way she had seen Finch do. Then Elesheva left the room.

Downstairs in the lot, she went to the truck covered in stickers. Checking over her shoulder, she untied the container marked: *BELIEVE IN AMERICA*.

The jerry can sloshed in her hand as she unscrewed the cap. She'd never smelled kerosene before. But she understood the word *flammable*.

The road was silent. Across it, the place where Rebecca's body had been left. And not far from here, the man who had left her there.

Elesheva rattled the matchbox in her hand.

THIRTY-ONE

Reaching Snow Shoe Lane, the past was spinning in Finch's mind like an old Discman – the day of Flora's death notice, Cochran removing his hat, the scream from Esther's core that followed. Then Ed's face turning white as he doubled over.

The street was dark except for the dappling of warm light from its houses – dinners, TV, family. To Finch, it was like flipping through a glossy brochure of far-flung destinations she would never see.

But none of that mattered now. The lives she could've had. The people she could've been. This was all her life was and had been – leading to this moment – to deliver this truth. Taking a deep, sick breath, she pressed the bell.

The door opened, its bell trilling joyously. 'You OK?' Ed's smile was crooked with worry. 'You're shaking.'

'Fine.'

'Come in.'

Finch sat on Flora's old kitchen island stool and felt the blood return to her fingers. Just like before, the heating was up way high.

'Are you sick, Dakota? I could get you a blanket.'

'I'm good.'

'Coffee, then?'

'No.'

She idly slipped her hand into the fruit bowl. Her fingertips brushed against a nectarine, feeling the delicate skin, the tiny downy hairs.

He sat at the island and closed his eyes, the silence churning.

'Are you ready, Ed?'

He took several breaths. 'As I'll ever be.'

'The Sugar Man was Lester Lamb.'

Ed put his head in his hands, as if this new understanding weighed on him. '*Lester?*'

'That's why they never caught him.'

'. . . You never found him because he was in the water. My God.'

'We think he couldn't live with what he did to Flora. He overdosed in his car. We're still not sure if he meant to drive into the water or not.'

'And because he did, we had to wait for an answer . . . I just still can't believe it was Lester. All these long years . . .'

'I'm sorry, Ed.'

'No, don't be. You're one of the only lights in all of this. Flora would've been proud . . .'

Finch nodded. 'Now you know.'

'Now I know . . .' He stood and went to the sink window for no reason. They looked at each other in the reflection. 'The house sale went through this morning. It's time, I think.'

'Yeah. It is.'

He turned to face her, a smile breaking through. 'You know what. I think this actually calls for a celebration. Head on into the studio, there are still some comfy chairs left.'

Without a word, Finch did as he asked.

The studio was cluttered with packed suitcases, countless moving boxes. His logic-problem books and code-breaking manuals stacked up in piles in corners. Boxes of flashbulbs, film roll, bottles of ammonium thiosulphate. Rolls of bubble-wrap everywhere. The music system was playing quietly, 'Tonight You Belong to Me' by Patience and Prudence.

Ed came in holding two glasses of wine. Pushing a box between the two chairs for a table, he handed one over and sat facing her.

'To Flora's champion. There's a poetry in you solving this. Not only did you never forget her, you dedicated your life to her. I can never thank you enough.'

Finch drank, then looked away with a sad smile. 'I'm glad this is over.'

'Me too.' He lost his smile. 'When will they announce it?'

'Soon.'

Ed's eyes glazed over. 'I haven't seen Esther in years. But she'll be happy. If I can get through to her.'

'She deserves some peace.' Finch downed her wine and went to the window. 'Actually, there's something she said when I went to see her. It's been bothering me.'

'I wouldn't get caught up in her words too much –'

'*The umbrella was dry . . .*'

'Hm?'

'How *could* it be dry?'

'What do you mean?'

'That evening she disappeared, it was raining hard. When Esther found out Flora was gone, she went looking for her. And you did, too. But when you got home, your umbrella was dry. Esther saw it.'

'So?'

'So, you told Cochran in your statement that you were searching for Flora with your umbrella because of the heavy rain.'

He put down his glass and stood. 'We both lied that day, Dakota. You know why.'

'Because we were together.'

Ed stepped into her space. 'Listen, I know what this is really about.'

'Do you?'

'You feel guilty. And I'll be honest, I do too. All these years I have. I never meant to start what started between us. Flora deserved better than that. And you did too. But I *loved* you, Dakota. I always have. Even now.'

She closed her eyes and shook her head. 'You never should've –'

'I know, baby. But I didn't choose it. I didn't choose it any more than stars choose to constellate. And yes, we didn't tell the whole truth that day to the cops. To protect ourselves, though. Not because of any *guilt*. She's not dead because of you. Or me.'

'She *saw* us, Ed. I understand that now. That's why you panicked so much. She saw us, and she screamed and she ran – right into the killer's path. It *is* our fault.'

'And we've paid for it. All these years, we paid.' He nodded gently, his green eyes drawing level with hers. That old smile that scrunched up whole lifetimes to waste paper. He put his arms around her, like it used to be. She smelled his aftershave. Sandalwood. Rock. 'But Lester is dead. You're back in my life,' he murmured. 'I want it to stay that way.'

His wrist grazed along Finch's mouth.

Bone. Vein. Muscle.

Surrendering, she kissed it, her lips rolling up his sleeve. And there, at last, she saw them – scratch marks. Clear. Beautiful. Pink as peonies.

Shunting him away, she drew her gun. 'I *knew* it.'

'What?'

'You fucking *know* what, you son of a bitch. Back five paces. Interlock your hands behind your head. Kneel. Right now.'

'. . . Why?'

'*You* killed Rebecca Frey. *You* killed Flora. Now, you comply.'

A bewildered frown. 'This is crazy.'

'*Monoceros*. The unicorn constellation. You tried to seduce Alana Wells. Same as me. You were Rebecca's admirer. *That's* why she didn't tell us. She never could.'

'. . . I don't know what any of this means.'

'Sure you do. Back five paces. Hands behind your head. Kneel.'

Ed obeyed. 'I have no clue where all this is coming from but it is ridiculous.'

'I don't have all the pieces of the puzzle but I see the picture. Rebecca was out here in Nectar the night of her death. Did she come to you, Ed? To talk? That was her *task*, wasn't it? Does Cochran know and kept his fat mouth shut?'

'Think about what you're saying. It doesn't make any sense. Nectar PD aren't geniuses but they can put two and two together, Dakota.'

'But they never tried to, did they? Burr Group. It kept Versammlung alive all these years. Nectar, too. Cochran was never gonna bite the hand that fed him.' She nodded at the puzzle books. 'That's how you made your money. Invested at the right time, then hid in plain sight, a picture within a picture. *You're* Burr. Publishing, real estate, agriculture. It's you. It's all you. You *are* Nectar.'

'Burr was my mother's name. But my investments have nothing to do with this.'

'But they do. Because nobody can touch you when you own everything.'

'You have no proof I hurt Flora or anyone else. There *is* no proof.' He got up from his knees. 'Now, why don't we calm this down a little and —'

'I didn't tell you to stand. Don't test me.'

'OK, OK. Listen, we're just talking. I know what you're like when you make up your mind. That's all. I'm telling you that there's another side to this. Please, see it.'

'Side? Bullshit. Esther tried to tell me. *You* were the umbrella man.'

'She's not well.'

'How could she be? After what she's been through. But the question stands. How could the umbrella be dry?'

'Dakota, you're not making any sense – how many pills are you taking?'

'You're the one that killed Rebecca. You're the one that killed Flora. I see it now. You did it because you're scared. You killed to protect your secrets: *you're* the Sugar Man.'

'No. You know me.' He shook his head. 'That isn't possible.'

'Everything fits, Ed. Everything. You wore that long sweater indoors to hide your scratches. Despite having the heating on all the way.'

'Dakota, I have a cold.'

'Yeah. You got it when you were out in the rain disposing of Rebecca's body. And once the DNA under Rebecca's nails is matched to you, it's all over.'

'Cochran is in on all this crazy shit?'

'I won't be going to *them* with this. I'm going way over the heads of your little friends. And you'll fucking fry. Believe me.'

'Dakota, I know you're agitated. And I know what you're saying *feels* very real to you. But there isn't going to be any trial. Because this isn't reality.'

'No? So, what's this?' She took out the note from her body armour. '*I know what you did.* For years, I wondered if it was meant for Flora or for me. But it was written by Esther, on her headed church paper. For you.'

'OK. I made mistakes and I did things that were wrong,

that were low. I never hid that from you. I was never more myself than when we were together –'

'Stop the bullshit. Your puh . . . your poison doesn't work anymore.'

'I loved Flora with all my heart. Her death broke me. And you're accusing me of her *murder* because of Esther's ramblings? She isn't in our world anymore, we both know that.'

'She is broken because of you.'

'She is unwell, Dakota. That's all. You're assigning blame to me, to others. I'm hearing that but I'm wondering if you're doing that to avoid blaming yourself?'

'B-blame myself?' Finch laughed venomously. 'I could just as easily shoot you in the gut. We'll see how patronizing you are then.'

'Dakota, I'm not trying to patronize you. But you're scaring me.'

'You should be scared, motherfucker. Now, the note. Esther was building up the courage to confront you. Only, how could she untangle herself from you? The house, the kids. Most people would never know how convincing you can be. How real you can make something feel. B-but I do. I, uh. I . . . I know.'

'What are you saying? You're slurring.'

The gun was still trained on him, but it dipped. 'F-Fluh-Flora was the one that saw us that day. That scream . . . the one I convinced myself I didn't hear – that was her . . .'

'I was with you that afternoon. And we both lied about it. You know this.'

'You went after her . . . Yuh-you –' Finch stumbled.

'Dakota, you're rewriting history. I protected *you*. *You're* the one that did this. You made this. You think it was easy to choose you over my child?'

The gun dropped to her side, heavy in her hand.

'No.' She snapped it back up. 'Shut up.'

'Do you even have evidence against me?'

'Yuh-you . . . put something in my druh . . .'

'I think you have a substance problem. And we should stop –'

Finch pistol-whipped him.

Grunting, Ed fell against the wall, clutching his head. The rivulet of blood from his temple curled into his ear. He was back on his feet now, his face red. 'You crazy *bitch.*'

Fighting the darkness at the edges of her vision, Finch flipped off the safety.

'Wait! Wait! She gave me no choice!'

'Who?'

'Rebecca. All right? Rebecca. She tried to force her fucking kid on me.'

'Kid?'

'I told you, I was rebuilding my life.'

'. . . My God. Euh . . . Elesheva.'

'You think it's easy? Living in a world of whispered gossip. *Everything* I told you was true. I *was* in a good place. And then, God laughs in my face with this colony bitch.'

'Why?'

'She just turned up out of the blue, told me she had money for me, as if that changes anything –'

'You raped her. All those years ago. *That's* why she changed. Because of you.'

'She told me she'd had my kid. That the girl wanted to live out here, away from Versammlung. She was making threats, Dakota. What the hell was I meant to do?'

'She told you Eva wanted to start a new life . . . but that she couldn't follow her. She wanted you to look out for her. To be a father. That money was her *atonement.* To make sure her kid had a little in this world.'

357

'*Her* kid. I tried to reason with her but she wouldn't budge. Things got out of hand –'

'Bullshit. You knew Evie's arrival would push you into the light. People would see the real you. Dolores, too. She was back in your life but now she would understand who her father really was. *That's* why you killed Rebecca Frey.'

'Look, I reacted when cornered. I shouldn't have done what I did. But Rebecca came to me. I didn't plan this. I didn't plan any of it.'

'You muh . . . murdered her. And your own child. You'll burn . . .'

He closed his eyes for a moment, as if to better savour the music – Bernadette Carroll, 'Laughing on the Outside'.

'I imagined this moment for so long.' His sigh was resigned. 'I used to dream of it. I never pictured it this way but it's a relief.'

Finch was shaking, her tongue weak. 'The sugar at the scene . . . why?'

'The bag broke in the struggle.' He shrugged. 'Look, I wasn't *trying* to kill Flora.'

'No, just silence her.'

'I used the nectarine at first. I put it into her mouth. I'm not saying I'm a good man. I know that I'm not. But you lied, too, Dakota. We both did. Kept our silence.'

'I-I betrayed her. But I was a kid. I thought I luh . . . loved you.'

His jaw hardened. 'That afternoon, Flora was . . . out of control.'

Finch closed her eyes.

She was seventeen again.

Back in the Subaru, alone, her sick heart beating hard. She could still taste him on her lips. The smell of the little tree hanging from the rear-view turning her stomach like always.

Dakota watched Ed get out of the car, then dwindle in the rainy grey haze.

Their secret was out. It was over. Soon, everyone would know that she had taken her best friend's heart and stamped it into mud.

Dakota got into the back seat and curled up to cry.

When Ed finally returned, he was out of breath. She listened to him breathing hard through his nostrils for a while until he spoke.

I need you to go home, Dakota. But you don't say anything about us. Ever. If you love me, you tell them you were at home tonight.

'Drop it,' his voice ripped Finch back to the present.

Opening her eyes, she saw Ed rack a shotgun.

THIRTY-TWO

Chests rising and falling, the music switched to 'Earth Angel' by the Penguins. Finch felt whatever Ed had put in the wine through her nervous system, dancing in her blood with the exhaustion and Visprozan. Searching his green eyes, she saw smug victory coupled with total determination. He would protect himself at *any* cost, it was obvious.

Finch cursed herself for not clearing the room when she had the chance.

He grinned. 'You think you're smart with that horse-shit Lester story? Trying to play *me*? But you forget. I know you, Dakota. I've seen inside you. I can tell when you're lying. And you couldn't hide your hatred for me from the second you walked in.'

'I shuh . . .'

'Killed me? Shoulda, coulda, woulda. But wait,' he cupped his ear. 'No sirens? No back-up? You didn't tell anyone? Of course you came here alone. Like a moth to the light.'

'Fuck you.'

'You're a little on the old side for that. Now, drop the gun. You can barely stand.'

'They'll know what you've duh . . .'

'No, they won't know what I've done. I can tell a story a lot of different ways and the Neanderthals around here will just nod. You're going to drop that gun. *Now.*'

Finch obeyed.

'Attagirl. Now, come here.' As he wiped the blood out of his eyes, a strange, languid smile formed on his lips. It wasn't Ed Riddell's. This smile revealed different teeth. Used different muscles. It was one she had never seen.

Finch stood before him. 'Killing me won't make this go away.'

'I should've done this years ago.' He smashed the butt of the shotgun into her chin.

She tried to react but her balance was gone. Finch didn't even register the fall. Now the pain came. Beyond her own understanding. She could only picture Rebecca's destroyed face, the fear of her own imminent death overwhelming.

Finch's mind had accepted death long ago. But her body had not. It wanted to live.

'That girl came to me, yes. Just like you, she couldn't accept that the past is the past. Now, I know I've done selfish things, Dakota. But I'm not the devil.'

'No . . .' She moaned, her mouth bloodied. 'Just a cowuh . . .'

'Coward? And you're still that scared little stray Flora brought home.' He crouched over her. 'Who thought the world had been so hard on her because mommy was a drinker and daddy ran away. Yet I was eight years old when my father beat the life out of my mom.'

'I found you . . . someone else wuh find yuh . . .'

'No. Nobody's finding me. I'm gone. Like you.' He lifted the gun. 'See you in the next life, honey.'

An alarm started to mewl. Fire.

Ed snapped his head around.

There was something audible over the alarm.

Crackling. And now the hollow popping of glass.

'My flashbulbs . . .'

The air smelled of burning plastic, acrid chemicals. Looking up, Finch saw it. Black smoke beckoning across the ceiling – coming from the kitchen.

'Who's here?' he snarled.

'I came alone.'

'Get up,' Ed motioned. 'Open it.'

Forcing herself up, Finch walked unsteadily towards the kitchen door. She opened it, and the fire roared, gorging on the new air. Flames raced up walls, withering backdrops, blooming across photo paper. The fairground stink of grease and smoke was unbearable.

Instinctively, they both retreated back into the studio.

But now a loud, metallic rasping sound – a jerry can sliding across the floor, its kerosene sloshing out. From the smoke, Elesheva Frey appeared, gun pointed at the gold puddle. Head shaved, hoodie caping out behind her, she looked like some offended god.

'Who the fuck are you?' Ed pulled Finch close to him, stuffing his gun into her back.

'You know who,' she replied calmly. 'Let her go.'

'I don't want to hurt her. Nothing rash . . . Wait. Don't I know you?'

'It is my mother you knew. That is why I am here.'

His expression changed with the realization. 'We can talk outside, all right? Because that liquid is very flammable. We don't have long until the fire –'

'I know. But you won't be leaving this place.'

Ed licked his lips. 'You're angry. That's understandable. Evie? That's your name, right? I can't let your friend go but we can talk. I know you must have things to say.'

Elesheva shook her head. 'Not one thing.'

'Listen. Your mother came here for a reason, right? Rebecca wanted you to have a life out here? For me to guide you? OK, I'll honour her wishes. Make up for what I've done.'

'. . . That is why she came to you?'

Finch's eyes lolled open and shut. 'Don't listen to him, Evie. He's a liar –'

He pushed the muzzle of his gun into her back hard. 'Shut up.'

'Let her go.'

'Shhh, forget her. She's not blood. *I am.*'

'You're nothing.'

'Do you realize how much you look like her . . .' He shook his head in wonder. 'Dolores, my child, you have her eyes, her nose. I'm your dad. Now, you wanted to leave this place? We can. Wherever you want. I know I've taken away from you – but I can give, too. Because you do have family. Your sister's name is Dolly. She'll take some adjustment but we can make it work. The three of us.'

'No, Evie . . .' Finch groaned as the drugs swallowed her. 'The serpent . . .'

'Shut your fucking mouth,' Ed snarled.

By now they were raising their voices over the spreading fire. Already, the flames were licking the fringes of the kitchen. Already, the heat was unendurable.

Elesheva looked down at the kerosene, then up at Ed.

'Evie! Look in my eyes. You're my daughter. Let's talk –'

'I told you.' The girl shook her head. 'There is nothing to say. Now let Dakota go.'

He raised the gun to Finch's head. 'Your choice.'

'Then we burn.'

'Baby, listen. You're angry, I see it, but you're young. Let's all walk out of here and work something out. When the flames come, the pain will be beyond your understanding.'

'You made me in pain.'

'If you shoot, I will too. But I don't want that.'

Elesheva met Finch's eyes. *Love or death.*

She lowered her gun.

'Good girl,' he nodded. 'That's smart. Now, why don't we –'

Finch shunted him.

Ed stumbled back against the counter.

Elesheva fired, hitting him in the shoulder.

He landed on his back, knocked out. Evie marched across the kitchen and put her gun to his crown.

'No,' Finch muttered. 'Don't, Evie.'

'He deserves it.'

'Yes, but you can't. Not *you*.'

'He-he must die.'

'I know, honey. But that is darkness. And if you wade in, you'll never come out. Ever. I know this because *you* taught me.'

Elesheva looked at her. Face blackened by the fire, a pure tear sliced its way down her face. 'But I have nothing else . . .'

'Evie, listen to me. You will. You'll have a life, you'll see turtles, eat ice cream. You'll have love for other people, in all shapes. It will come into your heart one day, even if it doesn't feel like it right now. This little man doesn't get to take that from you.'

The girl closed her eyes.

Ed snapped his open. He slapped the gun out of her hands. It spun off into the black smoke. The girl went at him with her teeth but he punched her hard in the gut and she doubled over.

Now, Ed was reaching for his shotgun.

Bellowing with a mother's rage, Finch was behind him, pulling with all she had – Flora's old necklace taut around his throat, the eye pendant cutting into his flesh.

With only one working hand, Ed flailed.

Finch pressed her eyes shut with the effort, his gagging sounds a stubborn dog pulling against its leash. Now, blood between her fingers, warm. His struggle slowed.

Until the necklace snapped.

Air rushed back into his body and he stumbled up, hacking and choking.

Elesheva was on her knees, clutching her stomach. Finch was on her back, nothing left in her.

The Sugar Man spat out blood, his voice wet. 'Shoulda . . . coulda . . .'

He picked up the shotgun. And noticed the broken necklace. The little gold pendant in the kerosene puddle, stippled with his own blood.

'Monoceros . . .'

An ember floated through the air and came to rest on his ankle – a molten angel.

He understood it too late.

It fizzed like a firework, then whomped to life.

As he slapped the flames out, his hands caught fire too. His green eyes, cooked pink now, were frantically searching for help.

The fire swallowed his feet first. One leg. Then the other. Then the body.

The music was still playing, 'Together We Are Beautiful' by Fern Kinney.

The Sugar Man's bellowing became squeals. Elesheva Frey closed her eyes for a moment to savour the music of her vengeance.

Then she dragged her friend up from the floor. Looping her arm, they hobbled down the burning hallway, amid smoke and fire fairies sparking gold around them. The home studio was now a blinding incandescence. An old banner floated down to the floor:

**FOR MEMORIES DONE WELL,
COME TO ED RIDDELL!**

THIRTY-THREE

Elesheva dragged Finch until they reached the safety of the wood. There, she propped her up against a tree, like a broken doll, and sat cross-legged next to her. With numbed, blackened faces, they watched the house burn, the inferno an iridescent jellyfish in the deep.

'*Shitshow*,' Evie whispered. 'That was the second word you taught me.'

Distant sirens were growing louder. Finch closed her eyes. She didn't know what would happen now. Just that, one way or another, and with the girl's help – she had done what she had to do.

'Eva . . .' She grimaced. 'You gotta go.'

But the girl was still transfixed by the fire. 'Killing him felt like nothing.'

'That's shock. Listen to me. They're going to find his body. I don't want them to touch you. You have to get far away from this place.'

She faced her friend. 'I'm sick of lies, Dakota. We killed him.'

'He killed himself.' Finch cupped the girl's cheek. 'You are going to leave this place and never come back. Be who you're meant to be.'

Elesheva's face had hardened with soot and hatred. But her blinks were still childlike, her voice small. 'Will you come with me?'

'For your own good, I can't be with you.' Finch smiled sadly. 'Maybe one day.'

Sirens screamed nearby now, fire trucks surrounding the blaze. The girl helped her friend up to her feet, and they hobbled deeper into the wood. They didn't stop until they came to the Testing Pool.

There, Finch slumped on to Flora's bench as the girl re-buried the gun. When it was done, she helped Finch out of her body armour. In the motion, her bloodied shirt lifted up.

Elesheva peered at the word *silence* carved into her bruised ribs, then traced it with her little finger. '. . . My father used to say the mouth is made for it.'

'He's wrong, Evie . . . Truth isn't in a book, or a preacher. It's only in you . . .'

Finch closed her eyes.

The girl let her friend sleep. She went to the place where Rebecca's body had been found a little over a week ago and wondered if she was at peace now.

The Testing Pool was still – a mist on it, pink as candy floss. Behind the shoulders of the Catoonah Mountains, the first feathers of dawn unfurled.

THIRTY-FOUR

Dakota Finch woke in the dark. But there were no tears. No nightmares. No fragments of memory. She got out of bed, crossed her apartment, and jumped in the shower. Her scar had been tattooed over. It was still a single word but now it read: *DEFIANCE*.

Afterwards, she sat in the window. It was a clear late winter morning in Detroit, the skies a sharp blue. Finch didn't feel like journalling but it was a part of her addiction recovery plan. With a resolute sigh, she flipped to the last entry.

In the end, Nectar was a maze. The deeper in I went, the closer to its heart I got, the farther away from the outside world I was. I see that now.

I also see what Ed Riddell was. How deeply in denial I was. That I had only ever gotten used to what he did to me. Never healed from it.

I still feel anger that the world doesn't know the truth about him. But exposing that would lead back to Eva.

Maybe, one day, the world will know who the Sugar Man is. Until then, only his traces are there. Like the stench after a house fire, lingering forever. For the time being, I'll leave Nectar to her secrets.

Now wearing her Detroit PD uniform, Finch drove north. Windows open, she listened to the year's first song of black-capped chickadees in the trees above. At the post office, she packed up Flora's old Discman in a box and slipped in a brief handwritten note to Dolores Riddell saying she was free to talk whenever/if ever it suited the girl.

Back in the squad car, she checked the time. Her shift had just started.

Fumbling in her pocket, Finch reached for a chewing gum – a new vice to replace the old. But her fingers brushed against a little paper slip.

She was now holding the Wisdom Wafer in her hand, its words faded.

No man ever steps in the same river twice. For it is not the same river and he is not the same man.

The dashboard radio crackled into life.

Attention all units: BOLO entered for wanted male – DOC escape and felony. Subject is Morgan Rush, five-eleven, Caucasian, associated with a teal 2000s Honda Accord, plate 015, Lima, Yankee Delta. Last seen moving at speed on Toledo Ave, request stop and detain.

That was five blocks from here.

Finch flipped on her turret light and sirens. Swinging a U, she felt contradictions deep in her heart: resignation to this grey, harsh loop of a life. But also, an inexplicable, bursting hope for the future.

THIRTY-FIVE

A warm breeze blew across Miloli'i Beach, cinnamon powder sand, cliffs rising up sheer as a tsunami of black and orange rock. Seal pups were playing in the reef. The girl had promised herself she would come here the first time she'd seen Hawaii on TV. And now, she'd kept that promise to herself, she'd seen the baby turtles.

The girl broke away from her kayak tour, which had stopped for a picnic. She was eighteen, her short, choppy hair dyed blonde, a tattoo of a sundae on her forearm.

Finding a secluded spot away from the group, she dug her feet into the wet sand, and opened her backpack. Inside, there was a large envelope from the university. She had carried it with her for a week now, waiting for the right moment to open it.

Closing her eyes, she ripped, recalling the other envelope she had opened years ago back in Nectar.

She wished Rebecca were here now and wondered what she would make of the person she had become.

Taking a breath, she opened her eyes:

Dear Evelyn Finch, I am pleased to inform you . . .

She breathed in the ocean, blue as the ocellus of a peacock.
Did she even want to go?
She could.

Or not.

She could go anywhere.

It was overwhelming.

But it was freedom.

'Dakota, you were right.' Evelyn stood up and looked out across the Pacific Ocean. 'So blue it hurts.'

Acknowledgements

On the writing side: amid the many wonderful Penguin folk, my warmth and thanks to the lovely Max and Bex, who listened to the buzzing from Day 1. To Joel, editor extraordinaire, who let such light into a darkened hive. And to my agent and champion, dearest Gordon (no tortured bee analogy, just gratitude). To Kane, PA, for its hospitality, particularly Brandy Schimp. You have my vote. Go Wolves! To Hal Sutton for, well, everything. Though we may never financially recover from this, I will always have your words. To Gracia Bokor for her language skills and all the rest. I will always be thankful to you. To Rebecca Hannigan. I told you so. Hashtag proud. To Nicole Gennetta for her bee wisdom, may your hives flourish. And to Hayley Shepherd for a steady hand amid those choppy waters.

To the beloved ones close to me, blood and friends: if I am the pen, you are the ink inside me. First and foremost, to my Bro; Thailand, Taiwan, Tighnabruaich – anywhere, everywhere, always and forever. A mis socios de la fila 6, aparte de *os quiero*, solo tengo dos palabras: *¡all right!* To my 'primos,' my lady brothers from other mothers; I count the days until the next terraza season. To Stewart 'Horsfield' H, an early visitor to Nectar and friend for life. To lovely Lily for the French. And most recently, to little Olivia. Vienes de las dos personas más dulces que conozco en este mundo. Te estábamos celebrando antes de tu primer aliento. Tuve la buena suerte de conocerte cuando tenías solo un día de vida. Y hasta mi último día, siempre encontrarás aquí un aliado.

With love always,
Nicolás
– Autumn, 2024, Madrid.